I'll Dance Across the Heavens

by
M.K. Fairview

PublishAmerica
Baltimore

© 2004 by Mary K. Marelli.

First printing

ISBN: 1-4137-2649-6
PUBLISHED BY PUBLISHAMERICA BOOK PUBLISHERS
www.publishamerica.com
Baltimore

Printed in the United States of America

I dedicate this book, first and foremost, to my family, for without them, without knowing their love all these years, I would be at a sad loss. Their support has made all of this possible. It has made me.

And to Mom, who continues to dance across the heavens....

The trappings of humanity. Our daily lives. Our demon inner being, emerging to govern our darkest thoughts.

Our deepest desires. Our dreaded fears. We live them daily. Embracing the gifts we are given, cherished or not, they make us weep.

We cry for something better. Searching inside for something that does not exist, yet is a part of us all. Fleeting. Always fleeting.

Life, love, happiness, true inner being. Fleeting.

We ask for more. We yearn for more. We weep when it is taken away.

Prologue

He stood among the ashes, staring at the charred ruins. Cole's entire life had been wiped out. Everything he treasured was lost. Everything he loved was gone in the blink of an eye, leaving a shattered, tortured man in its wake. Cole stood among the ruins, staring at the smoke that still drifted upwards. His family had perished in those flames. Their home, their safe haven, had been ripped away, leaving Cole cold and alone, and Sarah and their baby lying among the ruins. There was nothing left. Cole turned and walked away. There was no reason to stay. Without a word to anyone, he packed his meager belongings and left the only home he had ever known.

Chapter One

Leaning on the corral fence, Cole Morgan stared out over the horizon. Even on a good day, he sometimes could not shake the dark mood that set in. That is what happens when a body loses so much in such a short amount of time and has made one bad decision after the other in his quest for a new life. Feelings get lost, along with the person. Sometimes, there is just no way of knowing how to find your way back.

That was how Cole felt as he stood watching the sun sinking lower in the sky. Dusk was following quickly on the heels of the fading sun, but they still had a fair amount of daylight left. It was the second week of May and the days were already warmer. Sometimes, this time of year could be tricky in Montana. One moment it could be a bright, warm day, but with the blink of an eye, everything changes. One could almost smell the front as it rolled in from the west over the mountains, bringing yet another storm. It had been a hard winter and they were all hoping that the bad weather was behind them.

"Good thing, cause last year sure was a different story," Cole muttered to himself, unaware of the car that had just driven in.

"Now, if you're thinking of that infamous storm we had last year like I am, that was really a sight," Cole's long-time friend, Grissum 'Gris' Lavery said as he sauntered over to his side.

Cole jumped slightly, turning to face his friend. Leaning one arm on top of the corral fence, he grinned broadly. "Hey! I didn't hear you driving in! How's the sheriffing going?"

"You sure do have a way with words! If you're trying to ask me how my job's going, then it's going fine! The town is quiet, crime is at a nil and everyone is happy!" Gris bellowed heartily.

"That's good to hear! I was just standing here thinking how nice today was; we're lucky, spring came without any surprises this year! I remember going out with Brent last May, I think it was May 4, because we were headed down to Jacob's Perch to take a look at his stock," Cole regaled Gris with his tale.

"I remember that," Gris replied. "That was quite a wild week!" he snorted.

"Wild! Gris, it was more than wild! It was so nice that day, that I remembered thinking we oughtta have a picnic that following Saturday. Now, that was only two days away, mind you, but Mother Nature had a different idea!" Cole snickered.

"She sure did! Those poor women! They cooked and baked their hearts out that Friday! Who'd have thought that the very next day we'd wake to a foot of snow! In May!" Gris bellowed, shaking his head.

"May 6 to be exact!" Cole said, puffing out his chest.

"Oh, listen to the scholar!" Gris teased. "I'll never forget that one! Once old Will had all of us plowed out, we all gathered over at Ruth's for one heck of a party! Damn, Cole, that food was so good, I didn't care how much snow we had!"

Cole could not help but laugh as he listened to his friend. Gris was the Sheriff of Crater Mills, the tiny town they resided in. Tall, but stout, he was in his mid-fifties and had never married. His hair was thinning and he had to squint a bit more when he read, but he was determined to fight the ravages of time. He was still sheriff and he still sat tall in the saddle. That was all a man needed. Well, that, and a fishing pole.

Gris had taken a special interest in Cole from the time he arrived in Crater Mills over six long years ago. He had never seen a more broken, lost soul in his entire life. Cole was running, but it was not from the law. He was running from himself and memories that still tormented him to this day. Along with their friend, Ruth Rollings, who cared for Cole's young daughter Katie during the day while he worked the ranch, Gris listened.

Over the years, Cole slowly opened up to the two, sharing his heartache and torment, yet he still refused to speak of the fire. The only information he was willing to share was that his wife had been killed, but Gris knew better. He had read the reports of the fire, which sickened even him. His heart broke for people he had never met and he wondered how Cole had ever found the strength to continue on as he had. It was no wonder he refused to speak of any details, they were just too heartbreaking and grisly to contemplate.

At times, Gris and Ruth worried if Cole remembered the details at all, but quickly shoved such thoughts from their minds. He remembered. But remembering did not mean that he necessarily had to speak of it. He had lived it and that was enough. Cole's heart was forever broken, but with the help of close friends over the years, he slowly began living again. He still did not trust much and held most of the world at bay, and he still refused to speak of his hometown, which he left shortly after the fire. Old friends and what remained of his family were never contacted again. The land he had lived on all his life was forever haunted, as was Cole's soul. What had once made up his life, was shoved to the darkest corners of his mind.

Cole had a new life now. He had shoved the hurt aside the best he could under the circumstances, and stumbled on. With Gris' strong shoulder to lean on when times grew dark and Ruth's compassionate wisdom to help guide him along, he found his way. They made up an odd sort of family, yet, as Ruth was so fond of saying, it didn't matter what a family was made up of, it was the love they had for one another that mattered.

"You doing ok, son?" Gris asked, turning a worried look in Cole's direction.

"Yeah, I'm doing fine, why?" Cole tried hiding his feelings.

"You seem kind of down," Gris nodded.

"No, not really," Cole sighed deeply. "Just tired, that's all. Been a long day."

"Always is when raising a little one on your own," Gris winced, immediately regretting his words.

"Hey, don't sweat it," Cole quickly reassured his friend. "The fact of the matter is, I am raising my daughter alone. That's not your fault, it's a fact and we speak the truth of such facts. It's not your fault that I made so many mistakes and screwed up."

"Cole, you didn't screw up. We're not judging how that little angel arrived, we're just gonna spend our days loving her," Gris nodded.

"That's what I intend to do. Gris, I didn't mean...." Cole shuddered, thinking of Maggie once again.

"No son, you didn't mean it, and she knows that," Gris said. "Cole, we all go through this life and if we judge, then we're the ones who lose. We simply do the best we can with what we have. So, what do you say? Everything turned out all right in the end, Katie is doing fine and her birthday is in a few weeks! What could be better?" Gris said, trying to drag Cole out of his present mood.

"Nothing," Cole smiled, slowly turning his head and smiling. "Nothing at all."

Gris looked into Cole's deep, brown eyes, still seeing a tinge of sadness hidden within. Cole had carried that sadness around for the past six years, and Gris feared he would carry it in his heart throughout his life. Sometimes there was just no way for a man to purge himself of his personal demons. If only a friend could help take away some of the pain, but he could not. There was no way to assuage such pain, Cole knew that well. It was his burden to carry and he would muddle through life, shouldering it the best he could.

"Hey, know what you need?" Gris brightened, smiling widely.

Cole could only groan, "No, what do you think I need?"

"Boy, you need to go fishing! It's spring, the fish are biting and I sure don't feel like being cooped up tonight! Come on, the river's calling!" Gris urged.

The idea was tempting, but Cole was reluctant to accept. Today was Saturday. During the week Ruth ran his home and cooked their meals, but Saturday was different. That was the one day a week he and Katie spent together. Even though most of it was spent tending to the necessary chores around the ranch and grocery shopping, it was their special day. It was also the night Cole cooked his daughter's favorite meal, spaghetti. He was not the best cook in the world, but he did manage to find his way around such simple dishes as spaghetti and stews that only required one pot. Katie never cared anyway, her father was doing the cooking and he could do no wrong in her eyes.

"Gris, it sounds great, but I promised Katie spaghetti. It is Saturday!" Cole reminded his friend. "Why don't you stay and mooch some?"

"Now that sounds purely inviting! But I already promised Ruth that I'd have dinner over at her place. So, what do you say? You game?" Gris asked.

Cole was quiet for a moment, "Gee, I don't know, I mean I was going to spend the night with Katie," he shrugged.

"Son, you spend every night with Katie! And it won't be for long! Just wanna go down to the river and drown a few worms. You can get Ruth to watch that little darlin' for you," Gris suggested.

"Today is her day off and knowing her, she probably spent the day cooking, baking and cleaning! That woman never rests and I hate asking her to spend tonight working," Cole replied hesitantly.

"Oh boy, wouldn't want to be in your shoes if she heard you talking that way! She'd box your ears good! You know that she wouldn't be working, Ruth is never happier than when she's with you two!" Gris replied, his voice booming.

It didn't take long to make up his mind. Just the thought of relaxing and a few moments of peace and quiet was enough of a temptation. Plus, Cole simply could not deny Gris; the man lived and breathed fishing. Whenever anyone wanted to reach him on one of his rare nights off, they knew where to find him.

"All right, so she won't be working, but the thing is she does enough during the week and needs a quiet night!" Cole continued arguing.

"There's always Callie," Gris elbowed Cole.

"Don't go starting that! Callie's got enough with her own work and doesn't need to be spending her time watching my kid! She's got a life of her own!" Cole proclaimed.

"Uh uh," Gris replied, shaking his head as he grinned wickedly.

"Well, then she should!" Cole blurted out.

"But she doesn't, and you could—"

"I could nothing! Don't you go spouting off with your matchmaking bit! I don't need anyone in my life right now. I'm settled and am doing fine! Katie keeps me busy enough and I don't have time for anything else! So you and Ruth go prey on someone else!" Cole bristled, as he did each time Callie's name was mentioned.

"I do think you argue too much," Gris continued his teasing.

"No, I'm telling you how it is! All right, I'll see if Ruth can watch Katie at her place for a little while and will join you. I gotta admit, it sure will be good to just sit back and relax, it's gonna be a beautiful night," Cole admitted.

"That's why I suggested it! Now, can I talk you into joining us for dinner?" Gris asked hopefully.

"As much as I'd love to take you up on your offer, I already promised Katie that we'd have spaghetti and you know how much she likes my spaghetti!" Cole beamed.

"Son, that little one loves everything you do! The sun rises and sets on her Daddy as far as she's concerned! So, since I can't talk you into joining us, I'll be on my way!" Gris said, with a final wave as he left.

"Hey, be sure and tell Ruth we'll be over for dessert!" Cole shouted after him.

* * *

Crater Mills, Montana, a small town unlike any other as far as her inhabitants were concerned. Nestled at the base of the mountains, her lush green fields and pastures rolled on endlessly. For as far as the eye could see an infinite ocean of green blanketed the landscape until it reached the base of the mountains and began their ascent. Weaving themselves into the forest and patches of sage, they climbed high into the clouds that shrouded the majestic peaks. Everywhere you looked, you saw either tall green grass dancing in the wind as it stretched up to meet the sky, or dry prairie dotted with sage that melded into the vast expanse of horizon. Anyone who stood admiring her beauty knew that the old adage was right. Montana truly was Big Sky country. You knew it in your heart; you could feel it in your soul. There was no escaping this land. Her spirit inevitably became a part of you.

And Crater Mills had captured that spirit. She was a small town, one in which her people lived, loved, and worked the land together. They were modern day folk, but deep in their hearts, they were no different than their pioneer ancestors. They loved and respected the land with a fiery passion that burned like embers in their souls. That love had been passed down from generation to generation, never wavering and never questioned. They were a part of the land as much as the sage that dotted the prairies or the grasses adorning the fields.

That love was also passed down to all those who lived there. They were friends, they were neighbors, and they were pioneers. Every day was faced with their backs tall and proud and their eyes forged towards the future. Their love of family ran deep, and their hearts ran true. Cole felt that passion the day he first arrived in Crater Mills. He made it his home, something he had never regretted.

Most everyone ran a farm or a ranch, working the land in very much the same way as their great grandparents before them. Most of the surrounding ranches made their living raising cattle, yet Cole's heart belonged to the horses he bred and raised. Farms and ranches were not the only industry in town, but they were her backbone.

Crater Mills boasted one semi-retired lawyer; which was all they needed, since business was relatively slow anyway. The only client he had represented that anyone could remember was Cole when he purchased the ranch he now lived on. Other than that, things were basically quiet. There had not been a divorce in Crater Mills in over twenty years and any trivial disputes between neighbors were settled privately, amicably, and between the parties involved.

The only ongoing argument anyone could recall recently had been the one between Hec Jones and Sam Melton, and that had been over a game of checkers. To this day, Harold Becker, owner and proprietor of the general store, officiated over their weekly game.

Main Street itself was small; consisting of a general store, diner and post office on one side, with a bank and real estate office all rolled into one building on the other. There were a few specialty stores, such as a small gift shop, a florist, and a toy store, along with the feed 'n seed, which was located at the far end of town. Every Saturday afternoon the sidewalk was jammed with residents scurrying about as they ran their weekly errands. Men created a steady stream of traffic in and out of the feed store, either stocking up on necessary supplies, or just grabbing a chair by the woodstove so they could chat with their neighbors for a few moments.

It just felt good to get out. Most of the families in the area usually stayed to home during the week, running their farms or ranches. Saturday was the one day they set aside, affording themselves the luxury of a trip into town

14

and a chance to visit with friends. Women gathered around the gift shop, marveling at the latest crafts May had arranged, and the children stood outside the small toy store with their noses pressed up against the window, staring dreamily at the displays. About five miles out of town was a supermarket most of the residents frequented at least twice a month, and in between trips, they stopped in at the general store. There was really nothing special about Crater Mills. It appeared to be the same as every other small town in America, yet to its people, Crater Mills was special.

The most notable icon the town boasted, that still drew attention to this day, was the local pharmacy, which had become a legend in its time. The building was exactly as it had been when Milt James' great-grandfather first founded the store in the late 1800s. The old soda fountain was still in service and the walls were lined with dozens of wooden drawers, containing every kind of medicine as the newer, modern stores.

The over-the-counter medicines such as cough syrup and aspirin were actually behind the counter, dispensed by Milt himself, who had worked the store since he was a boy. He still took prescriptions over the old antique phone that hung on the wall and rang up the sales on a large, ornate, gold register sitting on the counter. And they still made deliveries. Only now, they were made by truck instead of horseback.

The thing that brought curious stares and double takes from strangers, however, was the sign Monty James had hung the day he opened the doors. 'Drugs, Guns and Liquor sold here.' The old sign was still there, only you couldn't buy all three. Milt concluded that back in his great-grandfather's time, it was simply convenient for folks to just walk in and buy whatever was needed.

Whether you were in the market for a new six-gun or hunting rifle, or you just needed some laudanum for your rheumatism, all you had to do was come into his store and Monty would take care of it all. Saturday had always been his busiest day, with sneaky husbands skulking around out front until the coast was clear. As soon as it was safe, hats were pulled down over their eyes and they would slip inside, where they would purchase a bottle of 'spirits' to wet their whistle after a long, hard week.

Then there was Doc Edwards, who held office visits in the downstairs part of his home and still made house calls when necessary. Most of the farms and ranches were far from town, but that never mattered to Doc, who believed that he should go to those sick, instead of them coming to him.

It was a rough life. Everyone worked hard and they played hard, carrying the love of the land and the spirit of their forefathers in their hearts. It was a rewarding way of life and it could be a dangerous way of life. They watched out for one another. At times it seemed like they were on their own, separated from the world at large. But that was fine, they had everything needed all wrapped up in one tiny little package called home.

Cole stood watching as Gris drove away. Pulling a carved wooden box from his pocket, he walked to the front porch and sat in the creaking, old rocker. Carefully removing the small blue amulet, he held it close, feeling a slight tug on his heart.

"I'll dance across the heavens with your mane as my reins," he whispered so softly that he barely heard his own voice. Looking back up towards the sky, he carefully placed the amulet back in its box.

It had been a good day, bright and warm. The long winter was behind them and May showed the promise of being a good month. The ranch was quiet. Cole had just finished his evening chores and was getting ready to start their dinner. It was not easy raising a three-year-old daughter alone, but Katie was a good girl and the light of her father's life. He also had help from his friends and neighbors and was never alone where Katie was concerned. Sighing heavily, Cole walked back into the house.

* * *

From her usual perch on the tall counter stool, Katie watched while her father prepared their dinner. Cole was not the most adept person in the kitchen, but he still managed to hold his own. At least he and his daughter did not starve, thanks to simple dishes like stews, where you just threw everything into one pot, and spaghetti, which was their personal favorite. Tonight, spaghetti was the dish of choice. Katie diligently tore the pieces of lettuce apart and tossed them into the spinner, which her father then placed in the sink for rinsing.

Helping gave her a sense of pride, and Cole treasured these times more than one would ever know. The years slipped by so quickly that every moment he grabbed seemed to fade into the recesses of his mind in a matter of seconds. Cole smiled at the way her tongue stuck out the side of her mouth as she worked, all her concentration on the task at hand.

She looked so much like her father that it simply amazed him. Both had light brown hair and brown eyes that often flashed dark when challenged, angered, or just feeling mischievous. Cole was tall and muscular. Standing at 6'3"; he tended to lean towards the slim side, not gaining an ounce of unwanted weight due to working hard from sunup to sundown. His skin was tanned to a deep bronze, as was his daughter's.

Katie loved the outdoors as much as her father did, with a passion for the land already instilled in her soul. Her long brown hair hung in ringlets cascading down her back, catching the golden highlights from the sun as she played happily in the yard. As long as the weather permitted, she could be found outside watching Cole working the ranch, or just romping in a pile of hay with a newly adopted batch of kittens.

Their differences were as vast as their similarities; where Cole was tall, Katie was small for her age. Tiny and petite, she possessed the same quiet strength as her father. Her eyes often twinkled mischievously, as did Cole's, and they both shared the same uplifted grin when they smiled, with the left side of their mouths curling upwards in a funny sort of lilt.

Her fingers were long and tapered, giving a delicate appearance that masked their hidden strength. She may have been small, but she was strong and carried herself proudly, even for her young age. Katie embraced life fully and held those who cared for her dear. She was not shy by any means, and faced life head-on with the same courage Cole, himself, had.

The last of the meatballs were dropped into the sauce, which Cole stirred and set to simmering. The pot of water sat on top of the stove, waiting until it was time to start boiling. Top it all off with some garlic bread, and their meal was complete. It had been a long day, starting with the usual chores one dealt with when running a house and raising a child by himself, followed by their usual weekly trek to the grocery store.

And his work did not stop there; once they returned home, Cole still had a long list of chores waiting for him. He watched his daughter as she worked, laughing to himself as he thought of their recent shopping trip earlier that day.

"Daddy, I don't want you to buy bugs," Katie had said, shaking her head as her father picked up the cellophane wrapped package of shelled pecans.

"What, honey?" Cole asked absently.

Turning his attention back to his daughter, he saw the brown ringlets that fell to just below her shoulders framing her soft face. To Cole's dismay, her tiny lips started quivering and tears began welling up in her dark eyes. She pointed a shaky finger at the package, shaking her head.

"Those are bugs, Daddy," she said, her voice unsteady.

Shaken by the tears that had formed and the stormy look that had crossed her face, Cole looked back at the package he was holding. He understood instantly and despite how upset her crying was beginning to make him, he could not help but toss his head back, laughing. His little angel had a firm grip on his heart, and her tears never failed to bring him to his knees.

He has loved his little treasure from the day she was born. It was just the two of them against the world. Katie's mother had simply walked out of their lives and never looked back. From the very beginning, Katie had been the sole priority of her father's life. Cole never ceased to take the time to explain things to her, and this was one of those times. Looking at her now, he saw that the look had turned from tears to utter confusion.

"Gee, you know they do kind of look like bugs all thrown in there like this, don't they?" he said, examining the packet closely. "Sort of shiny and flat lying there, looks kinda funny, huh?" Cole mused.

"They're bugs," Katie declared, now crossing her arms.

Cole could see that the tears had dried and defiance had taken over. "Well, they look like bugs, honey, but they're not bugs. They're not allowed to sell bugs!"

"Cause they're yucky!" she declared.

"Yeah, cause they're yucky," Cole agreed. "But honey, these are what they call pecans, they're some sort of a nut," he winced, thinking that he sounded like some sort of a nut. If Brent and Will could hear him now, they would be rolling in the aisle.

"You mean people eat them?" she asked, her eyes wide and unbelieving.

"Yeah, they eat them; but we don't have to!" Cole smiled brightly.

"I don't want to," Katie affirmed.

"Not even to try once?" he suggested.

"No, they don't look good," she remained steadfast.

Cole smiled, placing the package back. He certainly had no intentions on buying the nuts, they did look like a packet of bugs lying there all tightly wrapped and squished together. He also didn't worry about Katie refusing to even give them a try. She was a good little eater and usually sampled everything placed in front of her. She didn't always eat everything, but she at least tried. He also thought that the idea of having a child clean their plate was overrated.

Why turn something as enjoyable as dinner into a battlefield? You simply gave a child a tiny portion of what was being served and then there were no problems. Usually hungry, they would eat. Plus Cole always believed that a child knew when they were full and stopped eating. There was no sense in forcing them to finish when they simply felt that they could not handle it and pushed away from the table. Cole wished he had been smart enough to do that on the occasions when he overate. Holiday meals where the worst. Everything was so good that it almost seemed impossible to turn away from temptation. Anyway, they had it all settled; he would not be purchasing any bugs that day.

"You're not buying the bugs?" Katie asked questioningly.

"No, I'm not buying the bugs, leave them for Uncle Brent," Cole giggled.

"He likes bugs?" Katie squealed.

"He eats them all the time!" Cole laughed, knowing that the next time Brent visited, he wouldn't hear the end of it.

Their shopping was finished and soon they were home putting their purchases away. After a quick lunch, Cole helped Katie wash up and put her down for her nap. The rest of their afternoon was spent with Katie sleeping, Cole working in the corral, and a short visit from Gris. It had been a quiet Saturday and Cole found himself enjoying the late day sun as he started bringing the horses down into the smaller enclosure. This was the one day he refused to get involved in any work around the ranch except for the necessary daily care and grooming of the horses. Katie had been tired after their afternoon of shopping, so he had no problem getting her to sleep.

Cole had laughed to himself, muttering under his breath. "You never have a problem putting Katie down for her nap."

Sometimes she put herself down, usually in a soft pile of hay inside the barn, where she would sleep while he worked. Ruth would watch from the porch, where she either sat sewing, or snapping beans for their dinner. Right from the first, she sensed a loneliness in the man and took him under her wing, giving Cole something he desperately needed. In return, he gave Ruth a new reason to wake in the morning. She would never forget the lonely, tormented man that had arrived in town, lost to the world. His eyes held no sparkle and his shoulders were slumped. She could tell that Cole's spirit had been broken and was drawn to him immediately.

Slowly, a friendship formed and the two grew to care deeply for one another. Cole gave Ruth a purpose in life. She gave him someone that he could turn to when the world became too dark. She never judged and she never pressed for answers that he simply couldn't give. Sensing her caring and trust, Cole broke down over time, telling her everything. All Ruth could do was rock him in her arms as he cried the hurt out.

"Sometimes I just don't know how to go on; I don't know if I want to go on," he had sobbed as she rocked him back and forth.

"Honey, sometimes it seems to hurtful to go on. When those we love turn their backs on us, whether they mean to or not, it hurts beyond belief. We feel betrayed and we feel cheated. We experience a sense of loss that tears into our soul."

"I know that loss! I felt it when I lost Sarah! Then, for them too...." he sobbed brokenly, unable to continue.

"Shhhh, let it out," she soothed, patting his back.

"Ruth, I didn't kill her! I loved her! How could they say I killed her? My God, she was my entire life! I should have ... it should have been me," Cole finished, his voice finally breaking as the sobs tore through his body.

19

Ruth could feel him trembling in her arms, the grief all consuming. Cole had lost so much. That was why he had come to town in the first place. The loss of his first wife, Sarah, and their unborn child had been so devastating that he was unable to stay in his hometown. Alone and confused, he needed someone who not only understood that grief; he needed someone who could understand him. Ruth knew exactly what it felt like to lose so much, only not all at once; her losses came over a period of time throughout her life, yet they hurt just as deeply.

No one should be made to suffer in such a way. Everyone and everything Cole had loved and built his future on had vanished before his eyes. One moment his entire life stretched out ahead of him and the next it was gone, leaving a broken man in its wake. Cole left his home in Wyoming and came to Montana alone, not knowing why he had chosen to settle in Crater Mills. The only thing he knew was that he had to settle somewhere, so it might as well be here. Not long after, he met Ruth and found someone who cared. After everything that had happened, someone still cared.

Ruth more than cared, she loved Cole like a son. She was there when he bought his ranch and started working his horses again. Little by little his business grew, creating a comfortable life for himself. Yet, he remained alone. Life then took an unexpected turn, and nothing was ever questioned. All Ruth had ever wanted her entire life was a family to love and care for. All Cole needed was that same kind of love, and as they knew so well, fate has a strange mind of its own.

Ruth called it the Lord working in the mysterious ways he was so well known for doing, but Cole had stopped believing long ago. He just knew that the fate he followed blindly had given him a child to care for. Katie had no one else, and Cole needed no one else. To others, her birth may be looked upon as jaded, but Cole felt no such way, and neither did those who loved them.

To the people of Crater Mills, Katie was a blessing. She was another tiny soul brought into their fold to be treasured and adored, and that she was. At first, Ruth had to admit to being confused and angry, but those feelings were kept to herself. She had never passed judgement on Cole before and was not about to start. God help anyone who did. She had vowed to do whatever necessary to help her boy, and this was the one thing she could do.

People made mistakes, yet through their love for one another, they found a way to do what was needed. Besides, this involved a baby, which meant everything to Ruth. Her heart had always ached for a little one to hold in her arms, and now it seemed as if her prayers were finally being answered. After all these years, and in such a roundabout way, they were answered. She would never turn her back on a child. A baby did no wrong and only asked to be loved. That was the one thing Ruth had in abundance.

Soon, it was all over. Katie was born and her mother left. Cole never spoke of Maggie again, except on the rare occasion his fears with the world took hold, and he fought his own deep-seated guilt. That was when Ruth stepped in. She ran the house during the week so that he could work the ranch, and she took care of Katie's needs. Cole had raised his little angel by himself from the day she was born, and relied on Ruth for whatever help she could give.

But he was still stubborn. As much as he needed her help, was as much as he wanted to do things on his own. Ruth knew that life had been hurtful to Cole, thinking that it was that very reason he found it so hard to rely on others; trust was a hard commodity for him to come by. Still, Cole needed help, so she watched little Katie during the day, arriving early so that she could prepare breakfast and he could begin his chores. During the week Ruth cooked dinner for the three of them, but on Saturday nights, Cole preferred getting dinner on his own.

He loved the time spent with his daughter in the kitchen while they prepared their meal, which Ruth more than understood. She remained home on Saturday, getting caught up with her own work, and giving the two the time they so desperately needed for themselves. That did not bother her in the least; after all, she was needed. That was all she yearned for in this life, to be needed by someone.

It had been ten years now since her Gerald had passed on and Ruth has been alone. At 52 years of age, she found herself a widow, something she had not planned on at least until the age of 90. She would concede then, but at 52, it had been almost too much to bear. She and Gerald had never been blessed with children. After his death, Ruth found herself alone for the first time. Born and raised in Crater Mills, her life was rich with friends, but it lacked in other ways; ways that made one's heart ache in the cold, dark of night.

She was the one Cole turned to for help when he first arrived in town, and she was the one he turned to for help raising his daughter. He thanked the fates every day for bringing Ruth to him. For the first two weeks after Katie's birth, she had checked on the pair daily, knowing that Cole needed that time alone with his daughter. They all knew Maggie could not stay, but that did nothing to lessen the shock when she left.

Cole was left with the care of a newborn infant and the daily chores of a working ranch staring him in the face, knowing that he needed help. On one especially tiring day, Ruth breezed into the house, taking charge of the baby and sending a bleary-eyed Cole straight to bed. He virtually passed out, sleeping the remainder of the morning and not waking until later that afternoon. It was obvious to Ruth's trained, caring eyes that he had been running on adrenaline and nothing else.

'Now, you go on to bed and let me take care of this little angel for you. Don't worry about a thing, I'm here and everything will be fine from now on,' Ruth had said, her words a blessing to his ears.

Cole gratefully swallowed his pride. Having a baby and raising that child with the woman you loved was hard enough; babies changed everyone's lives, and proved to be a lot of work. They also proved to bring a lot of love. Raising Katie on his own had been more than culture shock for Cole, her unexpected arrival had sent him into a tailspin. Even though he had waited out the pregnancy with Maggie and knew that he would be raising his child alone, when the time actually came, he was instantly overwhelmed.

There were times when Cole thought he would not make it to the next day, and there were days where he felt too drained to go on. Yet, through it all, the love for his child remained in the forefront of his mind, helping him through the adjustments. With Ruth's help, and the love and support of his friends, Cole settled into a routine of sorts and soon everything fell into place. Still, he had his doubts, and wondered if he was doing right by his little girl.

Since that day, he found himself relying on Ruth more and more, even to the point where Katie now referred to her as Nanny. He shuddered to think of what he would ever do without her and simply didn't want to know. There had already been enough upheaval in his life the past six years; the last thing he needed was more. Ruth kept him on an even keel. She ran his house, did his laundry, and took care of Katie's needs so that he could work the ranch. Ruth finally had her little family, with each giving the other what they desperately needed. Life was turning out to be less lonely for all.

Cole's mind snapped back to the present, greeted by Katie's smiling face. She chattered and he tried listening, but his mind was still on the list of chores awaiting him before they went over to Ruth's. At least the horses were tended to for the night. They were up to eighteen in all right now, with three ready to be picked up by buyers in a little over a week's time … a week from that coming Wednesday, to be exact.

The horses were ready, but Cole still worried that he was not. There was so much at stake and he couldn't take any chances. Making it through the next winter hinged on how well he did this spring and summer with the buyers. Slowly, the ranch was starting to make money. His dream of turning the old run-down place into a working ranch was finally being realized. This was the second year in a row that Cole would turn a profit and with a little more work and more time on his hands as Katie grew older, he would be able to take on more horses, thereby expanding his herd.

Most of the major work was finished for the night; the stalls were already mucked clean, the grain bins were filled, and clean water filled the troughs. The only thing left to do was bring them in for the night and secure the barn. Cole preferred letting them out for a while longer to enjoy the warm night air, but since they would be going to Ruth's, he had no choice. He never left the house in the evening with the horses running loose out in the corral. During the day it never mattered much, there was always someone around, but at night, it was a different story. He simply felt uneasy about leaving his animals prey to the many predators the wilds of Montana attracted.

Taking a deep breath, Cole mentally checked off the chores listed in his mind. The horses were fed, dinner was cooking, Katie was tearing the lettuce for their salad, and the laundry was still piled in the bathroom. That thought alone was enough to bring him down; even though Ruth did most of their laundry during the week, there always seemed to be a mountain of it staring him in the face by morning.

"Shit multiplies faster than rabbits in the prairie," Cole swore under his breath, thinking of the overflowing hamper.

Now he knew that he would never get it done tonight. Plus, he still needed to clean the kitchen once they were finished eating, Katie needed to be bathed before they left, and the horses needed to be brought in. It never ended. Once all that was done, Cole would visit with Ruth a short while before he left Katie and went off fishing. He didn't want to think of what he had to do once they came back home. Katie would be ready for bed and would want to be read to as usual; no matter how tired he was, their nightly routine was never forgotten. And she would have to be tucked in.

Then came Cole's second favorite time of night; Katie would be sleeping, the house would be quiet, and he would rock in his chair, either reading quietly or watching the late news. In the fall, winter and early spring, a fire would be crackling in the hearth, with Cole sitting in front of the glowing embers while he unwound. Then he would retire for the night, only to wake as soon as his head hit the pillow and begin everything all over again.

"A man's work is never done," he snorted to no one in particular, smiling down at his daughter.

With the long evening stretching out ahead of him, all Cole wanted to do was bury his head under a pillow and sleep the night away.

* * *

"I'm done, Daddy," Katie proudly announced.

"Hey Katie bug!" Cole teasingly answered his daughter, sweeping her up into his arms. "Boy, that looks good!"

"I'm not a bug, Daddy!" she squealed with delight.

Her smile lit up his heart. They were running late this afternoon, which had suddenly turned into evening before Cole even realized it. The sauce was simmering, which had only been a matter of heating it up. Cole felt that he could kiss whoever invented homemade tasting jarred sauce. The invention literally saved his life. All he had to do was add a few of the frozen meatballs that he and Katie loved and they had their dinner. The rest of the meal was fairly easy, no one could go wrong boiling spaghetti for eight minutes, and the garlic bread took care of itself. All he needed to do was pull it out of the freezer, place it on a cookie sheet, and they had a gourmet meal. The only real work was putting the salad together, which was hardly a task at all.

Katie loved tearing the lettuce into tiny pieces while Cole sliced the onions and tomatoes. He would have loved adding such delicacies as chickpeas and olives, but Katie had tried that once and they were back to plain old onions and tomatoes the following night. The one thing that they did agree on was the dressing, Ranch with spaghetti and French with everything else. He had it all down to a science now and dinner went off without a hitch most nights. However, tonight was different; it had been a busy day and they were running late. By now, they would usually be sitting at the table eating.

The water was only beginning to boil and Katie had the lettuce ready. After running it through the spinner, Cole dumped it into the wooden bowl. Once the tomatoes and onions were added, he turned the salad over to Katie, along with a wooden spoon and fork so that she could do the tossing. In this manner, she was kept busy and he was free to prepare the rest of their meal.

The table was set and the spaghetti was drained. The dining room table, which was only used for special occasions, stood empty. On a day-to-day basis Cole and Katie preferred sitting at the small oak table in the kitchen, where they were able to enjoy the view of the mountains from the large windows. Sometimes he would just sit and watch the rippling water from the small stream that ran behind the ranch, and other times he and Katie would talk nonstop while they ate, his problems forgotten for the moment.

Cole tried hard; he never wanted his demons to plague his daughter, that just would not be fair to her. There were moments when he felt like giving in and just dropping away from the world when the darkness took over, but the one little glimmer of hope that made it possible for him to hold on was sitting on the counter with a smile spread across her face as she tossed their salad. Once he took in the sight of her tiny face, Cole was able to put everything else behind him. But in the dead of night when the world became quiet, the darkness would set in, once more robbing him of sleep. Then, there was no escape. He would just ride it out until the next morning, when he rose to face the day. Sometimes, Cole was just tired.

* * *

Just as they started eating, the phone rang. "Oh man, it never fails," Cole grumbled, rising.

Before he even had the chance to get out of his chair, Katie had already picked up the receiver.

"Hello?" her tiny voice answered.

"Hey Katie!" Brent's voice answered her back. "What kind of trouble are you getting into?"

"I'm not in trouble, Uncle Brent!" she giggled.

"No, but I bet Daddy is!" he teased, his bright blue eyes dancing with merriment.

Katie looked at her father, who waited patiently. "No, Daddy's not in trouble either! He's eating his dinner!"

"He's always eating! What did he make?" Brent asked.

Katie turned her face away from the mouthpiece for a second, "Daddy! Uncle Brent says you're in trouble and you're always eating!" she called out to him, much to Brent's delight. One of his favorite things to do was torment Katie into driving her father into a frenzy.

"Tell Uncle Brent to call back," Cole mumbled.

"What did he make?" Brent asked again, refusing to give up. At times, it seemed that Brent lived to annoy Cole, and he often found an unknowing ally in Katie.

"He made spaghetti!" she bubbled over.

"Hey, and you didn't invite me!" Brent feigned hurt.

"No, Daddy forgot! But he didn't make any bugs!" Katie announced.

Now it was Brent's turn to be confused, "What do you mean he didn't make any bugs?"

"Daddy says you eat bugs!" she replied brightly.

"Oh, he did, did he!" Brent frowned, trying not to laugh. "When did he say that?"

"When we were in the store! They were selling bugs and he said he would leave them there for you cause you ate bugs! Uncle Brent, how come you eat yucky bugs?"

"I don't eat yucky bugs, sweetheart, I think your daddy was pulling your leg!" Brent defended himself.

"No, he wasn't pulling my leg, he was talking to me!" Katie retorted.

"What kind of bugs did they sell?" Brent asked between bouts of laughter.

"Yucky ones!" she answered, turning back to her father. "Daddy! What kind of bugs do they sell?" she repeated Brent's question.

"Honey, let me talk to Uncle Brent," Cole pleaded, reaching for the phone before this went any further.

"No!" Brent's voice came over the line. "Katie, tell Daddy I want to talk to you!"

"Daddy, he wants to talk to me," Katie informed her frazzled father.

"No, he only wants to torment me," Cole groaned.

"Uncle Brent, what's torment?" she asked innocently.

Brent laughed before he answered, feeling sorry for his friend but unable to stop himself nonetheless. "It's something I do to drive your father crazy!"

"He drives you crazy," Katie replied back to Cole.

"Honey, do his eyes look funny?" Brent teased.

Katie studied her father's eyes carefully, "They're almost closed and he's rubbing the side of his head!" she answered.

"Uh oh, you'd better put him on before his head blows up," Brent said, pitying his friend.

"Daddy, here! Uncle Brent doesn't want your head to blow up!" Katie said, her eyes large as she handed the phone over. "Is your head going to blow up?"

"No honey, it's not going to blow up," Cole reassured his daughter, placing his hand gently against her face. "Why don't you go eat your dinner while I take care of your Uncle Brent?" he answered, with just a hint of malice.

"I heard that," Brent laughed as he heard Katie's bright 'ok, Daddy,' as she ran back across the room to the table.

"Good, now what do you want?" Cole grumbled.

"Nice way to greet a friend!" Brent pouted.

"When I'm talking to a friend, I'll be nice!" Cole shot back.

"Wow, you're in a mood! And you're eating late! What cooks?" Brent continued his torment.

"Spaghetti," Cole mumbled.

"Gee, now I know where Katie gets her wit!" Brent quipped.

"Brent, did you call for a reason or did you just want to torment me?" Cole rubbed his eyes.

"Seriously, I just wanted to say hi to Katie and see what you guys were

26

doing tonight. My mom made some pies this afternoon and she thought that maybe you two would like to come over," he offered.

Cole softened, he knew his friend's teasing side, and couldn't stay mad. "I'd really love to come, but Gris already invited me to go fishing with him after dessert."

"And you didn't invite me?" Brent whined.

"You wanna come?" Cole gave in, inviting him along.

"Nah, don't feel like fishing tonight! Just gonna gorge on pie and collapse in front of the tube!" Brent replied.

"Then why give me such a hard time?" Cole asked tiredly.

"Guess I had nothing else to do! Hey, maybe I'll get the chance to stop by tomorrow afternoon. Give Katie a kiss for me!" Brent said as he got ready to hang up.

"That, I will do," Cole found himself smiling at his daughter. "If I can get past the salad dressing smeared across her face!" he laughed with Brent.

"Oh that little one! She can steal your heart just by looking at her! Whether her face is smeared with dressing or not!" Brent replied.

"That she can, it's the one thing she's good at, besides spilling!" Cole winced as her glass of milk was knocked over. "I gotta go!"

"Have fun, Daddy!" Brent's laughter rang out as Cole hung up the phone.

"Katie, how do you manage to do that almost every night? I think I'm gonna glue that glass to your fingertips," Cole joked, picking up the dishcloth.

It was inevitable. He should have expected as much the moment he knelt to clean up the soggy mess. Katie was famous for spilling, especially on her father. The moment the thought was out, he shuddered as something soft and slimy plopped onto the back of his neck and slid down the front of his shirt. Looking back up at his daughter, he found her smile beaming back at him. Katie held her fork in her hand, with the remaining bits of lettuce and dressing hanging from the tongs.

"Sorry, Daddy," she shrugged, flashing him a bright smile.

"That's ok, Katie bug," Cole smiled, fishing the lettuce from the front of his shirt. "How in the world?" he asked, looking back at her again.

At times like this, Cole felt outnumbered. Katie ate her meal with a bright smile plastered across her face and he rubbed his tired eyes, returning the smile and digging into his own food. He felt slightly ashamed of his earlier impatience with Brent, knowing that his friend simply couldn't help himself. Ever since Cole moved here, Brent Williams and Will Robbins had been by his side.

The three had become close friends. Like Katie, Brent had a teasing side, which he could not hide. When in her company, that side came out, often leaving Cole on the receiving end. As frustrated as he became at times, he just couldn't get angry. Yet it was fun to gripe, especially when Katie was not around and Brent and Will ended up antagonizing one another. Cole didn't know whether he was the middleman or the straight-man, and usually ended up being the one to break up their arguments, which were good-natured and only took place in the absence of anything better to do.

Brent was totally different from Cole in appearance and stature. Although Brent was almost the same height as his friend, he was a bit stockier, sporting an extra 10 pounds on his frame. Yet, like Cole, he was solid muscle from the hard work a ranch demanded and the added weight went unnoticed. His blond hair fell impishly over his forehead, setting off deep, icy blue eyes. His smile was shy, yet his demeanor was impulsive and often brash. Brent was single and lived at home, where he worked the ranch alongside his father.

Will Robbins rounded out the threesome. Shorter than Cole and Brent, Will was of average height and weight. He sported closely cropped brownish hair that remained hidden under his worn hat, which rarely seemed to come off. Will had married his high school sweetheart, Lisa, and they had two sons, Lucas, 6 and Jordan, 8. Both boys were close friends of Katie's and enjoyed the times they were able to come over to the ranch and play. He, too, ran a cattle ranch, which had been passed down from his parents.

The last few years had been hard ones for Will. Due to a drought and a drop in the cattle market, he was barely making ends meet and was hoping that this year would be better than the previous two. So far he had been lucky; he had not suffered any major losses, yet he barely broke even, not making the profit hoped for. Like everyone else, Will forged ahead and did not let the hard times get him down for long.

Cole knew what a lucky man he was; he had been able to build a new life for himself, along with a family he loved and adored. At the center of that family was Katie, then it slowly spread out, enveloping practically everyone he came in contact with. The entire town had rallied around him, making him one of their own, and giving him the love and acceptance he so desperately needed.

His reverie was shaken by the inevitable 'uh oh,' coming from Katie's side of the table and the meatball that rolled from her plate, unceremoniously plopping onto the floor. Cole just smiled deeply at her, alternately staring between her and the saucy mess. Seeing the smile on her father's face, Katie kicked her legs happily while she tried scooping another forkful of spaghetti into her mouth.

Chapter Two

"Ahhhh, this is the life," Gris sighed as he leaned back against the thick trunk of the tree. "Just look at all those stars!"

"Yeah, it's nice," Cole answered absently. He sat up straight, knowing that if he leaned back, he would fall asleep immediately.

"Something wrong, son?" Gris worried.

"No, nothing really," Cole yawned, knowing that it was fruitless to fight.

"You seem pretty tired. You doing too much?" Gris asked.

"Gris, there's always too much to do at home. If the horses don't need something then Katie needs something. It never ends," Cole said, ashamed of his feelings.

"Katie giving you trouble? I find that hard to believe, she's always been a good little girl!" Gris exclaimed. He, too, had lost his heart to Katie's charms. Like Ruth, Gris now had a reason to go on. Cole and Katie were his family and he looked after both.

"Katie's not the problem," Cole said quietly. "Oh, I don't know! Sometimes the days pass by and everything falls into place and seems all right, you know?"

"Yeah, that about sums it up," Gris nodded agreeably.

"And other days, you find yourself thinking. Gris, what if I screw this up? I mean, when I think that her entire being depends on me, it still blows me away! It's scary, you know? If I make any mistakes with Katie, then I screw up big time! You can't make mistakes with a child! And I've screwed up a lot in my life," Cole blurted out.

"Oh my, it all still comes down to that, doesn't it?" Gris turned his worried eyes to Cole. "Son, first of all, you didn't screw anything up. You had a lot of hard knocks in your life, most of them undeserved, but that wasn't your doing! You can't change fate! It marches on with or without us! It has a mind of its own and all we can do is sit back and watch."

"You know what they say about the sins of the father," Cole began.

"Nonsense!" Gris blurted out. "A child doesn't pay for what her father has done. Especially if he hasn't done anything wrong!"

"Didn't do anything wrong? What I did wasn't wrong?" Cole said, aghast.

"Are you talking about Maggie, or…." Gris hesitated, staring intently at Cole

"Does it matter?" Cole asked softly.

"Son, it matters a lot. Cole, you can't change what happened to Sarah! No one can! You didn't cause it and you can't change it," Gris exclaimed.

"You should tell that to…." Cole stopped.

"Well, they were wrong!" Gris snapped. "And I think that they know it by now! You know, son, grief can cause people to act in ways that they would never act normally. Matt's thinking was clouded with grief. You have to remember that he wasn't in his right mind then."

"None of us were in our right minds! We were all faced with something that was unthinkable, but no one more than me!"

"Cole, it's been six years. That's a long time and people can change. Blind grief has a way of working itself out and we start looking at things differently. Son, in the heat of all that hurt, no one can think straight. Your worlds as you knew them all ceased to exist and no one could figure out why or how it happened. There just aren't any answers. You haven't called Matt or been back to Broken Arrow in six years, what makes you think that you're the only one still hurting?" Gris asked, looking over.

Both men were silent for a sliver of a moment. All Cole could do was shrug. Going back to Broken Arrow would mean going back to the hurt. Cole would rather remain separated from all that. Taking a deep breath, Gris continued.

"Cole, grief changes everything. Nothing in our lives is the same and sometimes we just don't know how to go on. Some of us turn from those we love and wallow in a wall of self-pity and others just leave. You did that, you couldn't face your loss and left the only home you've ever known. Your lives spun out of control and that's the hardest part to accept. It's hard to gain control again when it's snapped away like that. We all like to think we can control our own destinies, but when we find out that we're human and vulnerable after all, we find it hard to trust in ourselves again. I guess there's no worse feeling."

"We were grieving, but no one more than me! I lost so much!" Cole exclaimed, his nerves raw and on edge.

"You all lost; some more than others, but that really doesn't matter now, does it?" Gris asked, studying Cole intently. "Grief is grief, there's no way to measure how much someone suffers, it's just there. And in your case, it's affecting your self-confidence. Cole, I think this is more about Katie than it is Sarah," Gris reasoned, turning to look questioningly.

Cole bristled for a moment, then grudgingly realized that Gris was right.

"You know ... shit, you're right. Gris, I've been lost ever since Sarah and our baby died. I made some decisions that I've lived to regret. I don't want those mistakes coming back to hurt Katie. And I'm afraid that I'm going to make more wrong choices down the line where she's concerned. Gris, there's so much at stake! She depends on me for each and every need in her life!"

"And you will meet her needs as you always have," Gris sought to reassure Cole. "Cole, there are no guarantees in this life, and what happened between you and Maggie was a sad mistake, but I can understand how it came about. You both needed someone and you were there for each other. She was hurting too, but in a different way. That's no matter, though, cause hurt is hurt. When people are alone, it's only natural to reach out to someone. That's human nature, son! You can't change or help human nature, and you can't keep on kicking yourself your entire life. What's done is done and you have to go on with what you have and forget what has happened in the past and what you've done. Cole, Katie's growing older scares you. The choices and decisions are getting greater and she'll start asking more and more questions about the world around her."

"And I'll have to answer them," he said forlornly.

"You will, son, you will. Right now, it all seems so overwhelming. At times you don't seem to have any confidence in the decisions you make. You're scared, and that's only natural. Do you think you're the only parent who's scared?" Gris asked, turning towards Cole.

"You know me so well," Cole snickered. "And no, I don't think I'm the only one running scared."

"Son, raising a child is just about the scariest thing a person can do. Doing it alone is downright frightening. Just love her and everything else will fall into place. And remember, neither of you are alone," Gris said reassuringly.

"Ahh Gris, don't listen to me, you know how I can get at times. I tend to think too much and look back at things best left forgotten and worry them to death," Cole scoffed, tugging lightly on his line. "That's what happens when I'm tired, and tonight, I'm beat. It seems that no matter how much I do, nothing ever gets done. Have you ever felt like everything was pressing in on you? I feel like I spent the entire day running in circles and I don't think I've accomplished a thing," he sighed heavily.

"You still having trouble sleeping?" Gris worried, knowing how Cole's overworked mind sometimes led to sleepless nights.

"Sometimes. Not all the time, you know, but sometimes. Like I said, there's good times and there's still bad times."

"That's only natural, son. You'll always have bad spells, but how you deal with them is what's important now."

31

"How do I do that? How can I deal with anything, especially since I've made one mistake after another since Sarah's death? My life has been turned upside down; I don't even trust my own mind anymore. Look at my relationship with Maggie! That never should have happened! So tell me, Gris, how do I deal with things?" he asked, turning towards Gris, his eyes wide and questioning.

"Well, there's a number of ways. One of them is doing exactly what you're doing now. Talking about it! At least on some level you're getting it out," Gris nodded.

"And?"

"And the other ways you might not be so receptive to," Gris sighed deeply.

"Which are?" Cole asked warily.

"First, it might help to talk to someone else, you know...." Gris hedged.

"Oh no! I'm not going to talk to a shrink! I'm not nuts!" Cole cried out.

"I didn't say you were nuts, Cole! Just cause someone is at a point in their life where they need to talk to a professional doesn't mean they're nuts! It means you've suffered something so traumatic that it changed your entire life. You didn't know how to deal with it then and you don't know how to deal with it now! There's no shame in talking to someone," Gris replied.

"I am talking to someone," Cole found himself grumbling. "And I won't talk to anyone else. I don't mean to be blunt, but I know what your other thing is; you want me to contact Matt and talk things out. Well, I won't do that either, and there's no sense in arguing about it. As far as everything else, I can handle it."

"Can you really?" Gris looked over questioningly. "Can you really handle it? You're sitting here telling me that you still have bad spells and trouble sleeping, even after six years. And now you're letting that interfere with your relationship with Katie! You can't forget what happened, and you're so scared of screwing up where Katie is concerned that you're forgetting how good a father you really are! Cole, you're a good daddy and that little girl loves you! Son, you have to stop blaming yourself for things you had no control over a long time ago and you have to learn to finally put it behind you and go on with your life! You have a little girl who adores you!"

"And I adore her more than she will ever know," Cole smiled slightly, taking the matter in a different direction. "I guess I'm just in one of my moods tonight. I tend to get stupid when I'm overtired. And sometimes the thought of forgetting about Sarah completely scares me."

"No one's asking you to forget her, Sarah's death will always follow you. But that doesn't mean you have to continue blaming yourself! Cole, losing someone the way you lost Sarah is something that impacts a person's life, changing them forever. How you live with those changes is up to you. You can let them beat you down to the point where you stop living altogether, or you can look to the future and try your best to get on with your life. Sarah would want that, you know! And, you now have a little one of your own to go on for!" Gris reminded him.

"She sure keeps me hopping at times!" Cole scoffed, shaking his head. "Maybe that's my problem tonight. Gris, like I said, I'm just tired! It's been a long week and today was busier than I wanted it to be. We had a late start; we had to rush to the store and rush back to get things put away. Then Katie needed her nap and I had to get the horses taken care of and dinner to get."

"No wonder you're so tired! A woman's work is never done, I'm getting tired just listening to you!" Gris yawned.

"It's not always this bad, most days things go smoothly and I don't feel it as much. But tonight, it just hit me," Cole said, stifling a yawn.

"Raising a child by yourself is never easy, no matter how much help someone gives. You're still doing it all on your own," Gris nodded.

"Yeah, Lord knows her mother isn't any help. Hell, I wonder if she'll even remember that Katie's fourth birthday is in a couple of weeks." Cole turned his head towards Gris.

"Well, since she hasn't acknowledged her other birthdays...." he said matter of factly.

"Why should this one be any different? Right? I mean after all, she had her 'real' family to go back to," Cole snorted.

"That's about right, but if you ask me it's for the best. Would rather have no mother at all than have one who doesn't really care, yet comes around every once in a while pretending to," Gris exclaimed, feeling his fury building.

"You know, most of the time I can understand it, because she does have her family to think of. But damn it, Gris! She could have found a way to work this out!" Cole swore.

"Think about that, Cole, could she really?" Gris asked softly.

Cole sighed deeply, letting his shoulders sag. "No, she couldn't. I mean, if she claimed Katie, then we'd have a frigging mess because there's no way I'd let her go. And then we'd have the fallout with her family to consider. That would be messy as hell. Telling your husband and kids that a new little one is coming into the family but the father is another man is about the worst. But that doesn't make her a bad person!"

"No, and if you can see that it doesn't make her a bad person, why can't you seem to believe the same about yourself?" Gris shot back.

"I … oh hell, I don't have an answer to that! Because I should have known better! She was lost and needed someone...." Cole hesitated. "And I was just as lost. Not a good combination, if you ask me. Our coming together created more turmoil than anything. Gris, it's a frigging mess, you know?"

"Cole, she had to walk away from her baby. Maggie will always carry that in her heart," Gris reminded him.

"But she's the one who made this decision. She's the one who decided that things go this way so that she could protect her life. So, I went along with it. But Gris, I pray the day never comes where she comes back, cause I don't want her back. She denied Katie once, whether her intentions were just or not, she chose to deny her daughter. That's the way it is and that's the way it'll stay. Katie is mine, no matter what," Cole said.

As hard as he argued, Cole still could not shake Maggie's rejection of Katie, knowing his feelings were unjust and contradictory. The woman walked away from her own daughter, and he never wanted her to walk back. He and Gris sat quietly for a while longer, talking while they fished. Then fatigue set in and both men rose stiffly. The walk back was silent.

* * *

They returned to Ruth's house tired, yet triumphant. Gris bid a hasty goodnight since he had a batch of trout to clean and get into the freezer, and Cole just wanted to go home and put his feet up.

"Honey, you look tired tonight, do you feel well?" Ruth worried, placing the back of her hand against his forehead.

"Shows that much, huh?" Cole tried grinning.

"Are you sick, Daddy?" Katie worried.

"No, honey, I'm not sick. I'm just very tired and that's why we're going home and straight to bed!" Cole smiled tiredly.

"No story?" Katie gasped, her eyes wide and sad.

"Of course we're going to have our story! I wouldn't forget our story!" Cole answered, scooping her up into his arms. He tossed his head back laughing as she tickled his face with her fingers. "Were you a good girl?"

"Yes, Daddy," she smiled, teasing him. "Nanny made cookies and a cake today. She says we can have some tomorrow!"

"We can?" he smiled over.

"Yes, after our dinner!" Ruth beamed. "And you're not going to say no! I want the company and you need the break after cooking dinner tonight! I'm making a roast chicken with all the trimmings and dinner is at three, so don't be late!" she answered, her voice broaching no argument.

"Well, looks like we're going to be coming here for dinner! But right now, we're going home to get ready for bed!" Cole said, grabbing Katie up and kissing Ruth as he went out the door.

* * *

Sleep was fleeting and hard to come by that night. Katie was good, but not as tired as Cole had hoped she would be from playing in Ruth's front yard. She had spent the evening chasing fireflies until it grew late and Ruth brought her inside. Together, the two sat watching television until the men came back from fishing. Cole was dragging, Gris was ecstatic from his catch, and Katie was bright-eyed and wide awake.

The ride home was quick, they lived less than a mile from Ruth's place so there wasn't even enough time to lull Katie into a state of drowsiness. At first, driving over seemed silly, the walk wasn't much more than a short jaunt over the hill, but considering how tired he felt, Cole was glad that he did not have to make the trip home on foot. He doubted if he could even put one foot in front of the other. Katie bounced with excitement while he began their nightly routine, which started by getting her into her pajamas and then pouring a small cup of milk.

"Honey, please hold still!" Cole pleaded, trying to grab her feet to put her pajama bottoms on.

"I can't help it, Daddy! They don't want to stop!" Katie giggled, kicking her legs as she rolled across the bed.

As tired as he was, Cole just couldn't be mad. "You little weasel," he growled, diving onto the bed.

The wooden frame groaned under his sudden weight, making Cole fear it collapsing. But it held sturdy, much to his relief. The last thing he wanted to do tonight was retrieve his tools from the barn and spend half the night repairing a broken bed frame. He finally managed to capture his wayward daughter and get her pajamas on. With Katie tucked securely under his arm like a small sack of potatoes, Cole walked into the kitchen for her milk.

Grabbing their favorite quilt, he carried her into the living room, where they sat in the rocker. Wrapped in the quilt, Katie drank quietly while Cole started reading their story. It could have been the same story night after night and she would not have minded. Ruth had given them a book of nursery rhymes and fairy tales shortly after Katie was born and for as long as Cole could remember, he sat this way, reading while rocking his baby in his arms. Before she was old enough to drink milk from a cup, Katie snuggled in Cole's lap with her bottle. It made no difference if she understood what he was saying or not, all she needed was to be in his arms.

"Honey, which one will it be tonight?" Cole asked her softly.

"The billy goats!" Katie answered, stifling a yawn.

Cole turned to the page and started reading. Katie finished her milk and the cup was placed on the table, forgotten. They were visiting a very special world right now and nothing else mattered. Katie snuggled down into her father's arms while he read, his voice softly lulling her to sleep. He had to read two stories before she finally dozed off, yet he still sat rocking her, in spite of his own fatigue. The night was theirs; the crickets were singing, a soft breeze blew in from the open window and Cole rocked his baby in his arms, not wanting to put her down yet. If he did, another night would go by and another day would be earmarked into his memory. He just was not ready to let go.

Fatigue soon won out. As much as he hated to, Cole knew that it was useless to fight the hands of time; he had to put his little bundle down for the night. He wished that he could freeze the hands on the clock, thereby stopping the world from rushing by so quickly. Rocking Katie, it seemed as if they had an eternity to do so. Yet the seconds turned into minutes and soon it was almost an hour. Their time was now implanted in the recesses of his mind.

Cole was tired and needed to try and get some rest. Morning always came too quickly, with the horses and Katie all clamoring for his attention. Yawning loudly, he shuffled down the hall and put his daughter into her bed. After pulling the quilts up snugly around her neck and placing her bunny under her arms, he went into his own room.

* * *

Maybe it was because he was too tired, or maybe he just was not as tired as he thought. It had been a long day, but Cole had known longer. Sure, he had done a lot today, but he was used to starting early in the morning and working straight through into the night. No, his weariness stemmed from somewhere else. Funny, earlier he could have fallen asleep where he sat, now he lay in bed wide awake, staring at the ceiling.

He began dozing off, or at least he thought he had; sometimes it was hard to tell if it was the darkness that plagued his mind or sleep that was lulling him away. His eyes closed and he was falling. There was nothing to grab on to and with a sudden lurch, he hit bottom. Stifling a strangled gasp, Cole vaulted upwards in bed, covered in a sheen of sweat. His heart pounded and his head swam for a moment as fear filled his soul. Unsure of his surroundings, his own home became unfamiliar.

Trapped between sleep and wakefulness, Cole had no way of knowing which he wanted. He was tired, but falling asleep seemed like too much work. He tried sitting up, but his eyes were too heavy to stay open. Nothing worked; he would just have to ride this out the best he could. Sometimes this would only last a little while and sleep would eventually come, and other times it lasted straight through the night. He would find himself standing in front of his window staring out at the sunrise. When that happened, he wondered if he ever slept at all, or if he had simply stood here waiting for the day to begin.

"Hell, you could have slept where you stood for all you know," he grumbled, remembering that time only too well. It had happened more than once.

Cole lay on his back, trying to let his mind relax so he could drift off. Too restless and uncomfortable to stay that way, he flipped over onto his stomach. Not even five minutes later, he found himself thinking that it would be more comfortable on his back, so he flopped back. Then he tried staring at the ceiling; if he could only fixate on something, then maybe his eyes would close without even realizing it. Ten minutes later, he was still staring. Giving up, he turned onto his stomach once more, and then back over. Frustrated, Cole growled, throwing his feet over the edge of the bed and sitting up.

It was time to stop fooling himself, he knew that there would be no sleep for him now, if at all tonight. If sleeping pills weren't so addictive, then he would take them gladly. But sleeping pills were not what was needed. One needed peace of mind in order to sleep, and peace of mind was one commodity that Cole could not claim that night. Besides, if he couldn't sleep naturally, then he would rather not sleep at all. Why his mind tortured him some nights and let him be others was something Cole would never understand. He just learned to live with it. Knowing that this was not going to be an easy night, there was only one thing to do.

He went into his daughter's room and carefully sat on the side of her bed. With a sigh of relief, Cole saw that he had not wakened her. Katie's long eyelashes framed her small face, her almost heart-shaped lips fluttering softly as she breathed.

"You have a stuffy nose again, don't you, little Katie bug?" Cole snickered slightly to himself. "Just like your old man. Sometimes even when I'm not coming down with a cold my nose stuffs up at night and I breathe through my mouth. No wonder you sometimes cry for something to drink," he muttered, watching his daughter sleep. The wonder of this tiny being never ceased to amaze him. Gently reaching out, he brushed her hair back.

"I'll dance across the heavens with your mane as my reins," Cole said softly, almost wishing that he could hear her voice once again. "That's what I said to her one night, Katie bug. This giant horse swooped down from the clouds and I jumped onto his back. I soared into the heavens, hearing her laughter following me. She watched in wonder, stretching her arms out to reach me. We swooped lower and I grabbed her by the fingers and lifted her onto the horse's back. He reared, flailing his powerful legs in the air and stating his dominance before he turned, bringing us back up to the ends of the world. We rode on his back, soaring across the sky. We danced across the heavens, with me holding on to his mane. I could feel the power in his legs, his muscles rippling as we raced along. We flew from cloud to cloud, with her holding on to me the entire time. But she's gone now, and the horse doesn't do any more dancing. No one dances anymore," he said sadly.

Cole could feel the darkness setting in. As much as he struggled to fight it, his actions were to no avail. He was in a black mood, falling into a familiar, yet hated place. Katie was already asleep and he just couldn't bring himself to go into his lonely room. Even though it had been six years, there were times he still could not face it. The grief was as fresh as it was six years ago, the pain just as intense. Cole had hoped to draw comfort from his little girl, who slept soundly.

"I wish that you knew her, Katie bug, she was something else. She would have loved you as much as I do. I like to think of her as your mother, you know?" Cole whispered quietly. "I wish that...." he said, stopping.

"Oh hell, give it up. You wish what? You wish that you could turn back the hands of time? You wish that you could bring her back? Well, you can't and it's been six years! Six long years that have given you enough time to put things behind you and go on with your life. What the hell's wrong with you?" Cole swore inwardly.

"I'm sorry for what I might have put on you, Katie bug. That's what's wrong with me," Cole said softly as he stood staring down at his daughter. "I'm not sorry for you, no one could be sorry for you, but I'm sorry for the weakness that I carry that deemed the way you came into the world. I've done so much wrong in my life, and my wrongs have always affected those I love the most, Katie bug. I fear the day you think less of me. I only pray that the one wrong that scares me more than anything doesn't come back to haunt you one day."

Cole sighed heavily as he leaned back against the wall. "You're so little. So innocent! How can something as beautiful as you exist because of me? I'm sorry, Katie bug, but even you can't help me tonight," Cole thought sadly as he walked silently from her room.

* * *

He went outside, where he sat on the porch, deep in thought. If he had only been stronger that night. Being restless and alone was no excuse for what he did, yet it happened. For the life of him, it happened, and he prayed that Katie would not pay the price. He should have thought before acting, at least more than he did initially, yet, if he had thought differently and if his resolve had broken through, Cole would be alone right now. He would not have Katie. Again, the fates that had not made any sense in years brought him to this end. Joy and blessing from something that should not have been, was now his.

Chiding himself deeply, Cole strove to drive such thoughts from his mind. Ruth had reminded him time and time again not to think of Katie as an accident. A child was never an accident. A child just was. They came in their own time and in ways that sometimes made no sense, but they were never a mistake. If he kept on thinking in such a manner, and if his daughter ever heard or even felt his doubts, then she would be devastated, for no child wants to think of themselves as an accident. They are born feeling loved and wanted, Cole was not about to drive that feeling away. Katie would always remain treasured, no matter how he felt about himself.

Maggie and Sarah. Sarah and Maggie. Two women who had been a part of his life. Two women he had been unable to keep in his life. He could not shake either one. They were his greatest remorse and deepest sorrow. Now there was Katie. All three were instrumental in bringing him to where he was today. All three shaped his life as he knew it. Would he let his daughter down as he did the women who had crossed his path? Cole could only shudder at the thought.

He sat on the front porch of his small home staring up at the stars. Cole tried remembering Sarah's smile, but her image failed him. He had forgotten her face. That brought on another surge of sadness; after loving her all those years, now he could not even remember her face.

Why didn't you come to me? Why don't you come to me? They say that when we lose someone we love, someone that's close to us, they never really leave us. I'd like to think that you never really left me. It hurts too much to know that you're gone forever, but I know that you are, he thought tiredly, burying his face in his hands.

Cole had always believed that lost loved ones came back to a person in their dreams. They reached out, crossing back into our lives for that sliver of time. He never believed that this could happen during the day, although some believe that it can and does. When we are asleep, they come. We see their faces and hear their voices. They reach out, sharing a small bit of their lives with us again. The loneliness is forgotten for just a little while and sometimes, if a person is lucky enough, he wakes up with a renewed sense of hope that had been forgotten.

"You never came to me. Your voice never whispered across my ears and you never invaded my dreams, not even for a second. I know that I wasn't there for you when you died, but do you blame me? Do you blame me for what happened to you? Everyone else does, but if I thought you did then I don't think that anything could make me want to go on. Maybe that's why you stay away, you're disappointed in the person I really am. Now that you're not a part of this world, you see everything for what it is. You see a side of me you've never seen before. No matter how well you know a person, you never know everything. Now, you know everything. Is that why you don't speak to me? You don't like what you see?" Cole shuddered.

"I wish that I'd died instead of you; I'll always wish that. Sometimes the world is so dark and depressing, I find it hard to breathe. I feel as if I'm in a pit, surrounded by nothing but blackness. The floor falls away and I find myself crashing into nothing. There's nothing to catch me. I don't belong to this world and I can't come to yours. I'm trapped in a hellish nightmare I've created for myself. Or did I? Maybe it was created for me. All I know is that I can't breathe, everything comes screaming at me at once. You're gone, I'll never forget that. I'm trapped in the dark and there's no way out. I'm so tired that even with Katie in my life, I find it hard to go on at times. During the day when I feel everything pressing in on me again, one look at her face is enough to save me. But at night, she's not here and I'm alone. The demons start screaming at me. I'm their prey. I need you to help me during those times, but you don't come. I think that if it weren't for Katie, I wouldn't be able to go on. Without her, I'd have nothing."

"You still have nothing," Cole whispered softly. "You have Katie now, but can you keep her? Is something going to come along and take her from you? Maybe you were meant to be alone, only you're fighting your destiny and changing your fate. In doing that, you might have sealed your fate. Maybe the powers that be are just teasing you, letting you have a tiny bit of happiness and love, only to rip it away again. That's the problem with being truly happy, it's only fleeting … just a shallow, mirror image. Like a mirage, it doesn't exist. It only lulls you into a false sense of peace and just when you think that you have your life back and you let your guard down, they come back, ripping everything away from you. They always rip it away," he sobbed quietly, holding his hands over his face.

Chapter Three

The black times dissipated as quickly as they hit ... until the next round. They struck at will, guiding his life moment by moment. This moment, the sun rose and Cole greeted the day, grateful to feel his mood lessening. He still sat in his rocker as the first golden rays climbed over the hills, stirring as the warmth of the morning spilled down over him. It was a bright morning, just the type of day he looked forward to. It was only the beginning of May, yet the weather had turned unusually warm. Last night, there had not even been a chill in the air. Cole had kept Katie's windows closed, yet his were open to the gentle breeze flowing across the back pastures. In spite of the singing of the crickets and the warm night air that blew in softly over the head of his bed, he was unable to relax. Seeking refuge on the front porch, he was still there at first light.

Clad in the pajama bottoms and tee shirt from the previous night, Cole went inside to change. There were chores to attend to, and lounging over coffee all morning while still in his nightclothes was a luxury he could not afford himself. Plus, his hair was a mess and he knew he looked like hell. One glimpse at his reflection in the window was enough to attest to that fact; he would scare Katie to death if she saw him looking like one haunted.

He thanked God that Ruth would not be by that morning, she worried enough about him as it was. She seemed to have a certain sixth sense where Cole was concerned, and he learned long ago that it was useless to hide his feelings from her.

In spite of the lack of real sleep, he was not tired. He thought that odd; he should have been dragging, yet was full of energy and ready to tackle the day. The only reminder of sleeping in the rocking chair was the slightly stiff neck he knew would work its way out. Dressed, he tossed yesterday's clothes in the ever growing pile, hoping that he would have the chance to get at least one load finished before they had to leave for Ruth's.

"Grocery shopping and laundry, the two scourges of the American housewife," Cole snickered to himself.

His mood was lifting, yet the memories remained. Gris was right, how he chose to act on those memories was up to him. Drowning in self-pity never

41

did anyone any good, Cole had to remain strong for Katie. Whistling softly, he went into the kitchen to start the coffee. His mouth was like cotton and he poured a glass of orange juice while waiting. There was still a few minutes before he had to go out into the barn, so he used that time to just sit at the table, slowly drinking his juice.

Cole looked around his small kitchen; his home was not large by any stretch of the mind, but it was comfortable and it was attractive. Using the money from the sale of his land back in Broken Arrow, he had purchased the ranch shortly after his arrival in Crater Mills. Leaving his home had been hard, but it was the only choice he had. In spite of working day and night, trying to build a life for himself, Sarah and their unborn baby, Cole's dream was snuffed out the night they perished.

Unable to deal with the shocking aftermath of their deaths, he simply left. He did not know how to stay and go on as if nothing happened. His family had been the center of his life. When they were taken from him, Cole lost the will to live. After wandering aimlessly for a while, he felt the need to put down roots somewhere. Once he came to the tiny town of Crater Mills, Cole knew where he belonged.

If he thought Broken Arrow to be small, nothing prepared him for Crater Mills. It was about half the size of the town he had come from, which was not saying much. Other than that, the only noticeable difference was that after being born and raised in Broken Arrow, Cole knew everyone there. Even after his parents' death, he stayed on, trying to make a go of the ranch. Now he found himself in a strange town where he didn't know a soul. Like any other small town, though, the people of Crater Mills were friendly and caring, and welcomed him into their fold. It was not long before he was on a first name basis with just about everyone; considering that there were not that many people to begin with, Cole would have been ashamed if he did not become familiar with them.

Heading into town upon his arrival, the first thing that greeted him was the newly paved Main Street. He could tell that it had only been a matter of maybe a year or two since they had finally gotten rid of the dirt road that ran through, especially judging that the side roads were still nothing more than dirt lanes. There were no streetlights, none were needed, and the roadways weren't clogged with early morning traffic jams like most towns and cities were.

Those who worked in town walked to their places of business when the weather permitted, and everyone else worked the many farms and ranches that dotted the area. The largest part of Crater Mills' economy stemmed from those ranches, all of which were passed down from generation to generation.

Cole was lucky; his ranch had been put on the market about a week before he arrived. Shane Wilson, the previous owner, had passed on two months prior to his arrival. There simply was not an heir to pass the property down to, a fact that saddened many people in the area.

The one thing they prized more than anything else was family. It was the first and most important priority in their lives. Fathers proudly taught their sons and daughters to work the land, very much in the same manner as their fathers before them. They then worked side by side until it was time for the child to take over. That cycle continued generation after generation, with each new descendant proudly carrying on the traditions and teachings of their ancestors. It was sad not to have anyone to pass one's heritage on to. After Shane's death, the town declared themselves his family and gave him a proper service, promising that they would carry his memory within their hearts and would make sure that his deeds were never forgotten.

Upon arriving in town that first day, Cole found himself stopping at the general store. The large red cooler marked 'Coke' was what attracted him, with it taking two bottles of pop to cut the dust from his throat. It was the middle of summer and there had been no rain for weeks. Everyone moved a little slower and Cole wiped the sweat from his brow as he walked around slowly, getting familiar with the place.

"Can I help you, young man?" Harold Becker greeted him.

"You the store owner?" Cole smiled, extending his hand.

"Sure am, young fella. Harold Becker, at your service, like my father and his father before him. Only folks around here call me Hal," he smiled warmly.

"Name's Cole Morgan, nice to meet ya," he shook his hand firmly.

"What can I do for you?" Hal asked.

"Well, I really don't know where to start," Cole began. "I'm new to town, as you can see," he laughed with Hal. "And I'm in need of a temporary place to stay while I look around for a piece of property to buy."

"I think I can help you out with the place to stay. I have a few rooms out back where I can put you up for as long as you need.... Oh, do you have a family with you?" he asked, wincing at his words. The minute they were out, he saw the darkness descending over Cole's eyes like a curtain. But Cole forced himself to smile, shaking off the dark thoughts for now.

"No, just me," he shrugged. "And I don't need much. Just a place to lay my head and I'll be fine."

"I can offer you that! There's a nice room out back. This one's my favorite. It's small, but clean. Only has a bed, bureau, and a pitcher and washstand. For the winter, there's a woodburning stove in the corner, and a chair to relax in. Sorry, there's no kitchen privileges, the original one was just so outdated that I never did get a chance to put a new, workable one in. But I've worked out a deal with Sadie over at the diner where your meals are paid for with the room, so you needn't worry about that. We surely won't let a body starve!" he laughed at his own joke.

"That's good to hear!" Cole laughed, already warming up to the man.

Oddly, he felt at home. Cole had only been in town for a mere ten minutes, but it felt as if he truly belonged. He followed Hal into the back room, finding that he was indeed true to his word. The room was small, but it was clean and very comfortable. The wood floors looked as though they had just been swept, although dull and in need of sanding and refinishing. Not surprisingly, the walls were done in old, unfinished pine. The wood had been painted white at one time, but had faded over the years and was rough to the touch.

There were two windows, one over the bed, and one on the other side of the room overlooking the southern end of town. Cole breathed deeply, almost envisioning the cross breeze that would come into his room from the open range beyond, at night. The nightstand sat next to the bed, with a filled kerosene lantern sitting at the ready. A doily-covered antique dresser was placed on the far wall, and a washstand with an even older, cream-colored pitcher was placed against the opposite wall under the window. The overstuffed bed was covered with a homemade quilt, and Cole was informed that a trunk of extra quilts sat at the end of the hall, if needed.

"Uhhh...." he said, glancing around.

"Oh, the facilities! How in the world could I go and forget the facilities? Man's most important room!" Hal slapped his leg, bellowing heartily. "Come on, follow me down the hall, young fella! We sort of have a community bathroom, which you'll have to share with two other tenants, but since the other rooms are empty, you'll have it to yourself!" he said, opening the door.

"Now this room isn't as fancy as some of them there newfangled bathrooms you see in those newer houses, but that's ok. They're about as overrated as the houses themselves are. They just don't build things like they used to. This place can take anything the weather can throw at us and has weathered many a blizzard over the years. You throw one good strong wind at those other places and they fall down like a house of cards!" Hal nodded, trying not to brag too much.

His grandfather had founded the small general store in the late 1800s, with his father then adding onto it when he took over. Hal had been born and raised in these very rooms, and the only reason he was not living there now was that he had six children, too many to fit in the three small bedrooms.

They lived in a modest home on the outskirts of town, with Hal walking to the small store early in the morning, no matter what the weather.

No one could ever remember a time when his doors failed to open. Even during the worst winter blizzards, Hal kept a light in the window and a fire in the woodstove. He always slept over, ready to help out if need be. No one could ever tell what type of emergency would arise in the middle of winter, and Hal was truly dedicated to his job; it was his way of life. Cole felt as if he had gone back 100 years when he first walked into town; looking around his new surroundings, he was positive that he had.

Cole walked in, looking around the room. This was definitely a trip back through time. "Does this work?" he asked, fingering the pull chain that hung over the toilet.

"Go ahead and pull, you'll see! You ain't never seen one of them pull-chains before?" Hal beamed.

"Yeah, my grandmother had one," Cole pulled the chain, returning the smile. "Well, I'll be dipped!" he laughed, seeing the water swirling before it went down, flushing majestically. "Now my prayers are answered! I have a place to hang my hat and a working pull-chain! What more could a man want!"

"How about that old porcelain tub over there under the window?" Hal pointed.

"Now that's a beauty! Don't see many of them around anymore! You can actually fill the tub right up to your neck and soak!" Cole snickered. He had to laugh when he saw the old razor strap hanging from the wall. Looking further, Cole was oddly intrigued by the tray attached to the side of the tub, holding an array of shaving supplies and a mirror.

"That's something I came up with!" Hal said proudly. "I grew up here! I brought the misses to live here after we married, and we stayed until too many little ones came along! The one and only thing I loathed about this place was standing at the sink and shaving, especially in the winter. Boy, this room sure does get cold! In the summer it didn't bother me, but since we have more cold here in this part of the country than warmth, I purely hated standing here freezing my balls off just to shave! The woodstove just didn't reach in here that much and we didn't have these kind of heaters back then," he said, kicking at the small electric radiator with his foot.

"So, you shaved while you bathed?" Cole asked, with a halfway grin plastered across his face.

"You got it! I would lie back in the hot water and relax. I got so lazy that I even shaved in there during the summer! Only the tub would be filled with cool water so I didn't sweat my ass off!"

"You got it down to a science! How about your bathroom now? You still do that?" Cole asked curiously.

"Every day of my life!" Hal slapped his knee, laughing loudly. "Now, how 'bout it, young fella? You ready to move in, or what?"

"I sure am...." Cole replied, with both discussing the terms.

After paying the first month's rent in advance, it didn't take long to gather up his meager belongings and move in. The first thing that had been unpacked from the battered old suitcase Cole carried in had been a small, wooden box, which was placed in the top drawer of the bureau. After brushing his finger gently across the smooth wooden surface, he took a deep breath and closed the drawer as he looked around his new room.

Now, after six years, Cole was settled again. He had a small, but comfortable home, which he and his daughter were extremely happy in. It had not taken long for him to find the place, either. Ed Haskins, the only real estate agent in town, brought Cole here a week after his arrival. One look at the rolling green pastures and the stream that cut through the back of the property, he knew he was home.

The barn was in need of repair, with the roof leaking in a few places, only because Shane had been too old and weak to climb a ladder the last few years of his life to take care of it. Since he only had one mule left, there was really nothing to fix it for. He just kept Sweet Pea in the dry part of the barn and simply closed off the rest.

The house was also in reasonably good shape, although cluttered. Cole could tell that it had been hard for Shane to get rid of things. The man had been a virtual packrat. It took about a week to dig through all of his belongings; most of which were given to the people in town so that they would have something to remember their friend by, or donated to charity.

Sweet Pea now resided on Zeke Hill's ranch, and was so comfortable Cole didn't have the heart to uproot the poor animal and bring him back home. With Shane gone, it would not be much of a home anyway, so Cole let him be. The only items kept were the heavy oak kitchen table and chairs, the large overstuffed sofa in the living room, and the rocker that sat in front of the fireplace. The bed in the master bedroom was falling apart, so he opted for new.

Watching him moving into his new home with very few belongings was a sad testament to the tragedy everyone knew Cole had suffered. No mention of his lack of furnishings was made, and no one pushed him to talk about the fire. A man's home had burned, that was all anyone wished to hear. The one place where everyone remained safe and comfortably sequestered each and every day of their lives was what Cole had lost. They did not relish hearing the details. If Cole wanted to talk, then he would. Other than that, they kept their questions to themselves and their minds on other things. Cole either kept what Shane had left behind, or he went out and purchased new. The day he moved into his new home, he placed the small box from Sarah in his top drawer, where it had been since.

The simple, sprawling ranch style home, with low, elegant lines and a roofed porch running the entire length, was set against the backdrop of mountains. The paint was cracked and peeling, but it didn't take Cole long to scrape and redo the entire outside in a creamy, off-white hue. The window trim was done in a dark colonial green, with the inner trim offset by beige. The shutters matched the trim, and the deck had a tung oil finish of deep walnut.

Walking into the one-floor home, you came to a small foyer, which had an old coatrack, a table where keys were tossed, and a closet to the left. Turning to the right, you entered the living room, with knotty pine walls finished to a soft, golden hue, and a fieldstone fireplace. Two large windows stood on either side of the hearth, giving a majestic view of the vast mountain range beyond. Cole relished the nights spent in front of the fire while looking out over the mountains bathed in moonlight.

He then spent the next few months blocking out the memories and pain by throwing himself blindly into work on the house and outbuildings. The barn needed extensive repairs before he could even think of bringing horses in, and the house was in dire need of an overhaul. There were three bedrooms and Cole took the largest one. The bathroom was in the middle of the hall, between the master bedroom and the two smaller ones. To Cole's delight, there was an antique porcelain tub, much like the one at Hal's. He turned the larger of the two remaining rooms into a guestroom, knowing that was frivolous due to the fact that he never considered having guests in the first place. The last of the rooms was turned into a den, housing his desk, a large leather chair and a filing cabinet for his papers.

To the left of the living room was a small formal dining room which looked like it had not seen much use over the years and Cole knew that he would hardly use it himself. He had never been one to stand on formality, opting for the simpler things life had to offer. Further down the hall one entered the kitchen, which was large and square. A breakfast nook separated the small eating area from the main part of the room, with a heavy oak table facing the windows. The woodstove was located in the middle of the back wall and a butcherblock work island stood in the center of the room. The stove was electric, but it resembled the old, black cookstoves from years ago.

Cole could not help but snicker slightly; it was obvious that the stove was

Shane's small attempt to modernize the room, yet he was unable to break away from what he had probably been accustomed to. While scrounging around the old shed out back one day, Cole knew his line of thinking to be correct. Shane did indeed replace the old cookstove, but he had also been unable to junk it. Instead, the stove was placed in the corner of the shed, giving him an idea. It may not have been feasible to cook with any longer, but it was still solid, free of rust, and if need be, would be perfect for heating the shed during the winter.

The kitchen cabinets were old and handmade, and Cole instantly fell in love with them. He spent two weeks sanding them down and applying a rich, golden oak finish. The countertops were done in deep cranberry and the walls in between the countertop and the cabinets were brick, which Shane had retrieved from an old, abandoned house on the southern end of the property. The floor in the kitchen, like the floors throughout the rest of the house, was done in wide oak planking, and polished to a soft, wooden glow. The walls were also knotty pine, with the exception of the small eating area, which was oak siding halfway up, with flowered wallpaper above that. The wood trim was finished to match the cabinets. Cole's home was ready.

It had taken a lot of hard work, but he needed that work. Diving into each project was what kept him sane, or what he considered sane by the slimmest of margins. He would rise early, work as hard as he could until almost numb with fatigue, only to collapse and begin again the next day. Sitting at his table now, Cole was just finishing his second cup of coffee, not even realizing he had drunk that much already. So deep in thought about his arrival and remembering the first time he had come to his home, he suddenly realized that he had let an hour drift by while sipping the hot liquid. Looking at the clock, he knew that he had better get moving, and rose to start his day.

* * *

"Katie, I thought I told you to get your shoes?" Cole sighed, sitting back at the table.

"I did, Daddy, see?" she answered, holding one sneaker and one dress shoe in each hand.

"Honey, they don't match! Where's your other sneaker?" he asked.

"Daddy, Bunny ate it," she shrugged nonchalantly.

"Bunny ate it?" Cole's mouth fell open.

"Uh huh," she nodded, not seeing Brent coming in.

"Hey there, little angel!" Brent called out, scooping Katie up as she ran over. "What happened, did Bunny eat one of your shoes?"

"Daddy doesn't believe it. I hope he doesn't take Bunny out and shoot him," she said, her bottom lip trembling.

Cole jumped, seeing both Katie and Brent glaring at him. "Honey! Why on earth would you say something like that? I would never shoot Bunny! Where did you get such an idea?"

"I saw it on TV," she explained.

"You saw them shooting Bunny?" Brent quipped.

"You're not helping any," Cole grumbled. "Honey, what did you see on TV?"

"It was people with a gun and they were shooting animals," she said sadly. "Daddy, why did they do that?"

"Honey, I wished you told me that was on, you shouldn't watch things like that!" Cole exclaimed.

"I just wanted to watch my cartoons and you were fixing breakfast," Katie said in a trembling voice.

Cole pulled his daughter into his arms, "Honey, no matter what I'm doing or how busy I look, I'm never too busy for you! If you want or need something, then just come to me, ok?"

"Ok, Daddy, but why did they do that?" Katie asked.

"Did you see that this morning?" Cole wondered, seeing her answering nod. "Is that why you were afraid of telling me about your shoe earlier?"

"I thought you would be mad," she quivered.

"Honey, I would never, ever be that mad! And I would never ever shoot anything! Not even an animal! You know, I wish I saw that show, cause then I could have explained what happened. Did you watch all of it?"

"No, the guns scared me so I went in my bedroom," Katie replied.

"Honey, when you're scared, please come to me! I love you so much that whenever you're hurt or scared, I'm here to help! If you see something that upsets you or that you don't understand, then I can explain things to you. I don't know what you saw this morning, but some people hunt for food," he said, hoping that this would help. Knowing how sensitive his daughter was, Cole doubted that very much.

"Why can't they go to the store, Daddy?" she then asked.

"Honey, it's just that … well … maybe some people can't go to the store, that's all. Look, why don't you try to forget about what you saw and let's try and find your sneaker! Uncle Brent and I have some work to do," Cole smiled, putting his daughter back down.

"Uncle Brent, are you coming to Nanny's with us today?" she asked, hopefully.

"If your daddy invites me!" Brent replied brightly.

"You mean if Ruth invites you," Cole hissed.

"You know she loves me!" Brent teased. "There's always room for one more!"

"Don't you have a life?" Cole groaned.

"Not particularly," Brent shrugged.

"Figures, that's why you're always here. And why are you here? Your father finally get smart and toss you out on your ear?" Cole shot back.

"My dad would never do that! Remember who runs the place now," Brent crowed, puffing his chest out.

"Poor man, all his life's work...." Cole shook his head.

"Seriously, I just came over to see how you were doing. Thought that since you're coming over to our place the Friday after Katie's party to give us a hand readying the cattle for shipment, I'd return the favor. Ahead of time! You need any help round here?" Brent offered.

Putting his pride aside was hard for Cole, but he needed the help. There was no getting around it. Even though the horses were ready for the most part, there was always a lot of last-minute details that needed tending to. And Brent was right. They helped one another. Favors were always returned in one form or another, that went without saying. His friend could torment Cole to no end, but he had been Cole's first real friend since his arrival.

They all gave of themselves, pitching in and helping one another out. Brent was on hand to help out today, and a week from Friday, Cole would be at their ranch, giving them a hand in return. With the buyers coming shortly, Cole could not afford to turn any kind of help away; he was just beginning to make a name for himself, but there was still a long way to go. There was no time to waste by being prideful.

"Thanks, wasn't going to do much today but maybe try and check their hooves. Tomorrow am going to clean them real good and hopefully can get some turp put on them," Cole answered, clapping Brent on the shoulder.

"Daddy, what's turp?" Katie asked as she skipped back into the room. Cole smiled, noticing that she had her other sneaker in her hand.

"Bunny gave you your shoe back?" Cole grinned.

"Yep! And I had a long talk with him," she said seriously.

Brent had to turn away; he simply didn't think he could hold his laughter any longer. Katie was being as serious as a three-year-old could be and the last thing he wanted to do was laugh at her. But he just couldn't help himself, she always amazed him with some of the things she came up with.

She's sure giving her Daddy a run for his money, and she's not even grown yet, Brent snickered to himself.

"Is he going to listen now?" Brent asked, finally able to turn back.

"He's going to be good! Daddy, what's turp?" Katie asked, turning back to her father.

"Honey, it's short for turpentine. We have something called Venice Turpentine that we brush on the horses' hooves, it makes them stronger."

"How come?" she shrugged.

"Well, it's because they don't have any shoes...."

"Why? Did Bunny eat them?" Katie giggled teasingly.

That did it, Brent doubled over, sputtering as he broke out laughing. Katie leaned forward, staring at her father with a smile across her face as he finished tying her shoes.

"Katie...." he said, only seeing the way she shrugged her tiny shoulders.

"The horses are barefoot!" she continued her teasing.

Cole looked from his best friend to his daughter, thinking that maybe in some way she had inherited Brent's teasing streak. Either that or she had been hanging around him too long and it was starting to brush off. Whatever the reason, all Cole could do was look, seeing the teasing glint he knew so well in her eyes. He leaned forward, brushing his nose against hers.

"No, Bunny didn't eat their shoes, and no, they aren't running barefoot! Horses don't have feet!" he said.

"What do they walk on?" she asked, crossing her arms.

"Yeah, Daddy! What do they walk on?" Brent sat, crossing his arms too.

"Some friend you are," Cole hissed before turning his attention back to his daughter. "Honey, horses' feet are called hooves. They're hard, but they can crack and break. Some owners put shoes on their feet to protect them, but some people choose not to have shoes."

"But don't they break?" Katie wondered.

"Not really, honey! It all depends on where the horse walks. My horses are mostly in the fields and all around here and in the mountains. I prefer having shoes on my horses to help protect their hooves. But I don't put shoes on the horses that I'm selling unless the owner wants them. And they won't break because I don't take them in the mountains. They're just ridden in the fields where it's not so hard. The turpentine makes their feet stronger," Cole explained.

"See! They do have feet!" Katie declared happily.

"Yeah!" Brent fell back onto the couch, laughing helplessly.

"I meant hooves!" Cole answered, already feeling tired. "Honey, I meant hooves! Oh heck, all this talk about feet made me thirsty. Let's get a drink and go out to the barn," he said, putting a quick end to the conversation before things got totally out of hand. Things were already bad enough, Cole knew that he was seriously outnumbered.

* * *

The morning passed quickly, with both men making fast work of cleaning the horses' hooves. One horse had picked up a rock, and from the looks of things, it had been fairly recent. The area around the rock was not tender and the horse went back into the field with no problems. While the men worked, Katie frolicked in a large pile of hay with three new kittens. Her giggles had the men looking over, laughing at their antics. She lay on her back, with kittens climbing all over her, nibbling at her fingers and hair. One took a liking to the button on her shirt and alternated between biting and swatting at it.

"How do you keep up with her?" Brent shook his head.

"It's not easy!" Cole laughed with him. "If we could only harness and bottle that energy, then we'd be the richest people on earth!"

"The fountain of youth!" Brent nodded, grinning.

"That's about right, cause it's their innocence that keeps them going. Maybe that's why they don't get tired like we do," Cole surmised.

"How's that?" Brent wondered.

"Well, they face life differently than we do! They're naturally happy, where we're always looking for happiness. It just seems like a waste of energy, you know? I mean, look at her! She's truly happy, and she didn't have to go looking for it. She just trusts enough and that's what she is. I wish I knew how she did it," Cole said wistfully.

"That's cause the world hasn't touched them yet," Brent replied. "She hasn't known anything but her own little world here."

"Yeah, nothing has had the chance to hurt her," Cole said, his voice hushed.

"Cole? You all right?" Brent asked of him.

"Yeah, let's finish this up, this guy is fine," Cole replied, sending the horse back into the pasture.

Brent studied his friend for a moment. Aside from Ruth and Gris, he and Will were the only ones Cole had spoken with at length about the tragedy. Their hearts broke the night he opened up to them, letting out some of the hurt, but drawing them into the sadness he carried deep within. They grieved for everyone; not knowing the people didn't make any difference, they knew Cole and that was all that mattered. They knew him and they hurt with him. They had listened long into the night as he talked, with the only other noise in the house being the crackling of the logs in the fireplace and the wind howling through the valley.

It had been a cold, snowy day and both Brent and Will had come over earlier to give Cole a hand plowing paths from the house to the barn and tack room. They drove over in Will's truck, just so he could play with his new plow. For weeks now he had been waiting for the first storm to hit and this one struck with a vengeance. Earlier that afternoon, Will plowed out his ranch and took care of his own stock, making sure that they were settled in the barn for the night. He then plowed Walt Bremmer and Zeke Hill's ranches and finally made it over to Brent's place just as dusk was setting in.

Will doubted if he would make it home that night, so he put in a call to Lisa, letting her and the boys know that he would probably end up staying at Cole's ranch, which he planned on plowing next. His own chores were already finished, so Will had no worries there. After reassuring Lisa that the cattle were taken care of for the night and getting her promise not to venture outside, he then made his way over to Brent's place. Brent had been waiting and hopped into the passenger side so they could get underway. He, too, had just finished helping his father get their herd bedded down for the night and was anxious to get over to Cole's.

The three had become quick friends and were regular fixtures at one another's homes. One of them was always dropping in on the other either for a visit on the front porch on a warm night or to help out when chores piled up. Unlike Brent, who had his father to work with, and Will, who had his two teenage brothers-in-law Terry and Garth to help him on a daily basis, Cole was on his own, taking care of Katie and his ranch. The help he got from his friends was invaluable and he knew that he could never fully repay them for all they did. At times, even Terry and Garth came over to give Cole a hand after they were finished helping Will or anyone else in the area that needed it. The boys lived in town with their parents, but loved being on the ranch. Now that they had gotten their driver's licenses, they came over to Will's place on a daily basis.

Things really had not changed much over the years. Cole was barely getting started and hoped to make a success of his ranch so that he could have something to pass down to Katie one day. Brent's future was already set; he would take over the ranch when his father passed on, working it in very much the same way. Until then, he would live there helping his father work the land and taking care of his parents when they grew older. There wasn't a nursing home in the area and just the thought of one was unthinkable for just about everyone in town. Each took care of their own and they took care of one another, that was just their way of life. That caring spirit was passed down from generation to generation, proudly watching their children grow strong as they followed in their footsteps.

Soon Brent's place was plowed and the two drove off, saying goodbye by honking the horn and flashing the headlights. Brent's parents, Cal and Helen, stood at the window, watching them leave through the gloom of the storm. All the chores were finished for the night so they went out to eat an early dinner and spend the night in front of the fireplace, which was what just about what everyone in town would be doing. There would be nobody out tonight. This was a lonely time of year for all, and the most dangerous. They not only had the animals and their regular chores to still take care of, they also had bone chilling temperatures and mountains of snow to contend with.

Will felt the tires barely digging in, grateful that they were less than a mile away from Cole's place. His headlights cut dimly through the storm and the going was slow. What would have only taken five minutes at the most now took almost twenty. With the horn blaring, they pulled into Cole's lane, finding him shielding his face with his arm as he looked up.

"Hey! What the hell ya doing?" Brent called out, sticking his upper half out the window.

"Shoveling, genius!" Cole shot back. "I'm up to my ass in snow!"

"You and everyone else!" Brent answered as Will dropped the plow, cutting a path to the house. Cole stepped out of the way as he began clearing a walkway to the barn.

"Didn't think you guys would make it! It's even too bad out there for a plow to be on the road! You're both nuts!" Cole cried out over the din of the storm.

Brent jumped from the truck when Will stopped, putting it in reverse. Bounding over to Cole, he rubbed his arms against one another in a feeble attempt to ward off the cold. "We may be nuts, but we made it! We were beginning to think that we wouldn't for a while there! Damn, this wind cuts right through ya and I'm even dressed for it!"

"You can be dressed for it, but this isn't fit for man or beast! Tell ya the truth, I was worried and almost hoping that you wouldn't chance coming over!" Cole cried out over the wind.

"Ahhhh, nothing to it! Besides, wasn't far!" Brent grinned widely.

"Maybe not far, but when you get a good blizzard like this cooking, a man can even lose his way to the barn. Could end up wandering out into the open prairie and never find his way back! You should have stayed put and not worried about digging my ass out!" Cole argued.

"Hey, I wanted to play with my new toy!" Will flashed a toothy grin. Pulling up alongside the two men, he took a moment for a sip of coffee. "Want some?" he asked, handing the cup out.

"Thanks," Cole said, taking the cup between almost numb hands. In spite of the heavy gloves, the cold still seeped through.

"Thanks," Brent shivered, taking the cup from Cole.

"Let's get this show on the road! Got a roaring fire and some hot food waiting inside," Cole cried out, his stomach rumbling.

"Warmth! I was beginning to think I'd never feel that again!" Brent griped, stomping his feet. "You finished in there yet?" Brent asked, nodding towards the barn.

"Just about! Was in there earlier, got them all mucked out and fed, just wanna go in one more time to make sure everything's ok. Got 'em all blanketed, even though the barn is warm. Not taking any chances!" Cole cried out.

"Leg warmers?" Brent asked, his voice taking on a faux sultry tone.

"Yeah, cute black ones," Cole winked, elbowing his friend.

"Oh, he knows what I like!" Brent said with a drawl. "Come on, he's got the path cleared."

As Cole and Brent walked towards the barn, Will shouted that he would cut a path around the back of the barn and then would plow an area where the soiled hay could be dumped. Once the weather broke, they could push it back where it was usually dumped, but this would be good enough for now. Once he was finished, Will cleared a path to the tack room. There was a thin layer of new snow already lying on top of the cleared paths and all knew that in the morning the plowing would begin again. It seemed as never-ending as caring for the animals, themselves. During times like this, all yearned for spring, when their work would be made easier, at least they wouldn't have to battle the elements.

"There's no way you guys are gonna make it home tonight!" Cole told them as they gathered in the barn, shutting everything up for the night.

"I didn't think we would," Will agreed. "I already called Lisa and my stock is taken care of. Besides, Terry and Garth are with her so I know she and the boys will be all right."

"Yeah, and Mom and Dad have the house to themselves," Brent giggled lewdly.

"Yeah! I bet they're glad they don't have to look at your ugly mug tonight!" Cole snorted, leaving Brent sputtering as both he and Will trudged towards the house.

Soon their coats and boots were drying by the woodstove and they were warming their hands on steaming mugs of coffee. Cole gave both men dry clothes. Even though they were dressed for the weather, the stinging snow still came through their heavy leggings. Brent even managed to get snow down inside his boots and sat warming his toes by the fire before pulling on the warm socks handed to him. Camped out in front of the fireplace, the three talked long into the night.

"And that's why you came here?" Will asked.

"That about sums it up," Cole said.

The house was quiet except for the wind roaring down through the valley. The windows shook from the force of the gusts slamming into them. Looking out, all one could see was snow. Engulfed in a sea of white, they were cut off from the outside world. Cole had put together a hearty stew and served that along with the homemade bread and pies Ruth had baked the previous day.

Aside from the storm, the house was quiet. They ate in front of the roaring fire, feeling its warmth spreading throughout their bodies. Yet, they still couldn't help but shiver every time the walls rattled. At one point, something slammed into the side of the house, causing all three to grimace.

"Shit, don't wanna see what that was," Cole shuddered. "I ain't about to go out there, either!"

"Don't blame ya, no holes in the roof or the side of the house, so it'll keep till morning," Brent quipped.

"Don't think I wanna see then, either!" Cole laughed with them. "All it'll mean is more work in the spring!"

"Well, it's in the back of the house, no one sees that anyway," Will teased.

Pulling a quilt off the back of the couch, Cole snuggled down under the thick, warm, folds. Brent had already raided the trunk to the right of the fireplace and tossed extra pillows and quilts to Will. All three were used to camping out in the wild, so sleeping on the floor in front of a warm fire was definitely not a hardship. If they were warm, they were comfortable. Brent snagged the extra cushions from the chair and built his own nest to nestle down into. Leaning against the couch, he stretched out contentedly, unable to think of a cozier place to be at the moment. Will shoved the coffeetable to the side and made his own bed next to Brent. Between the fireplace and their body heat, no one was going to be cold.

The room was dark except for the soft glow of the fire. For a while all three men lay quietly, snug under their quilts, which were pulled up under their chins. Brent lay buried deep inside his blankets and cushions, with only his hair sticking out. Will curled on his side, watching the shadows of the flames flickering on the wood floor. Cole lay on his back, turning his head slightly to stare at the fire. The windows were blackened out, with frost beginning to form on the inside. Cole knew that they would find themselves buried in the morning and felt a momentary twinge of guilt that he had taken his friends from their families.

"Wasn't your doing," Will shrugged. "I knew that there was a chance I wouldn't get back home tonight, that was my doing. I know that Lisa and the boys are fine. She's tough and sure can take care of herself. Besides, Terry and Garth are there, remember?"

"Yeah, I remember," Cole said quietly, his mind wandering. "You know, I'm kind of glad not to be alone tonight," he added.

Brent remained silent, for he and Will had wordlessly planned on things working out this way. Both knew how hard being in a new place was, and neither could imagine the burden Cole carried deep in his heart. He just lost his wife and baby; being alone on a night such as this wasn't a good thing for anyone, especially someone as lost and lonely as Cole must have felt. They needed to be with their friend as much as he needed to be with them. If their presence could help, even if it was just a little, then Brent and Will wished to be nowhere else.

As the storm raged, all were lost in thought. Eventually, Brent noticed the small box Cole held in his hands. Elbowing Will, he motioned for him to look. They stared at one another, watching as Cole slowly slid the lid open. He pulled out a cobalt blue amulet, with the picture of a black stallion painted on the front. The mighty horse reared up against the heavens, flailing his powerful legs out in front of him. His majestic beauty was clearly seen, his power and grace felt just by holding the small piece in one's hand. Cole was quiet for a minute as he ran his finger across the smooth surface.

"I'll dance across the heavens with your mane as my reins," he said softly, his voice barely audible.

"What?" Brent asked drowsily, rolling onto his side.

"That's what I said to her when she gave this to me," Cole explained.

"Sarah?" Will asked.

"Yeah, it was my 29th birthday. She said that she searched for a week trying to find the perfect present. The morning of my birthday, she went out for a drive and found this little shop on the outskirts of some town. They had all sorts of homemade turquoise jewelry, dreamcatchers, and other items. Anyway, she found this in the corner, hanging on the wall. Said she was drawn to it, so she bought it and gave it to me that night," Cole replied, his voice hushed as he ran his fingers over the smooth surface.

"It's beautiful," Brent said quietly.

"Yeah, when I saw it, I felt myself soaring through the heavens on the back of a black stallion, his strength roaring beneath me. I became a part of him and together, we were invincible. We were immortal and nothing could touch us. Our souls became one, our hearts beat together and our minds linked. It was magical," Cole said, still holding the necklace in his hands.

"What was that you said, again?" Brent asked of him.

57

"I'll dance across the heavens with your mane as my reins," Cole repeated.

"That's something," Brent replied, too choked up to say anymore.

"This was … was…." Cole had to stop and take a deep breath before he could continue. Both men sat quietly, waiting for him to compose himself. "It was the last gift she ever gave me. She was gone before my next birthday came around."

"Oh shit," Brent swore, rubbing his hand furiously over his eyes.

Neither man was left untouched by Cole's story. At that moment, their friendship bonded and they only hoped that after all he had gone through, Cole could and would truly trust in them. They swore that no matter what came along, they would be by his side. And once Katie came along, both Will and Brent knew that they were there to stay.

"Well, that about does it," Cole wheezed, wiping the sweat from his brow. He and Brent stood back, leaning against the fence as they caught their breath. The chores were finished for now and it was almost time to go over to Ruth's for dinner.

"I'd like to work on the back deck some, but doesn't look like that's in the cards," Cole said.

"The hell with the deck," Brent replied. "Let's just go over to Ruth's and have a nice dinner and a quiet afternoon."

"We? You got a mouse in your pocket or something? I seem to remember that she invited me!" Cole began the argument.

"But she loves me too!" Brent whined. "Besides, Katie wants me to come, don't you, baby?"

"Not fair using my daughter like that," Cole glared teasingly.

"What do you say, Katie? Can Uncle Brent have dinner with you guys?" Brent pleaded.

"I don't think Nanny made any bugs, Uncle Brent!" she teased, giggling as she ran up to the porch.

"You know, I'm never gonna live that down, thanks to you! I hope you realize that, don't you? Soon, it'll be all over town that I eat bugs! Next time I go into Sadie's place, I'll be served a helping of bugs, thanks to you! I hope you're happy!" Brent grumbled.

"Uh huh," Cole grinned devilishly.

"You have no heart! You know that? No heart at all!" Brent's whining followed them into the house.

Chapter Four

Callie Marsh sat down hard after tending a horse with a stubborn case of colic. Any delusions of grandeur concerning her job had quickly diminished. So far, her day had been less than stellar. When she moved to Crater Mills to take over her uncle's practice upon his death, Callie did so with vigor and determination. Years of hard work were finally beginning to pay off. She would no longer be working in a large clinic where one was never on a first name basis with their clients or patients. Now, Callie had a practice of her own. And it was in a small town that consisted mainly of ranches and farms. She specialized in the larger animals, but would treat dogs and cats when needed. Callie was not one to turn anyone in need away.

Standing just under 5'4", Callie weighed in at 100 pounds soaking wet. She looked small and frail, certainly not what one would expect to see arriving when they called for a veterinarian, especially when it pertained to the larger animals. All of her patients stood heads over her, but she was the one in total control. No one in town ever doubted her for a moment. Callie's uncle had sung her praises for years, but that still did not mean that the lady vet didn't get her share of teasing.

"Want a stepstool, little lady?" was the running joke around town when she arrived to treat her patients.

One look at her steely, grayish blue eyes was enough to ward off further torment, for Callie was all business. She kept her long golden brown hair either in a large braid or ponytail, which hung down the middle of her back. On hot days, she wore a bandana around her forehead, keeping the sweat from her eyes as she worked. She had learned that trick early on when she treated Cole's horses one afternoon. Arriving at the ranch, she found him working in the corral exercising his horses. It was too hot for a hat, so he had opted for a blue bandana, which was tied securely around his forehead. It was the first time Callie had ever seen Cole Morgan, and she would never forget it.

Stepping out of her truck, Callie's heart lurched as pangs of passion slammed into her. She was literally caught breathless as she watched this dark-haired, muscular man racing across the fields on the back of a black stallion. She just stared, her heart in her throat as they ran along. He was one with his horse, both moving with a fluidity and grace that captured her heart and sent her soul soaring.

It was obvious to anyone who watched that Cole had a special kinship with the animal. He just didn't ride the horse, he became a part of the horse. Their minds and souls linked, each trusting and giving of the other. Cole had given of himself; he had taken a young colt, training him almost from the very beginning of his life. Most of the time the young animal had no idea he was being trained, he thought they were just playing. Then as time went on, his gangly clumsiness soon diminished, only to be replaced with a grace and beauty beyond compare.

The horse lost nothing of himself, Cole only brought out the power hidden within, harnessing it in a way that both man and animal could enjoy. He didn't break the horse's will only to have the animal bend to him, Cole let the horse to know that freedom was still in his heart.

Callie was awestruck as she watched them flying through the tall grass, the wind in their faces and the sun at their backs. The sight sent her heart racing; she had never seen a more magnificent animal in her life, something which was not lost on Cole. He knew that the animal was strong and proud and strove to make him feel he had lost nothing of what was deep in his soul. He only lent a part of himself to man, letting him be kin to a world that was special. Cole stood on the threshold of that world, getting a glimpse into their realm every time he climbed onto their backs.

It was a magnificent place to be … a place where one could run free and let his soul soar. The horse carried one up to the heavens and beyond. They became a part of you, accepting a part of you in return. They shared their soul, giving freely of themselves. Soon the fight for dominance was over. Neither dominated, and both had won. They had found a way to combine two different beings and two different worlds into one. Cole was now sharing that special place with his new friend as he raced along, oblivious to all around him. Leaning low and tangling his fingers in the animal's lush black mane, he let the reins lie unattended, allowing himself to feel the power and strength that this extraordinary creature possessed.

Spotting Callie as he turned the corner at the other end of the pasture, Cole gently nudged his horse forward and galloped over to greet his new visitor. He was confused, wondering why this young woman would be standing at his fence, watching him. Cole came to a stop, kicking up a cloud of dust as he reined his horse in.

"Help you, Ma'am?" he smiled down, melting her heart.

"My God, he's magnificent!" she said breathlessly.

"He sure is! He's one of a kind!" Cole grinned widely.

"I could watch you all day," she smiled back. "It's ... it's...." she blushed, finding herself tongue-tied by this handsome stranger, whose dark eyes drew her into their depths.

"Magical?"

"Yes! Magical! That's what he is!" she agreed excitedly.

"They are magical. Sometimes I forget that they are even of this earth; something happens when you climb onto their backs. You both cease existing as separate beings, and you become one with each other. He shares his power, compassion and love, taking you into a world that belongs only to them," Cole said wistfully.

"I never thought of a horse as magical before," she smiled softly. The stallion came close, demanding the attention that Callie gave willingly.

"I've always thought of them that way," Cole replied. "You don't own a horse, you share yourself with him. Each of you gives something to the other; you both give caring, trust and love. You bring your world into his and find that you need one another. That's real power! When you can reach out to another whether they're a horse or whether it's man, when you give of yourself, you have realized the gift of power."

"That's why horses are so magnificent," Callie said wistfully.

"They're always giving of themselves," Cole replied.

They stood quietly for a moment, tongue tied and unsure of what to say. Callie stopped stroking the horse's nose and extended her hand. "I'm sorry, I'm Callie Marsh. You called my office earlier?"

"You're the vet?" Cole squeaked, caught completely off guard. It took a few seconds, but he finally regained his composure. "Hell, you look like—"

"If you say I look like I should be sitting behind a desk answering the phones, I swear I'll throttle you!" she shot back.

"All right! At the risk of getting throttled, I have to ask. What the heck is a nice girl like you doing working a dirty job like this?" Cole laughed, holding up his hands as he backed away.

"You think a man can do it better?" Callie challenged.

"You strong enough to work with these guys? Hell, you can hardly reach their noses to pet them! Plus, you have to put your hands in places no man dares to go!" Cole exclaimed.

"Ah ha!" Callie bellowed. "Where no *man* dares to go, but a woman will do it and do it willingly! It's what my mother said all along! A man will shrivel and die at the sight of some of the messes made in this world, but a woman will come along and clean it up without even batting an eye, because she's strong! We do what's needed and think about it later!"

Cole rolled his eyes. He simply didn't know what to make of this spitfire standing before him, stating her dominance and confusing him with feelings that he shoved aside. There was no way that he was going to admit to them; his life was already confusing enough. Callie glared defiantly, and he relented. It was going to be a pleasure watching her in action, if she could reach the animals she had to tend.

"All right! I give! But I don't have anywhere today for you to stick your hand...." Cole stuttered, blushing profusely. He just stood, his mouth hanging open. "Ahhh ... I mean ... shit, I'm just gonna stop talking and show you to the barn."

Callie just shook her head, picked up her bag and followed along, his words haunting her. Cole was wrong about one thing, he did have a place she wanted to stick her hands, but it would only serve to scare the hell out of him. Knowing that she had just met the man, Callie steeled herself to behave, but she could let her mind go where her hands didn't dare; at least not yet. Watching Cole's backside as he walked away, Callie took a deep breath and followed along, thankful to have the task of giving his horses their vaccinations to occupy her mind.

* * *

Callie stood, wiping the back of her hand across her forehead, mindless of the mess. It made no difference anyway, she was filthy. It was growing warmer and that only served to make her feel all the more uncomfortable. She was caked with mud from head to toe after being head-butted by an ornery mule, kicked in the shin by a cow, and now was covered with something she just did not want to identify after administering an enema to a colicky horse. Sweat plastered her hair flat against her head, her face was streaked with grime and the strands of hair that managed to escape her rubber band now hung limply down the sides of her neck. She was hot, sweaty and grubby. And thanks to the horse, who was now feeling ten times better, she smelled like the barn floor. No, today was definitely not one of her better days. And who said that cows didn't puke? Callie had the mess splattered down the front of her shirt to prove that.

"Lovely," she groused, tearing the long latex gloves from her hands. "And I thought that this was going to be a glorious, admirable and a wonderful way to build a career."

Standing back, Callie seriously reconsidered her career options. Looking at what a mess she had become in the matter of only a few hours, anything had to be better.

"Could always switch to answering phones, Cole would like that," she snickered to herself, feeling the slight tug on her heart.

Right now, Cole was a sore spot with her. She had fallen in love with the man the minute she saw him on the back of his horse that day. Since then, she had not been able to get him out of her mind. Callie didn't set out to fall in love, she only went out to take care of his horses, which was her job. She had no intention of becoming attracted to the man, but her feelings had a mind of their own. Yet, Cole remained aloof. For some reason, he hung back, refusing to let her get close. Perhaps she intimidated him. Callie did have a habit of speaking her mind and coming on too strong at times. Or perhaps he was just not interested.

Then there were the rumors. At first, Callie refused to listen to them. They didn't last long, and soon the talk quieted down. Then four months later, the rumors proved to be true. A one-night stand turned Cole's life upside down and broke Callie's heart. She had known of Cole's night with Maggie, everyone in town knew. How Callie wished that he had turned to her that night. She wanted to be the one who held him in her arms, loving his loneliness away. She longed to show Cole that he could love and trust again. Instead, he gave himself to a stranger. To Callie, Cole was nothing short of polite. She loathed polite. Cole's eyes lit up whenever she came near, yet he pushed her aside. Every time they came in contact with one another, Cole pulled back. He pulled back and remained alone.

Like she had done since she met the man, Callie kept her feelings to herself. Even though things were over between him and Maggie, she knew that he had lost trust in life and was not about to try love again. He had already been hurt too much. At a time when Callie could be by his side, helping him through his turmoil, she found herself alone. She watched Cole's child being born and she saw him closing down.

The only person Cole did not remain closed off to was his daughter. He loved his little Katherine Sarah with all his heart. He was a devoted father. Nothing else mattered. Callie didn't matter. Cole opened up to his friends somewhat, but they all had the feeling that he was still walling a part of himself off from the world. After speaking profusely with both Brent and Will, the three came to the conclusion that Cole was hiding something. As time went on, they feared that he was also hiding that something from himself.

It was that secret that fueled Cole's fear of life. It was that secret he carried deep within, unwilling to share with those who cared, those who could help. Callie shuddered to think of a secret so dark that one felt it better to shove it back into the recesses of their mind rather than seek help from friends. Whatever the reasons, Cole was their friend and they would be there for him.

Callie's heart bled for him; she knew the heartache, but was unable to offer comfort. She prayed for the day when Cole could trust fully again. He had so much love to give, yet he was afraid to give it. And Callie loved him more than he could even begin to imagine. As time went on, she also began suspecting that he felt the same way about her, only fear kept those feelings at bay. Perhaps the day would come when nothing got in their way. How Callie wished for that day. She would wait forever if need be. She would also never give herself to another. Day after day, Callie felt her love for this man, and day after day, she watched him raising his daughter and helped out when she could.

So Callie did the only thing she could do; she loved Cole from afar and offered friendship, which seemed to be what he needed most. That was all everyone offered Cole ... love, understanding and support. They were there when he arrived, accepting him into their lives unconditionally. They knew a bit of the truth and that was all anyone needed. The gossip, if any, was slight; no one wanted to hurt Cole further, he had already been hurt enough. Speculation was unheard of. No one was about to pressure Cole for details about his past other than what he felt comfortable sharing. About the only thing there was to gossip about now in Crater Mills was the latest sizzling love triangle on the soap operas, or who was caught sneaking around Jake's shed on a Friday night.

Everyone in town knew that Jake had a still, it was almost as much a part of their tradition as Milt's old drugstore. And since Milt didn't offer spirits like his great granddaddy had, those looking for a nip after a long hard week usually made their way over to Jake's place. Lately, though, even the gossip mill was dying down. No one was seeing anyone new, nothing mysterious or sly was happening and it just wasn't newsworthy telling who was at Jake's the previous weekend. All the men went over to Jake's every once in a while, so where was the excitement in talking about that?

No, Crater Mill's gossip mill was in need of new fodder. Even so, Ruth refused to bring up the subject of Cole and the heartache he carried deep inside. In spite of being raised in a small town, Ruth was not a gossip. That did not mean she didn't turn a story or two over coffee, or that she turned a deaf ear when others started talking; it meant that when she held someone's confidence, that confidence would never be broken.

All Callie knew was that Cole had married and lost, then he lost once again when he blindly reached out, trying to replace something that had been ripped away. She hurt with him, and she ached to love his little girl. On the rare occasions she had babysat Katie, Callie found herself falling in love with her as if the child were her very own.

On those occasions, she would sit by Katie's bed pretending that very thing. She imagined that she and Cole were married, Katie was their child and she was there to love them both. She would never leave either of them alone, abandoning them for another life. She would not leave them alone in the world, only having one another to love. Katie needed a mommy and even though she and Cole were never together, they were close friends and Callie simply couldn't turn off her feelings. She adored Katie and loved her father beyond belief.

Only that love was never acted upon. Despite the glimmer Callie would sometimes catch in Cole's eyes, he looked away, dashing any hope that she might have had. Maybe he didn't share her feelings, or if he did, maybe he was just too scared to act on them. Nothing ruled a person's actions or decisions more than fear; it was the rawest, basic human emotion. It governs our lives, controlling every chilling aspect.

We steer clear of that fear, using whatever means possible, but it refuses to be denied. We cannot hide. It's always there, lurking. Some can see past that fear, going on with their lives by sheer faith alone. Others succumbed, warily eyeing the world around them as their days went on. Callie wondered if that haunted look would ever leave Cole's eyes.

"If he would only believe in himself," she muttered, shaking her head.

She needed to clear her mind, a long day still stretched before her. The one thing Callie could not afford herself was the luxury of pining for Cole, no matter how delicious the thought. She couldn't let her thinking cloud her judgement or actions; someone had to operate with a clear head.

"Some women have everything, then they toss it aside like it didn't mean a thing. Bitch," Callie muttered under her breath, her anger towards Maggie rising. "If she didn't come into his life, then ... oh hell, if she didn't come into his life, it still wouldn't change the way things are between you and him. And Cole would be totally alone because he wouldn't have Katie to love. She's the only thing I don't regret happening."

Putting her feelings aside for the moment, Callie went back to the task at hand. What had started out to be a quiet Sunday had slowly escalated as one emergency call after the other came in, and now she was something no one wanted to be near. Callie couldn't even stand being close to her own self right now. Stealing a quiet moment, she leaned against the fence, watching the horse that was now running free through the pasture. It had been a close call. Walt had come out earlier, finding the animal on his back, twisting back and forth in an attempt to ease the cramps in his belly. He whinnied painfully, his fright clear. There was no relief from the pain that gripped his midsection and Callie was called upon immediately.

"He's writhing on his back and whinnying something awful," was all Callie had to hear from Walt to know that there was no time to waste.

She only hoped to reach the horse in time. Once they were down like that, they ran the risk of their intestines twisting, or worse, rupturing. Then surgery was imminent and something Callie prayed they could avoid. Upon arriving at the ranch, she found Walt trying to calm the animal the best he could. One look said it all ... the colic had reached an agonizing, advanced stage. Running her stethoscope down the underside of the horse's belly and along his side, Callie hoped to pick up on any bowel sounds, already knowing that she would not. To her dismay, all was quiet.

"We have to get him up," Callie said quietly, with both she and Walt working at aiding the horse to stand.

That was easier said than done; the animal was in pain, he was scared, and he just wanted relief. To him, lying down would bring that relief. They finally managed to get him up on his feet and Callie immediately mixed some oil in a bucket of warm water that Walt's wife, Irma, had carried over. Working quickly, she put one end of a special pump into the bucket, shivering slightly as she advanced towards the horse's rear.

"One of the perks of my job," she grimaced, not missing the teasing grin that spread across Walt's face.

"Better you than me, little missy," he shook his head.

"Yeah, thanks ... I think," she said, soothing the animal as she lifted his tail. "Believe me, this is gonna hurt me more than it is you," she winced, pump in hand.

After a short wait in which to give the oil a chance to do its magic, Callie drew on her gloves and approached the horse, ready to finish the job. "Ok, big boy, nice to know you," she laughed, crinkling her nose as she lifted his tail.

* * *

"It sure is good seeing Patches doing well again. I thank you," Walt said.

Callie gratefully took the large glass of iced tea he offered. She had washed up the best she could with the warm water and cloths that Irma supplied her with, but she barely scratched the surface. All she wanted to do now was go home, fill her tub with hot, sudsy water and soak until she pruned.

"He's going to be fine, it's a good thing that you caught this when you did. Sometimes horses tend to go off into the field and you don't see them."

"I just wish that I was home yesterday; this obviously started then, it was so far advanced. When I checked him last night, he was standing quietly in his stall, but since it was growing late, I didn't give that a thought. Poor Patches."

"That's all right, Walt, we caught it in time, didn't we, fella?" Callie soothed the now happy horse.

"I sure do thank you. Would you like to join us for dinner?" Walt offered.

Callie threw her head back laughing, "Look at me! I think I'm coated with every bit of mess and grime known to man! Thanks, Walt, but I think I'll just go on home and take a long, long hot bath," she smiled gratefully.

"I understand, but the next time you're in the area just stop on in, the invitation still stands," he replied. "You have a good day," he nodded his goodbye.

"Thanks, Walt, and let me know how Patches does!" Callie waved, driving away. Lifting her arm, she winced at the smell, wondering if it was her or from one of her many encounters today. "All in a day's work," she cringed, rolling down her window.

* * *

Callie drove slowly down the dirt road, heading for home. As she topped the hill just past Ruth's house, she groaned, seeing Cole, Brent and Katie walking up the road. Getting a whiff of herself, all she wanted to do at the moment was sink down into the seat, never to be found again. The thought of driving past tantalizingly entered her mind, but that just would not do. Not only would it be rude, but it would also leave three people wondering why she simply ignored them. She couldn't do that to anyone, especially little Katie, who was waving furiously. She sat perched on top of her father's shoulders, holding on to his hair. Her legs kicked up and down slightly, catching Cole under the chin more than once. Judging from the smile on his face though, one could see that he was enjoying every minute of this, as was his daughter. Groaning, Callie pulled over, watching as they approached. Cole walked with a bounce to his step, singing an old song that had Katie in stitches.

"There was a man who had a frog and Bingo was his name, OOOHHHH," both men sang in top voice.

"It's not a frog, Daddy! It's a dog!" Katie giggled.

"B ... I ... N ... G ... O...." they continued singing, ignoring her.

"Daddy, it's a dog!" Katie exclaimed, leaning over. Peering down over the front of his forehead, all Cole could see was her smiling face, fringed by soft brown ringlets.

"You sure? Cause judging from the way Uncle Brent sounds, I thought it was a song about a frog!" Cole answered innocently.

"But frogs sound funny!" Katie insisted.

"So does Uncle Brent!" Cole replied back.

"And frogs eat bugs!" Katie said, clamping her hand over her mouth. Her eyes grew large as she stared over at Brent.

"See! I told you! There was a man who had a frog, and Brent was his name, oohhhh! B ... R...."

"Katie, don't listen to him! He's been out in the sun too long!" Brent groused.

They continued singing, accompanied by Cole's raspy imitation of a frog. Katie did more laughing than singing, while Brent tried singing along in his own way, dismayed to realize that Cole was right, he did sound like a frog. Now, if he could only dispel the rumor that he ate bugs before it spread all over the county, then he would be fine. Caught up in the moment, they were singing at the top of their lungs as they reached the crest of the hill, where Callie had pulled over. Katie's happy voice was the first to greet her. Callie hit her head slightly on the steering wheel as they approached. Hearing someone knocking at her door, she lifted her grimy face.

The smile that spread across Cole's face and the laughter that followed had her turning every shade of red. "Out for a Sunday drive?" he taunted, seeing the sorry state she was in. "Love your perfume!"

"Yeah, what do they call that? Eau de horsesh—" Brent grunted as Cole's elbow slammed into his ribs.

"New spring look?" Cole continued to tease.

"Hello Katie," Callie waved, ignoring the two.

"Did you fall in horse poo?" Katie asked, causing both men to double over.

Laughing so hard, Cole had to put his daughter down, but he never let go of her hand. "Yeah, did you...." he broke off. Every time he looked at her face all he could do was laugh.

"We'd ask you to join us, but...." Brent cringed.

"No, Katie, I didn't fall into anything, honey. I spent the morning taking care of some very sick animals," Callie said quietly, forcing both men to stop laughing.

"I'm sorry, is everything all right? Nothing serious, I hope," Cole worried. Their neighbors were more than friends, they all cared what befell one another. When someone was hurt or beset by hard times, everyone felt it.

"It was a close call. Most of the calls were minor, but Walt's horse was down with colic," she explained.

"Down?" Cole instantly worried.

"Is he ok? I mean, you caught it in time, didn't you?" Brent asked impatiently.

"Yes, Patches is fine. But I had to resort to some not so very nice measures, thank you!" Callie smiled coyly.

"Better you than me!" Cole burst out.

"You know, it must be a man thing! Walt said the same thing! Now, where would all you big strong men be without little old me?" she said in a sultry voice, batting her eyelashes at Cole.

"Whooweee," Brent hissed under his breath. "Come on, Katie, time for us to head on to Nanny's for some roast chicken!" he said, swinging her up onto his shoulders.

"Giddyap horsie!" she yelled, delighted at the snorting sounds he made as they galloped down the road. "Bye Callie!" her giggles rang through the air.

"Bye bye, sweetie!" Callie leaned out the window a little to answer. "She's getting so big," she said, almost wistfully.

Cole leaned on the side of the door, sticking his head slightly inside the window. "She sure is. You remember her birthday is coming soon, don't you?"

"Yes, I do! It's in two weeks and it's on a Thursday! I know all about the party!" she smiled up at him.

"You still coming?" he asked, almost hopefully.

"Cole, I wouldn't miss it for the world!"

"Good, cause she'd really miss you! Hey, we're going down to Ruth's for dinner, why...."

Now it was Callie's turn to blush, "Cole, look at me!" she whined.

"Yeah, so? Not like I haven't been covered with the same stuff myself! It's like perfume!" he exclaimed.

"Maybe your kind of perfume!" Callie burst out laughing with him.

"Seriously, why don't you come over with me? You can get washed up there!" Cole offered.

"No, as much as I'd love to join you, I really have a lot of work ahead of me. I just want to get home and take a long bath and change. Maybe next time, ok?" Callie answered, kicking herself for those very words.

"Ok, I understand; it's getting warm and you must be feeling pretty sticky and uncomfortable about now," Cole nodded.

His smile warmed Callie's heart, "Yeah, I do feel a mess! And I look a mess, and I smell a mess! I'll catch you next time, ok?"

"Sure! Will, Brent and I will be in town for the day Tuesday, maybe I'll see you around," he replied, standing back.

Waving, Cole stepped back while Callie pulled slowly onto the road. With a honk of the horn and a quick wave out the window, she disappeared around the next bend, leaving a cloud of dust in her wake. Cole stood, wondering why he felt so empty at the sight of her truck driving away. Shrugging it off, he walked slowly to Ruth's house.

* * *

Cole stood leaning on the railing of Ruth's back deck. Staring out over the late afternoon sky, he didn't realize how preoccupied he had become. Sometimes he was so tired, even the simplest of tasks seemed monumental. It seemed the more he did, the more there was to do. And the more he tried putting the pieces of his life back together, the more it fell apart. Cole wondered just what a person had to do to get real peace, real fulfillment, and happiness.

It should be so simple, yet it was fleeting. Every morning Cole woke, doing what he loved. He had the kind of job that most people could only dream of; the closest they ever came to being a real cowboy was watching them on a television screen. Cole had that; he got up in the morning and spent his day riding horses from sunup to sundown. He tended them and catered to their every need. The best thing of all was that he had no bosses to answer to, except for the horses. That was a dream in itself for most people.

Plus, he had a comfortable home, a beautiful piece of land and a daughter he cherished beyond belief. With all those things, how could a person not be happy? Cole wondered if he was so shallow and demanding that no matter what blessings were bestowed upon him, he would find himself asking, 'Is there more?' 'Is this all there is?' 'What am I going to do now?' It seemed that the blessings in his life either passed him by or he was just too blind to see what he really had. Instead of just embracing today, he seemed to always be looking for tomorrow, thinking that if only something different happened, or if he could only have this or that, then he would be truly happy.

But can we be truly happy? With all I have, I should be. I have my life, which is more than others have. I have a beautiful daughter and I have blessings that I can't even begin to count. True, money gets tight at times, but is money everything? What about the millionaire who works and strives each and every day just to make more? He doesn't really need it to live on, but feels he needs it to be happy. He sets goals that he has to achieve to feel fulfillment, but when he achieves those goals, he still feels empty. When you have too much, nothing means anything. But if you don't have enough, you despise those who do, saying 'Why not me?' And, I don't even know if this is about money or anything. Hell, I don't know what this is about. All right, I'm searching, but what the hell am I searching for? Cole thought, not realizing that Ruth had come up beside him.

Startled, he jumped as she gently took him by the arm. Looking down, he smiled slightly. The two stood, leaning against one another for strength and comfort. He could always find comfort in Ruth's arms, she knew how he felt and she understood. Ruth had felt this same loneliness for so many years, only Cole's went deeper. He was too young to have suffered such a life altering loss and had been struggling for years to get past that loss. Ruth feared that he was still struggling to this day. Of all the wishes one could be granted, she only wished that he could find a tiny bit of peace. If he could learn to trust the world around him, instead of only existing on a day-to-day basis, then everything would be fine.

"You're quiet today," Ruth spoke softly.

"Guess there's not much to say," Cole shrugged.

"Something happen that I should know about? Is everything all right with our girl?" Ruth worried slightly.

"Everything's fine with our girl," Cole smiled down at her. "Her father's just kind of doing too much thinking lately," was all he was willing to offer. There was no sense in lying to Ruth, she could always tell when he was covering things up.

"Her father needs to stop thinking so much and start enjoying things. Why don't you go down there? Looks like Brent could use some help," Ruth laughed, pointing.

Cole watched Katie and Gris chasing Brent down, with her tackling him around the legs. Crying out for help, Brent let himself fall to the ground, where his hands were promptly hog-tied by Gris. Katie stood over her prey triumphantly, her foot on his chest.

"I won!" she proclaimed, raising one fist into the air. "My castle is safe! I caught the dragon!"

"She watches too much TV," Cole giggled.

"No, she just has a good, healthy imagination. And what was all that talk about bugs?" Ruth looked questioningly at him.

Cole couldn't help but to laugh, "Well, it's something that Brent's not going to live down any time soon! When Katie and I were in the store the other day, she saw those packages of shelled pecans. She said that they looked like bugs and she almost started crying!"

"She was that upset?" Ruth's eyes grew wide.

"Poor kid! I mean, they didn't look like the most appetizing thing in the world, but to think that they were bugs! Who knows what goes on in a kid's head! Anyway, it took a bit of doing but I finally had her convinced that they weren't bugs, and we weren't getting them anyway," Cole shrugged.

"But where did she get the idea that Brent eats bugs?" Ruth laughed.

"Oh, that," Cole shook his head. "Me and my big mouth! I sort of told her that we'd put the bugs back for Uncle Brent, cause he ate them," he grinned sheepishly.

"You didn't! Poor Brent! He'll never live that down and I doubt if she'll forget that any time soon!" Ruth burst out.

"I know! But I just couldn't help myself," Cole laughed with her.

"Sometimes I just don't know what I'm going to do with you," she said, swatting at his arm.

Cole just grinned innocently again, sitting quietly with Ruth while they watched Katie playing. He wondered what he would do with himself at all. He wanted to tell Ruth how he had sat on the deck unable to sleep the previous night, but just couldn't bring himself to cause more worry for her. Cole was also scared, knowing that another long night loomed ahead.

* * *

There was so much more Ruth wished to speak with him about, but did not feel it was the right time. She saw the way Cole looked at Callie whenever she came around. Did he think no one noticed? Therein lay the problem, for everyone knew. Everyone, that is, except for Cole, himself. The man was just too stubborn to admit to his feelings, choosing to stay closed up, instead. If he remained aloof, if he remained alone, he remained safe.

Cole had spun himself into a little cocoon, containing his daughter and friends. Unfortunately, Callie was lumped into that category, always a friend, and nothing more. But Ruth knew better, she saw the way the two looked at one another. Callie couldn't hide the passion in her eyes either, and aside from Cole, Ruth had never seen anyone love Katie as much. She and Callie were forming a close bond; Katie reached out to her naturally, unknowingly filling the void left by her mother. Cole turned a blind eye to that, also.

"Honey, what are you going to tell Katie about her mother?" Ruth had asked one day.

"Who said I have to tell her anything?" Cole bristled, his spine prickling.

Ruth knew that she had struck a nerve. If there was one thing Cole feared, it was losing his daughter. Whether it was to her mother, or watching her walking away if his sordid truth was ever revealed, either way, he stood to lose.

"I know you don't like thinking about it, let alone talking about it. But honey, do you really think that Katie will go her entire life without asking anything?" Ruth asked.

Cole faced her, his eyes flashing darkly, "Ruth, what do I tell her, huh? Can you tell me that? Do you have an answer to this entire mess? cause if you do, you're the only one who does. How do I tell her that her parents never should have been together in the first place? How do you think that would make her feel? When she's older, she'll see all her friends with normal, loving families, and she'll see me, knowing that she came from a mistake! I won't have to tell her that, she'll know on her own! No matter what we say, no matter how I try to sugarcoat things, the ugly truth will set in, slapping her in the face! She'll know that she didn't come from a union blessed with love, but one driven by need and selfish choices! Damn it, Ruth! How the hell could I have done that to her? The whole goddamned truth is ugly!"

"Honey, how can a baby be ugly?" Ruth asked, grabbing at his hands.

"Having Katie isn't ugly, her birth wasn't sordid and it's nothing to be ashamed of. Katie is nothing to be ashamed of, but don't you see? She might think she is one day! If she knows, what will I tell her the day she comes to me asking why I never told her and why her mother never stayed? She'll think that she was something so shameful that her mother walked away, and I was the one left holding the bag," Cole said brokenly.

"Left holding the bag? Honey, do you really think so little of your daughter's love for you that she'll look down on you as someone simply left holding the bag? Cole, she loves you. The truth will be hard, but you'll find the way. As Katie grows older, she'll realize that people aren't perfect and that life has a way of making things happen. And when they do, we don't judge or look down on one another, we just continue loving one another just as you will continue loving her. She'll understand that her father only did what he wanted, he raised a little girl that he loved with every fiber of his being. She will remember that love. She'll always carry that in her heart," Ruth sought to reassure him.

"You think so?" Cole asked, turning tired, defeated eyes up at Ruth.

"Honey, I know so. Oh, children often strike out in anger, but even in the worst of times, they never forget our love for them. That doesn't go away. Now, don't you think that maybe you should make some decisions?" she gently prodded.

"Ruth, I know you mean well, but things are fine the way they are. My life is the way I want it, I have my ranch to run and I have my daughter," Cole said softly.

"But what about getting on with your life?" Ruth asked.

"What's there to get on with? I'm living the life I want! Ruth, I don't need a woman in my life to make it complete! I tried that twice already and look what happened! I'm just too damned tired to try it again!" Cole insisted.

"I know, honey, and I'm sorry. I just wanted to see you happy," Ruth lamented.

Cole took a deep breath and clasped Ruth's hand. "I am happy. Maybe I'm not happy the way people think I should be, but I am. And I have enough on my plate right now without stirring things up. Can't you just be happy for me?"

"Honey, what are you afraid of?" Ruth asked, seeing the veil clouding his eyes. "Are you afraid of losing Katie?" Ruth worried.

"Afraid? No! Ruth ... I...." Cole stuttered, turning away. He felt Ruth's hand gently cupping his chin.

"Honey, I know you and I know that you're still running. When will you stop and take a look around you? There's no need to run! There's no reason to be afraid! Look at everyone around us! Listen to your daughter's laughter. Look at the way she's running and playing under the blue sky. Cole, that's nothing to be afraid of! So, there are matters that need to be dealt with one day; if we learn to be strong now and believe in ourselves and the love we have for one another, we can face those matters and deal with them once and for all. Once it's said and done, we'll see that we really needn't have wasted all this time worrying in the first place," Ruth said, her love reaching out to Cole, saving him from himself once again.

He was quiet for a moment, letting Ruth's love in. "I know what you say is true, but it still scares me. One day it will come out. It will all come out. When that day comes, I can only pray that Katie remembers how much I love her. Ruth, how do you tell a child that their mother had no other recourse than to walk out of their lives? They don't care about the reasons, cause in a child's eyes, there is no reason for a mother going away. Mother's are supposed to stay with their babies, not disappear. There's nothing that's worse or does more permanent damage than rejection! No matter what the reason! A child carries that hurt around for the rest of their life. It ruins everything! If they don't blame themselves, which most of them do, then they have no self-esteem! They think that if they were prettier, or more handsome, or smarter or did something different or behaved better, than their mother or father would still be there. It's one hell of a burden for a child to carry! I've seen it with children of divorce! They never get over the pain and a lot of them act out and get in trouble, or worse!" he exclaimed.

"I know, I've seen it all too often. When I used to work at the Mental Health Clinic, I dealt with adolescents and teenagers. Some came from broken homes and they carried an awful lot of baggage. It's so hard to convince them that what happened wasn't their fault," Ruth agreed.

"See what I mean?" Cole almost cried out. "And this is so different. It's so complicated that I can't even begin to think of a way to tell Katie without causing harm! Then, what the hell do I do if she starts doubting my love? Can you imagine how she would feel? She'd know that her mommy didn't love her enough and left. What if she starts thinking that I'll do the same thing? God, I couldn't stand that! How do I make her realize that I love her, no matter what?"

"Honey, just keep on doing what you're doing and Katie will know that! Life isn't always smooth, and as she grows she's going to ask questions that are going to be harder and harder to answer, but you will find a way. She loves you and she trusts you, she will listen to what you say. You just have to have faith," Ruth comforted him.

"Faith in what?" Cole challenged.

"Honey, faith in yourself and in the Lord," Ruth said firmly.

"Ruth, I stopped believing in both a long time ago," Cole muttered.

It broke Ruth's heart to hear how someone so young had lost faith in so many things. She held her religion dear to her heart, finding peace and solace in her talks with the Almighty. Sometimes Ruth would just take a walk, talking to him as if he were an old friend; which to her, he was. One thing she would never do, though, would be to judge Cole. One couldn't push or force their feelings and beliefs on others, and she was not about to do that. She would also never judge. Perhaps that was why she was called into his life. Cole was lost and needed someone. When he turned his back on life, the Lord and on himself, the one person he did not turn his back on was Ruth. She was and always would be there for him. Maybe one day, Cole would find a way to go on that would bring him peace and comfort.

As they sat on her back deck watching the sun sinking lower towards the west and Katie running with Gris and Brent, Ruth and Cole sought solace from one another, not even aware they were doing so. All too soon, the shadows lengthened and dusk hovered just over the horizon. The sun was low in the sky, giving them a last few minutes of daylight before she retired to another part of the world.

"Thanks for dinner," Brent said, embracing Ruth. "It sure was good!"

"I'm glad you enjoyed it, honey. You come again, you hear?" Ruth smiled, returning his embrace.

"Sure will! Hey, I'll be by the ranch tomorrow to see if you need a hand with anything," Brent offered, turning towards Cole.

"Won't you be busy with your father?" Cole wondered.

"Not quite yet! Right now, the cattle are all in the pastures getting fat and sassy. By next week we'll be getting them ready for shipping and I won't get the chance to come on by. Besides, Dad's going off to take care of some business tomorrow so I'll kind of be at loose ends," Brent shrugged, flashing a lopsided grin.

"Thanks, won't ever turn help away! Maybe we can finish up that deck, don't have too much to do with the horses tomorrow except taking care of their hooves," Cole smiled gratefully.

"Feet, Daddy," Katie giggled.

"All right, feet," Cole laughed, knowing when he was defeated. His daughter knew the difference and that was what really counted. But her mischievous side had gotten the better of her again and she just could not help herself.

"Come on, you little weasel! Let's kiss Nanny goodnight and hit the road!" Cole whooped, swinging Katie up onto his shoulders.

"Night, Nanny!" she said, leaning over to kiss Ruth on the side of the face.

"Good night, sweetie! Now you be good for your daddy," Ruth smiled, waving as they left.

She stood on her front porch, her arms crossed as the trio walked away, singing their song in voices that would make anyone else cringe and run, but it was music to her ears. Shaking her head and laughingly waving them off, Ruth went back inside. It had been a good day.

Chapter Five

"Come on, honey, here's your milk." Cole snuggled Katie close to him.

They rocked quietly for a while, father and child just enjoying a few private moments belonging to only them. Cole looked down into Katie's eyes, his love for this little creature welling up. All he saw in those eyes was pure love and trust. She not only felt safe and secure in her little world, she was happy to be in her father's arms. The wonder of her never left him. He had not opened their book yet, however she was patient.

"Honey, Daddy has a special story for you tonight," Cole began, his voice soft and low.

The only other sound in the room was the squeaking of the rocker and the crackling of the fire. In spite of the warmth of the day, the night had grown overcast, taking on a chilly edge. Katie snuggled closer under the quilt.

"No book, Daddy?" she asked in a small voice.

"I can read one out of the book when I'm done, but I have a special story about a very special person. A beautiful maiden with a magic horse. Do you want to hear it?" Cole asked softly.

Katie's eyes grew large with anticipation, "Daddy, is she a fairy princess?" she asked in a voice that had taken on a breathless tone, the wonder of a princess filling her mind.

"No, she's not a fairy princess, but an Indian princess. She's from a tribe that's far away, but I used to know her once," Cole explained.

"You knew a real princess?" Katie asked breathlessly.

"Honey, she was the most beautiful woman I've ever seen," Cole smiled as he spun his tale.

"What was her name?" Katie asked.

"They called her Mak'a win, which means Earth Woman. She loved the universe and everything in it. She learned to take in the beauty of the world around her, not letting a day go by where she didn't at least take one beautiful thing to heart. She never let that happen, she saw earth's beauty the very first moment she woke, watching the sun rising in the sky. Colors of gold and red rained down on her, making everything look sparkling and magical."

"Oh Daddy, that sounds so pretty!" Katie gasped.

"It was, honey. Mak'a win would stand on the edge of the plateau where she walked every morning just so she could see the sun waking up the world. She would hold her arms out and turn her face up towards the heavens. She felt the warmth of the sun as it started rising, giving life to everything it touched. Then the colors came and she opened her eyes, seeing a rainbow surrounding the world. She looked at her skin, seeing the radiance that the sun brought. She looked at the ground, seeing the dew on the grass sparkling in the light. She saw the way the sunbeams danced over the lake, with the early morning fog rising and the world becoming brighter. She then looked out over the trees that dotted the mountainside, seeing the green leaves sparkling like jewels. The world was magical and she loved it.

"She took a deep breath, feeling the clean air filling her lungs, giving her life. She was one with the universe. She loved and treasured every living creature, from the tiniest little bug to the largest animal that roamed the forest, and the eagle that soared across the sky. She would listen to the sound of the owl at night as he hooted, letting the world know that he now ruled. Mankind was asleep, now it was time for the creatures of the night to come out. She felt pride when she heard the mournful cry of the wolf, knowing how strong and proud that animal was. She took stock in everything around her, thanking the Spirits for letting her have one more day in which to share the wonder of the world that they had created.

"But of all the creatures that ran the world and all the creatures that soared high in the sky and swam the seas, there was one creature that Mak'a win treasured above all others; even though she had never laid eyes on him."

"What was that, Daddy?" Katie asked, the book long forgotten.

"Katie, it was a creature that Mak'a win had only heard about in legends, but she knew he existed. She could feel him near. At times, he would be so close, she could feel his hot breath on the back of her neck. Sometimes she swore that she could feel the breeze when he raced by her. Mak'a win even claimed that she heard him calling for her from the heavens above, but she never saw him. There was only one other person who knew of him, and that was Skoso' ta, or Clear Eyes. They called him that because he was a proud, mighty warrior. He fought hard for his people so that they could live in peace in their little corner of the world. He loved his people and had the same respect for all things both living and gone that Mak'a win had. He also had a deep knowledge of the world around him and she would sit for hours just listening to his stories. One day, Mak'a win came to Skoso' ta, telling him how she felt."

"Skoso' ta, I come to you with something that troubles me," Mak'a win said softly, seeking answers.

"What is it, my child?" he asked, looking into her dark eyes.

"I have heard him," she replied. Sitting quietly, she watched the old man taking a deep breath, then sat back for a moment.

"He doesn't come for anyone often," Skoso'ta began. "He only came once that I know of, but I was not privileged enough to see. My grandfather once spoke of a mighty warrior years ago that he came for. That warrior fought long and hard for his people and was tired. Then he came, taking the warrior back up into the heavens with him. When he appeared, the earth became dark for everyone except this warrior, who they called Mato'zi, or Yellow Bear. To Mato'zi, the world became bright and golden, with the rays from the heavens glistening down upon him. Mato'zi saw the sparks shooting from his hands as he stretched his arms up towards the heavens calling to him. Mato'zi knew that he was the chosen one and was ready to leave this world and ride along the heavens until the day that his love would be brought to him.

"Mak'a win gasped, looking at the wise old man. She knew that she, also, was chosen. She knew that Skoso'ta spoke of her. She knew that her love waited for her and that when he was ready, he would come for her. So, Mak'a win went to the water where she prepared herself. She took a special soap and sank into the waters, washing her hair and skin. She lay back, her hair fanning out on the surface of the water as she rinsed, watching the suds washing away with the currents. She was almost ready. She dried off and dressed in the most beautiful gown you've ever seen. It was made of soft buckskin, which Mak'a win had tanned and worked over and over for almost a year to make it that smooth. The gown was almost cream in color and Mak'a win had spent many nights sewing small, blue beads into the collar and down the front. It wasn't fancy, but it was elegant. Mak'a win tied her hair back in one long braid and tied a beaded headpiece around her forehead. She was ready.

"Mak'a win bid goodbye to the older man. Neither said a word, something spectacular was about to happen and words were not needed. They knew what was coming and they waited. The old man stepped back, watching Mak'a win walking away. She went through the woods and climbed the small hill until she reached the plateau where she stood every morning. Skoso'ta waved, and the world grew dark. It was dark to everyone except Mak'a win, who stood, bathed in golden beauty.

"Mak'a win heard him coming, but he hadn't let himself be seen. This time, he was not alone. Mak'a win turned and looked up at the sky. A thunderous noise resounded over the earth, with everyone crying out in fear and confusion. Even so, they too, felt the magic of the moment. Mak'a win stood quietly, not showing any fear. She held no fear; something wondrous was happening, something that she had waited for all her life. She now knew what it was. Mato'zi, her love, was coming for her. He rode the heavens on the back of a magnificent stallion that spread wings and carried him through their world. They had flown from their world down to ours for over a hundred years, looking and watching. Mato'zi found Mak'a win one day; he had heard her crying upon her birth. Ever since that day, he rode the stallion down from the sky, with the horse's powerful legs propelling them on as they strode across the earth, just skimming the land. Mato'zi had watched Mak'a win growing. He had seen her laughing and had heard her tears. Mato'zi saw her when she played, he watched when she worked and he held her in his arms when she wept for the heartache of their people. Now, it was time to bring her home.

"Mak'a win held her arms out in front of her, lifting them towards the heavens. The magnificent horse broke through the clouds and flew down over the valley below, soaring just above the ground. Mak'a win looked down, clasping her hands to her heart. She smiled brightly as she watched her love coming for her. Mato'zi looked up, his black hair and dark eyes glistening in the beams of light. His smile reached her from down below, warming her heart. She heard the snorting of the horse and watched the strong legs as he started to rise, coming closer. He shot up from the valley floor, with strong plumes of breath spewing from his nostrils. He was mighty and magnificent, and he was proud. He had come to take her home with them.

"'Pis ko, come,' Mato'zi said softly, guiding his horse over.

"Pis ko, or Night Hawk as they called him, obeyed immediately and flew high in the sky, disappearing into the clouds. Mak'a win watched, her smile wide and bright as she waited. She could feel her heart pounding in her chest and the excitement running through her body. With a strong rush of wind, they burst from the clouds and soared over to her. Mato'zi smiled, laughing as they flew by. He leaned over the front of his horse, both of them one with the other. They shared each other's souls and gave of each other throughout eternity. Now, they came for her. Pis ko gave a mighty whinny and flew over so fast that the wind almost carried Mak'a win away. She squealed and held out her hand. She looked through half shut eyes, seeing his hand reaching for her.

"In one fluid movement, his hand caught hers and pulled her onto the horse. Mak'a win sat in front of Mato'zi, his strong arm wrapping around her waist as they flew upwards. She was silent, leaning back against the man she would be with throughout all eternity. Their love was deep and abiding, never to end. She was going home. Pis ko neighed loudly, bucking upwards as he flailed his legs in the air. Mak'a win held on to his mane as he snorted, taking off towards the heavens.

"'I'll dance across the heavens with your mane as my reins,' Mato'zi said to Pis ko as they soared upwards, bringing his bride home.

"From that moment on, they visited the earth every once in a while, soaring across the land below. No one ever saw them again, but they watched over the people they loved, protecting them as they went through their lives. Every once in a while, someone would hear a mighty stallion whinnying and snorting as he flew through the clouds. They would look up and see a bright light disappearing as the clouds wrapped around the three. When they turned to walk away, they would hear Mak'a win's soft laughter on the wind. The world belonged to Mato'zi, Mak'a win and Pis ko as they flew across the heavens for all eternity. They are still up there to this day," Cole said, finishing.

"Daddy, is she up there now?" Katie asked, eyes wide with wonder.

"She sure is, honey, and she's watching us even now," he said almost sadly.

"I wish I could see her," she said wistfully.

Cole propped Katie up more comfortably so that he could talk with her, "Honey, you can! All you have to do is use your imagination! With that, you can see and do anything you want!"

"What's magination?" she asked, puzzled.

"Honey, it's the most wondrous, magical thing; and the best thing about it is, it belongs to you alone. No one can tell you how to use it and no one can take it away. It's dreaming, honey. That's what imagination is. It's when you sit down and play with your toys. You take them and you make up a story as you play along. Each time you play, you use your imagination. It's when you paint a picture and you paint your horse blue...."

"Daddy, horses aren't blue," Katie giggled.

"They are when you use your imagination. Honey, when you dream, you can dream anything from a blue horse to being a butterfly that's flying through a bed of flowers. If you close your eyes, and dream hard enough, you can feel it!" Cole exclaimed.

"Can I do that now?" Katie asked, her eyes wide with wonder.

"What do you want to see?" Cole answered with a smile.

"I want to be a butterfly!" Katie gushed.

"Then you can be one! Close your eyes," Cole said, gently brushing his hand down across her face. He couldn't help but giggle with her.

"That tickles, Daddy," Katie laughed.

"I know, that's why I did it," he answered lightly. "There, now just pretend that your mind is a movie screen. You can see anything you want. What do you see?"

"Ooohh! I see a big, pink butterfly!" Katie gasped.

"What's she doing?" Cole looked down, trying not to laugh at the rapt look on her face.

"She's flying! Daddy, we're flying way up high!" Katie cried out.

"Can you see anything?" Cole wondered.

"I see you! You're waving to me!" she replied.

Cole laughed, holding Katie even closer. "I want you to come back to me, don't fly away!"

"I won't fly away, Daddy," she said, growing tired.

"I know you won't, sweetie, you're Daddy's girl," he replied, kissing the top of her head.

"Being a butterfly was fun," Katie yawned. "Can I see the princess?"

"All you have to do is close your eyes and you can dream about her. She'll come to you in your dreams," Cole answered.

Katie's eyes slowly closed; as much as she fought to stay awake and explore her newfound imagination, she found that she just couldn't. Cole watched her dropping off, knowing that tomorrow would be another magical day. He brushed her hair back, thinking of her dreaming of magical horses and beautiful princesses. He prayed that her dreams would always remain magical and never turn dark like his had. There used to be a time when Cole's dreams were just as special, but the world had taken that away. Now when he dreamed, he woke up screaming.

Cole thought of his princess as he rocked his little angel. She wasn't a princess, but a woman he had loved deeply, with a love he thought would never end. But it had ended, and she had been cruelly ripped from his life. How he wished she would come to him in his dreams. She would always be a princess to him, only instead of her love coming to him on the back of a stallion, she had given the stallion to him. Now the stallion lay in a box in the top of his dresser. The only time he danced across the heavens now was when he visited there with his daughter. Tonight he had brought a special princess into Katie's life, sharing his stallion and giving her a dream.

* * *

Cole was up and around earlier than usual on Tuesday morning. He felt good and was actually looking forward to going into town. Monday was spent with him and Brent taking care of a few odd jobs around the ranch, including managing to get a good portion of the back deck finished. But finding more time for the project would have to wait for at least another two weeks. Cole had horses to get ready for the buyers that were due the following week and Katie's party was coming up. It was going to be a busy two weeks, but Cole didn't mind. He would be lucky if he got the deck finished by mid-summer, due to another shipment of horses he needed to concentrate on.

Today he had plans to meet Brent and Will down at the diner for breakfast, which would give Ruth a break. The only thing Cole regretted was not being able to eat breakfast with Katie, but the change would be nice. His social life was virtually nil, so he looked forward to this one day a month. Every second Tuesday, Brent, Will and Cole met at Sadie's diner. They caught up with what was happening in one another's lives, the town's gossip, and any news that might be flying around.

Extra cups of coffee were poured once their meal was finished, affording the men time to relax that they did not have any other day. This had happened totally by accident. Shortly after Cole's arrival, he needed to go into town to run a number of errands, and the stockyard had a shipment of horses coming in that he had been anxious to check out. Not wanting to waste time with cooking and then having to clean up after himself, Cole opted for breakfast at the diner.

He would eat, go to over to the stockyard, make a trip to the general store for some much needed supplies, and lastly, run over to the feed 'n seed. Once he arrived at the diner, Cole was thrilled to find Brent and Will just sitting down. He joined his friends and had been doing so ever since. Purely by chance, both men had also come into town for the very same reasons as Cole, neither knowing what the other had planned. Helen had sent Brent with a list of items needed at the general store and Cal had called in their own grain shipment. Will basically had the same itinerary. What had started out as coincidental soon blossomed into a tradition.

Talking over breakfast, the trio decided that since they had a need to come in for supplies once a month, they should do it together. Now, they actually looked forward to their day in town. Working a ranch meant working seven days a week, there was no such thing as a weekend off. Their chores went on day after day without a break in the routine, caring for the animals was endless. The one day a month afforded the three some time to kick back and relax, which was a rare commodity. They met at the diner, had a hearty breakfast, and then went over to Becker's store. Cole always arrived with two lists, one for himself and one for Ruth. Once finished, the three went over to the stockyard to see what was going on. They usually milled around, watching the shipments or getting caught up in an occasional auction, but today they had a purpose. Brent and Will were readying their cattle for shipment in two weeks.

They were nervous, last year Will had barely broken even and Brent had lost money. Things had to be better this year, both were already feeling the pinch. Once all their business was finished, the trio would go over to the feed 'n seed, where they would spend the remainder of the afternoon. Ruth never expected Cole home before five, but she did not mind. Everyone needed to sneak away for the day every once in a while, and she had been known to do the same.

On this day, she made it a point to arrive early and sit with Katie until she woke. An early riser by nature, Ruth loved being there when the little girl tumbled out of bed, rubbing the sleep from her eyes as she staggered into her eager arms. Ruth now thought of this as her special day with Katie and looked forward to it almost as much as Cole. It was a break from the regular routine for them both.

As Cole shaved that morning, he was relieved that he did, indeed, look better. The dark circles from the past few nights had faded away. At least Ruth would be appeased. He had managed to get a good night's sleep the previous two nights. Ruth would only worry otherwise, something he hated putting on her. She knew of the sleepless nights and the nightmares he suffered; Cole just hoped to spare her this latest round. He was grateful that no one was witness to his night terrors, especially his daughter, who would be scared to death. To Katie, Daddy was the strong one. He was the one who made everything right in the world. Nothing bad was ever supposed to happen to Daddy, but something bad did happen and the only world her daddy could not control was his own.

Knowing that Ruth must have sensed his mood on Sunday, Cole was grateful that she would be spared any worry today. He just had a bad spell, something both were used to. She had sensed that he had not been sleeping simply by the quiet mood he had been cast into. When like that, Ruth just gave him the quiet understanding he craved. He should have talked to her, but it just wasn't necessary to burden her any more than need be. Lord knew that she had already done enough for him, Cole didn't relish the thought of adding to her worries. It was enough that she ran his home and cared for Katie, she didn't have to constantly go around picking up the pieces every time he fell apart. Cole preferred shouldering his load alone.

Wiping the steam from the mirror, he finished. With a towel wrapped around his waist, Cole walked to his room, whistling softly. Katie was still sleeping and there was time for a quiet cup of coffee before Ruth arrived. He was dressed and sitting out front when he saw her walking up over the hill. For all her 60-some years, which she would never admit to, Ruth still walked with a bounce in her step and her back straight and tall.

Tall and slender, her silvery gray hair was worn in a twist at the nape of her neck. With striking blue eyes and warm smile, the beauty of her youth was still present in her features. In the spring and summer, she wore a simple housedress, sometimes with a sweater or shawl around her shoulders, as she was so clad this morning. In the chill of autumn and the dead of winter, her style turned to long pants, warm boots instead of her simple shoes, and hand-knitted sweaters worn over a long-sleeved blouse. Layers were the only way to keep warm during a cold Montana winter. There was no room for false modesty.

Ruth was young at heart and had more energy than most people Cole knew. She chalked it up to good food, clean air, living in a place where one could find peace and tranquility in their surroundings, and hard work. Add friends and a small family to now call your own to care for, and you have all that is needed to keep one young, healthy and spry. Ruth walked from her modest, two-story farmhouse every morning the weather permitted and drove down on the days when it was just too rainy or cold to walk.

In the dead of winter, when the weather was frigid and the snow deep and deadly, she slept over so she could be with Katie while Cole tended the horses. Nothing challenged the body more than the heart of a Montana winter, threatening both man and animal with plunging, bone chilling temperatures. The nights were long and the days were short, with only a burst of sun every so often, if it could break through the dense blanket of steely gray clouds that seemed to shroud them until spring. Cole kept the horses closed up in the barn then, only letting them out if the temperature rose above zero during the midday hours and the biting wind gave them a brief respite. Even so, the animals were not allowed out for long and had a tendency to stick close to the building.

Other than that, the weather was just too wicked and deadly for either man or beast to venture out. Still, no matter what the conditions were, Cole had to go out to the barn at least three times a day. When blizzards hit, he kept a firm grip on the cable line he had strung from the house to the barn and made his way over in that fashion. It was only a short walk and he was on his own property, but when a body couldn't see more than a foot in front of his face, one misstep could send them wandering out into the storm for hours, possibly only to be overcome by the elements.

This morning though, those hardships were the furthest thing from Cole's mind. It was warm, it was the first week of May, and Ruth was walking briskly down the lane. He could see her smile from where he sat, and couldn't help but smile himself. Nothing made Cole happier or more at ease than knowing she was here taking care of things while he worked. Even though he would not be working today, Cole was still comforted knowing that Katie was in good hands and would be sitting on the front porch with Ruth, and whatever neighbor happened by for a visit, when he came home. And knowing Ruth, there was always someone there. Cole just prayed that this time that someone wasn't Callie.

"Morning!" Ruth called out, waving her arm.

"Morning! You look happy!" Cole replied, greeting her with a hug.

"It's a beautiful day, honey! How did you sleep? You look good!" Ruth exclaimed, relieved to see some color back in his cheeks.

"I feel great, so don't worry! It was just a hard weekend and I had a lot on my mind. Saturday I was overtired from shopping and everything else I had to do, but Sunday and last night I slept great. So you have nothing to worry about!" Cole reassured her.

"At least not with you," Ruth said quietly.

"What's wrong? What do you mean, at least not with me? Did something happen?" Cole asked, worrying instantly.

"Not really, but it seems.... Oh, don't listen to me! I'm just an old lady who worries too much and is seeing something in nothing!" Ruth laughingly waved him off.

"Well, something has you spooked!" Cole insisted.

"I tell you, something just doesn't feel right in my bones. You know me, I go by my feelings and something just doesn't feel right," Ruth nodded.

Cole knew Ruth's feelings and he did not take them lightly; if Ruth felt that something was wrong, then something was wrong. It didn't even have to be much, just something to come along and shake up the normal set of things was enough to make her uneasy. When Sadie and Gil went to Las Vegas for a vacation, Ruth was fine until around midmorning. Then for no reason at all, she began pacing the floors restlessly, going out to the porch and back inside again. She had a queasy feeling in the pit of her stomach and had no idea what it pertained to. That, she didn't know until after the event actually happened. All she knew was that something in her world was not right.

By mid-afternoon, Ruth was fine and back to her old self once again. She worked throughout the house as if she hadn't a care in the world. Nothing had happened to anyone as far as she could tell; Cole was out riding, Katie was happily playing with her dolls and her friends were fine. Later that evening, the call came. Sadie usually never called during her vacations, but she just had to tell Ruth how they had gone into a gas station just off of the interstate near Las Vegas. The attendant had told Gil that if they did not get their tires changed, then they could have some serious problems. Feeling that he was only taking advantage of tourists, Gil told Sadie to get in the car and they left.

They had only gone a mile when Gil had the funny feeling to turn around. By then it was around 11:30 so they decided to confront the mechanic. "I'm gonna make him put the car on the lift so I can see for myself," he vowed, turning back.

The minute the car was raised above their heads, Gil clearly saw what the attendant had been talking about. "See that, sir? If you drove a few more miles in this heat, then both of these tires could have blown out on you. I'd hate to see you folks have a wreck all the way down here on your vacation. Now, I have some good tires, they're not too pricey either, and I'll mount them for free," he offered, showing Gil how the steel bands had started wearing through.

"Hell's bells, those tires ain't more than a year old," Gil said, running a shaky hand through his hair. "I hate to think...." he hesitated, choking on his words. "You go ahead, young fella, and do what you have to do. I'll also apologize for doubting you, guess I'm just a foolish old man."

"No, you're just a little too paranoid for your own good," Sadie glared at her husband.

The mechanic smiled, threw the old tires out back in the pile, and within an hour had the new ones mounted and sent Gil and Sadie on their way. True to his word, he had only charged wholesale for the tires, but being the chastised soul he was and knowing his wife, Gil gratefully handed the man a $20 tip. By three in the afternoon they were finally on their way after a quick lunch, and Ruth had settled down, her feelings of woe leaving instantly. All was fine with her world again.

"Good lord, I knew that something was wrong," Ruth had said as she listened to Sadie's story.

Once news of this story spread, everyone in town knew of Ruth's 'premonition,' and took stock in her feelings. Cole was one of them and he listened to her now.

"I know you and I know that you wouldn't make a big deal out of nothing. Something has you upset," Cole stared intently.

"Like I said, don't listen to me," Ruth scoffed, waving him off. "It's just that this real estate bigwig came into Ed's office yesterday and started asking around if anyone had any land for sale. Seems like he's looking to buy a bundle. He's not saying what they want the land for, but the consensus around town is that he wants to put in a mall or some other sort of business.

Can you imagine that? We've been living this long without any of that fancy, newfangled stuff and we don't need it now. Progress brings nothing but noise, pollution, traffic and problems we don't need."

"I wouldn't worry about it," Cole soothed her. "Those guys seem to go all over places where they know there's large amounts of property to be had. They look for areas where they can help the economy by bringing industry in. They seem to think that we need it!" he snorted. "Sometimes they hit it lucky and find the owner willing to sell, but I can't see that happening here. Most he'll leave here with is a passel full of nos."

"I sure hope you're right, honey, because I don't like this at all," Ruth replied, squeezing his hand.

"Ruth, has he approached anybody?" Cole asked.

"Not that I know of, but Lacy says that he told Ed he'd like a list of all the ranches in the area, so I know that he's going to start nosing around," she replied.

"Then let him! I'll just turn his ass around and send him packing!" Cole said emphatically.

"I'll send him packing all right," Ruth sniffed.

"Now, be nice! The bastard's only trying to make a living!" Cole laughed lightly.

"Not off of us he's not! Let him go somewhere they appreciate his kind and what he wants to bring in! We never did need any of that and we don't need it now! All these folks have been on their places their entire lives! You're the only one starting new, and if Shane had any kin, they'd be running the place now! That's just the way it is; no one here's going to sell," Ruth said sternly.

"See, there's nothing to worry about then! But I gotta go, I'll call you later," Cole leaned over, kissing her on the cheek.

"Honey! Listen to me, I'm cackling like an old hen and didn't even fix you something to eat," Ruth chided herself.

"Don't worry! I'm meeting the guys at Sadie's, remember? It's your morning off! Give Katie a kiss for me and tell her I'll try and call later!" Cole called back over his shoulder.

* * *

The diner was noisy and busy when Cole arrived. Everyone dug into their meals, talking a mile a minute as they sought to get caught up with the news in town. Even though nothing much happened since yesterday, the air was still buzzing. The noisy clanking of forks and knives against plates and coffee being sipped filled the air, adding to the din coming from the kitchen. Bacon sizzled on the grill, along with eggs, hashbrowns, and sausages. The smells drifted outside, drawing anybody that walked by with an appetite, in. Gil knew what he was doing, sometimes no matter how cold it was, he purposely left a window open a crack so the odors wafted out. Hungry people by the dozens descended on them in the morning, more so than any other time of day.

Early risers by nature, some of the ranch hands drove into town for their morning meal before their busy day began. Lunch and dinner were usually slow, with only the occasional shopper and a few stragglers dropping by. Most of the hands were too busy at the ranches and farms to even think of getting away, and by the time they finished up later in the afternoon, most were either too tired to drive into town or it was just easier to grab something at home. Their days started early and lasted long, not finishing until well after dark, when they would be busy tending their animals for the night. Breakfast was the best meal by far, they had a hearty meal that stuck to their ribs most of the day, and the chance to socialize before their day began, something all looked forward too.

"Over easy, Gil!" Sadie cried over her shoulder.

"You said scrambled!" he groused back.

"Hey Gil, your brain is scrambled!" Brent yelled back.

"At least it's not b—" Cole started, only to be abruptly and painfully stopped by an elbow to the ribs.

"What'd you do that for?" Cole then whined.

"Cause Katie's not here! AND I DON'T LIKE SCRAMBLED!" Brent grumbled, yelling over to Gil.

"Yeah, yeah, you'll eat what you get and like it!" Gil argued back, waving his spatula while he continued working.

"You'll get over easy, sweetie," Sadie flirted, glaring at her husband. "He's getting hard of hearing."

"I heard that! And I heard you before! Here, over easy!" Gil unceremoniously plopped a plate on the counter, along with an extra helping of hashbrowns and bacon.

Brent rubbed his hands together before he began, "Hah, I got more! Damn, am starved," he said, digging in.

"Doesn't your mother ever feed you?" Cole frowned.

"You know, you're just jealous cause I got more and you have to cook for yourself," Brent mumbled around a mouthful of eggs, followed quickly by a bite of bacon and piece of toast, all in one fluid, orchestrated movement.

"God, you eat like a caveman," Cole groaned. He had finished his breakfast and was enjoying a cup of coffee while Brent and Will ate.

"What's the matter, you got no appetite? Feeling sick or sumthin'?" Will asked of Cole.

"No, not feeling sick, guess I have something on my mind," Cole replied.

"You got a mind?" Brent muttered.

"Just keep on shoveling eggs into your mouth and mind your own business," Cole muttered. "It's just something Ruth said earlier that's got me feeling kind of bothered. Any of you guys hear about someone going around asking to buy land?"

"Yeah, name's Peter Sinclair," Sadie answered, having listened in. She never meant to; but the diner was small, the town was small, and everything discussed in public was shared by the public.

Cole was lost in thought for a moment, "No, name don't sound familiar, but...."

"But what? So he's asking. Lots of times we get someone nosing around every few years or so looking to buy up some land. Nothing new," Will shrugged.

"Yeah, I know but this is.... I don't know; I guess I've been listening to Ruth too long and am starting to have her feelings," Cole hedged.

"Ruth don't feel right about this?" Sadie instantly worried.

"Well, not about Pete Sinclair per se, but she's just got her back up that someone has the nerve to come into town and try to take us over," Cole explained.

"Don't blame her there, don't cotton to folk coming around trying to change us," Sadie agreed.

"I came and bought up Shane's land," Cole said quietly.

"Honey, that's different! If poor old Shane had had someone to pass his land on to, then he would have done that. And you didn't come to town trying to buy someone out. This is different, Shane had no one to take over and he'd be mighty proud to see the job you're doing out at the place," Sadie soothed him.

"Yeah, we like you," Will smirked, shrugging at the glare Brent threw at him. "What?"

"Don't go giving him an ego," Brent grumbled.

"Don't listen to him, honey, cow must'a kicked him in the head," Sadie said, glaring at Brent. "And we gave you extra," she said with a slight snort of indignation.

"Hey, I'm sorry! You know the problem I have with my big mouth! Didn't mean nuthin' by it. Just that when I get nervous and all I tend to get kind'a stupid," Brent shrugged.

"You think?" Cole glared.

Listening to the two argue, it would be hard for an outsider to believe that they really did care about one another. Deep down though, where it counted, all three cared deeply and respected one another unconditionally. It was a code of honor that seemed to belong to men alone, they were absolutely loath to admit their feelings. Torment was a much more desirable pastime. When push came to shove though, Brent and Will would be there for Cole and the same went for Cole where they were concerned. All three would fight to the death for the other and God help anyone who caused trouble or heartache for any of them.

Upon Cole's arrival all those years ago, it was Brent who showed up at his doorstep one morning, with a casserole, a pie, and a handshake at the ready. "Mom did a bit of cooking and baking, hearing as we've got a new neighbor now," he smiled brightly.

It didn't take long for Cole to fit in. Ruth was first to arrive that morning, introducing herself and giving him her phone number, along with a dinner invitation for that night. Brent was the next to arrive, carrying gifts of food and offering a helping hand. Between the two of them, they had almost all of Cole's meager belongings moved in, when Will showed up.

"Will Robbins, I got that spread just the other side of you," he introduced himself with a toothy grin. "Any time you need anything, and I mean anything, just holler!" he grinned. Picking up two large boxes, he carried them into the house.

"Make yourself at home!" Brent called out after him, and it all began.

The three had been inseparable ever since. And when Katie came along, Cole knew that without the help and support of his close friends, he never would have been able to hold things together on his own. He simply could not deal with the demands of a newborn baby and a dozen or so horses alone. Something had to give; but thanks to his friends, he had been able to hold on to his dream and raise his daughter. She had the life that Cole dreamed of for her; there was the ranch to run and play on, and two good friends to call uncle watching out for her.

"You say that something about that guy is bothering you?" Will asked, getting no response from Cole. "Hello! You in there?" he said, resorting to snapping his fingers in front of Cole's face.

After a few seconds, the noise registered and Cole stirred from his trance. He had been sitting with his coffee to his mouth, but only held the cup between his hands, not drinking a drop. His mind had wandered back over the years, remembering how his friends had come to him. There was more to it, too, only he couldn't place his finger on it. The bit of news that Ruth had given bothered him. Cole did not know of a Pete Sinclair, but he was determined to find out. Maybe the man meant no harm; like he and Ruth had discussed earlier, he was only out making a living. Yet, if that's all there was to it, then Cole found himself wondering what it was about the man that had set his nerves on edge. Ruth was right, something was out of kilter in their world.

"Sorry, what'd you say?" Cole stammered, shaking his had slightly.

"He asked you what it was about that guy that bothered you. You know him from somewhere?" Brent jumped in.

"No, not necessarily. Never heard of the name, never met the man. But I intend to find out! Wanna know if he's working by himself or for someone else," Cole answered absently, still deep in thought.

"What the hell you mean about him working for someone?" Will wanted to know.

"Just that," Cole shrugged. "Most times, it's usually a large company or some developer who sends these guys out to buy the land for them. They act as spokesmen. They might have plans like putting in industry, or maybe some malls or even developments."

"Hell! We don't want any of that shit here!" Brent swore. "Things are fine just the way they are and Petey Sinclair's gonna find that out soon enough!"

"Yeah, little Petey's gonna find out what it's like to have his ass run outta town on the end of a rail," Will snickered menacingly. "Either that, or he'll get the rail shoved so far up his ass that—"

"I get the picture," Cole moaned, rubbing his temple.

"Hah!" Brent burst out, causing both men to jump when his fist pounded the table.

"Will you stop that!" Cole cried out.

"Just like I told Katie the other night! Your head's gonna explode!" Brent declared victoriously.

"If it is, it'll be cause of you," Will reasoned. "Give the man a break! God! You damn near made me spill my coffee!"

Chapter Six

Pete Sinclair pulled up outside of Walt Bremmer's ranch, stopping before he drove under the large, curved arch. "The Circle B" was the name emblazoned across the top. He wiped the sweat from his brow, taking a breather before encountering his first, hopefully, potential client. It had been a long ride, but that never bothered Sinclair. He often spent weeks on the road scouting out an area before approaching the prospective sellers with an offer. Getting the true lay of the land was not possible from a plane, Sinclair preferred seeing it firsthand from the front seat of his little gray Civic. Culver was right, this could be a tough one; but that didn't deter Sinclair. He had been in tough deals before and walked out a winner; he was not about to let his boss down.

He got out of the car for a moment, leaning on the top of the door as he scanned the ranch. Nothing but flat pasture and rolling green hills with the vast mountains in the background met his eye. The sky was blue, with nary a cloud in sight and that only added to the slowly building heat of the day.

"Big sky country," Sinclair spat, cursing. "They're right, all I've seen so far is sky and nothing but vast, empty land. One minute it's all green and lush and the next it's barren and empty, nothing but that fucking sage and dirt. Who wouldn't want to get the hell out of here?" he said, shaking his head.

Sinclair wasn't a large man by far, standing at only 5'10" tall. He was also thin and frail-looking and his clothes hung on his frame. There wasn't any meat on his bones to speak of and if a strong enough wind came along, he would be rolling across the prairie like the tumbleweeds he had driven over during his ride in. His wire-rimmed glasses had slipped down over his nose and he pulled them off, wiping his face. A few strands of hair fell from his nearly bald head, so Sinclair brushed them back, trying to make it look like he had something there after all. Glancing in the mirror, he frowned; it looked ridiculous. When he returned home after this trip, he would give in and finally shave his head. At this point, no hair would look better than the few strands he had left to work with; it was time that he stopped fooling himself. His father had gone bald early in life and he took after the man; there was no sense in wasting good energy trying to fight nature, it was a losing battle.

Sinclair sat in the car, patting the large briefcase sitting on the seat next to him. It was filled with the usual contracts and deals, with offers ready to be made and checks ready to be issued. Culver was right about another thing, there was nothing here and that was what he wanted, virgin land to build yet another empire on. He would buy out the entire area if so desired and would make something out of this place.

Besides, Sinclair was not about to return a failure. Randall Culver wasn't someone you wanted to let down; he was a sore loser and hated taking no for an answer. The man had been born without a conscience and would stop at nothing to get what he wanted, no matter who he had to step on in the process. Sinclair wondered what Culver's mother must have been like, he could not imagine a gentle, loving woman spawning something as heartless and cold as his boss.

Culver sat behind his desk throwing his money around to anyone willing to stoop low enough to carry out his orders, and he had found that in Sinclair, who was shocked the first time he laid eyes on the man. Culver's reputation preceded him. Sinclair did not know whether to expect some giant ogre sitting behind a desk chomping on small souls for a snack, or a fire breathing dragon sitting amid a pile of ashes of those who were unable to fulfill their appointed tasks.

Putting his imagination on hold, Sinclair struggled to stifle his laughter the first time he walked into Culver's office. The booming voice on the phone belonged to a man who was nothing more than average. That was the only word to describe Culver. He wasn't meek and frail-looking like Sinclair himself was, and he wasn't the large hulk of a man that Sinclair had expected to find sitting there. Culver was an average-height man, who sported just enough weight to allow him to move around comfortably, and looked more like some mild-mannered school principal, rather than the ruthless businessman Sinclair had heard so much about.

The man's hair was thinning, but he was far from bald. Sinclair snickered inwardly on that one; Culver kept on running his hand through the black strands, something Sinclair envied him for. Despite all his power, Culver still fell prey to the same human frailty that plagued so many others ... he was unable to control his own thinning hair. But at least he had something on top of his head to run his hands through.

Culver's face was taut, with worry lines creased across his forehead and eyebrows that seemed to grow together, curling up at the outside corners when he frowned. Judging from the way that they now seemed to stay permanently curled, Sinclair deducted that Culver tended to frown quite a lot. The pallor on his face had Sinclair wondering just how much he ventured outside. Maybe he never saw the light of day, which would explain a lot, at least in Sinclair's wild imagination. Maybe the man could not face the sun and remained hidden in his large, dark office, sitting behind an ornate mahogany desk. With all the open range and land Culver owned, one would think him tanned, healthy and very rugged from time spent outdoors.

One look at his pasty complexion, however, betrayed that fact. Culver's skin was waxy and his mouth was nothing more than a thin line drawn across his face. How someone with such tight, rigid features could address a person with as much force as Culver did was also beyond Sinclair. Sitting there, the man looked like he couldn't harm a fly. However, the one thing that betrayed Culver was his eyes. They were almost black. Sinclair had never seen anyone with eyes so dark before. He wondered if they held any color when he was a child, if Culver ever was a child. If so, they no longer held any resemblance to anything human, to Sinclair, they just looked cold, dead and black … the perfect image for a man without a conscience. Looking into Culver's eyes was something a person did not want to do, as Sinclair quickly found out. He suppressed the chills that ran up and down his spine as he took his seat, nodding at the man.

The eyes that looked back at Sinclair brooked no nonsense; Culver was a man who knew what he wanted and was used to getting his own way. He was brash, he was callous, and he was not afraid to go after what he wanted, thinking himself above both the laws of mankind and the law of the land. People were only an obstacle to the man, and the right amount of pressure and money always insured their easy removal. But if push came to shove, Culver could be deadly. That wasn't lost on Sinclair as he met with Culver one last time the morning he was slated to leave for Crater Mills.

"Hell, they're easy prey! Those people are probably sitting there so bored out of their gourds that they'll practically give everything away!" Sinclair had said to Culver as he rifled through his notes.

"Don't underestimate them," Culver replied dryly. "You forget, the land they're on has been passed down from one generation to the next. Those cowboys tend to get sentimental and that can lead to trouble. Especially one, and he's the reason I picked this place," he said, frowning as he sat back.

"One? Who the hell is the one?" Sinclair demanded to know.

"Cole Morgan's his name. He bought the place six years ago. Seems the previous owner had no family to speak of so when he kicked the bucket, the place went up for sale," was Culver's reply.

"Why the hell would he be any trouble?" Sinclair asked, not knowing of Culver's past dealings.

"All you need to know is not to take any shit from him. I made the mistake of turning my back on the bastard years ago, thinking he was an easy target. Well, he's not! Son of a bitch beat me once. He won't do it again. I'll kill him this time," Culver finished, refusing to divulge any further information.

Sinclair knew better than to push. He did what he was told; took what information was needed and went off. If Culver said to watch out for this Morgan fellow, then he would keep an eye on him. Culver had to have a good reason and that was enough for Sinclair. He certainly wasn't above using whatever force needed in order to get what he had set out to accomplish. In spite of his size, Sinclair was a formidable opponent and never shrank from a challenge. His mother had always said to watch out for things that came in small packages.

"Could be poison," Sinclair snickered, thinking of her for a moment.

"What the hell you spouting off?" Culver asked, his tone impatient and harsh.

"Sorry, Mr. Culver, I was just making a mental note to myself," Sinclair quickly covered for himself. "Don't you worry about this Morgan, whoever the hell he is, I'll take care of him. I'll call you next week after I start the wheels rolling," he answered, standing and snapping his briefcase shut.

Culver was quiet as he watched Sinclair leaving. Pete was new to his organization. He didn't know a thing about his past dealings, and Culver preferred to keep it that way. But Sinclair was shrewd and easily bought, which made a very good combination for Culver. Get a greedy man with no heart to work for you and he did whatever requested, no questions asked. Sinclair was working out fine.

"Nope, Cole Morgan won't be a problem at all. I'll deal with him personally this time if I have to," Culver sneered under his breath. The door closed and Sinclair was gone.

* * *

With that conversation fresh in his mind, Sinclair started the car and drove down the lane leading to the main house, where he was greeted by a middle-aged man walking slowly over, a puzzled look on his face. Sinclair surmised that they probably didn't get too much company around here. And with good reason, they were the furthest from town, which was why he came here first. He would start with this ranch and work his way in. Besides, Walter Bremmer had one of the largest spreads in the area, and if he could be convinced to sell, then others might follow suit. Sinclair looked around, spotting a slim woman with mousy brown hair and sharp features, who obviously had to be Walt's wife, standing on the porch. A true hick, in Sinclair's book, clad in a simple flowered housedress, with an apron tied around her waist. The only other person present was a younger, lanky, darker-haired youth, who was busy with the cattle.

Sinclair figured that to be their teenage son, Zachary. He prided himself on knowing as much as he could about the families he was dealing with, Sinclair believed in being totally prepared. There was no room for surprises where he was concerned. With a smile on his face, he picked up his briefcase and met Walt, extending his hand. Sturdy, wispy salt and pepper hair and blue eyes, with hands callused by years of hard work, Walt took Sinclair's hand firmly, staring intently for a moment. He was not an overly large man, but Walt's structure was foreboding. Yet, his demeanor was friendly.

"What can I do for you, young man? You selling something?" Walt asked with a small smile on his face.

"No, sir, but I would like a moment of your time," Sinclair began.

"You know, word does get around this place pretty fast, even though we are miles from one another, and I don't mean to be rude, but I've heard tell that there's a young man going around town asking a lot of questions about land being for sale. And if you're that man, then I have to tell you that you're wasting your time. My land never has been and never will be for sale. I inherited it from my father, and he got it from his father before him. I've lived here my entire 42 years and intend to pass it down to my son when my time comes," Walter explained firmly, broaching no argument.

"Name's Peter Sinclair," Sinclair still forged ahead, offering his hand.

"Walter Bremmer," Walt took his hand.

"It's true. I have been going around asking about land being for sale. So before you send me packing, as you folks would say, I only ask that you listen to my offer," Sinclair continued.

"Son, you can't offer me enough. Money's not an issue here; it's the land that means everything to me and always will. Some folk can't seem to understand that, but it's as much a part of me as my very soul. I wouldn't sell it to you if I didn't have a penny to my name. There's just some things that money can't buy," Walt stubbornly held his ground.

"Sir, my client is prepared to offer a very handsome settlement, indeed. If you would just give me ten minutes of your time, I know that I can change your mind," Sinclair replied.

"Now, if you wanted to sit and chat the morning away jawing about the weather, how stubborn teenagers are these days," Walt laughed, glancing at his son, "or the market price of meat, then I'd give you that ten minutes and more. But, since you only want to talk about an offer that I have no intention

97

of accepting and no interest in hearing, then I must bid you a good day and send you off," Walt said, turning to leave.

Sinclair had never been put off so abruptly before, and knew that Culver would not take his failure lightly. "Mr. Bremmer, if you could—"

"Good day, Mr. Sinclair!" Walt turned back once more.

"Good day, Mr. Bremmer," Sinclair replied crisply. "Hope one of your fucking cows stomps on your foot," he muttered under his breath.

As he drove off, Sinclair knew that he had to report this to Culver, who would be far from pleased. He also knew that Culver was not one to give up, so he knew he would be back. If not, then they would have to take other measures. Sinclair was not opposed to other measures.

* * *

"Hey, hey, hey," Will elbowed Cole, getting his attention. "You recognize that car?"

Cole lifted his head, looking up from the chair he had tilted against the wall of the building. "Nope, no one I know. You know anyone in a gray Civic?" he then elbowed Brent, who was also napping in the same fashion.

"Nope, no one here drives an economy car," Brent sneered. "We drive trucks! Gotta be that real estate guy," he said, sitting up straighter for a better look.

It had been a fairly quiet day and after a quick lunch, the three walked over to the feed 'n seed. While their trucks were being loaded with sacks of grain, they each leaned a chair back against the wall, dozing and looking about. Now that their trucks were ready, no one was about to move. It felt good to sit quietly in the middle of the afternoon, almost as good as it felt when younger and sneaking away from school. Some might think sitting on the front stoop of a seed store boring, but it was amazing what you could pick up around town when just gazing about; something the three were about to find out.

Of course, they had their petty squabbles; that went without saying. No one ever saw them around each other for any length of time without some sort of an argument. They wanted to play checkers, but were not allowed without adult supervision. Even Hec and Sam were better behaved than these three, their fights over the game becoming almost legendary. Gris had no choice but to intervene, taking the game board away and leaving three sulking men behind. To this day, the board remained locked in his top desk drawer.

He knew that their arguments were good-natured, they just couldn't seem to help themselves. Even so, Gris derived a perverse sense of satisfaction from the power he wielded over the trio. They were letting off steam and meant no harm, except to the checker pieces themselves. Sometimes wayward children just needed to be reined in.

Being nosy paid off. All three perked up when Pete Sinclair drove in, catching their attention. Will had been the first one to notice and elbowed a napping Cole. Before Cole could utter more than a grunt, Ed pulled in alongside Sinclair and the two walked into the office together. It was almost 2:30, something that didn't go unnoticed by the three.

"Son of a bitch works better hours than a banker," Will sneered. "I oughta tell my wife, she's been bitching that I work too much and hardly spend any time with her, and when I do, I'm too tired!"

"And she's complaining about that?" Brent began his torment. "At least it saves her the trouble of pleading a headache!"

"Shut up, asshole, when's the last time you got laid? No wonder you spend so much time with those cows," Will hissed.

"Been wondering 'bout that myself," Cole snickered. "You know what they say about cowboys and all those long, cold winter nights!"

"Look who's talking!" Brent struck back. "At least I can remember my last date!"

"What date? You don't date! You sit home with Mommy eating pie! Cole, would you believe I called him Saturday night to go to the Branding Hole and he said no? Said he was just going to watch TV and eat some pie. Can you believe that?" Will said in disbelief.

"Yeah, he called and invited me over to join him, but even I had better things to do!" Cole teased.

"See if I invite you over again!" Brent replied in a huff. Sitting back, he crossed his arms and turned his argument back to Will. "What, was Lisa letting you out of your cage for the night?" he replied, unable to stop himself.

"No! I didn't need her permission! I just thought that we could go and blow off some steam! I wanted to take her dancing, but she was tired after a long day with the boys," Will shot back.

"How are Lucas and Jordan anyway?" Cole switched gears, feeling the familiar throbbing on the side of his head. "You should bring them by one afternoon to play with Katie."

"Oh, you're not gonna let our little angel play with his—" Brent replied.

"Hey, watch it!" Will sneered. "Lucas and Jordan happen to like playing with Katie!"

"Do they dress up and play tea party?" Brent sneered, giggling.

"No, asshole, that's your job! Everyone knows how you go home nights and dress in your Mama's dresses when no one's around!" Will argued back.

"God, will you two just shut up!" Cole burst out, finally putting an end to their arguing.

"What? We were only having a little fun!" Brent whined.

"Yeah, what else is there to do?" Will asked, as they both turned to gape at Cole.

"Nothing but watch what that asshole does. God, I don't trust him and I don't know why," Cole shivered, watching Sinclair through the window of Ed's office.

Since the three had seen Sinclair following Ed inside, they watched through the large picture window in the front of the building. Between arguing with one another and watching Sinclair, they were pleasantly entertained. Cole looked at the man, trying to jog his memory. His demeanor did not go unnoticed by Brent, who had fallen silent, studying his friend.

"Cole, you ok?" he worried.

"Yeah ... just watching those two," Cole hesitantly replied, nodding towards the building.

"You know him from somewhere?" Brent asked about Sinclair.

"No, not that I can think of," Cole drawled, rubbing his chin. "But there's just something about him. I mean, look at the little bastard! He's hardly bigger than a flea, but don't let that fool ya. I just got a bad feeling about that guy."

"That little shit?" Brent exclaimed. "Hell, we can roll right over him!"

"Like I said, don't let that fool ya. I don't think he's working alone. Not that I'm saying he's up to something, but some of those guys can; well, let's say that they're very good at getting their way," Cole replied.

Both Brent and Will's eyes flew open as heads turned back towards the office. They looked at Sinclair, who was now sitting at Ed's desk. Things had seemed to take a turn, Ed didn't look happy and ran his hand through his hair as he talked. He then got up and slammed the file drawer shut, and Sinclair left. Neither man said goodbye or shook hands, which further puzzled the nosy trio. That didn't help Cole's suspicions any.

"What the hell do you think that was all about?" Brent asked.

Cole looked between his two friends, "I don't know, but I sure intend to find out. In the meantime, let's just leave him alone and see what he does. Don't want to put him on guard; but I won't take my eyes off of him for a moment either. From now on, let's all keep our eyes and ears open."

"You think he's up to something?" Will's mouth fell open.

"Probably not, Will. Who knows? He and Ed could have been arguing about a million things! Maybe they didn't agree on the price of a house!

Maybe they're just arguing about some deal; hell, Ed's got his hands into just 'bout anything," Cole explained.

"And into anyone," Brent snickered.

"Maybe that's what they're fighting about!" Cole joined in. "We've all heard the stories about the women Ed brings out to see all those houses that are so far out of town!" he laughed, emphasizing those last words.

"Yeah, maybe his wife finally put a contract out on him and Sinclair's the man to do the job!" Will laughingly agreed.

Cole laughed with his friends, trying to dispel his uneasiness by joking. He only hoped that they were right, but he seriously doubted that. Peter Sinclair hadn't come to town for any of those reasons. He had something else on his mind, and Cole vowed right then and there to watch every move he made.

"He looks like a shrewd bastard," Cole hissed, watching the man through narrowed eyes. A few minutes later, Sinclair drove away.

* * *

Later that evening Brent followed Cole home for dinner. Ruth had been expecting him and had everything ready. The smell of chicken and dumplings greeted them upon arrival. The minute Cole stepped out of his truck, Katie was flying into his arms. She wasn't used to her daddy being gone all day long and had waited patiently. He scooped her up, laughing as her fingers tickled his face.

"Were you a good girl?" he asked of her.

Katie just nodded, but her smile told all.

"It smells like you and Nanny have been baking!" Brent joined in. "Got a hug for your Uncle Brent?"

"We made cookies!" she replied, finding herself being passed to Brent's arms. Wrapping her arms around his neck, she squeezed tight.

"My Lord, you're getting strong!" Brent gagged playfully, eliciting giggles from Katie.

"Daddy, Callie's here," Katie smiled.

Cole looked, seeing her truck parked alongside the fence. In his excitement to see his daughter, he hadn't even noticed. Cringing, he tried not to frown. Not missing his reaction, Brent smiled devilishly, elbowing Cole in the ribs. A tired groan escaped his lips, for he had been poked and jabbed by either Brent or Will all day long and just knew that he would soon be sporting a batch of new bruises. He also knew what Ruth was up to; yet he couldn't be mad. She meant well and only wanted him to be happy. Why she kept on insisting on throwing him and Callie together was beyond him, though.

It made no difference that she made his blood boil or his head swim whenever she came around. Any hope of coherent thought flew right out the window whenever Callie was near. Cole became tongue-tied, knowing that he blushed profusely. And God forbid if they touched, just the mere feel of her hand sent sparks shooting throughout his body. When she passed him by, their bodies did not even need to touch; yet Cole could feel the heat of her passion. Chastising himself and shaking off these thoughts, he walked to the house.

They were just friends, after all. Cole had to keep reminding himself of that fact each time Callie's blue eyes looked right through him. He had to completely wipe her smile from his mind before he even thought of facing her. Just thinking of the times he had let love into his life was all that was needed to suppress his feelings. He had lost once. It has been six years and Sarah's death still hurt as much today as it did then. Then there was Maggie. Afraid of making another such mistake, Cole avoided the issue altogether now; the last thing he needed was to confuse love with need again. There was no sense in going down that same road a second time, and he was just too tired to even think of a relationship with anyone, no matter how he felt. To love someone meant work. Cole did not have the energy to work at another relationship.

"Sarah loved you and you just walked away. Are you happy now, Cole? You didn't care enough about your own wife and now she's dead! It was easier for you to just walk away. You just walked away!" the cold words came back to him.

That was the moment that the light in Cole's eyes was extinguished completely. He had lost everything; all he held dear in his life was gone. He was completely and totally alone. His wife, his friends, and life had abandoned him. He lost all trust in himself, in everyone around him and in the powers that be. There was nothing left to go on for and he wondered why he couldn't just pick up his gun and end it all right then and there.

Later that evening, after the funeral, Cole walked into the barn and sat on a bale of hay. His mind had shut down and his body felt like it had ceased functioning. He looked at the horses without really seeing them. His cousin had been coming over to care for the animals ever since the tragedy struck. Now Cole just sat and stared. He looked up at the rafters of the barn, knowing how strong and sturdy they were. He picked up a length of rope, which he held in his hands. It would be so easy to end all the pain.

"This oughta do the trick. What the fuck? No one's gonna miss me anyway. Might do the world a big favor," Cole sneered, fashioning a noose.

His eyes closed, he envisioned himself throwing the end of the rope up and over the beam. He then fastened it tightly … it had to hold. He was not going to fail at this like he had failed at everything else in his life. If they came into the barn and found his lifeless body swinging at the end of a rope, no one would give a damn anyway. Pulling the noose down over his neck, Cole gave it a quick twist and it snapped snugly, the sinewy coils already biting into his skin. Closing his eyes, he gulped, took one last breath, and jumped from the ladder.

The rope caught and he gagged, his body lurching violently. The ladder was kicked over as spasms sent his body twitching wildly in the air. His eyes bugged out and all air was closed off from his lungs as his windpipe collapsed, crushed under the dead weight of his body. It wasn't fast, but it was over in a matter of seconds. His eyes glazed over and his fingers twitched spasmodically a few more times. Within minutes, he was hanging quietly, the rope creaking as his body swung in a slow, lazy circle.

Nice thought, Cole now admonished himself silently. *You got Katie waiting for you in the kitchen, your friends are here, and that's what goes through your mind? Shit, this has gotta stop. Gonna drive yourself insane if you don't get a grip and do it now. You didn't do anything wrong and nothing that happened was your fault. It's all over now and you gotta learn not to dwell on things so damned much,* he said to himself as he went in to get washed up for dinner.

Standing over the sink, Cole still couldn't shake the dark thoughts that threatened, plunging him back to a familiar, yet dreaded place. He never could kill himself; something had always stopped him. Some unseen force always stepped in, steering him in another direction. To Cole, that was just another failure, which was no surprise. He failed miserably at everything else, so why not fail at this, also. Lacking the courage to carry out the only wish he held deep in his heart, Cole did the only thing a coward knew how to do. He shut down, both emotionally and physically. For the duration of his stay in Broken Arrow, which was only a matter of days, he avoided everyone and never spoke to another soul.

There was just nothing to say. No one could take away the pain Cole was pitched into. There was no escape. At times, the grief was so immense that it literally tore him apart, leaving him gasping for air at the uselessness reality brought. Nothing made sense anymore. The word forever was branded into his heart and soul, making the present unbearable. Forever. It stretched on with no end in sight. Forever was a dark, dismal place one's mind wandered to when the world ceased making sense. It stretched on endlessly, never bringing any peace and driving one to the brink of insanity with the enormity of its meaning.

Forever meant that there was no escape, no matter how hard the heart and mind searched for peace. It brought no comfort to a shattered soul, only a torment that was never-ending. It meant that he would never see Sarah again. Never. Another word that instilled a deep-seated fear in Cole's heart. He would never see Sarah again. He would never stop feeling the pain and he would never be the man he used to be. Everything was gone. Forever. How Cole hated that word. There was no hope in forever and no peace in the present. Tears no longer came.

It hurt too much to think of forever and it hurt too much to cry. Everything was gone except for the hollow emptiness that had become a part of his heart and soul. The tears had stopped long ago, but the hollow emptiness that had settled into his soul refused to give Cole peace. Even his aunt and cousin no longer recognized him. Cole no longer recognized himself.

All trust in the world around him had been shattered, along with any confidence he might have had at one time. Cole no longer believed in life, he ran from love, and trust was a word he no longer had any use for. His world had collapsed, along with any memories of that tragic night. The only thing Cole knew how to do was to block everything from that time out and leave. He no longer carried any conscious thought of the fire and Sarah's face was nothing more than a mere blur in his imagination. That part of his life was over.

It had been a long, hard struggle, but Cole was slowly making his way back into the world again. For a long time he merely existed, holding everyone at bay. He built up a wall, shielding himself from hurt. If you let people in, you inevitably got hurt. Ruth saw through his defenses, sensing the lonely man hidden deep inside. With love, patience, and a gentle hand, she slowly led Cole back into the world. But there was only so much that she could do. Cole had lost the ability to trust.

He shrouded himself with the familiar. He had his ranch, he had his daughter and he had the people of Crater Mills as his family. That was all he needed. That was all he wanted. Yet, he felt threatened. Something was infringing on his safe world and Cole did not take that lightly. He didn't know Pete Sinclair, but he had an uneasy feeling about the man. Cole took offense at someone coming around, trying to buy people's homes out from under them.

If a person wanted to sell, then he would go to the realtor, not the other way around. To do otherwise was to push and Cole did not like being pushed.

He didn't like strangers and he didn't cotton to anyone coming around threatening his way of life. If need be, Cole would push back. He had worked too hard to get to where he was today and nobody was going to take that away from him, no matter how hard he had to fight or what the cost. Cole just had the feeling that Pete Sinclair would not go away easily.

* * *

They found Ruth and Callie in the kitchen, putting their meal on the table. Ruth came over, embracing Cole and Brent, while Callie stood back, smiling her greeting. Cole tried hiding his nervousness, while Callie fought to hold back. All she needed to set her heart racing and her face aglow was Cole striding into the kitchen. At first, Callie had resisted Ruth's invitation, but the older woman persisted and she found herself giving in.

"You look better than the last time I saw you," Cole snickered wickedly.

"Yeah, you smell better too," Brent jumped in.

"All I know is that I look and smell a heck of a lot better than the two of you!" Callie sniffed, tossing her hair back.

"What are they talking about, honey?" Ruth asked, placing her hand on Callie's arm.

"Oh, they just saw me after a hard day at work," was all Callie had to say. "So, what's your excuse?" she challenged, staring blatantly at Cole. She loved seeing him squirm under her gaze and wasn't about to let him off the hook easily.

"Never mind us, it was a long day," Cole sighed.

Ruth looked to make sure that Katie wasn't listening. Seeing she was sitting at the table with a pad and pencil, she turned to Cole. "We'd better talk after dinner," she whispered.

"Something wrong? Is Katie ok?" Cole worried first thing.

"Honey, she's fine! You can see that! No, this can wait; we'll take our coffee outside and talk while Katie plays in the yard," Ruth nodded.

Neither Cole nor Brent cared for waiting, but they had no choice. Katie was ready for her dinner and would wonder why it was being delayed. Cole made it a point to keep upsetting things away from her, she was way too young to understand anyway and would probably think something was wrong with either him or someone they were close to. Katie was sensitive, yet she was strong.

One day when she grew older, Cole knew that he would be including her in their conversations; but they had a long time until then. Ruth and Callie had the rest of the meal set out and the men took their seats. Cole tried not to blush when Ruth sat Callie in the chair next to him. Their legs brushed together and he fought not to shoot out of his seat. Trying his best to calm down, he picked up his fork.

"Pass the chicken?" was all he managed to choke out, dismayed that it was Callie who handed over the platter.

* * *

"God, I'm gonna explode," Cole groaned, sitting in the rocker with his coffee.

"Daddy, are you going to blow up?" Katie giggled. She skipped over, her hair shining in the rays of the setting sun.

"No, honey, I just ate too much, that's all! Think I'll just sit here until I can move again," he groaned.

Brent and Callie weren't doing any better. Even Katie had done justice to her dinner, but seemed to know when to stop. Cole wondered who the wiser of them was. Ruth's cooking was unsurpassed, as they all proved tonight when they dug in. And Callie had opted for a second helping, something she rarely did. Cole finished his third and Brent put an amazing four helpings away. Ruth beamed proudly; Cole knew they were making gluttons out of themselves, she just saw it as people loving and appreciating her efforts. For Ruth, there was no greater pleasure.

Ruth took her seat on the other side of Cole, while Callie and Brent pulled over two spare chairs. Cole kicked himself for his thoughtlessness. The least he could have done was bring the chair over for her. He blushed, but her smile was forgiving. Besides, no one stood on ceremony to begin with, friends just made themselves at home.

Coffee was brought out and everyone literally collapsed into chairs on the front porch. Katie ran down to the lawn to catch fireflies and the rest sat back to watch. This was what Cole was waiting for. "Care to tell me what happened today?" he addressed Ruth.

"Honey, I didn't mean to get you all worried. Nothing happened here; I'm just concerned about something I heard from Frannie. It seems that this real estate fella went over to Walt's today."

"He went to Walt's?" Cole's mouth fell open.

"First thing this morning. Of course, Walt already figured out just who he was and sent him packing. Wouldn't even hear him out."

"Did he leave peacefully?" Brent asked.

"Oh, he didn't put up a fight, and that's what has old Walt worried. You have to remember, we come from the old days. Back then and in our parents' time, things like that weren't taken lightly. Sometimes if a person wanted something bad enough, he pulled out all stops to get it," she replied firmly.

"You really think he's going to resort to violence?" Callie asked. Her eyes had grown wide with fright and Cole took her hand before either of them even had the chance to think about it.

"I doubt that; the most he'll probably do is come back and try again. This isn't the old days, haven't heard of a range war since my grandfather's time. Don't worry, he's just trying to pick up some land. Once he realizes that no one's going to sell, then he'll be on his way," Cole squeezed her hand.

Callie's smile was forced and she tried relaxing for her own good. She did not want to upset anyone, but she had seen Pete Sinclair around town and she just didn't like the man. Being a friendly person by nature, Callie usually didn't pass judgement so quickly. But something about the odd little man bothered her. Brent didn't like it any better, and the foursome became uneasy.

"Listen to us," Ruth clucked her tongue. "Aren't we a bunch! Someone comes to town trying to make a deal and look how he has us all in a tailspin! And what did this person do? Nothing more than go to one of the ranches and ask if they were interested in selling. Then, he left peacefully. I say let's not go borrowing trouble."

"I agree," Callie nodded. "Let's just give him the benefit of the doubt."

"You really think he'll give up and leave peacefully?" Brent asked.

"What the hell kind of talk is that? Brent, I swear either you've been herding cattle too long or you've been watching too many westerns! This is 1985! Yeah, we may still ride the range like our fathers used to, but we don't go packing six guns anymore! Hell, you act as if a range war is coming," Cole shuddered, in spite of himself. What he hated to admit was that he had been having the same thoughts Brent found the courage to voice.

They grew quiet; each was afraid to unveil their own thoughts, and all were slightly ashamed of themselves. Cole seemed to be the one this bothered the most. He had no idea where the feelings came from; Pete Sinclair hadn't done a thing against him or anyone else in town for that matter, but he couldn't help how he felt. Some long forgotten thought nagged at the back of his mind.

"Come on everybody, it seems that we've all had a long winter to do nothing but stir up our own imaginations," Ruth laughed lightly.

"Funny you should say that, cause Katie and I were just asking about imagination last night," Cole replied. Truth be told, he was beginning to feel uncomfortable talking about Sinclair, and desperately searched for a change of subject, which Ruth had amicably provided.

"What did you tell her?" Callie leaned forward, smiling.

"I told her that her imagination was something special she had that was hers alone. I just told her it was a way to dream and let our minds soar."

"She soared all day today, because all she kept on talking about was that Indian princess you told her about last night," Ruth said.

"I wanna hear about that," Brent immediately brightened.

"Use your imagination," Cole laughed, much to his dismay.

"Then I'll go ask Katie!" he replied, jumping from the porch.

"While he does that, I'll be leaving for home," Ruth smiled at the group.

"I'll walk you," Cole offered.

"No honey, there's no need," Ruth argued.

"Yes, there is a need," Cole argued back.

"Honey, you have that little baby to get ready for bed and all," Ruth exclaimed.

"She'll be in good hands and I won't be gone for long. I'm not about to sit here and let you walk home alone. And don't say that you've walked this road many times this late at night and later! I know you have, but I feel better taking you. Besides, I ate too much tonight and I think it'll do me good to move around!" Cole stretched as he stood.

"All right, since you put it that way, then I'll let you walk me home," Ruth relented.

"You know, I could use a walk myself," Callie joined them. "This way, you won't have to walk back alone."

Brent smirked, looking away. Ruth strode off the porch with a knowing look on her face. She and Callie had spent the entire afternoon talking; she knew exactly how the woman felt, but was helpless to do a thing about it. Callie had shown up with some supplies Cole needed for the horses and one thing had led to another. Soon, they were talking over coffee and the afternoon wore on. Katie sat with them and they joined her in coloring and doing puzzles. Then there was just the small talk. But Katie soon tired and was put down for her nap. Ruth took advantage of the quiet and put a pot of coffee on, brought out the pie she had made the previous day and sat with Callie for a good old-fashioned talk.

"Just give him time, honey, that's all you can do," Ruth had said earlier, patting Callie's hand. "He's been so hurt and lost for so long, that it's going to take a while for him to trust again."

"Will he ever?" Callie asked, sighing deeply.

"He will. The thing is, will you still be here?" Ruth asked.

"Ruth, if I have to spend my life alone, then I will. I can't imagine being with anybody else. I've never loved a man the way I love Cole, I felt it the first time I laid eyes on him. I just wish I knew how he felt," Callie replied.

"Doesn't take a rocket scientist to see that. The man feels the same way and possibly more; he just isn't willing to admit that to anyone yet, including himself. He needs time," Ruth nodded.

So, time was one thing Callie had that she was willing to give. She would wait, she would give Cole the time needed and would snatch moments like this as they came along. She joined Cole and Ruth as they walked off the porch, going over to where Brent and Katie were.

"Brent, would you mind staying with her while I bring Ruth home?" Cole asked of him.

"You know I love to watch this little princess," Brent smiled lovingly at Katie.

"Am I a princess, Uncle Brent?" she smiled.

"You sure are, sweetie. You'll always be a princess to me. Now come on, why don't you and I go inside and sit down? You can tell me your story there! Maybe we can draw a picture!" Brent suggested.

"Ok! Bye Daddy!" Katie said quickly, breaking loose and running into the house.

"Gotta go, she's a livewire," Brent laughed, running after her.

"Thanks!" Cole waved at his retreating back.

* * *

Dusk was setting in when they left. By the time they reached Ruth's house and bid her goodnight, the crickets were singing loudly and the first stars of the night were just starting to come out. They walked side by side for about a quarter of a mile without saying a word. But it wasn't an uncomfortable silence; each was enjoying the other's company, like this was something that they did every night.

"Make a wish," Callie said softly.

"What?" Cole looked at her, puzzled by her request.

"Haven't you ever taken Katie outside to wish on a star? I used to do that all the time with my father. We would sit on our porch and look up. When I saw the biggest, brightest star, then I would make a wish," Callie fondly remembered.

"Did they ever come true?" he grinned crookedly.

"Some of them did! But not all of them! The unicorn I wished for never came! And I wished for my baby brother to turn into a toad and hop away," Callie laughed.

"Why in the world did you wish for that?" Cole's exclaimed, his mouth falling open.

"Cause he was a pain in the ass and he still is! But I love him and wouldn't trade him for the world," she giggled, reluctantly admitting.

"I know you've missed him ever since he moved to South Carolina," Cole said quietly.

"It's hard," Callie admitted. "South Carolina seems like the other side of the world, and in a way, it is! It's completely on the other side of the country. With both of us having such demanding jobs and very little time to ourselves, it almost seems impossible to visit. It was different when my folks were alive; at least then he would come home for Christmas. But since they died and I moved here, Parker and I sort of lost touch with each other. It's hard, you know?"

"Yeah, I guess that would be," he said sorrowfully. "I don't have any brothers or sisters, so don't know how it feels. How's your niece?"

"Elizabeth? She's fine! She's about five by now. She was around two the last time I saw her. So funny, she's living her life and I really don't know much about her. Oh, Parker writes me once a month and all, but he has his own life, which I know very little of. It's all passing me by," Callie replied with a hint of sadness.

Cole could feel her sorrow and wrapped his arm around her shoulder without thinking. The minute he did that though, he froze, but left it there. "Hey, no more sad thoughts tonight, ok? We've had them all day with this Sinclair guy and then again tonight. Let's talk about something fun. Hey! What about Katie's party? I haven't shown you what I made her for a present!"

"No, you didn't!" Callie exclaimed, feeling how natural and right it was to be in his arms. "What is it?"

"Not gonna tell! You have to come see it. I'll show you when we get home, since Brent has her in the house with him," he said mysteriously.

They walked the rest of the way in silence, with Cole's arm still around her.

* * *

Looking towards the house, Cole watched Katie and Brent through the front window. The television was on with some silly show that had them both in stitches and he could see the paper and crayons strewn across the coffeetable onto the floor.

"Looks like somebody had fun," Callie laughed. "I'll help you clean up."

She had turned to head into the house when she felt Cole's hand on her arm. "Never mind that! It's just a few crayons and paper. Believe me, she's done worse! Besides, I'll make Brent clean it up!" he laughed with Callie. "Come on, I wanna show you something before they realize we're back."

"Where are we going?" she asked, growing more excited by the minute.

"Shhh! You don't want them to hear us! Just out back to the shed! Brent, Will, Gris and I have been working on something for months. The only one who knows is Ruth. She helped! She made the curtains and tiny quilts and all," Cole excitedly replied.

"Tiny quilts? What in the world would she make tiny quilts for?" Callie asked as she followed Cole into the shed.

He couldn't help but laugh at the confusion in her eyes. "For this!" he announced.

Callie's eyes grew large. With her hand covering her mouth she gasped, moving forward. "Oh Cole, this is beautiful! Look at this!"

"You like it?" he asked, standing proudly in front of the little house. "I mean, from a girl's point of view, you think she'll like it?"

"Oh, she'll absolutely adore it! Look! Little people! Did you make them?"

"We made everything you see," he announced, his chest puffing out with pride.

Callie sat on the chair in front of the table, admiring the house. It was a little girl's dream come true. They had fashioned an old style, two-story Victorian, complete with a large wraparound porch with a roof, which stood as tall as Katie herself. Every tiny little detail was seen to, from the shingles on the roof down to the tiny windows, which were trimmed, and even slid open and shut. Cole had painstakingly cut tiny little panels of glass, which he mounted into the small panes. The windows alone had taken over a month to complete, but it was worth it. Ruth would come by nights just so he, Brent, Will and Gris could go out to the shed and work on their project.

Looking from the back, one could see the hallway just inside the front door. To the right of the door a wooden staircase led to the upstairs. There were four bedrooms, a den and a bath complete with a tub, sink and tiny toilet, all of which Brent and Will had whittled in their homes during the long winter nights and brought over to be mounted in the house. The project started late last fall and they worked diligently throughout the winter. Cole carved the table and chairs for the dining room, and an everyday table in the kitchen. He and Brent then carved tiny trunks for the rooms while Will did the endtables, coffeetable, and the dressers. One of the nicest touches of the master bedroom was the canopy bed Cole designed, along with a wood-trimmed mirror, which hung over the dresser. Gris was the painter of the bunch, claiming his fingers were just too thick and clumsy with a knife to do

111

any worthwhile whittling.

"Hell, 'bout the only thing I can do with a knife is gut and fillet a fish," he had laughed with them.

So in his own masterful way, Gris blew them all away with his painting skills. Seeing how he tended to each and every tiny detail of the home and the wood trim that needed staining, Cole willingly turned that project over to him. He was about as good with a paintbrush as Gris was with a knife. So while the others spent their long nights whittling the tiny characters and furniture, Ruth busied herself with the needlework and Gris took the house home so that he could work his magic. Soon, it all started pulling together.

Then Ruth added her own special touches. A trip to May's was in order, where she picked up tiny samples of wallpaper that they used in the rooms. The master bedroom was painted a colonial white with a wooden handrail running around the room and matching wood trim. The other bedrooms were each done with different wallpaper, all trimmed with wood. She then made an array of braided rugs that were scattered throughout the house, along with curtains for every room. The trunks really opened and were actually a bit larger than ordinary pieces one bought in the stores for dollhouses, which were not done on such a grand scale. Cole had wanted the house to be big enough for their large fingers to easily work with and for Katie to be able to really play with. Each bed in the house was made up with sheets, handmade quilts and matching pillows. Tiny pillows were made for the living room couch. He had wondered how in the world he would ever make the couch; then thanks to Ruth's brainstorm, one was soon finished.

She simply had him make the base with a solid back, on which small pieces of foam were glued. Ruth then finished the couch off very much the same way one upholsters a real couch. By the time she worked her magic, Cole was awestruck and had talked her into making a matching chair and loveseat. Laughing, Ruth willingly obliged. Working on the house gave them all a respite from the long, winter gloom. Most of the time television reception was nil due to the severe weather and reading became tiring. One needed something to occupy their hands when the nights began shortly after four in the afternoon and the cold and the dark set in.

During those times, the animals were tended and settled early. By dark, most of the ranchers had their livestock back inside, if they had been let out at all. That was rare; during the deadly grip of winter when the temperatures plunged down to 40 below zero, the stock was kept sheltered, only to be let out when things warmed up to about zero. Even then, they were only let out for a small portion of the mid-morning until around two in the afternoon. Most of the horses preferred staying close to the barn, where the door was left open for their convenience. Their legs were wrapped and all wore blankets on their backs. Suspecting their lack of truth, and considering how horror stories found a life of their own, Cole had even heard of tales where a horse would stand in the biting winds and suffocate when his nostrils froze over, packed with blowing snow. Plausible or not, during the extreme cold and wind, he kept his animals out of the elements as much as he could, as did many of the others.

That was better for the animals, which were safe and warm; but it made for a long day and night for the ranchers, who needed to find things to do with their idle time. That was when Cole found himself sitting in front of the fireplace one snowy afternoon, drafting out plans for the house while Katie slept. He just started doodling, and an idea was born. The next thing he knew, he was on the phone talking with Ruth, Brent, Gris and Will. They became as excited as he and even started making plans of their own.

"MA! WHERE'S THE PAPER AND PENCILS?" Brent yelled, yanking the junk drawers open.

Will had made himself scarce in his den, kicking back in his large leather chair while he sketched. Chewing on the end of a pencil, he propped his feet up on his desk and dreamed. This was just the diversion he needed to channel his restless energy. What had looked like it would be a long afternoon now passed with ease.

Unable to make it over to Cole's that day due to the snow, which had been falling steadily throughout the morning, Ruth spent the remainder of the afternoon and evening with her own plans. Knowing that a house needed curtains, towels and a variety of other things, she began searching through her sewing box. She even came up with a pattern for tiny linen napkins, which were kept in the drawers of the dining room hutch.

Cole was excited; while Katie slept he had made exact diagrams of the house. If anyone didn't know better, they would think that he was making blueprints for a home of his own, instead of a child's dollhouse, but he wanted it to be perfect. He wanted Katie to have something she could carry throughout her entire life. When she tired of playing with it, he knew that it would be a treasured keepsake in her room. When she married, Cole hoped she would bring the small house with her and eventually pass it down to children of her own. He dreamt big, and the plans grew on a grand scale.

After her nap, Cole bundled Katie up and brought her out to the barn with him. The snow had stopped and he had shoveled a path to the barn earlier while she watched out the window. Cradling Katie close, Cole walked through the small path, his head bent low against the wind. Inside the warm barn, she curled up in a pile of hay while he went about his chores. He made quick work of mucking out the stalls, which proved almost impossible to get rid of in this weather. Luckily, Will had come by the previous day with his plow, once again cutting a path out behind the barn where Cole could dispose of the manure. In the spring, what soiled hay remained would be pushed back to the edge of the woods as soon as the weather broke.

Once that chore was done, Cole set about making sure all the outer doors were latched securely against the wind and then went to the inner part of the barn, where the horses were housed. They were almost as warm as he and Katie were in their home. The barn was constructed solidly, with an inner area for the animals where they mingled, using their shared body heat for extra warmth. With legs wrapped and blankets on their backs, they were ready for the cold winter night. Cole set out the grain, replaced the water with fresh and closed the inner doors. Once he knew that the animals were safe, warm and secure, he then latched the outer doors and carried Katie back inside where they called Ruth to let her know that they were safe and inside for the night.

Ruth hated being separated from them. Usually when a storm hit, she stayed in the spare room Cole set up for her just so she could be with Katie while he tended the animals. If she hadn't come down with a touch of the flu during this latest round of bad weather, she would have been there. But Cole was on his own; everyone had their own places to take care of and he knew that he had to just trust that Katie was fine. Cole hated this; he should be able to handle things without constantly relying on Ruth, there had to be a way.

During the height of the blizzard he had no other choice than to bring Katie out to the barn with him, which was almost as dangerous as leaving her in the house by herself. There was just no other choice; as dangerous as conditions were, Cole bundled her up and wrapped his coat around her tiny body. With one arm securely around her waist and the other holding the cable guiding their way to the barn, he felt her clinging tightly as he forged ahead against the wind, his heart in his throat the entire time. There had to be a better way, but unfortunately, there weren't that many options. Once Katie was older, she could remain inside while he trudged out to the barn, but for now, they had to brave the elements together.

After that harrowing experience, Cole had simply decided that the best way to do his chores when inclement weather struck, was early in the morning, which he did on a normal basis anyway, and later in the afternoon while she napped. As a rule, Katie never woke once she fell asleep, but that did nothing to lessen his worry. The animals were taken care of before dark when the weather grew too bad to bring Katie out with him, and Cole kept to their regular schedule when he could bring her. It was hard, but it worked.

It had to work.

Now, they all had something to keep them busy. In between fighting the weather, keeping in touch with the outside world when the phones were working, and tending the animals, Cole and his friends spent their long nights working on bits and pieces of the house. Sketches grew into plans and plans grew into individual, scale drawings. Once they were done, the actual construction began taking place. During the day Ruth would care for Katie while the men snuck out to the shed.

Cole would never forget those afternoons. The world was hushed and dark. The sky was a dull gray and a carpet of white blanketed the land, muffling every sound. Everyone and everything just seemed quieter, more relaxed, and at peace with themselves. The only problem was, they all hungered for something to occupy their hands and minds. After lunch, Cole would slip outside to the shed, where he would start a fire in the woodstove Shane had left behind, and wait for his friends.

They had thermoses of coffee and whatever treats Ruth had baked the previous night to keep them sated. They talked quietly … three friends gathered around a wooden table bathed in the soft light from a lone bulb hanging above them. Some days the wind was strong, shaking the sides of the building and seeping in through the cracks. Cole would just pop another log into the stove and they were warm and comfortable.

A hint of woodsmoke could be detected inside, but they were used to that smell. They relished that smell; it was like home to the men. Sometimes a rare ray of sunshine would stream in through the windows, illuminating the smoke in the room, further lending to the grayish atmosphere. Cole had brought out a radio for them to listen to, but all they did was keep it tuned to the weather station, keeping aware of any alerts. Music wasn't needed, they preferred to talk.

All three soon learned to look forward to and welcome those afternoons. At night when they returned home, the only thing anyone could think of was going back to the shed the following day and resume working. Sawdust filled the air, dust invaded their nostrils and the sounds of a saw still echoed in their minds, but they treasured every minute spent there. Not a one of them could remember enjoying anything as much as they enjoyed working on that house. It not only served as a catalyst to keep them occupied; it bound them even closer together. Laughter filled the air, teasing was a given fact, and Cole, Brent and Will would talk for hours.

At night, they worked on their own special little pieces that each brought home. Furniture was made, little people were born, and a house was decorated, right down to the tiniest detail on the wooden children. And now

Cole stood proudly, showing off his work for the first time.

"Cole, this is breathtaking!" Callie gasped, lightly fingering every little piece. "Look at the tiny lips on their faces! And their hair and eyelashes are real! How in the world?" she turned up her face, smiling wonderingly at him. She was awestruck by all the love everyone had put into the small house.

"That's all our hair! I cut off a lock of my hair for the daddy, and Ruth glued those sickeningly minuscule pieces on for their eyelashes! I'm not even gonna ask how she did that!" he laughed with her. Without even realizing it, he leaned in closer, placing a hand on either side of Callie. His warm breath blew across her cheek.

"What about this one?" she asked, holding up a little boy.

"That one is Will, as you can tell from the brown hair and brown eyes! And this one is from Brent. I lopped off a hunk of his hair when he wasn't looking! Boy, you should have seen him dancing around! You'd think I scalped him!" Cole laughed so hard, his sides ached. "Oh man, that hurts," he wheezed.

"Now that...." Callie laughed just as hard. "That, I'd have paid to see! What about the Mama?"

"Ruth! She happily donated a lock of her hair! And see this little girl? Guess who the unknowing donor is?"

Callie's eyes narrowed, "You didn't?" she asked, fighting hard to suppress her giggles.

"Yep! None other than Katie herself! When Brent found out that I lopped off a piece of her hair when she was sleeping, he refused to take his hat off when I was around!"

"Well, I don't blame him!" Callie countered. "I'm inclined to think twice myself the next time I see you come bearing scissors! I treasure my hair!" she laughed, her voice catching in her throat when Cole unwittingly wound a piece around his finger.

"I wouldn't cut yours," he whispered softly, letting the strand fall.

Their eyes locked for a moment. Cole started leaning forward, then caught himself abruptly. Clearing his throat, he broke the moment, but failed to still the pounding of his heart. He feared talking, hoping his voice didn't sound choked and stinted.

"Here, I'll show you the rest of the house."

Callie let out the breath she didn't realize she was holding. She turned her attention back to the house but still couldn't get the reality of the closeness of his body out of her mind.

"I love the trunks, they really open!" she exclaimed, continuing her venture.

116

"Yeah! All of them do and you can really use the stuff! Look! Even the closets open and shut! So do the dresser drawers!" Cole proudly announced, showing off their handiwork.

"You even have little towels and clothes! Look at the clothes!" she said, pulling a dress from the closet. "I can't believe this!"

"Ruth made the clothes," he answered. "It was her idea to make things a bit larger than usual, but not too large to be ornate, funny-looking, or gaudy. She said that what good was having dolls if you couldn't change their clothes? And she was right. It would suck if Katie couldn't change their outfits and they went to bed with their clothes on!" he snorted.

"Good point," Callie chuckled. "There is imagination, like you said earlier, but it's more fun to be able to carry out that fantasy! She'll have so much fun with her little family!"

"I hope so," Cole replied wistfully.

"My God, when I think of all the love and all the work that went into this project.... You all thought of every single little detail! Even the hangers! How did you do hangers?" Callie asked, her eyes full of wonder.

"Would you believe out of chicken wire?" Cole exclaimed, his voice squeaky due to the excitement coursing through him, both from Callie and the house. "We twisted the ends tight and crimped them so that no sharp edges poked through. Then Ruth wrapped felt around them. Aren't they great?"

"I can't believe it! And all the dolls' arms and legs work! She can really dress and undress them!" Callie said, awed.

"She can even sit them at the table, see!" Cole showed off their moveable joints.

Callie searched even further, taking in every detail. Just when she thought she'd seen it all, another discovery was made. "I can't believe it! Their shoes come off! And they have real boots! How?"

"Tom over at the shoestore did them! He made them out of leather. Aren't they great?" Cole replied with a huge grin plastered across his face.

He tried to hide his feelings, but failed miserably. Cole couldn't help himself, he was so proud of the work they had done and so excited about presenting the house to Katie, he was literally quaking with excitement. His muscles rippled slightly as shivers ran up and down his spine, making him wonder if his reaction was simply because he was showing off their handiwork for the first time, or if Callie had something to do with it. Clearing his throat, Cole turned his attention back to the house.

If he was this excited about the house now, he could just imagine how he would be climbing the walls at Katie's party. And Cole wouldn't be the only one; as her party drew nearer, all they seemed to talk about was the house. No one could wait to see the look on Katie's face as she discovered each and every little treasure hidden behind its walls. The reaction of their friends was something they couldn't wait to see either, they were proud of their work and could not wait to share it with everybody.

"They're more than great!" Callie gushed. "Cole, she's going to absolutely love this! She's going to spend hour after hour playing with this and never get tired! It's like having your own little people! She's going to have an entire new world to explore."

"You think she'll like it?" he asked with bated breath.

"Are you kidding? A little girl can get lost in a house like this for hours on end and never grow tired of it! When she grows older, she'll still visit and talk with her special people! They're going to share a lifetime together! They're going to laugh, cry, talk and just have fun! They're going to celebrate every birthday and Christmas, and be there for her first day of school! Cole, you didn't just make her a house, you created a legacy!" Callie replied almost dreamily.

"I never thought of it that way," he said softly, his eyes welling up. "A legacy! She'll have a lifetime to pass on to her children and they'll continue the legacy! Long after we're gone, her legacy will live on! Can you imagine the life this house is going to get?"

"Just like the one your house will get, and Katie's house will get one day, and her children's house will get. This house will go on just like that! Cole, every time she looks at this and picks up a quilt or one of the little people, or a piece of the furniture, she'll remember how much her father and friends truly loved her! She'll see all of you in every little detail. That will never be forgotten! When she's young, it will just be a playhouse with a special world she can visit; but when she's older, it will be an entire life that she shared and these little people will be her special friends! She's one lucky little girl; she'll never forget how much her daddy cared."

"That's what I want her to know, how much I care. It's gonna be hard on her when she realizes the truth about her mother one day, and I want her to be strong enough to realize that it was all Maggie and had nothing to do with her. I don't want Katie to ever feel unloved and insecure."

Callie could feel her blood beginning to boil at the mere mention of Maggie. "That woman! How cold...." she hissed, stopping herself. "Cole, it's going to be hard on Katie when she learns the truth. And there's no way of hiding it either. She's going to start asking questions one day and you have to be there with the answers."

"What if I don't know the answers?" he asked helplessly.

"Just take one day at a time and one question at a time. You'll find the answers when needed. Right now though, you don't have to worry about it, that will all come in good time. First, you have to finish this house, have her party, and let a special little girl know how much her daddy loves her," Callie gently reassured him.

"That will never stop," he said softly.

As much as she wanted to stay and explore the little house, Callie knew it was growing late. They all had to get up early and Cole had to get Katie into bed. They closed up the shed, locking the door so that Katie would not unknowingly wander inside. Walking over to the house, they couldn't help but see how quiet things had become. Once inside, they found Brent snoring softly with Katie curled next to his side. He had pulled a quilt around her and she slept soundly. The only thing Brent had forgotten was her pajamas, which Cole knew he would have to do. It would be like dressing a doll; Katie never woke once she fell asleep like this.

"Guess there won't be any reading tonight," he smiled over at Callie. "I wonder if Sleeping Beauty will make it home?"

"Doesn't look that way! He already parked his boots at the door!" she couldn't help but giggle. "Do you need any help with Katie?"

"No," Cole's eyes twinkled when he smiled at her. Bending over, he picked Katie up in his arms. "I'll just get her into bed and then come out and tuck this one in," he said mischievously. "Maybe I'll take him out back and stick him up in the crook of a tree, let him wonder how the hell he got there when he wakes up!"

"God, you guys are bad! How do you survive each other?" Callie couldn't help but shake her head.

"I have no idea!" Cole answered, laughing with her. She would never know how good that felt.

"Well, I'll see you around this week, ok? Don't forget, I'll be by this weekend to give the horses a final going over to ease your overwrought mind, ok?" Callie couldn't help but giggle at his nervousness.

"Ok, and thanks. I know that the horses are ready for the buyers and are doing well, but you know me!" Cole scoffed, walking her to the door. "Will you get home all right?"

"I'll be fine! God only knows how many times I've been out late at night!" she said nonchalantly.

Cole knew, yet he worried nonetheless. "I know it, just be careful, ok?"

"I'll be careful! Plus, Harve watches out for me! I swear he wakes up when I leave and watches that I get home safely!" she said, talking of her neighbor.

Harve Meuller was the elderly widower who lived directly across the road from Callie's modest home. Knowing that she often kept such late, erratic hours, Harve had appointed himself her anonymous bodyguard years ago. He always watched, making sure she was safe no matter what time of day or night it was. The way everyone cared for each other and watched out for one another never ceased to amaze her. In the city, Callie could walk among a throng of people and not be seen. Out here, someone was always looking out for her welfare.

"Well, goodnight," she said, turning away. Reluctantly, Callie walked to her truck.

"Night," Cole said, his voice barely above a whisper.

He stood by the open door until she drove out of sight. He watched from here and Harve would be on the other end making sure Callie arrived home safely. Sighing, Cole locked the door, pulled the curtains shut and went to get Katie ready for bed. Once that was done with, he grabbed an extra blanket from the cabinet, covered Brent and propped his legs up onto the overstuffed couch, plopping a pillow under his head.

"Huh, just like Katie," Cole mused, smirking at his sleeping friend. "Neither of you moved a muscle when I got you tucked in," he snorted, putting out the light. Minutes later, Cole was also asleep.

Chapter Seven

"Morning honey," Brent grinned sheepishly as he came into the kitchen, his hair askew and clothes wrinkled.

"Sleep good?" Cole answered.

"Like a baby. It was so sweet of you to tuck me in," he taunted.

"Just didn't want to hear you bitching in the middle of the night cause you were cold," Cole replied quickly.

"Ahhh, aren't you so kind."

"Coffee?" Cole offered a cup.

"Just a quick one. Gotta run or Dad's gonna kill me. That's why I got up early, wanna get home before he starts the chores. What about you? You always get up this early?" Brent asked, looking over the rim of his cup.

"Yeah, come on out to the porch. She'll be asleep for hours yet; she never gets up this early," Cole whispered as the two walked out.

Brent grabbed his boots and followed. "Man, sorry to crash out on you like that."

"Must have been all that chicken," Cole laughed. "And thanks for watching Katie. Looks like you two had a good time!"

"We did! She's just great. She even told me about her princess story!" Brent beamed. "Hey, you and Callie were gone for a while," he eyed Cole suspiciously.

"Not what you think!" Cole defended himself. "I took her to the shed...."

"Oh?" Brent raised his eyebrows.

"To show her the house!" Cole exclaimed.

"Ohhh, the house! Likely story!" Brent nodded teasingly.

"Likely story and the truth," Cole replied adamantly. "As a matter of fact, she fell in love with the place. Told me that I was giving Katie a legacy and every time she plays with it, especially as she grows older, she'll remember how much we all love her and she'll see us in every piece."

"Wow! And I thought it was just a house," Brent whistled.

"Yeah, me too. But according to Callie, a girl forms some kind of a special bond with things like that. Says Katie will tell them all kinds of things," Cole said wonderingly.

"Like secrets and stuff?" Brent wondered.

"Yeah, and things like her dreams and sharing what happens in her life. Callie says she'll talk to them when she's happy and cry to them when she's sad. God, I hope she has very few sad days," Cole wished fervently.

"It would be nice if we could protect her from the harshness of the world," Brent replied.

"That would be nice, but it's not a reality. I guess all I can do is let her know that I'm here for her no matter what; that she can and should always come to me. There's nothing she won't be able to tell me," Cole said emphatically.

"Nothing?" Brent tested him.

"Nothing. I don't care what it is. She's my little girl and that's unconditional," Cole replied.

"Wow, intense," Brent shook his head. "Well, hate to break the moment but I gotta run, or my Dad's love won't be so unconditional," he laughed with Cole. "Thanks for the couch," he yawned, rising to leave.

While Brent drove away, Cole went to the barn to begin his day. It was going to be a long one, beginning with the usual round of chores that greeted him each and every morning. Flinging the doors open, he let the animals out into the corral and proceeded to muck the stalls and set out their feed. Soon, all were in and eating and he went back to the house. Once Ruth arrived and they finished breakfast, Cole would come out to start brushing and grooming the animals. Today he had to check their teeth and clean their ears. He also had to exercise three of the larger ones this morning and later that afternoon would take some of the others out. It wasn't exactly a job to turn one's nose up at, leaving Cole to wonder just how many people would look upon what he did as work.

It was work and it was necessary; if he didn't ride the animals, they would just graze in the pastures, getting fat and get lazy. To anyone else, it looked as though he was spending his day riding as if he hadn't a care in the world. How he wished that were true.

This morning, Cole had been reluctant to mention Sinclair to Brent, but something about the entire situation still made him uneasy. He had seen how some developers could strong-arm people into selling. They'd had a similar encounter in Wyoming. Although he hadn't sold out then, a lot of his neighbors did and some of them didn't seem happy about it either. Cole never thought that any of them would part with their land, but after a few months of a developer nosing around, they had given in.

"Guess sometimes it's hard to turn from that kind of money," Cole said sadly as he stepped into the shower.

That same developer had offered him almost twice as much as his place was worth and he turned them down. The land had been his grandfather's, who had struggled to start a small ranch. It was eventually passed down to his father, who then bought the adjacent lot, which contained water rights. Cole knew what a rarity and what a blessing that was, every rancher dreamed of owning a piece of land with a large lake. He also knew that it could be as much a heartache as a blessing. It brought out the worst in some folks when they came around, wanting to buy you out. Even though the mist was hot and steamy, Cole couldn't suppress a shudder.

"Mr. Morgan, my boss is making you a very generous offer! It's worth twice the value of the land. You'll never get another offer that comes close," Wayne Mitchell argued.

"Look, Mr. Mitchell, my wife and I talked long and hard about this. We just don't want to sell. I'm just now getting this place up and running the way I want. Besides, my grandfather started this ranch, I can't just turn my back and walk away!"

"You'll be sorry," he said, trying not to sound as menacing as he felt. He knew that Mr. Culver would not like what he would have to report. He wanted that land, and didn't care how he got it. He also knew how heavily Cole had mortgaged the land in order to get his first stock shipped in.

"You know, a lot of ranchers just starting out run into money problems. You take out loans to finance your stock, and then you need money for feed and vet bills and whatever little problem pops up. And with animals, a lot of little problems pop up."

"Are you threatening me?" Cole said darkly, his eyes narrowing as he leaned forward.

Mitchell didn't even flinch, *"I don't threaten, I just point out the facts."*

"The fact is, my finances are none of your business. So you can just go back and tell your boss no deal," Cole stated coldly, staring just as intently.

He never wavered or flinched himself. He stated his feelings and stood his ground. Time seemed to freeze for a moment while both men stubbornly stared, their eyes locked and firm. Finally, Mitchell was the one who gave in. He snapped his briefcase shut and stood, abruptly leaving. He was never heard from again. Three of Cole's surrounding neighbors had sold. Cole was the only one who held out. He didn't care, though; he wasn't going to sell, no matter what.

Cole snapped out of the past, realizing that the water had turned cooler. The hot water had been used up, with the change in temperature bringing him out of his reverie. Why he had even thought about Mitchell and times best forgotten was beyond him. He didn't want to remember, so he shoved the thoughts back where they came from. That time was best forgotten. Nothing good had come of it and Cole's life had fallen apart soon after. He didn't need the reminders.

As much as he had argued with Mitchell that day, Cole had turned around and sold anyway. Just a few short months later, he simply signed the papers, no longer caring what became of the ranch. His dreams had died with Sarah. He never knew who had bought the place or what had ever become of it. At that time, nothing mattered anymore; Cole just wished that whoever the buyer was, they had better luck with the place than he did. He regretted leaving the ranch his grandfather had started, but he had nothing left. His entire family was gone, with not even a brother or sister to help him through the hard times. Cole was alone in the world.

Shaking the water from his hair, he shivered as he reached for a towel. He had other things to tend to today. What happened to Sarah was over; it had been nothing but an unfortunate accident that no one could have prevented. Lately, Cole found himself dredging up the past more and more. Thoughts of Sarah ran rampant through his mind, coming unbidden no matter the time of day or night. Bits and pieces of the past also surfaced, shaking him to the core. Sinclair's arrival seemed to have thrown Cole into a tailspin, dredging up similar experiences he'd had with a buyer back in Broken Arrow. There was no reason to compare the two; one had nothing to do with the other. He had never seen Sinclair in his life. Broken Arrow had been another lifetime, lived by somebody else. There was no room in his life for the memories

Cole remembered very little of that time. Everyone in his life now knew of the fire, but out of respect, never spoke of it. Sarah had been killed. His baby was gone before it had a chance at life. No other details were needed, or given. That was all he would say ... that was all he could say. No one had ever questioned him, reasoning that the tragedy was just too painful to speak about, and Cole prayed that the past was where it belonged ... in the past. It did not belong here. Culver, the fire, and the reason he left Broken Arrow had nothing to do with Crater Mills and his life as it was now. The funny thing was, the more Cole tried shoving those thoughts away, the more they screamed at him.

Don't let it happen again! reverberated through his head more often than not.

"Don't let what happen again?" Cole asked of himself, feeling the shadows creeping in, tucking away all thoughts that sought to become conscious. Some things were best kept hidden.

Cole forced himself to think of other things. He had enough on his mind with everything going on in his life right now and there wasn't room for anything else. Anxious to start his day, he quickly dressed. There was no need in letting Katie or Ruth see him like this; both would know that something was wrong and Ruth would want him to talk. He didn't want to talk anymore. He just wanted to forget. Cole was becoming a master at burying the truth. And why not? He had buried his family and the truth soon followed.

Let dead things lie, that's what Cole lived by now. Let dead things lie. If they remain buried, they couldn't hurt you. No matter what, though, the past always had a way of finding him. All it took was a stranger like Sinclair coming to town, bringing back a time best forgotten.

* * *

This was the start of an almost typical day for Cole, in spite of the earlier intrusion of dark thoughts. He hated interference with his daily routine, especially when it had to do with memories of Wyoming. Yesterday he was relieved to get away from the everyday grind and go into town, and today, Cole was just as happy to get back to the ranch. As he sat on the porch sipping his coffee, he saw Ruth walking up the road. Her warm smile was something that he looked forward to every day.

"Morning!" he called out, waving.

"Good morning honey," Ruth waved back, beaming brightly.

"What'cha got there?" Cole asked, curiously eyeing the small basket she carried.

"I made us some biscuits to go with our breakfast this morning. It was such a beautiful day that I rose early and got to baking!" she answered.

Lifting the checkered napkin, Cole breathed deeply of the aroma, his mouth already watering. "Do I have to wait?" he asked eagerly, nosing through the basket.

"No, you don't have to wait. But I find it hard to believe that you have any room left at all after last night!" Ruth exclaimed brightly.

"Yeah, me too! But when it comes to your cooking, we always find room!" he laughed along with her. "I'm surprised that Brent could even move this morning after all the chicken he packed away!"

"Brent stayed the night?" Ruth asked.

Cole followed her into the kitchen where the basket was promptly deposited on the counter and she set about getting things ready. Katie was due to wake soon and while Ruth prepared their breakfast, Cole would get her washed and dressed for the day. They still had a few minutes to themselves yet, so they talked quietly.

"Yeah, when we got back here after walking you home last night, I took her into the shed...." Cole answered, seeing the same knowing look on Ruth's face that Brent had sported earlier. "Will you quit it! God, I swear you're just like Brent at times!"

"Inquiring minds...." Ruth said under her breath.

"You mean nosy minds!" Cole shot back. "Anyway, I showed her the dollhouse and it took longer than we thought. Brent was asleep on the couch by the time I got back in so I just let him be," Cole finished explaining.

"So, how was Callie?" Ruth couldn't help but ask. Someone had to knock some sense into Cole's thick head.

"Callie is just fine, thank you. And I know that you mean well, but there's nothing between us but friendship," Cole replied, trying not to blush.

"Uh huh ... friendship," Ruth repeated.

"Yes, friendship! Ruth, I know what you were doing yesterday!" Cole accused lightly.

"Me? Now what on earth could you mean by that?" Ruth answered evasively.

"Ruth, I know that you're only looking out for my best interests but I'm really doing fine the way I am. Callie and I are just friends and friends are what I need right now! My life is fine the way it is! I have Katie, I have you guys and I have my ranch. It's all going good! Besides, I'm really not interested in a relationship right now, and doubt if I'll ever be. They're too much work and I have enough of that, thank you!" Cole answered, putting an end to the subject.

"Suit yourself," Ruth quipped.

"I think I'll go get Katie dressed," Cole said, making his escape.

Ruth shook her head as he practically ran from the room. She was just about the only person who was able to even broach the subject of Callie, and even then he usually avoided the topic all together. Brent and Will tried at times, but Cole only cut them off or changed the subject before they could get started. If Ruth didn't feel that the two cared about each other so much, then she wouldn't even push the issue. But it was plain to see that there was an attraction neither could deny, no matter how hard they fought.

Cole could turn his back on the issue as much as he wanted, but that still did not change his feelings; they just didn't disappear because he chose not to address him. Then Ruth thought of Katie; she adored Callie and the two were so good together. Katie hungered for a mother's touch and Ruth knew she could get that from Callie; who already loved the small child as her own. In a way, Ruth had to remind herself at times that Katie was indeed Maggie's child; she spent so much time with Callie as it was, it just seemed natural that the two be together.

Callie filled a void that Katie needed desperately; her father worshiped the ground she walked on, but she still needed the loving touch only a mother could provide. Cole could fight and deny his feelings all he wanted, but it did not change the fact that whenever Callie came over, she and Katie were instantly drawn to one another. That was one fact Cole could not avoid.

* * *

"Hey Gris! Long time no see! How was your trip?" Cole excitedly greeted the man.

"Long and boring!" Gris wheezed, climbing out of his car. "Christ, it's gonna be a warm one today. Too damned early in the year to be this warm. Ruth and Katie inside?"

"Yeah, they're in the kitchen," Cole answered, nodding towards the house. "Sounds like you're in a mood. What gives?"

"What gives is this bullshit I have to put up with once a year when the powers that be decide to play games; and I'm not talking about the man up above, either. I'm talking about the damned yokels we elected to congress that sit with their heads up their asses thinking what stupid stunt they're gonna pull next. I guess part of their oath is 'who can I screw over now?'"

"I don't like the sound of that," Cole said quietly, sighing deeply.

"I didn't either when I got there. As usual, our taxes are going up and my budget's being cut. So, we drive the same old cars for the next year, I cut out all mandatory overtime and just have my fellas standing by in case they're needed. Seems that someone came up with the harebrained idea that we're such a quiet town and such good, model citizens, that nothing ever happens here! We don't need to be protected!" Gris replied.

"Don't surprise me, guess we're on our own. Hell with 'em! We'll take care of ourselves. But that's gonna be a tough one for Ted and Troy to swallow. You still able to keep them both on?" Cole asked worriedly.

"Oh yeah, but they won't be happy about things. No, I have the distinct pleasure of telling them that they're not going to get their cost of living raise again this year, not like they were expecting it though. They even made a bet with me that it wouldn't come through. Looks like I'll be spending my tomorrow washing their trucks in front of the office for the entire town to see," Gris laughed, in spite of his mood.

"Now that I gotta see! I should bring Katie and Ruth down to cheer you on! Too bad they aren't making you do it wearing a woman's dress and a flowered bonnet!" Cole roared with laughter.

"You just keep your mouth shut, you hear? Don't need to be needling those eggheads on!" Gris glared warily at his friend. "So, what's been going on here?"

"Nothing much, I spent the day in town yesterday. Just ran some errands and spent the better part of the afternoon sitting in front of the feed 'n seed watching the world go by. Oh, and there's this little bit of news that has everyone buzzing," Cole answered.

"What's that?" Gris' interest was piqued.

He had just spent the last three days at a budget meeting upstate. Year after year, it was the same old story. Taxes went up and their salary remained the same. Even if they were lucky enough to get a small increase, something else was ultimately taken from them, leaving them right where they started. Nothing ever changed, and nothing ever would. Once again, Gris found himself the bearer of bad news.

His head ached, he missed everyone and he was in desperate need of one of Ruth's creations. All he wanted to do was relax over a hot meal, spend an afternoon visiting with Ruth and Katie, and catch up on what had been happening around town during his absence. He listened with keen interest to what Cole had to say.

"Nothing much," Cole explained. "I'm probably making a mountain out of a molehill, but there's been this guy, Peter Sinclair I hear his name is, who came into town the other day or so. Can't remember exactly when, but I heard that he came with the intentions of buying up some land. Must be right cause yesterday he went out to Walt's place and tried making an offer."

Gris' curiosity was now definitely on the rise. "Oh? Hell, that must'a been a waste of time! There's no way old Walt and Irma would leave the place! Shit, he was born in the bedroom he now sleeps in! He's known nothing else!"

"I know that, you know that, and everyone else in town knows that! But this Sinclair went out there anyway, and at first didn't take no for an answer!" Cole exclaimed.

"He give old Walt a hard time? Cause if he did...." Gris fumed.

"Nah, just pestered him a bit. You know how rude some of those city folk can be, can't take no for an answer; but he eventually got the message and left," Cole replied.

"Good, he can just hightail it right out of town! Don't know a soul who'll end up selling their place. Man's just wasting his time," Gris nodded.

"Yeah, but he's still here!" Cole said. "Don't know whether he's gonna try it again or if he's gonna start canvassing the area. All I know is that if he shows up here, he's gonna be run right off! The only way I'll leave this place

128

is in a pine box. And even then, my spirit will come back and roam around forever! This place is mine and I just ain't a leaving!"

"Hahahaha, gonna have to call in them ghosthunter guys," Gris chuckled. "They can bring in all their fancy equipment and hunt you down!"

"They won't stand a chance against me! I'll scare the hell outta them all and send them screaming into the hills!" Cole threw his head back laughing.

"You know, that's a sight I just don't wanna see! You're scary enough in real life, but afterwards...." Gris shivered.

"Gee thanks," Cole grumbled. "You gonna torment me all day, or can I have some peace and get on with my chores?" Cole shot back, cinching the saddle firmly.

"Go on! 'Bout time you did something anyway! Ruth in the house?" Gris nodded his head towards the door.

"Told you when you first came that she was! Must be getting old!" Cole shook his head. "They're probably in the kitchen stirring up some trouble."

"Just what I need! Some of Ruth's trouble," Gris replied, rubbing his stomach.

"That's the last thing you need!" Cole laughed, patting Gris's stout belly.

"Hey, watch your own business," Gris grumbled. "And get your ass to work! I'm gonna go inside where I'm appreciated."

"You do that! And tell Ruth I'll be in for lunch!" Cole waved as he mounted his horse and rode off.

Gris watched until he was out of sight, shaking his head. The news from Cole made him somewhat uneasy and he didn't like being uneasy. He also didn't like strangers who came into town poking around where they had no business being. Tourists were no problem. They minded their own business and helped keep Crater Mill's small economy going during the summer months when they came through, stocking up on supplies before heading out to the river to camp.

The last new person in town had been Cole. Before him, Gris just couldn't remember anyone new moving in for the life of him. People were beginning to settle in the new development just outside of town in Marshalls Peak, but Crater Mills was still untouched and they preferred keeping it that way. Cole's arrival was different; he was looking to see if there was a place to settle on. Gris knew that if nothing had been available Cole would have moved on. All he had wanted was a home; he was not trying to take someone else's.

Judging from what Cole said earlier though, this Sinclair was not looking for a home and that left Gris wondering just what he was looking for. From the little he had heard, Gris felt that the man obviously wasn't working for himself. Sinclair did not want a ranch of his own, he seemed more interested in buying up what he could and that was what set Gris on edge. Some bigwig probably earmarked their area for some big project and had the idea that it would be easy buying people out of their homes. What they didn't know was that they were wasting their time.

Most of the ranchers were just barely skimming by. Last year's cattle market had been hard on everyone, with Walt being the only one to turn a profit. Will barely broke even and Brent and his father Cal had lost a little. Three of their prize breeding bulls had taken ill and half a dozen of their calves died over the winter. Yet, they still plugged along, living off of their profits from the previous year and borrowing from the bank when necessary. Everyone prayed that this year would be better for all, and so far it looked promising. If this stranger thought that he had any chance of using money as a way out for those burdened, he had another thing coming. Being burdened meant being challenged, and no one out here was willing to turn their backs on a challenge.

"Gonna have to look that Sinclair fella up later on," Gris muttered to himself on his way into the house.

* * *

Cole made his way down the south pasture where his property ended and the open range began. Stretching out for miles around was nothing but blue sky, flat grasslands and a few clouds that cast their shadows over the tall grasses. A slight breeze blew, bending the blades in half, but offering little in the way of relief from the early spring heat. Cole wiped the sweat from his brow. As he rode along he admired the land, breathing deeply of the fresh air and taking comfort in the lush green beauty that was just beginning to stir. Everywhere he looked buds were in full bloom and patches of wildflowers were springing up all over the place. An array of color greeted him.

"It's like a rainbow on the ground," he had told Katie one spring morning as he took her for a ride through the pastures. "Look at all the colors!"

Katie's eyes were wide as she looked around, grasping everything her father pointed out. He held one strong arm around her waist as he introduced her to the world. This turned out to be a ritual that started when she was one. That first spring, he saddled Ontario and mounted, bringing Katie along with him. Ruth thought she was too young, but this was their way of life; everyone here was born to the saddle, often riding before they could even walk. Katie barely toddled along, only able to venture as far as the couch or coffee table would take her. For anything else, she still needed a guiding hand. Most of

130

the time, it was her father's strong hands that reached out, helping her along. Ruth knew that for as long as Katie lived, her father's hands would be there for her. That morning, the weather was clear and warm, beckoning Cole out for a ride.

The only thing that Ruth had insisted on was that he wait until the weather broke for good and the chill had left the air. Cole agreed willingly, he would never bring Katie out where she could catch a chill and take sick. On the morning of their first ride, the sun shone brightly and the air was warm and inviting, with just the tiny whisper of a breeze rustling through the trees. It had been almost two weeks now and spring was finally here to stay; even at night the temperatures never went down to a level where they had to wear their coats and jackets again. Cole had slept with his windows open, but Katie's were still kept shut. He knew that today was the day and he brought his little girl out for her first spring ride. It was right, she had just turned one the previous day and he was ready for their journey.

"Katie, today Daddy's going to introduce you to spring," he smiled, only getting her smile in response. "Cat got your tongue?" he laughed, seeing her sticking her tongue out in front of her.

A serious look crossed over her face as she strained to look down, hopefully finding her tongue still attached. Just to make sure, she squeezed it with her fingers and turned a smiling face back up towards her father. Shaking her head no, all he could do was throw his head back, laughing heartily. Cole knew then and there that he was in for the ride of his life; at the tender age of one, Katie's personality was shining through and a spark of humor and wit was beginning to emerge.

With innocent wonder filling her eyes, Katie looked at the world unfolding in front of her. The grass was lush and green, after a long winter of stark, cold white. The land was being reborn right before their eyes. Leaves were just opening on the trees and birds flew about making nests for their new families. She laughed with delight as Cole pointed out a robin flying away with a large piece of grass hanging from its beak.

"She's going to make a nest for her babies," he explained, telling her about the blue eggs.

Cole looked down at his daughter, wondering what was going through her mind. Her face was radiant and her eyes darted all around her. He swelled with love and pride; a tiny human being, his tiny human being, was seeing the world around her for the first time ever. Cole could not imagine how Katie felt at that moment as the magic of nature thrilled her, yet he could see the wonder dancing in her eyes and feel the excitement as she kicked her small legs. She squealed at the birds that flew overhead, staring at an eagle as he soared by. She jumped, clapping her hands and screeching loudly when he stirred up a nest of grasshoppers, sending them flying through the air.

"They're grasshoppers, honey!" Cole laughed along with her. "And look at the eagle! See how he's just circling the mountains? They're special, it's really an honor to see an eagle, they're the most magnificent sight I can imagine. I know that you won't understand this now, but one day you will. Eagles are considered sacred by some. They remind us to stand brave and tall, for us to gather our courage and take pride in that. Through their grace and knowledge, we can learn about ourselves and the world around us if we are open enough to hear their message," he spoke softly as they rode along.

"Look at the blue sky!" Cole pointed out.

Katie's head tilted up as she watched the clouds, squinting against their brightness. "Gonna have to get you some of those fancy sunglasses like all the actresses in Hollywood are wearing these days!" he laughed.

Then Katie pointed, crying out in delight. Cole's eyes followed her finger, seeing a field of colorful wildflowers in full bloom. Vibrant red, yellow, orange, gold and purple hues burst forth, dotting the land. Mingled within was a dainty tiny white flower, which melded into the massive explosion of color. Katie clamped her hands over her mouth and stared. Cole couldn't help himself, he had to stop and bring her over. Tying Ontario off on a tree, he held Katie close as they walked into the middle of the field. Everywhere they looked, color burst among them. He stood Katie on the ground, holding her hand until her wobbly legs found their balance. The flowers were almost as tall as she was, burying her in a sea of beauty. Her golden brown hair shone in contrast to the glorious hues as she turned, looking around.

"They're wildflowers," Cole explained, kneeling beside his daughter.

Katie reached out with a chubby hand, lightly touching the frail buds. Even at her young age she sensed the fragile beauty that surrounded her and did not grab at or crush a bud. She laughed as they danced around her, the wind tickling them across her face. Cole laughed also, sneezing when a flower got him in the nose. That alone sent Katie into peals of laughter, especially when Cole lay on his back, sneezing wildly and tickling her at the same time. They were in a world of their own, something they both sensed.

Cole quieted down, holding Katie against his chest. Her hair blew softly across his face as she settled her head against him. Together, they looked upwards, seeing nothing but the blue of the sky above and the colors of the flowers cascading down over them. Katie grew quiet, her eyes silently taking it all in. Cole was breathless as he watched; if it was this magical to him, then he could only imagine what if was like for his daughter. She was one, and the world was as fresh and new as she was.

"Honey, it's a rainbow on the ground. Look at all the colors! Remember the rainbow I showed you?" he asked, not getting any real answer other than the feeling that she was listening. "It's in your storybook and it has all the colors you see here! I don't know the names of the flowers but will one day; maybe when you're older and can understand all I am showing you today a little better, we can get books and find out what kind of flowers they are. But I do know the colors! That's blue, there's red and this one is violet! And over here, this one is lavender...." Cole went on, with Katie taking in every word.

Now Cole rode through the field, noticing that the time was right for their ride. He had done the very same thing on Katie's birthday ever since that first ride, making their excursion a yearly ritual. It was something special that they could share amongst themselves that no one could intrude on or take away.

"Honey, soon you can see your rainbow again," he said softly as he rode along.

* * *

A lone figure came riding hard and fast. Squinting, Cole stared out over the horizon, his heart in his throat. Reining in his mount, he stood tall in the saddle trying to make out the face almost hidden in the cloud of dust. Whoever it was needed help and he needed it desperately; anything could happen out in the open range, and that was what sent a shiver of fear coursing down Cole's spine.

"Shit! That's Zach! What the hell's going on?" Cole swore under his breath. Without a second's hesitation, he urged his horse on, racing over to the boy as fast as he could.

His mount snorted, bucking slightly as Cole abruptly reined him in. A million scenarios played through his mind; Zach was alone all the way out here, which was odd. The youngster also had a wild look in his eyes, which scared the life out of him. The first thing Cole had to do was calm him down enough to talk. The animals were skittish as he reached over, taking hold of the reins.

"Zach, what's wrong? Is it your Dad?" he cried out.

"Cole ... gotta get Dad!" he shouted frantically, trying to break loose.

"Whoa, there! Zach, what the hell happened? Are you hurt?" Cole worried, feeling his heart in his throat.

It was obvious that something had put the boy in a panic. At the age of 15, Zach was handy around the ranch and had been born to a horse; but he was still young and he still acted impulsively. Cole tried his best to calm the boy down; it was quite a ride over to Walt's place and if help was needed, Cole needed to know what had happened to get Zach worked up into such a state of hysteria. He could help now; Walt could be reached later.

"Tell me what the hell has you so spooked. You got one long ride to your place! What are you doing out here to begin with?" Cole asked.

Something had the young boy scared. With school over for the year, at this time of day Zach would be doing chores around the ranch, not riding the range alone. Not unless something was very wrong. Still, Cole doubted if Walt would consider letting Zach ride out this far on his own. Once you reached the open range, you set yourself up for any kind of danger.

Zach started talking, gasping for air the same time. "Cole, the cow … Dad's prize cow … stuck."

"What do you mean? Show me!" Cole ordered, letting go of Zach's reins.

Both were off in a shot, heading down towards the wetlands. Wanting to become familiar with his surroundings shortly after moving in, Cole spent days riding the range and exploring his own land, as well as the vast open fields. At first, it was puzzling as to why no one had ever bothered buying up this section. It would have been the perfect way to expand; the land bordered the open range beyond Cole's property, Walt's ranch and one corner of Brent's place.

It seemed to be prime land and the perfect opportunity. But upon further exploration, the reason soon became apparent. Once one passed through the open fields, the ground grew mushy and soft. A swampy marsh covered a good portion of the bottom country. It was not feasible to build on and definitely wasn't a good place to let cattle or horses graze. As beautiful as the open range was, was as dangerous as it could be to one not prepared. Cole had been warned, so he had been on the lookout when he went exploring.

Once they hit the wetlands, the danger soon became obvious. Just on the other side of the basin was a mud bog, which ranchers in the area feared. It showed no mercy, acting very much in the same way as quicksand. Everyone who knew the place knew that there was no difference; once you went in, you rarely came out. The more you struggled, the more you sank. It was there that Cole saw the real problem.

"It's Mazie! She went wandering last night and we've been out looking! I found her but she started running and went right into the muck! I couldn't pull her out, so I lassoed her and tied it off around the tree!" Zach explained as Cole grabbed his own rope and ran over.

"Shit, let's get this around her and you hold it tight. Pull it in the other direction. Don't want her to strangle and choke on the one line. If you hold it out the opposite way, she won't be able to thrash around as much, it'll keep her steadier," he said.

Taking another rope, Cole tied it firmly around his saddlehorn, and fastened the other end around his waist. Zach's eyes grew wide with fright. Mazie was held securely for now and had not sunk any deeper, but she still couldn't get out. The boy was almost paralyzed with fright and seeing Cole heading closer towards the bog didn't help. It made no difference that they were rescuing a cow; they didn't see Mazie as a cow as much as they saw her a part of their family. When man or beast needed aid, help was always at the ready, given willingly and without question.

"Cole!" Zach cried out, his stomach knotting in fear.

"It's ok! I'm tied off ... ain't going anywhere," he gasped. "Hand me that rope you're holding and then take the other one you have tied to the tree and put it around your saddlehorn. Then grab hold of one yourself. I don't care which one, just as long as you're pulling. I'll pull from here and try to keep her steady, she's gonna flail like hell! You guide the horses back."

"I can't!" Zach cried out, unable to move.

"DAMN IT! YOU CAN AND YOU WILL! NOW MOVE!" Cole shouted, snapping Zach into action. "PULL!" he screamed, feeling the ropes growing taut as the horses strained.

The animals backed up slowly, snorting and shaking their heads at the sudden burden thrust upon them. Mazie lunged forward, but floundered in the mud, falling face first. She struggled, flinging her legs wildly but not getting any grip. Cole pulled, only to slip on the muddy bank and go sliding down towards the bog. Zach screamed, but Cole had to ignore him. He stood, feeling the rope still tight around his waist. His heart hammering, Cole had to swallow past his fears.

All that stood between he and the bog was a thin rope, something he did not care to dwell on. It seemed so minuscule and so fragile, yet it served as his lifeline. Cole prayed that the rope held; if it let loose, he would go tumbling into the bog and go under, leaving an almost hysterical boy out here alone. If that happened, Cole doubted if Zach would be any help at all; he was only a kid and he was scared to death. He struggled to keep Zach calm, shouting for the horses to keep on pulling while frantically fighting to yank Mazie loose.

"PULL!" he cried out, feeling Mazie coming a few feet closer.

Cole stood, easing himself up the bank. Mazie still was unable to get a foothold, so both he and Zach tugged frantically at their lines. Mud flew from her hooves, splattering them both. Clumps flew through the air, hitting Cole in the face and head, covering him from head to toe. His clothes were encased with the muck, which he spat from his mouth.

"PULL, DAMN IT! WE'RE ALMOST THERE!" he screamed above the cries of the cow.

The horses whinnied in protest but struggled anyway. They slowly backed up, finally making headway as the muck started losing its grip and Mazie was able to put her front hooves on the solid ground of the bank. She fell forward once again due to her back feet still not having anything to dig into, but her body landed on solid ground and was soon able to get back up, bawling loudly as she fought.

Cole pulled with all his might, as did Zach. Another few feet, another prayer from both men and with a burst of adrenaline, Mazie was free, with all four feet planted firmly on solid ground. She started to run, only to realize that escape was impossible; there was no way either Cole or Zach were about to remove the rope from her neck. All they wanted to do was bring the wayward cow home. Cole collapsed onto the ground, wiping a muddy arm across an even muddier face. He gasped, looking up at Zach and smiling widely. The relief on the boy's face was eminent.

"She's out! I can't believe she's out! Cole, thank you! Thanks so much! You saved her!" Zach cried out happily, running around as he checked the wayward cow out. "She's ok!"

"She sure is," Cole gasped, still too shaken to get up. He shuddered, staring down at the unforgiving mud. The thought of leaving this world with a lung full of muck was not his idea of making a dignified exit. "What do you say we get her on home?" he asked, gratefully taking the canteen handed to him.

"I can't thank you enough," Zach smiled again. "Thought you'd like to get that shit out of your mouth!"

"Mud, I hope," Cole laughed in spite himself.

He rinsed three times, spitting out a brownish mixture of mud and water. It was only after the third time when the water spat came out clean, Cole finally drank.

"You ok?" Zach worried.

"Yeah, I'm fine," Cole reassured the boy. "What do you say we get this one home to your father?" he suggested, standing on wobbly legs.

"You'll come home with me?" Zach brightened.

"Yeah, after hauling her ass out, there's no way I'm gonna stand by and let her get into any more trouble! You have any idea how she got loose?" Cole asked.

"No idea at all! The fence was shut securely when we went to bed last night. I double-checked it! I hope Dad's not mad at me," Zach said forlornly. "He left it up to me to make sure that things were closed up."

"Hey, take it easy on yourself! You probably did close everything up! But these animals are tricky! They're really escape artists at heart, it's what makes life interesting!" Cole laughed, ruffling Zach's hair.

He had the uneasy feeling that Walt had no idea his son had wandered out so far. Knowing Walt, he probably sent Zach out looking for Mazie, with explicit instructions to stay close to home. But being a boy, Zach got caught up in the moment, his father's warnings forgotten as he followed the cow down towards the bogs. Cole knew that Walt had to be frantic by now and wanted to make sure that both Zach and Mazie were delivered safely.

"Really? You don't think my dad's gonna be mad?" Zach asked hopefully.

Thinking of his own daughter, Cole just smiled and took Zach by the elbow, guiding him over to his horse. "Let's get mounted and head on over there. I can guarantee you that he's not mad. As a matter of fact, nothing will make him happier than seeing you riding in safe and sound."

"Ok! Let's bring her home! Thanks, Cole," Zach smiled, happy once more.

Cole laughed to himself and shook his head. Nudging his horse gently in the ribs, they started off. It was a quiet ride, with each lost in thoughts of their own. Zach had learned a little about life, a father's understanding and forgiveness, and Cole learned how to pacify a child. No matter what their age, he knew that they still needed their folks.

Chapter Eight

Ruth paced the porch, looking endlessly out over the horizon. It was well after lunchtime and Cole was never late. She worried; as much as she tried to hide it, she knew that she failed in her efforts. Katie had become sullen, choosing to sit in the rocker and color quietly. She couldn't tell the time, but she knew when her daddy was supposed to be home and he had yet to arrive. Ruth had tried feeding Katie her lunch, but the child refused. She would not eat until Cole returned. She instinctively knew when he was supposed to be working and when he should be home. When he was in town yesterday, Katie knew that he was supposed to be gone. Today, however, he was working the ranch and never missed lunch.

"Ruth, he probably just lost track of the time," Gris tried to reassure her, failing to do so. It could not be helped, he himself was worried; this wasn't like Cole and they both knew it.

"Gris, I don't have a good feeling about this," Ruth hissed in his ear. "What if he fell from his horse and is hurt?"

Gris shifted his feet restlessly, running his hand through his hair. "I'm gonna call Brent, maybe he went over there."

"He had no reason to go over! He said he had horses to exercise and so far has only done a few. He wouldn't leave and go over to Brent's unless it was an emergency; and then he would phone and let us know. No, something's not right," Ruth worried.

"Then I'm gonna call him anyway. Perhaps he can help," Gris said, picking up the phone. "Hello, Helen, Gris here. I'm fine, how are you? Glad to hear that nasty lumbago isn't bothering you, good thing winter's over. Knew you were in some misery there," he spoke amicably for a few seconds, so as not to alarm the woman. "Say, Brent wouldn't happen to be around, would he?"

"Hey Gris, what's up?" Brent's breathless voice came over the line a few minutes later.

"Brent, you seen Cole?" Gris asked hopefully.

"No, I haven't seen him since I left his place this morning. Why?" Brent instantly became alarmed.

"Well, Ruth and I are a bit worried; seems he left a few hours ago to exercise one of the new horses. Was supposed to be back for lunch and hasn't shown up yet," Gris explained.

"Shit," Brent swore under his breath. "Gris, I know where he goes to ride, goes on down through Elijah's Meadow. I'll head right on over there. You stay with Ruth, she must be beside herself."

"She's not the only one, I'm pretty worried myself. You go on ahead, but if I don't hear from you soon, I'll be following after. Maybe we're making a mountain out of a molehill, but it's just not like him. If Cole says he'll be back for lunch, he'll be back; especially since he knows Katie's waiting for him," Gris replied.

"She ok?" Brent asked.

"She knows something's up, she's sitting here awful quiet," Gris explained. His heart catching as he looked out the window, seeing just how still she had become.

"I'm on my way," Brent finished, hanging up without further pretense.

Something had happened; Brent just hoped that it had nothing to do with the fact that Cole was exercising a fairly new horse, which was enough to make anyone nervous. True, Cole knew what he was doing, but everyone had accidents. If he had been thrown out in the open range, he could lie there for hours.

"Can I help, son?" Cal offered, catching a bit of their conversation.

"I don't know, Dad, maybe ... yeah, you better come along. Cole hasn't been back yet, if he's hurt one of us can stay with him and the other can go for help," Brent replied, clapping his father on the shoulder as they turned and ran from the house.

Mere minutes later both father and son were thundering down back towards the west end of their ranch. At times like this, Brent felt the fear catch in his throat at the thought of what could have happened. They could come across anything from something as simple as Cole nursing a horse gone lame, to finding his friend injured from a fall. Just the thought made Brent's blood run cold. Too many times over the years they have had to go out looking for one of their own after an accident had befallen them.

Just three years ago, Zeke Hill suffered a skull fracture after striking his head on a rock after a fall from a horse. To this day, he suffered from short-term memory loss; something they all found hard to deal with. Nevertheless, everyone helped Zeke in whatever way they could. Shortly before Cole arrived, Will was thrown from his animal and suffered a compound fracture to his left leg. Luckily, he was close to his house and his horse wandered back into the corral, sending everyone out searching. Aside from the suffering caused by the break itself, Will was in shock and had lost a lot of blood, but had made a steady, uncomplicated recovery.

Now Brent and Cal were scared to death, wondering what they would find. Racing side by side, they saved time by cutting across Mason's Pond and along Saddle Ridge. It wasn't long before they neared the north end of the meadow. Knowing that Cole would be down around the area of the bogs, they spurred their mounts forward. Just to the north of them was the back end of Walt's property. Looking at a map, all the larger ranches bordered one another, with Cole's in the middle. Most of the open range ran directly behind his and Walt's land.

A river cut through the south pasture, feeding the two ranches and winding down through the woods until it ran alongside the William's ranch. From there it ran through the woods, not meeting any of the other neighboring ranches. Will had his own lake, with several small ponds scattered throughout his property. All were spring fed and provided plenty of water, even during times of drought when the river ran low and the adjoining creek beds had a tendency to dry up, worrying his neighbors. Being Will, though, he offered to let all their stock water at his lake, which went low, but was continually fed by aquifers.

Water splashed from the horses hooves, splattering their riders as they cut through the lower end of the river, taking a well-known shortcut over to Cole's pastures. Skirting along the outer edge Brent and Cal looked up, spotting two distant figures on horseback with an obstinate cow in tow coming towards them. With his heart in his throat, Brent cried out, ordering his horse on.

"Heeeyah, Whiskey, let's hit it," his shouts instantly obeyed.

Both he and his father galloped to the rider's sides, only slowing down when they recognized Zach and Cole, who were covered with dried mud from head to toe. Their mouths went dry, knowing that somehow the two had done battle with the bog. And judging from the state Mazie was in, they knew exactly how, where, and why the battle ensued. Zach was the cleaner of the two, which wasn't saying much, but it was obvious he had not come close to harm. After seeing Cole, though, Brent knew that his friend had gone down into the mud in order to save the animal.

As with everyone else, these animals were like family to Cole. They were the backbone of their financial success, with their futures resting firmly on the well being of their stock. To leave an animal to drown in the bog was unheard of by all. Every rancher around had done battle with the bog at one time or another, with a few losses. Even though no people had come to harm that Brent or his father could recall, they were still scared to death of the place, and with good reason.

Cole's white smile met them as they rode closer. Seeing the way Brent reined his horse in and just leaned forward on his saddlehorn grinning wickedly at him, Cole knew that he would have a hard time living this one down.

"Good afternoon, gentlemen," Brent drawled. "Lovely day for a mudbath, don't you think?" he leered, elbowing his dad, who grinned just as deviously.

"I can explain...." Cole stuttered.

"Oh, he can explain, Dad," Brent continued his torment. Now that the worry was gone, a release was needed. "You know, here we are, working our asses off and then we get a call to come looking cause Cole's missing...."

"Shit! Ruth and Katie! I promised...." Cole slapped his head.

"Yep, he ditches work, goes wallowing in the mud and stands up the two most gorgeous women in the world. Now, how do you like that?" Brent glared menacingly.

"Damn, I promised Zach I'd bring—" Cole sputtered.

"Never mind! Here," Brent broke out laughing, handing Cole his canteen.

Shaking his head, Cole joined in the laughter and accepted the canteen of cold, fresh water handed him. "Thanks," he managed to mutter.

"Everything ok?" Brent asked, finally turning serious.

"Was one hell of a time," Cole answered breathlessly, after taking a deep drink of cool water. "Mazie here took a walk last night and when Zach tried rounding her up, she took a wrong turn...."

"Right into the mud," Brent finished for him. "Damn, that must'a been fun."

"Have had easier days," Cole snorted, grabbing the fresh bandana Brent handed him.

His was used up long ago, hardly making a difference in removing the mud. This wasn't the best way to cut through the muck, but it was better than nothing. Cole planned on stopping by the river before they rode into Walt's place. It would be too cold for a good dunking, but he could at least rinse his face and hands in the clear water. Anything was an improvement at this point. After swiping uselessly at the grime, Cole gave up and poured the water directly on his face, still making little progress. It was going to take a lot more than just a quick rinsing to get back to normal.

"Hmmm, don't know whether it made things better or not! Now we can see your face!" Brent teased, sending Zach off into peals of laughter.

"Now we can see your face!" he hooted, pointing at Cole.

Cole turned, glaring at the boy until he sobered up, looking properly chastised. "Sorry," Zach muttered, trying to keep from laughing again.

"Ahhh, don't listen to him, Zach, he's just an old grump," Brent pacified the boy.

"He sure saved my ass though," Zach brightened, his eyes still twinkling with mischief.

"Hey, don't mention it," Cole sought to reassure him once again. "All in a day's work!" he smiled comfortingly. "And my muddy face is still an improvement over yours," Cole just had to get one more shot in at his friend.

* * *

"You don't mind stopping by my place and letting them know I'm all right?" Cole asked of Brent.

"Are you kidding? And miss the chance to see that little angel again? Besides, I'm hungry, maybe Ruth has something good made," Brent could only hope.

"All right, good deal. I'm gonna rinse myself off in the river the best I can," Cole shivered.

"Better you than me! You wanna freeze your balls off, be my guest!" Brent exclaimed, trying not to laugh.

Even though the air was warm, it was still early spring. The land was only now coming into bloom and the sun had yet to warm the earth and her waters. Cole did not relish the idea of a cold river, what he yearned for was a long, hot soak in his tub.

"Well, maybe not," Cole couldn't help but laugh with the others. "I think I'll just escort Zach here home and will be back shortly. Thanks," he smiled over at his friend.

"For what?" Brent wondered.

Cole was silent for a moment, almost too overwhelmed to speak, "For caring enough to drop everything and come looking for me," he said, extending a grimy hand.

"Hey, no problem! We can't let our little princess down, now can we?" Brent smiled widely, staring at the mudcaked hand for a few seconds before deciding to accept it. "What the hell," he laughed with his father.

"Thanks, Cal," Cole grinned, repeating the handshake.

"Son, we all gotta watch out for each other out here. Sometimes it seems like nothing has changed in 100 years. Help is far away and we're pretty isolated. If we can't depend on each other, then who can we depend on?" Cal smiled, solidly shaking Cole's hand.

"I know," Cole blushed, thanking God that he had layers of muck still clinging to his face so they couldn't see the crimson tinge to his cheeks.

"Well, we better be off, afternoon's slipping away," Cole said, urging his horse on after a final goodbye.

The rest of the ride was quiet, with Cole and Zach taking an obviously hungry, tired cow home. Mazie had lost her fight long ago and was feeling the urge to be back where everything was familiar. She decided that the outside world was not all it was cracked up to be. She was caked with mud and would rather not have that episode repeated. Plus, there was no fresh hay or feed for her to munch on and she didn't like that one bit. She also missed Walt, who had raised the cow from a bottle shortly after her mama died. Yep, Mazie was more than ready to go home.

So was Cole; but he had not only promised Zach, who was relieved to have his company, he wanted to see for himself that both boy and cow were delivered safely. It had been quite a trying afternoon for Zach, who had performed well once Cole was able to get him past his panicked state and thinking clearly. Zach had grown up a little that day.

Every inch of his body ached. Cole pulled a muscle in the back of his leg during his struggle and sitting in the saddle didn't help matters any. Plus, he ended up using muscles he never knew he had. He missed lunch, his stomach was rumbling, he was tired, and the mud was beginning to irritate him.

Brent was right, all it took was one hand plunged into the icy waters running from the snowmelt on the mountains to know that it was just too cold to do any more than rinse his face and hands. Everything else could wait. However, Cole couldn't resist filling their canteens and drinking deeply of the cold, sparkling water. His parched throat relished every drop as it slid down, cutting through the filmy taste still present in his mouth. The mountains did not warm up as quickly as the rest of the world, but after drinking, Cole didn't care. He was fortified for now.

What he really needed was a long, hot bath. Nothing else could compare and nothing else could make his aching muscles hurt any less. After a hot meal and an evening relaxing on the couch once the chores were finished, Cole knew that he would feel as right as rain. Now, though, he stood stiffly, the dried on mud caked to his clothes making it hard to move.

"Well, that's about it for now," Cole said, the last few droplets of water dribbling down the front of his chin. "Let's get you home," he grinned at a very tired Zach.

* * *

"Oh Lord, that's good to hear," Ruth twisted her handkerchief in her hands. "Then he's really all right? He didn't fall or get hurt in any way?"

144

Brent squeezed Ruth's hand and winked at Callie, who came to join the vigil. She only intended to drop off the poultice promised Cole for one of his horses, but after hearing of his disappearance, there was no way she could tear herself away. She and Ruth sat side by side on the porch looking over towards the open pastures. They prayed for everything to be all right, their hearts literally stopping at the sight of Brent and Cal riding up alone.

"Oh no," Callie gasped, running from the porch. In her frightened haste, her feet barely touched the ground.

Unable to move, all Ruth could do was stand there and cry.

"Honey, let's go into the kitchen with Papa," Gris said, lifting a confused Katie up.

"HEY! HE'S ALL RIGHT!" Brent yelled out, for all to hear.

Not knowing if she heard right or not, Ruth took a step forward, holding on to the thick front pillar. Brent jumped off of his horse, handing the reins to his father. He ran to Callie's side, knowing that the women feared the worst.

"He's all right! Just helping out a kid in distress," Brent laughed, the mere sound of it setting off a round of fresh tears of relief. "Gee whiz, you tell them good news to spare their feelings and all they do is bawl anyway," he grinned crookedly, shaking his head.

"What happened? Where is he?" Callie gasped between tears.

"Honey, it's really all right, you can stop worrying now! And you too, Ruth! Cole was out on the range and he ran into Zach. Seems that one of their cows was stuck in the bog and Cole offered to help," he explained, seeing a very relieved Gris standing on the porch.

"Hey Katie," Brent smiled, holding out his arms.

"Where's Daddy?" she asked, running into his embrace.

Brent scooped her up, swinging her into his arms. "Your daddy is over at Mr. Bremmer's place. He helped rescue one of their cows who was stuck in the mud."

"Is the cow hurt?" she wondered.

"No honey, the cow's not hurt, Zach's not hurt, and your daddy's fine," Brent said, following everyone up to the porch. "But he couldn't get word here and he couldn't leave poor Zach alone, kid was totally spooked. Anyway, Cole helped Zach get Mazie out of the mud and is heading over to their place as we speak. He told me to tell you that he'll be home soon."

"Oh praise be," Ruth bristled. "Well, he may object to this, but I'm cooking another special dinner for him tonight. It's been a long day! Everyone, you're all invited to join us if you wish," Ruth smiled around at her friends.

"Thanks Ruth, but Brent and I gotta be heading back," Cal nodded, handing her an empty glass. "I thank you for the snack though," he smiled back.

"You're more than welcome, Cal. And I thank you two for going out to find Cole and coming back with such good news!" Ruth gushed, literally beaming. "Well, you're staying, aren't you, Gris? And Callie?" she asked, turning to the rest.

"Ruth, as much as I'd love to stay I think I better get over to Walt's and check on Mazie. I swear, between her and Patches, those two are sure going to drive that poor man to drink!" Callie laughed with the others.

"Well, if you change your mind, dear, I'll have enough ready," Ruth smiled back. "Now, we all better get moving!"

"You heard Nanny, little one, it's time we got moving," Gris chuckled, heading over to a rocking chair.

Laughing at the sight, Ruth just didn't have the heart to interfere. She quickly cleared away the tray with the remnants of their snack, grateful that Katie had been willing to eat a little something. Gris then took her and the two sat on the rocker with her on his lap. Together, they started coloring a picture for Cole. Gris settled back chuckling, the twinkle was back in Katie's eyes. He had missed her and was going to spend the afternoon making up for lost time.

Ruth bustled into the kitchen to start their evening meal, glad that she had taken the time to make a chocolate cake that morning. Callie got into her truck and drove on over to Walt's, chiding herself the entire way. She knew that she would be going straight home afterwards instead of over to Cole's for the evening, where she would rather be.

She also knew that she should keep her distance as much as possible; she just wasn't going to push herself on Cole, he had a lot of issues that were better worked out alone. "Besides, he's a big boy," she chuckled as she blushed. "He knows where to find you when he makes up his mind."

Looking to the left, Callie pulled out onto the road after seeing the coast was clear. With her windows down and the radio blaring, she drove on over to Walt's to see if there was anything she could do.

* * *

After a weary ride, Zach and Cole finally arrived at the western slope of Walt's ranch, where they saw him looking out towards the mountains, his horse at the ready, tied to the fence. Cole had the feeling that he had been out looking for Zach as well, and nudged the boy.

146

"Your dad's looking for you," Cole smiled knowingly.

"Dad," Zach said, urging his horse on. "DAD!" he cried out, waving wildly.

"SON!" Walt's relieved voice came to them. "ZACH! SON!"

Cole rode in with Mazie following tiredly behind, watching as father and son embraced heartily. He could hear the plaintive cries in Walt's voice, knowing that the man had been worried beyond reason. His son had been gone longer than he had felt comfortable with and Walt had probably been out searching.

"I was about to call out all the neighbors," Walt said, his entire body trembling. "Cole, thank you!"

Cole jumped down from his own horse, taking Walt's extended hand firmly. Walt pumped his arm up and down, unable to show enough gratitude for the safe return of his son. "Didn't Ruth or anyone call you?" Cole wondered.

"If they did, I have no way of knowing! Irma left yesterday afternoon to go visit with her sister and won't be back till the 'morrow. I wasn't able to hear the phone if they tried, I suppose I should have stayed in the house but it's hard to just stand idly by when your son's missing. Lord, the thoughts that went through my head," Walt cried, embracing Zach.

"I'm fine, Dad, thanks to Cole," Zach grinned widely, blushing at the attention.

"I don't know how to thank you," Walt gushed. "I was expecting the worst when he didn't come back sooner."

"Walt, you don't have to thank me, everything's fine. Mazie's none the worse for wear and with a bit of cleaning up, I think she'll be fine," Cole reassured the man.

"Guess you had yourself a touch of spring fever, huh, girl?" Walt turned his attention to his cow. "She wander into the bogs?"

"She ran smack dab into the middle of them," Cole laughed.

"Looks like you had your own little run in," Walt nudged Cole in the ribs.

"Yeah, am a bit messed up myself," Cole chuckled.

"You wanna come in and get washed up?" Walt offered.

"Thanks, but think I need a bit more than getting washed up," Cole laughed with the two.

The sound of a truck pulling in not only captured Cole's attention, it put him on guard. He should have known; whenever there was trouble, especially when an animal was involved, Callie was there. Even if her services weren't asked for, they were offered. She just did not believe in taking any chances and wouldn't rest until she knew for sure that everything was fine. Callie was not only thorough; she had a caring, compassionate side. Besides, she just had to see the mud-covered cow and the two tired cowboys who had dragged her in for herself.

Cole couldn't take his eyes off of her as she pulled in and climbed from her truck. Biting his tongue, he resisted the urge to ask if she needed a stepstool in order to climb down. He had learned long ago that Callie was a force to be reckoned with and there was no way he would come out a winner. Smiling, she strode across the yard. The way her hair flew out side to side behind her as she bounced over to where they stood, set Cole's heart racing. Then he wanted to sink into the ground at his appearance. In spite of his earlier, haphazard attempt to wash up in the icy river, only his eyes and mouth were visible beneath a layer of muck, and it wasn't the most pleasant smelling stuff either. He now truly regretted the way he had tormented her last Sunday, knowing that he could never clean up looking half as good as she did.

"Uhh, hi," Cole stammered, averting his eyes.

"Hi to you, too," Callie answered, crossing her arms. "It's been one hell of an afternoon!"

"Yeah, we had things stirred up pretty good," Cole nodded sheepishly.

"Looks like you're the one in need of cleaning up now," Callie teased, getting her own revenge after last Sunday.

"Guess I had that coming, huh?" Cole grinned sheepishly.

"Uh huh," Callie nodded, giving a half smile.

"Well, how about dinner and some birthday shopping Friday night?" Cole brazenly asked, his skin prickling.

The words just burst out before he could change his mind. He couldn't help himself and nothing could have been more impetuous or ill thought of as those words. They just happened; before Cole knew it, they were out, taking every bit of resolve out the window with them. In one brief moment of insanity, Cole put himself on the spot and everything changed. He had no idea what brought that on or where the idea even came from. The last thing he had planned on doing when he woke that morning was to make plans to take Callie, or any woman for that matter, out on a date. He didn't date. Dating was for teenagers, not used up men like him. He choked up then, wanting to take the words back, but found himself unable to do so.

They had obviously taken Callie by surprise as much as they did him; even Walt and Zach watched, with shocked expressions on their faces. They, too, had been waiting for Callie and Cole to get together, and now Walt found himself nudging Zach and nodding knowingly. They were seeing history in the making and had something to brag to the rest of the town about.

148

"Well, I think Friday's ok," Callie stammered, not wanting to sound too eager.

"Hey! Just a thought," Cole shrugged. "I know that it's short notice and I don't even know if Ruth can watch Katie."

"You know she will!" Walt burst out, very much against his own will.

Cole turned, smirking at the man, "Yeah, she probably can. Why don't I ask her and you check your schedule?" he asked, turning back to Callie.

"That sounds good," Callie breathed an inner sigh of relief. "But first, I have a muddy cow to check out!"

"Ok, you go check out your cow and I'll be hitting the road," Cole tipped his hat.

Walt walked over to the horses with Cole, wanting a quick word with him. Zach was still upset over what happened, and followed along. "Dad, I'm sorry, it's kinda my fault. I thought I shut the gate last night," he said, hanging his head.

Walt came to his son, placing his hands on the boy's shoulders. With one hand, he lifted Zach's head, forcing his face upwards. "Son, it's all right. Accidents have a way of happening and Lord knows that I made enough of them myself growing up," he smiled lovingly. "The important thing is that you're all right. There's nothing to worry about, things like this happen to the best of us. Why don't you run into the house here and get Cole a cold soda?" he nodded his head towards the door.

"Thanks, Dad!" Zach immediately brightened. "Be right back!"

After Zach went into the house, Walt turned to Cole. "Damndest thing, can't figure out how they got out, except that I did find the gate opened a bit."

"Lose many?" Cole asked.

"Nope, only eight got out but we got them all back now that you guys brought Mazie home," Walt replied.

"That's good to hear," Cole smiled, accepting the bottle of pop. "Thanks, Zach, this is sure gonna go down good!"

"I better go help Callie!" Zach turned, running the other way.

"Kids," Walt shook his head.

"Yeah, no matter the age, they sure keep us hopping," Cole groaned.

"That they do and you're just starting out!" Walt was quick to point out. "How about coming in for something to eat?"

"Look at me!" Cole's mouth gaped.

"So? What's a little dirt? The floor can be vacuumed and the kitchen chairs are wooden!" Walt shrugged.

"Thanks, Walt, but I better get on home, Ruth's been having a fit since I didn't show up for lunch!" Cole exclaimed.

"Thanks again, son," Walt smiled, firmly taking Cole's hand. "You need me, you just call."

"I'll remember that," Cole replied, returning the handshake.

"You better! I shudder to think of what could have happened if Zach had tried getting her out by himself," Walt sobered, shoving such a disturbing thought from his mind.

"I'm just grateful it didn't come to that. Now, I better get going," Cole climbed onto his horse again.

"I'll phone Ruth and tell her you're on your way!" Walt called out to Cole's retreating form.

Waving, Cole rode away, tiredly heading towards home. It looked like the rest of the horses would have to wait until morning to be exercised; he had used all his energy wrestling Mazie loose and all he wanted at this point was a long, hot bath and something to eat. He also suddenly remembered that he had asked Callie out. Moaning, Cole felt like riding off in the other direction, anything was better than facing Ruth's knowing glare.

"Maybe it's time I came to term with things, maybe it's time to.... Nah...." he finished, shaking his head.

* * *

"Daddy!" Katie's excited cries greeted him as he rode in.

Cole reined in his horse, turning it over to Gris. "Thanks," he smiled widely.

"You look like hell," Gris snickered, then became quiet as Katie approached, running as fast as her legs could carry her.

"Hey, Katie bug!" Cole cried out, grabbing for her.

It had been a long, worrisome day for both father and daughter, with her missing him immensely. He missed having lunch with her yesterday and knew that she had missed him today. He felt bad about scaring her, but it couldn't be helped. In spite of the mud that covered him from head to toe, he cradled Katie close.

"Oh, look at you two," Ruth chuckled, shuddering at the sight.

"Daddy's all mud," Katie giggled, seeing the stains on the front of her clothing.

"Come on in, honey, let's get you cleaned up," Ruth said, leading both up to the porch.

"Don't know where to start," Cole snickered, sitting down. "Don't want to track any of this sh ... stuff into the house," he chuckled.

Ruth disappeared, only to return minutes later, with a fresh shirt for Katie. "I have the tub filling," she smiled comfortingly.

With a clean shirt on, Katie turned her attention back to her father. "Daddy, are you hurt?" she asked.

"Honey, I'm not hurt. Daddy just helped Zach and got all muddy!" Cole replied.

"Is Zach muddy?" Katie wondered.

"Not as muddy as me! Only Daddy had that pleasure," Cole tiredly explained.

"You need a bath," Katie said, crinkling her nose.

"I sure do! I bet I smell pretty bad, huh?" he teased, grabbing for her.

Katie laughingly dodged his grasp and ran to hide behind Gris, who stood protectively over her. Ignoring them both, Cole pulled his boots off, depositing them on the porch. His pants crinkled when he stood, dropping dried clumps of mud all over the porch. He cringed, thinking of walking through the house like that; it wasn't that he was a picky housekeeper as much as he loathed dirt like this being tracked in. However, the fight was lost when Ruth grabbed him by the elbow and pulled him inside.

"That's why God invented vacuum cleaners," she clucked.

"He's the one who did that?" Cole quipped, earning a swat on his backside. "I'm going! I'm going! But I don't now which to do first, bathe or eat! I'm starved!"

"You just get washed up and I'll have dinner on the table by the time you're finished," Ruth said, pacifying him.

"Just a soda?" Cole pleaded, sticking his head back out the bathroom door. "Thank you!" he replied, reaching for the bottle handed to him.

He couldn't even wait for the tub to finish filling. Peeling the clothes from his body, Cole itched everywhere. Scratching furiously, he stood naked for a moment, before giving in. Regardless that the tub was barely half full, he sank into its depths. Sliding on his back, he pulled his head under, feeling the first layer of grime rinsing off. Closing his eyes as tight as possible, he shook his head under the water, letting a hearty cry of relief loose as he burst through the surface.

The water was almost black with mud, which Cole had no desire to soak in. Pulling the plug, he stood while the mucky mixture swirled away. Sediment was rinsed and this time, Cole waited patiently for clean, hot water to reach the desired level. He lay back, just soaking in the warmth. The ache slowly left his muscles, but he would be stiff the rest of the night. Feeling the steam on his face, Cole closed his eyes and rested.

Once washed and dressed, he sat at the table digging into his meal. Katie had refused to eat her lunch earlier and now asked for seconds. Ruth's appetite had returned, as did Gris'. They'd had a scare this afternoon. Some might think their worry and actions exaggerated, but living as secluded as they did and knowing that the person you were worried about had ridden off on the back of a horse, a million scenarios ran through one's mind. Both Ruth and Gris kissed their prayers up to God, thanking him for bringing them all together again. They finished their meal, with Cole rising to go to the barn.

"Cole, just go sit down," Gris pleaded.

"No way, got to get the animals brushed, fed and settled for the night," he argued back.

Shrugging, Gris quickly looked Ruth's way before following Cole outside. He was more than willing to care for the animals, but Cole was stubborn and not one to turn his back on his responsibilities. In his philosophy, if you were able to walk, you were able to work. Not even a bad fever could keep him from trying to carry on with his chores, as Ruth had found out the first year he moved in.

The entire town was caught in the grips of a flu epidemic, with Ruth, Irma and Gris being among the lucky few who managed to dodge the bug. Cole had an especially hard time, with Ruth insisting that his already taxed system was compromised due to the stress he was under. She knew that he had just lost his young wife and baby, so it was no wonder he had succumbed so quickly.

Where many others recuperated within a week or so, Cole had fallen prey to pneumonia, which seemed to hang on. Even then, he fought them, insisting on caring for his animals on his own. Ruth had taken matters into her own hands the morning she found him alone in the barn. Gris had been coming over on a daily basis to help with the chores, but as stubborn as he was, Cole rose even earlier and stumbled out to begin his work.

"Land sakes! You are the most stubborn damned man God has put on this earth! You may not care very much, Cole Morgan, but you're not going to kill yourself as long as I'm here! I don't intend on coming here one morning and find your bones lying on the ground. Honey, I know you're hurting deep inside and on some level you probably don't care what happens to you right now, but this is no way to be! Let me take care of you," Ruth urged softly, herding Cole into the house.

Somehow, her words had broken through; Cole did want to live. He could not shake the dark mood that plagued him and he didn't even know how to go on, if he could go on at all. All he knew at that moment, though, was that he simply did not want to die. Why he wanted to live was beyond him; if he died he could be with Sarah. Something, however, had intervened, keeping him rooted to this earth. Cole gave in, letting Ruth get him settled in bed, call for Doc Edwards, and stay on for the next three days, nursing him through the fever, which had risen to 104.

Cole had listened then and recovered slowly, but he had no fever now, so there was no way he was going to sit on the porch and watch others do his work for him. Halfway to the barn a truck pulled in, startling him. Cole shook his head, knowing he was beat at his own game. Zach ran over on gangly legs, with an excited smile plastered across his face. Walt followed, albeit a bit slower.

"What are you two doing here?" Cole groaned, almost afraid to ask.

"Cole, this was my son's idea, and there's no stopping him," Walt beamed proudly. "But I was thinking along the same lines myself."

"Yeah! You helped me out this afternoon and lost a lot of time you could have gotten your own work done. I told Dad over dinner that I wanted to come over and help with your horses. I can muck the stalls and set their feed out," Zach rambled on excitedly.

Cole knew the feeling; Zach was young and learning a lesson about life today, no matter how much Cole hated someone else doing his work for him. Zach was on the threshold of manhood and Cole remembered how very special that felt. He was not yet a man, but he was getting too old to be a boy. The exhilaration Zach felt at shouldering his own responsibilities, as well as helping others out, was an invaluable lesson the boy would carry with him throughout his entire life. When one was in need and someone reached out to him, that favor was returned in a million little ways. Zach's way was showing up tonight to help bed the horses down. Cole could see the gleam in the boy's eyes and did not have the heart to turn him away. This wasn't only a way for Zach to help Cole out, it was a way for the boy to rebuild his fragile self-confidence.

"Thanks, Zach, I really appreciate it," Cole sighed. He was sore and everyone knew it, no matter how loath he was to admit to that. Another lesson learned for Zach today.

"Ok! Why don't you go sit with Dad and I can take care of things for you? You can check the doors and gates if you want," Zach laughingly blushed as he ran towards the barn.

"Don't worry, I think you learned your lesson!" Cole called out teasingly. "Well, I guess I better go sit down." He turned back to the porch once more.

Before he could even reach the house, Brent and Will drove in. "Who called out the cavalry?" Cole groaned.

"We thought you could use a hand," Will exclaimed, flashing a toothy grin.

"Nope, Zach has everything under control," Cole replied, nodding towards the barn.

"Oh yeah? Good kid!" Will saw the pride spread across Walt's face.

"Was totally his idea, he wanted to thank Cole for helping him out this afternoon," Walt said proudly.

"That's why we came," Will explained. "Thought you could use a hand, plus I needed to get out for a bit," he stretched, yawning.

"Sounds like you should be in bed," Cole taunted.

"No, just a long day. Got my chores finished and decided to see what was kicking over here," Will replied, his voice heavy and tired.

"Me too," Brent quipped. "Thought I'd see if you'd managed to scrape all that mud off!"

Between the laughter and teasing about his earlier sorry state, and the obvious relief that a scary situation had turned out fine for all involved, the men sat on the porch while Zach finished up in the barn. After an hour, he closed the outer doors and latched them securely. He joined the others on the porch as they talked, helping himself to a cold glass of milk and a thick slice of cake. Tonight, a young boy felt like a man.

* * *

There was so much to talk about, but they kept the talk light so as not to worry Ruth and scare Katie. Pete Sinclair was in the back of everyone's minds, yet they held their tongues. Only when Ruth excused herself to bathe Katie, did the men talk a little.

As soon as the door closed behind them, Cole turned to Walt. "Hear you had a visitor," he began.

"You and everyone else," Walt snorted. "You know anything about him?"

"No, name's not even vaguely familiar," Cole said softly. "I just don't like that someone has the nerve to go door to door trying to buy someone's home. If you want to sell, than that's different, you call someone and put up a sign. I don't like the way these guys come poking around."

"Sounds like you've had something like this happen before," Gris leaned over.

Brent and Will gathered closer. "Well, sort of," Cole replied. "Back in Wyoming there was this developer who was trying to buy up some land for one of those newfangled housing developments. Couldn't see the sense in it out there, neither did anyone else. Fella didn't take too kindly to being turned away, but he eventually left."

"Give you any trouble?" Brent worried.

"Well, let's just say he was persistent. He sent one of his stoolies out a few times trying to get me to sign the offer, but I had no interest in selling. We did have words a few times, but it never went beyond that...."

"Is that all?" Gris knew he was holding out.

"Well, I can't prove anything, but I was jumped one night when I was on my way out of one of the bars in town. Went there with Matt and he left a few minutes before me. I stayed behind to finish up a hand of poker. Anyway, the parking lot was dark and when I went to unlock my truck, I was jumped and roughed up a bit. Nothing major, bloody nose, a shiner and split lip, that was about it. What bothered me, though, was that they didn't take anything! Didn't want my truck and didn't take my wallet, which had a fair amount of money in it. They took nothing! Just kicked my ass and left!"

Brent turned, looking worriedly at Will. "What then?"

Cole just shrugged, "Nothing, then. That was it! I just chalked it up to some drunk I must have pissed off. There were a lot of guys in on that poker game and there'd been a few arguments. It was dark and they sucker punched me; I went down like a ton of bricks and never shook it off. Couldn't even tell you what they looked like, just saw their fists," he tried joking.

Everyone, including Zach, had grown quiet. He'd crossed a line today in many ways and was now included in their serious talk. It scared him, but knowing that something bothered his father and not knowing what it was frightened him even more. They all had a bad feeling about Sinclair, even though he hadn't done or said a thing to anyone else.

"You think?" Zach asked quietly.

Cole reached over, ruffling his hair. "Hey, Zach! That was a long time ago and the guy was just a ruthless, greedy bastard. I don't know what became of him cause that was right before...." he swallowed deeply.

"I understand, Cole," Zach said, sounding older than his years. "That was right before you had to come here."

"Yeah," Cole answered, choked up. "So I don't know if he ever bought any of the land or took his development elsewhere; I just didn't pay any more attention to him. And this Sinclair fella had nothing to do with them. I've never seen him before and am sorry I got everyone riled up. The two things aren't related," he reassured the boy, and hopefully everyone else.

"Whether they're related or not, it needs to be addressed," Will broke in. "And you didn't get anyone riled up; Sinclair did that when he came to town looking to take our homes out from underneath us. I don't care if he's paying or not, you leave a man and his home alone. We don't take kindly to that. It's rough out here, and we're not ones to be toyed with or take things lightly. We've been thinking about everything you said since he went to Walt's."

155

Cole looked towards the door, grateful to see that Ruth was still in Katie's room. "Tell you what, we'll get together Friday night for a meeting. If nothing else comes of this Sinclair guy, then we'll just sit around shooting the shit and playing poker. Either way, we need to talk about this and keep our eyes and ears open. There's nothing to be afraid of, I don't want to get anyone spooked or stir up any trouble. But I can tell you, if anyone and I mean anyone, comes around and tries to buy me out, he'll get his ass booted out of here. And if he takes it a step further, he'll be sorry. I lost everything once before and it took me a long time to get where I am today. I'll kill anyone who tries to take it away again," he said coldly, looking at the steely glares he got from his friends.

"Take it away, Cole?" Brent asked softly, staring with his head cocked to the side.

Cole shook Brent's question off, "Never mind, didn't mean take away. No one took my place away, we all know why I came here," he hedged. "Guess I just got my words mixed up. What I meant was that I lost everything once before and don't feel like starting over again. I've already started over once and I'm here to stay."

They all saw a different side of Cole that night, a side that they didn't turn from. A side that they had themselves. There wasn't a man sitting on that porch, Zach included, that wouldn't fight to the death for his home.

* * *

Everyone left shortly after that, with Gris driving Ruth home. Cole felt the soreness in his bones, but he also felt the burning need to spend some special time with Katie. He missed her. Used to working around the ranch and glancing her way every once in a while, Cole would sometimes lean on the fence, just watching her as she played in the golden sunshine. He loved the way she danced around the yard, with the sunlight illuminating the golden highlights in her hair. To him, there wasn't a more beautiful sight on this earth.

Cole had missed that today, and hadn't had a moment to breathe since he came home, let alone spend time with Katie. After the commotion of his homecoming, dinner, and all their company, his head was spinning. Now the house was quiet, the crickets were singing and Katie was fresh from her bath, rubbing her eyes. She was dressed in pajamas and Cole held her close, breathing in the scent of powder and lotion that he had grown accustomed to associating with his daughter. He loved this tiny being with everything in him.

"Tired, honey?" Cole asked, her nod being his answer. "I know, it was a long day. Daddy's tired too. But we're still gonna read," he said with a soft smile.

"Milk, Daddy?" she yawned.

"Of course, honey! Daddy wouldn't forget your milk," Cole smiled lovingly.

Carrying the small cup, Cole got settled in their chair. Katie yawned again, nestling close. He just now realized how much she had missed him today, as much as he had missed her. She drank her milk, with him slowly rocking her. Taking the empty cup, Cole set it carefully on the small table to his right and felt her nestling closer. Her one arm reached up, trying to wrap around his neck, but she was only able to reach the base of his throat. Cole chuckled, hearing her delighted giggles when he kissed her fingertips.

"Tickles, Daddy," she laughed softly.

"I know," he teased, tickling Katie softly under the chin before he snuggled close again. It was too warm to wrap their quilt around her, so Cole bunched it up, letting Katie hold it in her arms. They rocked for a few minutes before opening the book. "Which one tonight?"

"I want the billy goats," she said, her eyes already closing.

"Then the billy goats it is," he said lovingly, reading slowly as he began to rock.

The stars had come out and the sound of crickets came in through the screen door. The only other sound in the room was Katie's soft breathing and her father's voice as he read quietly. The rocking chair squeaked on the wooden floor, and there was no fire tonight. Even though she was asleep, Cole read on. He would always read to his little girl. Finished with the story, he laid the book down and just rocked Katie close to his heart until his own eyes started to close.

Chapter Nine

"Oh shit!" Cole cried out, springing up to a sitting position in bed.

Whoever said that the mind works better at night than it sometimes does during the day, was right. It was especially true with Cole and he could literally kick himself. Looking at the clock, he saw that it was a little after four. In spite of the early hour, he felt good. He didn't want to rise so early; he still had an hour and a half to sleep, so he just lay back thinking of the predicament he had unwittingly painted himself into.

"You asshole! You asked Callie out for Friday night. What the hell did you do that for? Then you forget and go and tell the guys that you all should have a meeting Friday night and they agreed! Of course they agreed, asshole! The only one who knew about the date was Walt, but he even forgot! Shit, shit, shit! What the hell am I gonna do now?"

Cole groaned, lying back. How he ever got himself into situations like this was beyond him. Every day of his life Cole tried teaching Katie to think before she acted. But did he? No. He just plunged right in, living moment by moment and not remembering anything from the previous one. Being muddled didn't surprise him one bit. Now he wondered why he even asked Callie out. No, deep down he knew why he asked her out; he just wondered why she even bothered to accept in the first place.

"Who you trying to kid? You got feelings for her, there's no denying that. Think you can go on the rest of your life not facing them? God, sometimes I feel so close to just going to her and professing my love and other times I just want to run into the mountains and hide. But, since I can't run and hide, I thought I'd try and ... and ... oh shit, what the hell were you going to try?" Cole cursed himself silently.

Lying on the bed, he covered his eyes with his arm, groaning loudly. "What a frigging mess, I go and ask her out and then I go and plan a meeting. I don't want to break the date, cause let's face it; I'm getting tired of being alone. True, not ready for marriage! No way! Probably won't ever get married again, in spite of what everyone thinks. Don't need that. Let them think that cause I'm free and single, I'm looking to get hitched. Let Brent get hitched! He's just as single, and just as free. Even more so! Besides, I've already been there, done that, don't want to head down that aisle again. I just don't want to be alone all the time. I have needs too. Just want to go out with a pretty woman I think the world of and treat her to a nice dinner. That's not too much to ask! And she said yes! Now what the hell do I do?

"If I go to her and break our date, I'll hurt her feelings and I don't want to do that. Besides, I asked her first. But if I go to the guys and tell them that I have to change the date of the meeting to Saturday, they'll eventually find out why and I'll never hear the end of it either. Is it going to be worth it? I mean, I want to go out with Callie. But do I want to hear their shit when they know? Oh hell, how did everything get so screwed up so fast? If you only took the time to think, then none of this would have happened," Cole chastised himself.

He lay back, trying to figure a way out of his present predicament. If anyone could paint themselves into a corner, he sure as hell could. He had done a good job of that within a matter of hours yesterday. The sun started peeking over the horizon, turning the sky a light tone of pink. Cole rose, pulling his pants on over his boxers before padding softly out into the kitchen to start the coffee. Going into the bathroom, he stood over the toilet, staring at his reflection in the small window. Groaning again, he lightly pounded his head on the frame over and over.

* * *

Their morning went quickly. After having his first quiet cup of coffee, Cole greeted Ruth and then went in to finish dressing for the day. Katie was dressed, they had breakfast together and Cole was soon outside saddling the first horse. He still had to exercise them and couldn't let what happened yesterday stop him. Katie was reluctant to see him leave, but Cole had to make her realize that sometimes things just happen.

"Honey, I didn't mean to scare you yesterday and nothing bad happened. I came home, didn't I?" he pleaded, hoping to ease her mind.

"I missed you," she pouted.

"And I missed you, but the horses are counting on me. Honey, it's my job to take care of them and they need to be exercised. They can get really sick if they just stand around all day, and this is the only way to do it. You do understand, don't you?" Cole patiently explained.

"Are the horses sick, Daddy?" Katie wondered.

Looking in her wide eyes, Cole's heart softened, "No honey, they're not sick; that's why Daddy's taking them for rides. Ok?"

"Ok, Daddy," she smiled, pacified for the time being.

"Will you and Nanny make me a good lunch? I'm going to be really hungry," he beamed at her.

"I'll make you a sandwich with ketchup!" Katie immediately brightened.

Cole tried not to wince, wondering what a sandwich with ketchup would taste like and shuddering at what she would be putting under the ketchup. "That sounds good, honey," he said, kissing her goodbye.

Katie ran up to Ruth and took her hand. Both stood on the porch waving as he rode away. Heading in the same direction as the previous morning, Cole's mind whirled with his latest problem. Good or bad, one thing riding afforded was plenty of time to think. Cole still hadn't mentioned anything to Ruth and for that, he was grateful. He thought of telling Callie that he couldn't find a sitter on such short notice, but she would see right through that. Not only that, all she would have to do was talk to Ruth once and she would know that he never even asked; so that wouldn't work.

Cole hadn't spoken to Ruth at all, knowing that she would hound him constantly about his plans. No, he intended to wait until at least Friday morning, and then spend the day making himself scarce around the ranch so that he wouldn't have to listen to her. Now he did not know what to say. He could just see the look on her face when he told her how he had screwed up. He could also hear the torment he knew would be coming from Brent and Will, especially when he cancelled the meeting.

"Damn, back to square one; still don't know what to do," Cole mumbled to himself. "Go with Callie and have a great time, or go to a meeting and spend the evening with a bunch of cowboys who smell no better than their horses," he giggled wickedly, thinking of Will and Brent. "Wouldn't that start a round between those two?"

As he rode along, Cole was almost afraid to look ahead. The last thing he wanted to see was Zach riding up to him again. Looking up slowly, he settled back smiling; not a soul was in sight. Maybe today he could get all the horses exercised and then tomorrow, could get things ready for Callie on Saturday. She was coming with their annual boosters for Rabies, Encephalitis, Tetanus and Strangles. Once that was over, then he would give the animals a good going over on Sunday, complete with a much-needed bath and rechecking their hooves and teeth. After that, a brushing down would be done on each, and they would finally be ready for the buyers to come for them the following week.

"Gonna be good getting some money coming in for a change," he sighed, slightly feeling the pinch.

There was still a bit of money in the bank to buy groceries with, get the supplies for Katie's party the following week, and to at least pay the electric and phone, but it would not go much further than that. Anything else would have to wait until at least the middle of next week, when Cole would have three of the horses sold. He would then pay off his bill down at Mel's feed 'n seed, the balance of the bill owed Callie, and put some money in the bank for an emergency fund.

He groaned, thinking of the bills staring him in the face; Callie would never even ask him for the money, but it was owed her and he would pay. If she had her own way, his animals would be cared for free of charge, but Cole was having nothing to do with that. He would pay his way and that was all there was to it. And Mel had carried him since late fall, not asking for a penny. Cole knew that he carried practically all the ranchers and farmers through the long winter without expecting any type of payment until their first round of stock could be sold, and Cole would be doing that very thing next Wednesday. At the same time, Will and Brent were readying their first shipment of cattle for the stockyards, with Walt following after. The price of cattle was holding steady and for that, everyone, including Cole, was grateful. Last year almost all of them had lost money and they now had the chance to make it up, the outlook was good.

Shaking his head, Cole cringed as he thought of the way consumers griped about the cost of beef and milk these days. What they didn't realize was the sheer cost to the farmer and rancher to produce the goods needed. Sometimes the vet bills and cost of feed alone were enough to put one under, especially after a particularly hard winter. They all felt the pain when turning on the news and seeing yet another farm or ranch succumbing to auctions. The family stood staring dully as their livelihood was sold out from underneath them in order to pay the bank. It was a sad state of affairs, with no end or solution in sight. They were needed; there was no doubt about that, yet they barely made enough to survive.

It was different for Cole, his business was mostly for pleasure. He provided no food or drink to the market, only a luxury afforded by few. People loved to ride, and as long as people loved to ride and looked for high quality, well-trained horses, Cole had it made. He wasn't at the mercy of the market; people would always pay a high price for a good horse. His dream was to one day have a ranch so successful that the name Morgan would become a household word synonymous with well-bred, strong, magnificent horses. Snapping out of his reverie, Cole pushed all worry about bills from his mind for now and turned back to the ranch. This mount had had enough riding for one day and he needed to get another saddled and out.

Riding back in, Cole greeted Katie, grabbed a cold drink and set out on the next horse. The process was repeated three more times and by the time he arrived after exercising the fourth horse, Cole was pleasantly tired, stiff and more than ready for lunch. He only hoped that Katie had forgotten all about making her ketchup sandwiches.

"Daddy! Nanny says lunch is ready!" his gracious daughter bellowed from the front porch.

Before he could even reply, she turned and ran back into the house. Shaking his head, Cole wished he could harness an ounce of her energy; she was like a mini whirlwind swirling about the place, making him dizzy just watching.

"Doesn't she ever just walk?" he muttered to himself.

Once he got the horse brushed down and turned loose in the corral, Cole limped towards the house, rubbing his backside the entire way. Ruth watched laughing, biting her tongue as he came into the kitchen. She was just dying to ask if he needed a pillow to sit on, but smiled sympathetically instead. Sometimes no matter how used you were to riding, sitting a horse for six straight hours was enough to make a body sore. Walking around a little and taking a break worked the kinks out, and then one was ready to go back.

"Ahhh, homemade chicken salad," Cole grinned, rubbing his hands together. At least Katie had forgotten the ketchup.

* * *

The rest of the afternoon passed quietly enough. Katie played on the front porch with her dolls while Ruth cleaned the kitchen. She had full view of the porch from the kitchen window and smiled as she heard Katie singing to her little family. A warm breeze blew in through the open windows, giving a clean scent to the home, which had been closed up all winter. It just felt good to open things up again, letting the clean, fresh air in. Ruth finished the dishes and went to get Katie for her nap.

"Come on, honey, let's get you down," she said, holding out her hand.

"Ok, Nanny, can my dollies come? They're tired," Katie yawned, rubbing her eyes.

"Of course they can, honey," Ruth smiled lovingly. "I'll tuck them in with you."

She led Katie into her bedroom and covered her with a light quilt. Her dollies were clutched to her chest when Katie turned to her side, stuck her thumb in her mouth and fell asleep with Ruth gently stroking the hair back from her face. Like with Cole, Ruth's love for this child was overwhelming. She now knew how it felt to be a grandmother, thinking at one time that this particular pleasure would be denied her. Ruth had never been able to have children of her own, not that she and Gerald hadn't tried, but early in their marriage, Ruth had suffered three miscarriages and a fourth pregnancy that had resulted in a stillborn baby boy.

Ruth thought that she would never get over that. Gerald almost hadn't. The child's death had hit him harder than she realized at the time. He grew sullen and quiet, and the rest of their years were spent alone on their small farm. Ruth sewed and made quilts in her spare time, or in the winter when the nights were long. The money they brought in supplemented their income from the farm, and she and Gerald lived comfortably until his death at the age of 55.

Doc Edwards said that his heart just gave out one night. Ruth knew better though; Gerald was just too young to have had his heart give out. No, she would always believe that Gerald had simply died of a broken heart. At the age of 52, Ruth now faced life alone; her Gerald had gone on to be with their babies. How she wished that he could be here with her right now, sharing in this new part of her life. Gerald would have fallen in love with Katie the minute he had laid eyes on her.

Those days passed quietly for Ruth, with her working part-time at the mental health center in town and doing bookwork for some of the local businesses. Her quilts still brought in money and were the most popular items at the local fairs and flea markets. She kept as busy as she possibly could day in and day out, yet when night closed in, so did the reality of the loneliness that was now her life. As rich as she was with friends, Ruth was still a lonely woman deep inside. At night, her house was quiet and she rocked in front of the fire, designing another masterpiece.

At the start of every morning, Ruth got dressed and went out to the back field where her small family rested. Gerald's grave was in the middle, with their baby on one side, and a marker for the other little ones lost on the other. All their graves were tended with love; this was the only thing she could do for her little family. Every winter they were decorated with pine boughs and after Christmas Ruth would place the strings of cranberries and popcorn that had adorned her tree out over the graves for her children to see.

She often wondered why she even bothered with a tree at all; she was the only one who saw the decorations and the magic of twinkling lights. Ruth just hoped in her heart that her little angels looked down from the heavens each year and took joy in the season with her, even though she couldn't see them. Tears flowed unchecked as she told them about her holiday; she had never seen the light in her children's eyes when they saw her tree.

That all changed the day a broken man came into her life. It was as if the fates and the powers that be all combined, bringing him to her. Ruth needed someone to take care of, and Cole needed that very thing. He had given up on life and Ruth had just found a reason to go on. Cole fought to withdraw from the world and she fought tooth and nail to give him a reason to stay with them. Eventually Cole started trusting her more and more and a friendship was forged.

Then came the fateful night he spent with Maggie. Ruth bit her tongue, not saying a word when Cole came to her, pleading help. She knew that in his own way, Cole had been searching to replace something he had lost so tragically. She held no blame for that night, her boy had been lost for so long, and now it was her turn to help. That was what a mother did, a mother helped her child and a mother never judged. Ruth loved Cole no less than if she had given birth to him herself, and she was there throughout the entire ordeal. Like a typical mother, she was there for her wayward child, ready to pick up the pieces where they fell.

She cared for Maggie during her pregnancy and never said a word. Cole was her boy; she would never turn her back on him, and Maggie was with child. There was no force on this earth that could turn Ruth away from a child. She was there when Katie was brought into the world and she was there when Maggie quietly slipped away, climbing aboard a plane that whisked her out of the country, leaving Cole and a tiny baby behind.

Then Ruth knew her real calling; one morning she marched into Cole's house and masterfully took over. It had been two weeks since Maggie left. At first Ruth had helped out here and there, but she also held back, giving Cole precious time with his new daughter. She was never more than a phone call away and was always there when summoned. This morning however, Cole did not have to call.

Ruth had awakened knowing that today was the day. Cole needed to get back to his work at the ranch. Everyone had been helping out with his stock as much as they could, but she could tell how much he balked at that. His friends did not mind and would have helped out as long as they were needed, but Cole took exception to the fact that he was not meeting all of his responsibilities. He was overextended, overworked, overwrought, and exhausted almost to the point of sheer collapse.

Katie was a good baby, but she was a baby. Babies cried a lot, especially at night, and babies needed a lot of attention. They had to be fed, changed, bathed, rocked and walked. They needed to be sung to and talked to, and they needed to feel your presence. They knew when they were alone and cried to bring you to them. The world was strange, open, cold and lonely after coming from a place where everything was quiet, small and warm.

This strange new world took a lot of getting used to and they needed their mommy and daddy as much as they could get. Only, Katie didn't have a mommy; she had a daddy who ran ragged day and night taking care of her, cleaning the house, caring for the horses, and kept the formula ready and the laundry done. Bottles needed sterilizing and her tiny clothes needed to be folded; but the problem was, Cole had forgotten to dry them.

The last clean sleeper had just been used and lay in a soiled pile on the floor. Cole had no idea what to dress Katie in. About the only thing he could think of was to use one of his tee shirts for a nightgown, but that was miles too big, and it was the smallest item he had. Not knowing what to do, he just put Katie's diaper on her, wrapped her in a blanket and collapsed into the rocker, desperately trying to quiet her cries. He still needed to dust and vacuum, one could write their name in the thick layer of dust coating the furniture.

Sleep had been almost nonexistent ever since Katie had come home, and fatigue was finally taking its toll. Cole was used to waking early in the morning; he had done so every day of his life. What he wasn't used to was being woken up every hour or so during the night by a crying baby. Sometimes it seemed the minute his head hit the pillow, Katie began to squawk. He had never been so tired in his life.

"What do you have, radar or something? Every time I lie down and close my eyes, you take that as your signal to wake up! It's nighttime, baby! We sleep during the night! See? It's dark outside! That means we lay our heads down and close our eyes until the sun comes up! Then you can cry!" Cole had pleaded with Katie the previous night, to no avail.

His eyes were heavy and leaden, his head ached and he was hungry. He had not had the chance to go grocery shopping and didn't even have so much as a cup of coffee that morning. He had skipped breakfast because Katie just would not stop crying, no matter what he did. Cole was ready to give up when Ruth swept into his living room, took the crying baby from his arms and sent him to bed after handing him a sandwich from the basket that she carried in.

Cole did not know whether to eat or collapse from sheer exhaustion, but hunger quickly won out. He sat on the edge of his bed and chewed slowly. Too tired to sit at the table and not ready to lie down yet, every bite was savored as he leaned against the headboard. A cup of cold, day-old coffee sat on the nightstand and just as he was reaching for it, a fragrant, fresh cup from Ruth's thermos replaced the drink. She patted his hand reassuringly, flashing a smile he would never forget.

Ruth's words were like a comforting magic to his ears. *"I'll take care of everything, honey,"* was the last thing he heard before closing his eyes, sleeping through lunch, sleeping through the late afternoon chores out in the barn, and sleeping until it was time for dinner. When Cole finally did wake, he stumbled into the kitchen, his eyes almost falling out of his head. The counters shone, the floor sparkled and the inviting aroma of roast chicken filled the air. There was also a cake on the counter, iced and ready for dessert. Coffee simmered on the stove and his mouth fairly watered for a cup.

Ruth greeted him warmly, but the thing that caught his attention most was the sheer silence of his home. Katie was sleeping peacefully in the cradle that Brent made for her and moved into the corner of the kitchen, close to the warmth of the woodstove. Will was just closing up the barn and Brent sat quietly rocking the cradle. He had been a regular fixture at the house since the day Katie was brought home; one look at the little girl and Brent's heart was gone. Will was no better. Katie had two uncles who would be there for her the rest of her life, and Cole had a family.

He stared, his mouth gaping. The entire house sparkled from top to bottom. He hadn't even heard Ruth when she vacuumed her way through the rooms. Neither had Katie.

"See, babies aren't scared of loud noises," she explained. "When they are used to them, they don't even give them a thought. I vacuumed her room while she was sleeping and then went out into the hallway into the living room. She's a good baby! She didn't give me a bit of trouble."

"But the laundry!" Cole exclaimed, his mouth falling even further.

"It's all done and it was no problem," Ruth shrugged.

"But ... but how...." Cole sputtered.

"Honey, you're a new daddy and that's hard. Plus, you're doing it all by yourself! You have a house to take care of, laundry to do, a ranch to run, and a baby. Cole, you need help and that's why I'm here," Ruth said, leaving no room for argument.

And there was no argument. Cole ate heartily that night and spent the rest of the evening sitting quietly in front of the fire. Will had gone home after enjoying a slice of cake and a cup of coffee, but Brent lingered a while longer to drive Ruth home. From that day on, Ruth showed up first thing in the morning. When the weather was bad, cold and rainy, she drove down. When winter storms were forecast, she stayed in the spare room that Cole had converted for her. She kept extra clothes in the spare dresser and slept in the bed he purchased especially for her. Ruth now had her family to take care of and had been doing so literally from day one. There was no greater calling and there was no greater blessing.

Looking down at Katie now, Ruth brushed the tears from her eyes. She was truly blessed; the good Lord had given her someone to love. She could not believe that it had been four years already. Katie was a joy to watch. How Ruth cherished the days spent taking care of her and her father. Her love was returned tenfold. The first time that Katie called her Nanny, she had to turn and wipe the tears away.

"Nanny," Katie spoke softly one night as Ruth was getting ready to leave.

"What, honey?" Ruth asked, turning back. She stared at Cole, who was just as shocked and surprised.

"Nanny, are you coming back?" Katie asked, giving a small smile.

"Honey, I'll always be back," Ruth reassured the tiny child.

"I'll see you tomorrow, Nanny," Cole smiled softly.

"Tomorrow, honey," Ruth said brokenly, squeezing his arm. Turning, she spoke softly in his ear, "You don't know what this means to me. I've been waiting all my life to hear someone call me Nanny," she smiled, dabbing at her eyes.

Smiling understandingly, Cole squeezed her hand. He, too, needed Ruth as much as she needed them.

"Sometimes the good Lord does know what he's doing," Ruth now said softly as she rose, tiptoeing from Katie's room. "He gave me a family again."

While she relaxed on the porch and Katie slept, a strange car drove in. Cole had not yet returned and Ruth did not like seeing a vehicle she didn't recognize. Rising, she felt the hair prickling on the back of her neck as she went inside, hooking the screen door shut. The act in itself seemed futile, the lock certainly provided no form of protection at all since the door could have easily been kicked in, but the act in itself made Ruth feel better. Standing inside, she watched the short, odd-looking stranger walking up. Knowing instinctively who the man was, Ruth fought the urge to slam the door in his face.

"May I help you?" Ruth asked, coldly.

"Mrs. Morgan?" the odd man smiled.

"No, there is no Mrs. Morgan," Ruth said coldly, glaring at the man.

"Then perhaps you can help me. I'm looking for a Cole Morgan," Peter Sinclair addressed her.

"Mr. Morgan isn't available at the moment. Good day," she replied stiffly, turning to leave.

"Ma'am, would you please give him my card and tell him to call me the first chance he gets?" Sinclair asked quickly, straining his neck, with the slamming of the front door and turning of the lock being his answer. "Yes, and a good day to you too," he cursed, placing his card on the small table between the rockers. "Shit, this fucking town's getting on my nerves."

168

* * *

"I'm sorry, Mr. Culver, but I still don't have any good news to report. You see, I haven't gone back to the Bremmer place, I'll do that tomorrow. Thought I'd give him another day to think things out," Sinclair explained.

"Don't waste too much time or he'll think that you simply gave up and weren't serious at all. I want his land and Morgan's land; they're vital to my plans. They have the only river around the area running through them, and without that water, I have no lodge. I have to have that property! In one direction you have a useless swamp, that's better-suited for Morgan, in my opinion, and once you follow the river in the other direction, it leads to state protected gameland. It's the perfect setup, no one can build around me and the folks that come to the lodge can not only hunt and fish, but they can buy special permits that I can arrange with the state, and use the gameland, also. Either way, I make money. If either man holds out, then I'm sunk. The more ranches you can buy out, the more I can expand. Just think of how my business will boom if I put in a modern mall! 'Bout time someone took those brainless hillbillies out of the dark ages and planted them in the real world. But it won't work if you can't swing the deal for me! Folks don't come to a fishing lodge in Montana only to sit on the front porch counting tumbleweeds," Culver replied angrily.

"I'm sorry, sir, but I thought that I would give Bremmer just one more day. Meanwhile, I went to Cole Morgan's place earlier, but he wasn't home. Some broad was there; rude bitch if I may say so myself. Slammed the fucking door in my face," Sinclair cursed.

"Then start slamming back," Culver screamed, feeling the vein on the side of his head beginning to throb. "I can't afford to waste any more time! If those cowboys don't start accepting offers, then I have no choice but to send Murphy and Howard up. They know how to get things done. Start hitting some of the other ranchers in the area, that might shake them up. Begin with Morgan's friend, Brent Williams. He and his father had a bad year last year; if we can drive them out, the rest might follow suit."

"Sir, just give me a little more time, I have some plans and just need a bit more time. I have my own ways of getting them to listen. I know that the Williamses had a rough year, and Bremmer's wasn't much better, he only made a margin of his usual profit. Neither can afford any more losses. They'll soon start seeing things my way. I checked it out, Williams is already overextended at the bank and Bremmer isn't far from that. Morgan is barely breaking even, he's only starting out. Williams is the one to hit hard; like I said, he's already in hot water with the bank and is hoping to pay his loan off with his next shipment. If it arrives," Sinclair said menacingly.

"Just do what you have to do; I don't give a fuck about them cowboys up there, I just want them the hell off my land. And Morgan has been a thorn in my side for years. He fucked me over good in Wyoming and I'll be damned if he'll ever do that again. When I found out he left, I thought he'd found a hole somewhere and crawled off to die. Bastard's back and in my face again; this time I won't be so nice," Culver swore.

"Don't you worry about Morgan, he'll see things my way soon," Sinclair said, hanging up.

The thought of a quarter of a million-dollar bonus was all the incentive he needed to lose his shyness and start pushing back. Sometimes, talk alone just wasn't enough. He would pay one more visit to Bremmer first thing in the morning, but tonight he was going back out to Cole's ranch.

* * *

Finished for the day. Those words were music to Cole's ears. The horses were exercised and now roamed leisurely through the lush green fields. There had been no unexpected surprises; Katie was inside with Ruth, and Cole even managed to squeeze in a few minutes of time to straighten out the tack room. One day he would give it a thorough cleaning, but this was good enough for now. He leaned on the fence sipping the soda Ruth brought out for him, and watching the horses as they romped in the fields. Hearing a car driving in, Cole turned, seeing Sinclair's gray Civic pulling up.

Not a move was made to greet the man. Cole's anger towards the intrusion simmered just below the surface as he stood watching the unwelcome stranger bend over, picking up his briefcase. Sinclair then pulled something out of his pocket and headed towards the porch. Cole knew that the man had seen him by the fence and why he chose to ignore him was reason enough to go over. Katie burst through the door, excited at the prospect of a visitor. She stopped short, her shyness taking over when she realized that this man was a stranger to her. She hung back, but Sinclair approached, with a smile pasted across his face.

"Well, hello little miss. Would you like a lollipop?" Sinclair asked, extending the treat towards Katie.

"NO! SHE WOULD NOT!" Cole yelled, striding up.

Before Sinclair could react, Cole snatched the treat from his hand and threw it in the dirt. Startled, Katie turned and ran back into the house crying for Ruth. Cole then stood between Sinclair and the front door, staring coldly at the smaller man. His sheer size alone should have been enough to drive the smaller man away, but Sinclair was shrewd and didn't give it a thought. He stood his ground and stared Cole down.

"I don't know who the hell you are or what you want, but no one comes here and bribes their way into my home by using my daughter. Now, turn back to your car and get the hell off my land," Cole seethed, fists clenched.

"Mr. Morgan, I meant no harm. Was being neighborly," Sinclair began.

"I know neighborly, and you're not neighborly. If you wanted to speak with me you could have come over to the corral," Cole seethed.

"I'm sorry, the sun was in my eyes, I simply didn't see you there. Again, believe me, I was not using your daughter to get to you," Sincerely apologized.

"Oh no? Then why the lollipop? You seem to know an awful lot about someone you never met before," Cole coldly accused.

"I have a stash of them in my car, kind of addicted to the things myself," Sinclair shrugged. "Then I saw your little girl on the porch and didn't think it would hurt. But it was stupid of me and I apologize again. You are right, our children should not accept anything from a stranger, and that's what I am."

"And will remain. I had a long day and have plenty of work yet to do. Goodbye," Cole turned, feeling Sinclair grabbing his arm. Turning, he glared menacingly.

"Mr. Morgan—"

"That's the second time you called me by name, and that puts me at a disadvantage I don't like," Cole said, feigning ignorance. "I don't seem to share in the same privilege."

"I make it my business; I know all the ranchers in this area. That's why I'm here. Name's Peter Sinclair, I'm interested in purchasing your land," Sinclair replied.

"You're interested in purchasing my land?" Cole asked, his eyes narrowing.

"Yes, sir, I am," Sinclair nodded firmly.

"You. Alone. You must be a mighty rich man; first Walter Bremmer's land and now mine," Cole stated.

"Well, not me exactly," Sinclair tried to regroup. "I'm representing a land developer; he has prepared a very handsome offer for you, if you care to review it," he said, reaching for his briefcase.

"No need, don't need to review any offer to make up my mind. Simply not for sale; isn't now and never will be," Cole stood his ground.

"But sir—" Sinclair sputtered.

"But nothing. Now quit wasting my time and get out of here."

"Mr. Morgan, if you would just give me a chance, you might be surprised. Just think of what that amount of money could mean to you. You can send your daughter to the best college one day—" Sinclair went on, only to be cut off again.

"My daughter will do just fine, thank you, and I will do it myself. She's not your concern, so don't mention her again if you value your teeth," Cole hissed, his face turning red with rage. "Just who is your boss anyway?"

"He prefers to remain anonymous," Pete answered.

"Well, Petey, I don't do business with anonymous," Cole answered. "If a man can't come forward with his name, then the only reason for that is he is either ashamed or he has something to hide. I don't cotton to either. I also don't deal with a pawn he sends to do his business," he spat, spinning on his heels.

Going inside, he slammed the door, leaving Sinclair alone. The subject was closed as far as Cole was concerned. Sinclair stood staring at the door for a moment before climbing back into his car.

"Stupid shit kickers," he swore as he drove away.

* * *

Coming into the kitchen, Cole pulled a distraught Katie up onto his lap. Ruth set about quietly putting dinner on the table while he watched. Both had a lot to say, but remained quiet; this was not anything for Katie to hear. Besides, Cole had said everything needed when out on the porch. From her perch at the table, Ruth could hear every word through the open window. She shuddered at the mention of an offer for the land, balking at the way Sinclair refused to gracefully back down. They ate in silence and then sent Katie in to color while she watched TV. Ruth refilled Cole's coffee cup before she sat down.

"Don't know if it's me, or maybe I'm just prejudiced; but where I come from people just don't go pushing themselves off on others. They also know when to back down and take no for an answer and don't go around trying to put folks out of their homes," she sniffed angrily.

Cole found himself taking her hand, "Ruth, no one's trying to drive us from our land and take our homes," he tried comforting her.

"It sure seems that way to me. Seems like that Sinclair fella can't take no for an answer," she angrily replied.

"He left," Cole said, staring intently.

"All right, so he left!" Ruth exclaimed. "But it still riles me! To even think of coming to decent, hardworking folks and try to take them off of the only home they've ever known! And this is every bit your home as anyone else's here! To me, it seems like you've been here all your life. The nerve of some people!"

Neither had heard Katie coming out into the room. "Daddy, are you and Nanny mad?" she asked, her eyes wide with fear.

"Honey, no! We're not mad, especially at you!" Cole said, jumping up.

"Was that man bad?" Katie asked, now frightened. She had never heard her father and Ruth in such a state before.

"No, honey, he's not a bad man; it's just that he came asking for some information that Daddy tried to help him with. But I'm not mad at you," Cole smiled, tickling her chin as he held her close.

"Can I go watch TV now?" Katie asked, immediately brightening.

"Yes! Please! Go watch TV!" Cole laughed, playfully pushing her out of the room. "Now, you and I have something to talk about," he said, piquing Ruth's interest.

One reason was that Cole wanted to change the subject. He still needed to discuss Sinclair and his visit, but not with Ruth. He didn't want to alarm her needlessly, and he wanted to get his decision out in the open. He had decided that he would face the music with Ruth and deal with his friend's teasing once and for all. The meeting would have to be changed until Saturday, but tomorrow night, Cole had other plans. Biting the bullet, he took a deep breath and explained.

"Ok, now first of all I don't want to hear anything like 'it's about time', or 'I told you so', ok?" he implored.

"Now, would I say anything like that?" Ruth asked, feigning innocence.

"Yes, you would! Now, just listen, I'll mention this once and don't go reading anything else into it, ok? First of all, Callie and I are just friends!" Cole said, standing his ground.

"Jus—" Ruth began, only to be cut off.

"And I asked my friend out for dinner tomorrow night. It's no different than when I go out with the guys," Cole tried convincing himself. "I'm simply taking her out to dinner because I need to get away for a few hours and have a nice night. I was wondering if you could watch Katie for me."

"Honey, I'd love to watch Katie for you!" Ruth answered happily.

"I'll bring her over to your place after I finish with the afternoon chores, and thanks," Cole smiled back.

"Why don't you let her stay the night?" Ruth offered, excited at the prospect of having Katie over.

"You don't mind?" Cole asked of her.

"Honey, I don't mind. This way, you don't have to cut your date short.

You just go out and have a good time, ok?" Ruth smiled warmly.

"It's not a date! It's just dinner with a friend!" Cole huffed, as he rose to go out to the barn.

While Cole tended the horses for the night, Ruth bathed Katie and had her ready for bed. The sun was just setting low in the west and she met Cole on the porch on her way out. Katie was lying quietly on the couch, waiting for her daddy to read to her. It was early, but she was tired and Cole was looking forward to an early, quiet evening for himself. He kissed Ruth goodnight and watched until she disappeared from sight, wondering just what in the world he would ever do without her. He had been so lost and lonely when Ruth came into his life, giving him the type of love he had lost when his mother passed on so long ago. Cole desperately clung to Ruth and her love, needing her more than she would ever know. He, too, thanked the fates for letting her into his life.

With a cup of milk in hand, Cole settled Katie on his lap and read two stories that night. As usual, she fell asleep in his arms and they rocked for a while longer. The sad thought of Katie being too big for him to hold like this one day caused him to hold her just a little closer. They were little for so short a time. One minute they were in your arms, and the next they were out in the world. Cole already missed her. Reluctantly, he settled Katie in her bed, already making a memory of tonight.

Leaving her door open, Cole walked into the kitchen and double-locked the door. He then locked the windows and went to the front door. That, too, was locked and he went to the phone, dialing Brent's number.

"Hey, what's up?" his friend's voice came to him.

"Nothing much, just wanted to fill you in on a few things," Cole spoke softly.

"Shoot," Brent quipped in his usual manner.

"Well, I had a visitor tonight. Actually the bastard came twice," Cole began.

"Sinclair? What the fuck did he want? Like I have to ask!" Brent exclaimed, seething with anger.

"He wanted what you think; he came earlier and Ruth slammed the door in his face—"

"Good one, Ruth! Way to go!" Brent whooped, cutting Cole off.

Cole couldn't help but to laugh also; he knew Ruth when she got her dander up and when Sinclair came nosing around, the man was met with the likes of a mother bear protecting her cubs. "Yeah, she wasn't too hospitable to him! But more importantly, I think he scared her."

"Did he try anything?" Brent asked, jumping out of his chair and pacing around the living room. "You should have called me! I'd have been right there!"

"Brent, everything seems fine, there really was no need to call you and get things riled up any more than they already are. I want everyone to be aware of what's going on, but I don't want to go starting trouble where there isn't any. And to answer your question, no, he didn't try anything, just stood on the porch and talked through the screen. Didn't even try to come in, and when Ruth slammed the door on him, he left quietly. He came back tonight though, and that's what has me pissed off."

"Why? What did he do?" Brent asked, not skipping a beat.

"What did he do? I'll tell ya! Bastard knew I was standing in front of the corral, he says the sun was in his eyes and he didn't see me when he pulled in, but he's a damned liar. The sun was setting, it wasn't in his eyes. No, he ignored me and went straight to the porch. Katie came running from the house and he tried giving her a lollipop!" Cole cried out, angrier than he'd ever been.

"He what! He tried giving Katie a pop? That son of a bitch," Brent swore. "He better stay the fuck away from her."

"That's what I told him; I ran over and got between them. Threw the pop in the dirt and scared the hell out of Katie. She ended up running back in the house to Ruth," Cole explained in detail.

"Is she ok?" Brent worried.

"Yeah, Brent, she's fine. I read her two stories and she's about forgotten the entire incident. She did ask me if I was mad and who that man was, I just told her he was someone who came asking Daddy some questions," Cole replied.

"Good! Don't want her scared, but you gotta have a talk with her. It's scary that someone would offer her candy or something, she's so little yet...." Brent shuddered, afraid to put his thoughts into words.

"Believe me, I've thought of that a million times," Cole shuddered, thinking of all a child faced from the world in general. "I'll have to tell her about not taking something from someone she doesn't know and to run and get either me or Ruth right away. I don't want to scare her, but she has to know."

"We'll have to talk about Sinclair tomorrow night," Brent reminded him.

"Well, that's the problem; we'll talk about Sinclair, but instead of tomorrow night, let's make it Saturday, ok?" Cole asked.

"Why Saturday?" Brent quipped, popping a peanut into his mouth.

Here it was, the moment Cole dreaded. He might as well dive in and get it over with. "Cause I sort of ... I sort of asked Callie out for dinner tomorrow night," he said quickly, cringing as each and every word rolled off his tongue.

"HOT DAMN! It's about time!" Brent whooped, spilling the can of peanuts over his lap. "You and Callie! I bet Ruth—"

"Ruth, nothing!" Cole quickly cut in. "And don't go making anything of it! It's not a date, we're not a couple and don't need you or any of the other old hens around here yammering nonstop about it! Don't go making something out of nothing!"

"Who you calling an old hen?" Brent squeaked.

"You for one! And you're about the worst! And then there's Will. He runs a close second. I know that the minute we hang up you're gonna call him, so go ahead! But be sure to tell him that there's nothing to it! It's just a night out having something to eat with someone who's a little more civilized than you!" Cole shot back.

"Hey," Brent hiccuped, pounding on his chest as he belched. "I'm civilized!"

"Yeah, in a pig's ass," Cole snorted back.

"I think I resemble that," Brent joked.

"You mean resent," Cole closed his eyes, rubbing his head. Brent was doing it again. "Why the hell do I even call to talk to you?" he groaned.

"Cause I'm the only one who really understands you and you know it!" Brent beamed.

"Sorry as that sounds, you are," Cole gave in. "So, you gonna sing like a canary and let everyone know to meet at Walt's Saturday at eight?"

"You bet! Have fun tomorrow night! Where's the little rugrat gonna be hanging out, or do I need to ask?" Brent asked knowingly, popping a retrieved peanut into his mouth.

"She'll be at Ruth's for—"

"For the night! HELL'S BELLS! Cole has the entire night to get Callie! Man, wait till Will hears this!" Brent shouted, slapping his knee.

"GOODBYE!" Cole shouted back, hanging up the phone.

He shook his head, laughing to himself. Brent meant well and Cole wouldn't have him any other way. As a matter of fact, he not only endured Brent's teasing, he almost looked forward to it at times, thinking that he needed his head examined for feeling as such. In only six short years, Cole had carved out an entire new life for himself and secrets from the past had no place here. Brent turned out to be a well-loved, trusted friend he just did not want to live without. They were family and that was the only thing that mattered to Cole. He and Brent were true brothers.

That saddened Cole for a moment, there was a time when he had thought of Matt that way. But that was a long time ago. There was no sense in going there now; yet he couldn't stop it. The long night was just beginning to press in, robbing him of sleep. He went out onto the porch and leaned back in the rocker, hooking his hands behind his head.

* * *

The dark mood was fighting to gain control of his psyche. Cole could feel its familiar icy fingers threading their way through his soul, seeking to bring him back into the dark abyss that he knew so well. He didn't want to go there; he trembled as he held his head in his hands, slightly rocking back and forth. Sometimes it seemed that no matter how hard he fought, Cole still fell prey to his own, private demons. Little by little, he felt himself slipping away.

When things were going well, he was able to keep a handle on his emotions. But when things turned on him, causing undue stress and anxiety, Cole struggled. It never failed; during times of adversity, he ultimately fell apart emotionally. If he didn't doubt himself, he was too hard on himself. The only annoyance in his life right now was Sinclair, but that shouldn't be causing this kind of a reaction. Cole was also nervous about the upcoming sale of his horses and the buyers who would be arriving next week. Deep down, though, he knew what he was doing and he was confident. Then there was the excitement of Katie's birthday party.

None of those reasons warranted the mood he was slowly tumbling into. Cole then groaned; he knew exactly what was causing the way he was feeling right now, and in a way, it was the scariest thing he could do. He was taking Callie out. That meant that he could no longer deny his feelings for her. After years of successfully shoving them aside, they taunted, refusing to be ignored any longer. His pleas fell on deaf ears ... his own. He had asked Callie out and like it or not, they were going.

He was going on with his life and someone did not approve. That had to be the only reason for feeling this way. His mind wandered back to his time with Sarah. Cole tried remembering her, but she was a vacant, blank face in his mind. Then her face was replaced with Matt's, whose own stark confusion stared back at Cole. That shouldn't be, Matt and Cole were closer than brothers. They grew up together, sharing everything that a boy faces as he grows. Shuddering, Cole closed his eyes as he slipped into another time and place....

They raced through the field, clearing the fence and going further down the back pasture. Cole leaned low over his horse, the wind whistling around his ears as he nudged his mount faster. He took a split second to look back,

177

feeling Matt close behind but not knowing exactly where he was. He cried out, spurning his horse faster when he realized that Matt was moving up on the left side of him. They were in big trouble, but neither boy cared. They had cut school shortly after ten and snuck back to Cole's house. His parents were in town for the day and the boys had a terminal case of spring fever. It was only Monday, and the prospect of being closed up in that classroom until Friday was unthinkable.

When classes changed, both boys skipped the rest of the day and took off. They were only freshmen, but already sported a reputation. They were far from bad, just a restless handful. They managed to keep passing grades, but their minds were always elsewhere. Matt dreamed of taking off for the rodeo and spent a lot of his time fantasizing about that very thing. Cole had visions of running the largest, most successful ranch in the country. People from all over the world would come to buy his horses. Their teachers were constantly yelling at the boys, trying to pull their heads out of the clouds. More than once, they were caught cutting classes and going down to the stockyards where they watched the cattle being loaded and unloaded in one section, and the wild horses being brought in from another.

"Gonna ride one of them broncs one day," Cole said wistfully.

"You're gonna break your fucking ass," Matt cried out, slapping the hat off of Cole's head.

"I can do it now!" Cole declared adamantly.

"You? Never!" Matt taunted.

"Can too!" Cole argued back.

"Your old man will skin your hide! Cole, what do you think he'll do to you if he finds out that you ditched school to come here riding broncs?" Matt asked.

"Can you really tell me what good school is? I mean, you want to ride the rodeo and I want to run a ranch! Who the hell cares what Napoleon did hundreds of years ago! How's that gonna help?" Cole replied, thinking that he made good sense.

"Who the hell knows! How's it gonna help if you break your ass here and they have to call your dad? Come on, I'm hungry," Matt exclaimed, slapping Cole on the back of the head. "We can hang out here after lunch and then sneak back to school before the buses leave."

That had been the previous week, and both boys missed their bus and had to walk home as their punishment. Their fathers refused to pick them up, thinking that it served both right. It was dinnertime by the time Cole arrived home hungry, tired, and dragging, but he was made to do his chores and wash up before he was allowed to sit and eat. That night, Cole sat at the table alone; his father had refused to wait for him. He also refused to hit his son.

Seeing the crestfallen look on Cole's face, Seth Morgan had a hard time keeping a straight face. He also fought the urge to relent, Seth knew how hard it was being cooped up in school all day instead of being outdoors with the animals one loved so much; but he had to hold his ground. Even though Cole didn't see the sense in school right then, one day he would thank his father for making him tow the line.

Cole did learn from that experience; he learned to be back in time for the bus home. Matt had received the same treatment from his folks, and took the lesson to heart just about as much as Cole had. Their fathers loved and respected both boys, but they couldn't rein them in. They were restless and they wanted to be outdoors. Today, their wild streak had taken over again. They ran down the back road leading out to Cole's ranch and quickly saddled two horses. Cole grabbed a few cans of soda, which he put in their saddlebags, and they took off, heading into the sun.

The next thing both knew, they were racing across the fields and heading down towards the lake. It was mid-May, just about the hardest time of the year to be in school. During the fall and winter, when the weather was just too severe to be outside, school was a welcome relief from being stranded and snowbound at home. Once the weather grew hot, though, there was no stopping the boys. They took off every chance they got, and accepted their punishments when found out. And they were always found out. Cole knew that his folks would be home around 5, so they had a few hours to swim.

Cole was the first to reach the lake, jumping from his mount and yelling his victory, "In your face!" he shouted at a sullen Matt.

"Wait till next time!" Matt mumbled.

"No next time! Your ass is filled with lead! Weighs the horse down," Cole teased.

"Yeah? At least my ass doesn't sink like yours when I go in the water," Matt threatened, grabbing Cole around the neck.

Before Cole knew what hit him, Matt had wrestled him down towards the water's edge, trying to toss him in. It didn't take long for him to regain his senses and fight back. They grabbed at each other, wrestling like two large bears.

"Let go! My old man's gonna kill me if I ruin these boots!" Cole grunted, slipping out of Matt's grasp.

"He's gonna kill you anyway," Matt answered breathlessly, collapsing onto the ground. "Too fucking hot to screw around, gonna go swimming," he gasped, stripping down to his boxers.

179

Cole was right behind him, diving headfirst into the cool water. They swam for over an hour, splashing one another and constantly fighting as one would inevitably dunk or pull the other under. That act in itself led to revenge on the part of the other party, and the fight ensued. Yet, it was a good-natured fight; neither boy could ever be really mad at the other. They had been the best of friends since kindergarten, and had promised to never turn their backs on the other. ...

"Sometimes life fools ya," Cole muttered, sitting back against his front porch and closing his eyes.

Matt did turn his back on Cole, something Cole never thought would happen in a million years. Never had he needed his friend more, and never had he seen such a naked hatred in his entire life as he did in Matt's eyes that morning. He had known that his friend could never forgive him. Standing at the funeral, Cole was almost reluctant to attend. It was his wife, but he felt like an outsider. All his friends tried their best to offer what comfort and support they could at the service, but the cold words spoken by Matt had said it all.

"It should have been me," Cole had muttered at the gravesides and had thought ever since. "It shouldn't be them. How the hell could it be them?"

This time Cole forced himself back to the present, not wishing to dwell on things anymore. Yet every time he closed his eyes, Matt was there....

"You ready?" Matt asked, sitting before the fire.

"Why are we doing this again?" Cole cringed, seeing the knife shining in the flames.

Matt turned the knife over in his hands, letting the blade sterilize itself in the fire. "It's to make us bloodbrothers," he had explained. "There's no stronger bond, we could be born brothers, and the bond couldn't be stronger. It means that no matter what and no matter where we are in life, we are bound by our promise to always look out for one another."

"How?" Cole shrugged.

"By the mingling of our blood. When we do that, our lives run together. We may be separated by the choices we make later in life, but our lives will still be entwined. We will be one; brothers of blood till the end. No matter what, I pledge that I will be there for you," Matt solemnly vowed.

"I pledge the same thing," Cole winced, biting his tongue so as not to cry out.

Matt had pulled the blade lightly across his palm and handed the knife to Cole, who did the same. The boys looked at their hands, seeing the shiny red sheen glistening in the firelight. Looking intently at one another, they promised each other their life and held their hands up high, clasping tightly

180

as their blood mingled. After a few minutes, Matt dropped Cole's hand.
"There, it's finished. We are brothers from here on in...."

"No, Matt, that's where you are wrong. We were not brothers from there on in, we were just kids playing a game and acting out legends we had heard stories about while growing up. We thought that we were brothers for life, but we were so wrong. Life has a way of taking things from you. I looked away one day and everyone just vanished. One minute you were all there by my side, and the next, I was alone. It's my fault; no one has to tell me that. Maybe I did take the easy way out, maybe you've known that all along and Sarah knows it too. And now I'm paying the price. I've done nothing but make one mistake after the other, and now I'm raising my little girl alone. I'm scared to death that I'll find a way to mess that up too. God, I'm so alone and I don't like being alone, but I don't know how to be anything else," Cole said brokenly, his voice barely above a whisper.

He sat for a few more minutes, trying not to give in to the sobs that threatened just below the surface. Cole thought that he would never cry again; at times he vowed he never would. Whoever said that men don't cry hasn't had their heart ripped out and handed to him. Cole had never cried before; his father would punish him, and he never cried. Bullies would beat him and he never cried. When he fell from his horse and broke his arm, or when he didn't heed his father's warning and stepped behind a horse that was being shoed, he didn't cry. That time he took a nasty kick to the side of the face, breaking his nose and knocking three of his top teeth out. To this day, he wore a partial plate to repair the damage. And he never stepped behind a horse that way again. Still, he never cried. Nowadays, it seemed like he never stopped crying.

* * *

The night dragged on. Cole had given up sitting out on the porch and came inside, opting to lie in bed. Sleep eluded him, but that was no surprise. He was thinking too much. He always thought too much and he wasn't helping himself any now. He needed sleep, tomorrow was promising to be a busy day, and therein lay the problem. The mind was sometimes a hard thing to shut down. Cole was one to play his day over and over for hours, wishing that he could get up and get on with things instead of just thinking about them. He hedged, though, because getting on with tomorrow meant getting on with his date.

Cole was nervous and was driving himself into a chaotic frenzy. He wasn't sorry that he had asked Callie out, but that did not stop him from being scared to death and it did not stop him from hashing and rehashing every notion that came into his head. This was one trait Cole prayed he didn't pass on to Katie. It was bad enough he tormented himself with his own self-appointed brand of insanity, the last thing he wanted was to drag Katie down with him. He had to lighten up, but that was easier said than done.

A long night was getting longer as Cole lay in bed, trying to quell his nerves. Tomorrow night he would be going out on a date. He could feel his heart pounding and his mind racing. He felt as if he was a teenager scared to death of his first kiss. Images of him doing or saying something infuriatingly stupid flashed through his mind. He almost half expected to wake the following morning with a huge zit on the end of his nose, something which would have been devastating to a teenager. And since Cole felt no older at the moment, he knew that he would be just as crushed. His cowardly side wanted to call it quits while he ran and hid for the evening. Then he chided himself; he wasn't a teenager anymore, he was a grown man. A grown man who needed something in his life other than just working the ranch and spending his nights lying in bed staring up at the ceiling.

For the first time, Cole had to admit that he was lonely. He wasn't ready for marriage by any stretch of the imagination, but he needed someone back in his life once again. He wanted to feel the magic of getting to know someone again. He wanted to share intimate moments when he could look into Callie's eyes and laugh at the merriment he saw there, knowing that she was the only person who knew what he was laughing at. He missed the small jokes and innuendoes that a couple shared, leaving the world guessing what they were talking about.

He longed to have someone to hold and share his feelings with. He also longed for a woman's touch again, no matter how loath he was to admit that. Cole never chose to be alone, and he knew that it was about time he stopped fighting his feelings and faced them truthfully for the first time.

It was time to stop running and hiding behind a wall of pain. That wall would always be there, but if Cole didn't want to instill that in Katie, then he had better pull his own self together first. She needed to see that he was truly happy and strong enough to fully work his way through a hurtful past; one which he would tell her about one day when she was old enough. There was so much he wanted to share with his daughter, and when the time was right, he would. But there was also so much he wanted to share with Callie, and it was about time that he did.

That didn't help tonight, though. Cole's nerves had him on edge and his mind would not let him rest. All sorts of feelings slammed into him as he lay in bed wishing that he could sleep. But as night pressed in and his muddled mind started racing, Cole wasn't able to put anything to rest. Nights were the worst, and when he was nervous, they became unbearable. His anxiety then escalated into another realm, dwelling on anything that popped into his head. He simply could not shut his mind down to sleep. Cole tried shoving all thoughts of his parents, Matt, Sarah, and even Maggie, from his mind.

He had to stop dwelling on the others and Maggie had no place in his life. Their short time together barely constituted a relationship; what they had together had been nothing more than jumping into bed, taking from each other and then it was over, leaving both shattered in the end. Cole slowly picked up the pieces and went on. Mistakes were best forgotten and put in the past, and loneliness was not a good basis for a relationship, as Cole had learned the hard way.

They had spent one night together, and then Maggie went back to her real family, until Katie came along. Once that chapter in her life was over, she walked away, and Cole was not about to let her walk back into their lives. Maggie was out of his life; not that it was a big loss, but it was a loss. Cole already had too much loss in his life.

How he survived, he had no idea. There were plenty of times when he didn't want to survive, even after Katie was born. Then he started fearing that he would destroy her life, as well, and would eventually have to face the day she turned her back on him, her eyes filled with hatred and disappointment. That would be just the thing to push him over the edge.

"What the hell's wrong with you?" Cole cursed, flinging back the light blanket. "Lying here thinking all this shit when you should just put it out of your head and get to sleep."

Yet he knew that there wouldn't be any sleep that night, and what little he would manage would be fleeting. Cole lay back, dozing without realizing it. A short while later he woke, cursing himself. The vicious cycle began again. He tossed and turned, dozed and then woke again, swearing. He tried telling himself that he was lying down and his body was resting, but Cole knew that he would be feeling the effects of no sleep in the morning and decided not to fight it any longer. Rolling over onto his side, he stared out the window until he fell into a fitful sleep an hour before dawn started breaking through.

Chapter Ten

Clothes were strewn about the room. Cole stood in his boxers and socks, staring at the mess. Ruth had taken Katie over to her house an hour earlier, with the promise of making cookies and coloring with Papa. As soon as Gris heard the news of Cole's date, he made one of his own. His time with Katie had been limited lately and he promised to come over with a new coloring book, crayons and ice cream. Katie was almost too excited to take her nap that afternoon, but succumbed to sleepiness anyway. Once she woke, though, she was like a mini whirlwind running through the place.

"Daddy, can you braid my hair with pretty ribbons?" she pleaded, her eyes bright with excitement.

The look on her face warmed Cole's heart; he loved when Katie had something to look forward to, and tonight was special for her. It was also special for him, although he was an absolute lout about admitting that. One part of him was scared, but he supposed that was only natural. Cole knew that the reason he had asked Callie out went beyond friendship and had for years, but they would have to tar and feather him before he would give Brent, Will, Ruth, or Gris the satisfaction of their convictions.

"Why fight it?" he told himself all afternoon. "Maybe everyone's right after all, it's just what you need. Lord knows you're not the brightest man on the face of the earth, so you might as well give in and listen."

What if they're all wrong? his inner insecurities fought back.

"No, they're not wrong; you can see that in Callie's eyes and it's about time you looked. And it's also about time you admitted it to yourself. You turned to Maggie so you wouldn't be alone and you didn't even love her. The only thing you shared was loneliness, you didn't even share Katie. But Callie is different; if you were so willing to reach out to someone you didn't care about, what's keeping you from someone you do?" Cole reasoned, carrying on the same argument that had been racing through his mind the entire day.

He had decided to just work around the ranch today; the horses were exercised and he could very easily get back to that again on Monday. Tomorrow would be spent with Katie, doing their regular Saturday chores and sneaking some special time together. It was also their spaghetti night,

185

something Katie didn't let him forget. The day was spent with Cole brushing down the horses, puttering around the interior of the barn and giving the tack room a going over. He paid extra attention to the stalls, replacing each one with a new layer of freshly bailed hay.

"There fellas, I even had my sheets washed today;" Cole snickered to the horses. "Looks like we're all gonna sleep in clean beds tonight."

He continued putting things back in order, satisfied that everything was taken care of. Brent had promised to come over and bring the animals in for the night, since the days were getting longer and warmer and Cole just hated locking them up early. He usually led them back in just before sundown, but tonight he wanted to get an early start.

Looking at his watch, Cole saw that he had time to go into town like he had hoped. After all, what was a date without flowers, and he wanted to make tonight special. Cole not only wanted to show Callie how much he cared, he wanted to let her know just how very important she was in his life. Whenever he needed her, whether it was for an emergency with his horses or he was feeling down and needed a friend to talk with, she was there. Many nights were spent talking on the phone like school children; especially over the winter when the evenings were long and outside contact with others was almost nil. Callie had already given so much of herself to both him and Katie, that Cole needed to show her how he appreciated every moment.

"I'll be back soon," he called out to Ruth. "Come give me a kiss, Daddy has to go into town," he said, sweeping Katie up into his arms.

"Can I come, Daddy?" she pleaded.

"Not this time, pumpkin, Daddy has some business to take care of," Cole winked.

"What's bizzes?" she asked, wrinkling her face in confusion.

"It's secret stuff," Cole answered, whispering in her ear. "Now, you go and be a good girl."

He put his daughter down and waited until she was safely inside the house with Ruth. He could hear them in the kitchen laughing about Daddy's secrets. Cole shook his head, almost pitying Ruth, for Katie would have her guessing about his secret business until he returned home.

Arriving at the small flower and gift shop at the end of town, Cole was looking at the various assortment of trinkets and gifts, when he had an overwhelming idea. He not only wanted to show Callie how important she was to him, he had two other very special women in his life, also. Ruth was his rock; she had filled the void he'd had ever since the loss of his own mother, and he loved her just as deeply. Cole simply couldn't imagine his life without her and he couldn't let tonight go by without letting Ruth know in a special way.

Then there was Katie, the light of his life. She was everything to him; she was what gave him the will to wake in the morning and face yet another day. Even when his world turned dark, as it often did, just her smile or the mere thought of her gave him a flicker of hope, eventually drawing him out of his mood. Cole needed to let her know how special she was to him; he wanted her to know that Daddy loved her and thought of her even when they weren't together.

It took a while; Cole simply had no idea of what kind of flowers to get. He would have loved to get roses for Callie, but he couldn't afford them at this time. If everything went as planned, within another year or so his ranch should start bringing in larger profits, then he wouldn't have to think twice about such things. For now, though, finances were pretty tight. Just the thought of the bills sitting in the drawer at home was testament enough. And he puzzled over what to get Katie. Walking through the aisles, Cole remembered how she loved to wear pretty things. She was delighted with new barrettes and hair ribbons; the simplest things in life were what thrilled her the most.

Then he saw it. A small box sat on the counter, containing a tiny wrist bracelet with little silk wildflowers adorning the back. Cole was awestruck, they were the color of the flowers they saw each year when on their ride. They weren't big; they were small, delicate replicas of the real thing, and they were perfect. He could just see the light dancing in Katie's eyes when she saw them, and he had to have it. It was a little more than he wanted to spend, but Cole had a change of heart that he couldn't help.

In a split-second decision he decided to use his credit card, something he hated to do. He rarely used it, and even then it was only for emergencies. This wasn't an emergency, but he had decided to use it anyway. He had already put some money aside for dinner at the restaurant that night, so at least that wasn't a worry. This way, he could get both Callie and Ruth the flowers he really wanted, and he could pay it off after the first three horses were sold.

"Let's see, I have three going out this week, and the money should take care of Callie's bill, the feed 'n seed, and I can still get more grain. Can pay another portion of the ranch, pay the electric and put enough aside for groceries, gas, insurance and the phone bill till the next batch goes out," he figured, running his finances through his head.

One thing Cole was careful to do was to pay at least four months of his mortgage at a time; this way if things got slow, he wouldn't have that particular worry. Every time a shipment of horses went to buyers, the house payment was at the top of his list. Then came the electric, which he budgeted for each month, the phone, the insurance, and the living expenses, which seemed to get higher every time he went to the store.

"I don't care, this will get paid somehow and tonight is special," he said, taking the box to the counter.

"Cole! How nice to see you here," May smiled brightly at him. "How's Katie doing?"

"She's doing just fine, thanks," he smiled back.

"I take it this is for her?" May winked conspiratorially.

"Yep, it sure is. And I'd like to get some roses," he winced, especially after seeing the knowing expression that came over her face.

"Some roses? What kind?" May smiled deviously, yet asked politely.

"Well, actually two batches...." he cringed.

"Oh! Two batches! Looks like somebody has a big night planned," May smirked. Leaning on the counter, she waited for his reply.

Cole could feel his face burning; thankful that no one else was here to watch him squirm, especially Will and Brent, who would be rolling in the aisles right about now. If his friends were present, he would turn tail and run, completely forgetting about tonight. Now he really was a goner; it was bad enough that Ruth and Brent knew, with just them things would get all over town quickly enough. But to have May tell her tale of how he came in buying roses and flower bracelets, Cole knew that it was over. He would never live any of this down.

"I'll ... I'll sort'a take some of those white ones," he stammered. "You know, about half a dozen in each batch."

Cole couldn't help himself, his shirt felt uncomfortable around his neck as he pulled on the collar, squirming. May laughed, squeezed his hand, and left for the back room. "I'll have them ready in a minute, Cole. Oh, and my lips are sealed!"

"Yeah right," he muttered under his breath. "Only until I'm outta here."

Minutes later, Cole had his packages in hand and walked as quickly to his truck as humanly possible, his eyes glued to the ground the entire time, refusing to look at a soul. He should have done this under the cover of dark, feeling every eye in town on him. Without looking back, Cole drove towards home.

* * *

Katie was dancing across the porch when he pulled in. Cole watched for a moment, smiling at her antics. He had never seen anyone so free, happy and uninhibited in his entire life. There wasn't a shy bone in her body, and her imagination knew no bounds. Even if she didn't have anything to play with, Katie could always amuse herself as she was now doing. He could hear the silly song she made up as she twirled, her arms held over her head. Ruth sat in the rocker watching Katie and smiling as she saw him driving in.

"Daddy!" Katie cried out, running over. Before he knew it, she was in his arms tickling his face with her fingers. Cole closed his eyes, savoring the moment.

"Hey Katie bug," he giggled. "Why don't you run onto the porch with Nanny?"

"Ok, Daddy!" she agreed, running back up onto the porch.

"And close your eyes!" he called out after her.

"Daddy, then I can't see you!" she cried out.

"But Daddy has a big surprise and he wants your eyes closed. And no peeking!" Cole said, trying to be stern but failing miserably.

Cole laughed as he watched Katie sitting next to Ruth, her hands pressed tightly over her eyes. Her smile was wide and her legs swung back and forth as excitement took over. Ruth glared, giving him a why-did-you-do-that smirk when she saw the bundles of flowers he carried in.

"Now, what did you go and do?" she asked of him.

Katie still sat, squirming in her seat. "Daddy, can I open my eyes?"

Cole hid her package behind his back before finally relenting, "Ok, honey, you can look," he smiled.

Her eyes opened then grew wide when she saw the flowers. "Daddy, they're so pretty!" Katie exclaimed.

"Yes they are, and they're for Nanny," he said, handing Ruth her bundle.

Ruth had to sniff away the tears that threatened as she took her present with shaking hands. "Oh honey, now why did you go and do this?"

"Because of everything you've done for me since the day I moved in here. You not only help me with my daughter and run my home, you were there when I needed someone. You knew my pain, yet you didn't push or judge. You were just there, giving me what I needed. I just wanted you to know how much everything you do means to me," Cole said, his own voice breaking.

Beyond words, Ruth wept as she pulled Cole into her arms, holding her flowers close. Katie watched, confused, yet happy. Turning a smiling face up at him, she tugged on her father's arm.

"Hey! Did you think I forgot you?" he asked, winking at Ruth.

"Do I have flowers, too?" Katie asked breathlessly.

Ruth smiled while Cole reached behind his back and pulled out a brightly wrapped box. Katie's eyes all but fell out of her head when she saw the package, which she grabbed excitedly.

"Look, Nanny! I have a present!" she squealed with delight.

"Go ahead, open it," Cole replied, also shuddering with anticipation.

These were among his favorite times, watching the light shining in his daughter's eyes. Cole didn't know who was more excited, he or Katie, whose little fingers flew in a flurry as she tore at the paper.

Her delighted cries rang out across the yard when she pulled the bracelet from the box, "Daddy! It's flowers! It's our flowers! Look, Nanny!" she cried out with glee.

"Oh, aren't they beautiful," Ruth exclaimed, touching the petals gently.

"Honey, they're silk," Cole explained. "That means that they aren't real flowers, but they are made to look like real flowers. Only the best thing is, they won't die! They'll last forever and ever!"

"Can I wear them, Daddy?" Katie asked breathlessly.

"You sure can, give me your hand," Cole said softly.

"Can I wear them and show Papa tonight?" she smiled widely.

"Yes, you can wear them to show Papa! You can wear them whenever you want!" Cole replied.

"What if they get dirty?" she worried.

"Then we'll wash them!" he shrugged, overcome by her excitement.

Looking at the happiness in his daughter's eyes, Cole didn't regret the purchases one bit. Sometimes there were just some things more important than money, especially when his daughter wrapped her arms around his neck, thanking her daddy. As Cole had learned, things always had a way of working out.

* * *

A short while later, Brent stopped by for a quick visit and to reassure Cole that everything would be taken care of. Plus, he just wanted to see his little angel for a few minutes. Pulling in, he was assaulted by Katie, who launched herself into his arms, her face bright and shining and her smile wide. She proudly held up her wrist, which was adorned by a colorful array of flowers.

"Well, what do we have here?" Brent smiled widely.

"My daddy gave them to me," Katie said proudly.

"My, my, my! Pretty flowers for an even prettier lady," Brent said softly, admiring the bracelet she displayed. "If they aren't just about the prettiest thing I ever saw!"

"They're like my flowers," Katie said quietly.

Brent's voice caught, he knew of the rides that Cole took Katie on once a year, and in a way, he envied his friend. Brent looked forward to the day when he would have a child of his own to share the wonder of the world with. He wasn't opposed to marriage; he just hadn't found the right woman yet. But he kept his eyes and his options open, hoping that one day, it would happen for him. Montana could be lonely, and Brent just wanted to have someone by his side for the dark, lonely times. The only time that he was glad to still be single was after hearing what Cole had suffered. He doubted if he would have been strong enough to face such a loss, let alone put it behind him and move on.

Cole was stronger than he ever gave himself credit for. No one believed that more than Brent. He saw something in his friend that Cole didn't see in himself. Brent saw a quiet strength that enabled Cole to wake in the morning and face yet another day. At the darkest time of his life, he had found a way to go on. Even though he was alone, Cole still forged ahead. Brent knew of the time in the barn when Cole held the rope, thinking of ending it all. That had scared him half to death, not only for his friend, but also for himself. He wondered if he would have been too weak to turn away and would have slipped the noose around his neck. Shuddering, Brent immediately shoved those thoughts from his mind.

Today was not a day for morbidity; it was a day for new beginnings. It was a day where everything in their lives was falling into place and they all had bright, promising futures to look forward too. Next week Brent and his father would be taking their shipment to the stockyard and Cole had his buyers coming. Walt and Will would also be shipping their herds out. Nothing could ruin things for them now.

Placing Katie down, Brent watched her dancing back to the house. Cole met him in the yard, with both men laughing at the way a tiny flower bracelet seemed like the entire world to a small child.

"You'd think I gave her a million dollars," Cole said, his eyes growing misty.

"Yeah, she sure loves her flowers. That's cause her daddy gave them to her!" Brent replied, his voice a little raspier than usual.

"She's so easy to please," Cole said, with Brent agreeing.

"I know! It sure doesn't take much to make that little one happy! So, tonight's the big night! Doing anything special?" Brent asked, not missing the way Cole turned red. His friend just ignored the teasing glint in his eyes.

"I'm taking her to that new French restaurant over in Millvale," Cole informed Brent, seeing the knowing, leering look that came over his face. "And don't think it! We're—"

"Just friends?" Brent glared intently.

Cole deflated, sitting down. He knew when he was defeated. "If I tell you something will you tell anyone else?" he looked at this friend who had taken a seat next to him. "Of course you will, but I'll tell you anyway," he conceded.

"You know me so well," Brent exclaimed.

"Brent, I've been having a hard time for years now, as you well know. Hell, if it hadn't been for you, Ruth, Will and Gris to confide in and pick up the pieces when I crash and burn, I don't know what I'd do."

"Hey, we're there for you," Brent said sincerely. "What's up?"

Cole turned sideways, smiling at his friend, "What's up is I'm tired of fighting my feelings and I'm tired of being alone. I just can't fool myself any longer. And I wasn't planning on this happening! It just happened, and I have no idea how things came about! But I've been alone and not by my choice. It's not fun, let me tell you. What's worse is I feel abandoned."

"Oh shit," Brent muttered, at a loss for words. "You ok?"

"Think I'll be, but it's been hard," Cole quietly replied.

"I know it's been, it's not easy going through all you did," Brent nodded.

"Anyway, what I'm trying to say is that I'm tired of fighting things. I think I've been lying to myself and that's making things harder," Cole admitted.

"What things?" Brent wondered.

"Things like not being able to sleep at night, not being able to fully put the hurt from the past behind me and things like not trusting in other people, life, and myself fully like I used to," Cole answered.

"Hey, you can trust in us! I know how empty that sounds cause of what happened once," Brent replied, reluctant to mention Matt. "I know how much all of that hurt, but you have to know that sometimes things happen that we can't help or control. I've told you before I bet they're all hurting like you've been all these years. I bet it's even worse for them, cause they have to live with what they did. I know that if I'd done that to a person, I couldn't live with myself. You know, seeing what you've suffered cause of them, I know that I could never do anything like that to you, or anyone. I might get mad enough to beat the shit out of you," he tried joking, seeing from the slight smile that crossed Cole's face that he had succeeded.

"Now, that, I can handle. Hell, Matt and I've had some arguments growing up. Everyone does! Friends argue at times, I'd rather you kick the shit out of me! That doesn't hurt as much! But this was different. I don't even think it was anger, as much as it was...."

"Was what, Cole? Grief? A hurt so deep that it's a wonder anyone survived? Cause that's what it was, you know. You can't think straight at times like that. You can't function. Words no one realizes saying have been said, and like in some marriages, when close ties suffer a deep, traumatic loss, instead of turning to each other, people turn away from each other. Nothing destroys more than grief. Sometimes it can make a relationship stronger, sometimes, it all falls apart," Brent shuddered.

"Sounds about right. Anyway, enough of that! What I'm trying to say is that I'm tired of living in the past," Cole said simply, wrapping his feelings up in one simple sentence.

"So, you do have feelings for Callie?" Brent teased, elbowing Cole lightly.

As much as he hated to admit it, especially to Brent, the town crier, Cole had to give in, "Yeah, I do have feelings for Callie—"

"I KNEW IT! HOT DAMN!" Brent jumped up excitedly. "I just knew it! Hell, everyone but you could see!"

"You telling me everyone knows?" Cole exclaimed.

"Yeah, and I didn't even have to open my mouth! We can see it! It's as plain as day the way you two look at each other! It's about time you finally saw it for yourself!" Brent grinned.

"Yeah, guess it is," Cole snickered. "About time I stopped being alone, too."

"Does that mean…?" Brent glared slyly at him.

"It means I'm taking a woman I care about out on our first date! Don't go planning any weddings or sending out any announcements! That's a long way off! Right now, marriage scares the hell out of me and I'm not sure I'll ever be ready to take that step again! Plus, I not only have myself to consider, I have Katie!" Cole argued, setting Brent straight.

"But Callie loves Katie, and vice versa!" Brent argued back.

"All right, I'll admit to that; but the thing is I'm still taking it slow! VERY SLOW!" Cole emphasized, standing his ground.

"Well, it's a start," Brent agreed. "And you're right, go have fun and take it slow! Don't do anything I wouldn't do!"

Cole shuddered, "Hell, no human in their right mind would do what you would do!"

"With that thought in mind, I'm gonna be a man and bow out gracefully before I start arguing that point! You go get ready for your date and I'll take care of things here! Oh, and tell Katie that I'll stop by Ruth's later and they better save me some ice cream!" Brent laughed as he strode over to his truck.

"Oh, you heard about that, huh?" Cole shot back.

"You bet!" Brent called back over his shoulder. "She was so excited she had to call me earlier and tell me! Here I was covered in cow shit from head to toe after cleaning out the barn and getting the little buggers out of the mud down on the south end, when I'm called to the phone! Her timing was terrible, but she made my day!"

Cole couldn't help but laugh; no matter what he was doing, Brent always dropped everything for Katie. He couldn't resist her charms; Cole knew the feeling. He knew of very few people who could resist Katie's charms. No, there was one person, and Cole felt sorry for what she was missing out on. For his part, though, there was a lifetime of memories already stored up. Whistling, he went back into the house to get Katie ready to walk home with Ruth.

* * *

Cole stood on the porch as they left, waving to Katie as she turned back once they reached the top of the hill. Ruth's house was just on the other side, so the walk wasn't far. Besides, Katie had so much pent-up energy that nothing could hinder her today. Minutes later he was still standing there, even though they had disappeared from view. What had started out as a small bout of nerves all day was now turning into a full-fledged panic attack. His stomach tightened with knots and his mouth went dry. And his hands were clammy. Cole brushed them on his jeans, swearing.

"What the hell! No matter what I do, when I get nervous my hands get sweaty. Gonna be great, just real fucking great. Gonna take her hand and she'll slip right out of my grasp," Cole swore, pacing the porch.

What the hells the matter with you? It's not the first date you've ever been on and you've been with women before, none of this is new to you, so why the nerves? his inner self fought.

"Cause this is new to me! I grew up with Sarah! We sort of came together! It just happened! Besides, I was a total wreck then too! Sarah got tired of waiting for me to ask her out and finally took matters into her own hands! I was never any good at this. And Maggie was different; she came to me at the bar and we just sort of flopped together. Plus, she didn't matter; but Callie does! This is the first real time I've asked a woman out!"

But you're friends! You two have known each other for years now! Hell, it's not like she's a stranger! She's already seen you at your worst when you've been covered with mud and shit from head to toe. Hell, you've seen her that way, he tried joking, remembering last Sunday. *Anyway, she's spent nights sitting by your side in the barn waiting for one of your mares to foal. And she's been here to help out with Katie too! Can't count how many times you woke in the morning to find her here taking care of things with Ruth,*

194

giving you both a break! She babysat for you, she worked your horses side by side with you, she's gone riding with you and she's laughed and cried with you, Cole argued with himself, remembering the time they had lost a mare when she foaled.

See? Cole still continued fighting with himself. *You and Callie sure aren't strangers to one another, she's been there for you a lot over the years and you're close friends! It's not like you're rushing into something like you did with Maggie. You care about and respect Callie! You never respected Maggie! But what about Sarah?*

What about Sarah? his mind raged. *Sarah's been gone for over six years; if she was still here you'd be with her, but she's not here. Your vows were 'till death do you part' and she's gone now, Cole; you're not doing anything to dishonor her memory or to hurt her. Besides, do you think she'd want to see you alone the rest of your life? Hell, if the situation was reversed, would you want her to be alone?*

No, I'd want her to be happy; I'd never want her to hurt like I do and face nothing but long, cold dark nights the rest of her life, Cole thought sadly, knowing he was right.

See! Sarah loved you, she wouldn't want you to be alone!

But does she still love me? Does she really still love me, or does she blame me? Cause she still never comes to me! She never calls out to me in my sleep or appears to me in my dreams like other people's loved ones do! Their loved ones come to give them comfort! They let them know that everything's all right and they can and should go on! Sarah never did that! She never comforted me! She never told me that everything was all right! She never came to me!

DON'T! he sharply corrected himself. *Just don't go there! The dead are dead! They can't and don't come to us! You never did believe in ghosts, so why would you believe that she would come to you? Perhaps she did! Perhaps she's come to you in ways you can't see or aren't capable of seeing! Maybe she came to you by bringing you Katie! So you had a one-night stand with Maggie. Big deal. You did get Katie out of that and she gave you the will to live again! Maybe Sarah came to you in that way! She didn't want you to be alone then and she doesn't want you to be alone now! But you're still so crippled inside that you can't see that! Maybe she's the one who brought Callie here!*

You think so? You really think so? Cole thought, trying to still the pounding of his heart. *Maybe you're right, maybe there is something to it. Lord knows something stopped me from hanging myself that day in the barn and something drew me here! No, something brought me here! I mean, when*

195

you think that I could have ended up anywhere else in the world but I wound up here, there must have been greater forces at work!

See? I told you so! There's a reason for everything, but there's gonna be no reason for being late, so get off your ass and get yourself ready! he chided himself.

* * *

That was easier said than done. Cole took his time showering and then carefully shaved. He brushed his teeth twice and then rinsed with mouthwash. Looking in the mirror, he combed back his wet hair, knowing he would return once dressed. Walking to his room with nothing but a towel wrapped around his waist, Cole felt an odd sense of freedom. His daughter was at Ruth's, so he need not worry about walking around naked, which felt pretty good. And he was going on a date. He felt young again.

Now, all he had to do was get dressed. He looked at his old suits and cringed, they were, indeed, old. None of them would do. "Shit, might as well give these to charity; hell, they won't even want them," Cole muttered.

He pulled out his black one, immediately tossing it onto the floor in the back of the closet. That was the one he wore at Sarah's funeral; he should have burned it. Next, he pulled out a navy blue suit, which he tried on. Looking in the mirror, he cringed.

"Look like Captain Kangaroo," he cursed, pulling the suit off.

Next came his brown suit, which Cole had always hated, but tried on anyway. "What? Did you think it got better-looking over the years?" he sneered, frowning at his image. "Shit, you didn't, so why should the suit?"

Ripping that one off, his options were slim. He had a few new pairs of pants and would have no problem picking out a shirt, but they were going to a fancy restaurant. He needed a jacket.

"SHIT! Why the hell didn't I think of this sooner!" Cole exclaimed, slapping himself on the forehead. Rummaging through the back of his closet, he soon found what he was looking for.

"HERE IT IS!" he whooped with glee.

Standing there, he pulled out the black corduroy sports jacket Ruth had given him for Christmas one year. He had never worn it and wondered when or where he would get the chance. Nevertheless, he had kissed her for the gift then and he could now kiss her again. It was perfect. It would go good with the black pants he had purchased last month, even if they were nothing more than a pair of jeans. With a white shirt, a bolo around his neck and the blazer, no one would know the difference. Whistling, Cole grabbed his clothes, splashed some cologne on and quickly dressed. Minutes later he was standing in front of the mirror, adjusting his hat.

There! Finished! And not so bad if I say so myself, he thought, kicking aside the pile of clothes. *Will take care of this mess tomorrow. Hell, gonna have to go clothes shopping one day! About time I stopped wearing nothing but work jeans and shirts!* Cole beamed proudly in the mirror, pleased with what he saw.

* * *

The case of nerves wasn't lost on Cole alone; Callie was battling her own jitters. She hated her hair, her face was too bronzed by the sun and she couldn't find anything to wear. In her mind, she was either too short, too round, too thin or too plain. Images of Maggie flashed through her mind, no matter how hard she fought. Maggie was an elegant woman who could carry anything off. If Maggie swept her hair up, all of it stayed. Callie tried that very thing, only to have the tendrils fall loose and go tumbling down her neck. She cried out in exasperation, throwing the brush across the room.

"I'll just wear it down!" she fumed, tugging at the pins that held her hair in place.

Then her face was too shiny from the exertion. *Just great! Look at you, you look like a teenager with an oily face! No, you look like a workhorse sweating hard after working the field. Why not? He's always seeing you covered in something! What makes you think he'd see you any differently? To him, you're just one of the guys!*

Sitting at her vanity, Callie sighed, staring hopelessly. *No matter what, you won't look elegant. Maggie is elegant.*

Maggie again, I should have known, her inner self chided. *It's always been Maggie, even though you know that they were together only one night. Why the hell should you let one freaking night bother you? The only reason she returned was because she had a secret to hide from her family; she never came back for Cole, and he never begged her to stay! Hell, they haven't seen each other in years. Why do you still feel threatened?*

Because of what they shared together and because she's probably still elegant and that's what drew him to her in the first place, Callie exhaled deeply.

You think so? If it was, it sure as hell wasn't enough to make it last ... for either of them! And don't sell yourself short. You're beautiful in your own way, her inner voice argued back. *You must be doing something right! He asked you out!*

197

Who says it's a date? Maybe he just wants a friend to go out with for a little while. Besides, who knows what would have happened if Maggie had left her husband? Or what will happen if she suddenly shows up with a change of heart! Where will that leave me?

Alone if you keep up this kind of attitude. I swear, you say Cole is the only one closed up? Honey, you're as scared as he is. You both spend so much time and energy running from one another, when you should be running towards one another. Oh, what the insecurities of life can do to us. Listen to you! You know deep down how Cole feels, and you also know that if Maggie showed up today, things wouldn't change. She's his greatest fear! You all know that! Let your love loose! Let it reach him and help him over the heartache he's had. It's about time that man knew real love again, he hasn't felt that in a long time. And neither have you! So stop being silly and get on with things! This is more than just a trip for burgers and you know that! If he simply wanted to go out for a burger with a friend, he wouldn't be going through so much trouble, now would he?

"We'll see," Callie sighed, picking up her mascara.

She opted for a plain black skirt with a white silk blouse, elegant yet simple. You just couldn't go wrong with the basics. "Even you can't screw this up," Callie muttered, smiling at her reflection.

She was finally ready. Now the only thing to do was pace nervously, hoping that she could hide her sweaty hands.

* * *

Sinclair lurked in the brush just behind the barn as Cole drove off. He had been hiding for the past two hours, watching the heartfelt scene when Cole presented Ruth with the flowers and Katie with her bracelet.

"Such a good daddy," Sinclair snickered menacingly. "Just not good enough. Not smart enough to know when to take the money and run."

Brent arrived and walked over to the corral with Cole. The two men leaned on the fence and Sinclair leaned forward in his hiding place, listening. He knew of Cole's plans to date the lady veterinarian, smirking at how he now had another piece of ammunition to use if and when needed. Right now, though, things were falling into place nicely. Cole planned on selling three of his horses on Wednesday, and Sinclair had skulked around long enough to know which three they were. Imagine how shocked he would be when the buyers backed out after hearing how their prized animals had taken ill. Nothing like hitting someone in the pocket, where it would hurt. Maybe then Cole would be more hospitable when he visited again and would be receptive

198

to his offer.

Plus, there was an unexpected bonus in the plan. Brent meant the world to Cole; he was a close, trusted friend who was slowly becoming an unwitting pawn in Sinclair's quest. If a wedge was driven between the two men, the results could send them both reeling. They wouldn't be thinking right and that would only serve to make things easier on Sinclair when he swooped in for the kill. There was nothing better than having an unknowing ally. Brent was playing into Sinclair's hands very nicely.

It wouldn't take long to break Cole; Sinclair was banking on that. The man had left his home once before and he would soon be leaving this one. Cole had lost more than his wife back in Broken Arrow, he had lost his home. He chose to leave rather than rebuild. In the wake of the tragedy, he had no reason to rebuild. Cole not only blamed himself for everyone's suffering, his confidence had been shattered. That was how Sinclair would strike. Maybe a few more losses would be just enough to drive him over the edge.

"Just imagine the shock when you realize the truth about your so-called friend," Sinclair snickered to himself. "Why, you left him to take care of your stock and all of a sudden they turn up sick! Gonna have to randomly hit one or two of the other horses too, really make the bastard's head spin," he laughed menacingly.

Sinclair lay back waiting; he didn't particularly like the outdoors, and the wilds of Montana were proving to be too much for him, but the quirks Culver was willing to pay insured that he would stay anywhere and do anything needed in order to collect. Once this deal was sewed up and the cowboys were eating their own dust, Sinclair planned on retiring on some far away tropical island. All he had to do was wait for Brent to finish up with the horses later on and leave. Once he was gone, Sinclair would sneak into the barn with his little bag of goodies.

"You fucking cowboys think you can push me around; you all may be bigger than me, but you're a hell of a lot dumber," Sinclair snickered, staring up at the sky.

* * *

The turn-off loomed just ahead. Cole couldn't do it. His hands stuck to the wheel and he could barely swallow. Just one little turn to the right and he would be on Callie's road. He just couldn't pull in. Instead, he drove straight, passing it by and going on with no destination in mind. His thoughts whirled and his nerves were acting up again. Beads of sweat broke out on his forehead, which he quickly wiped away.

"Glad Mama taught me to always carry a handkerchief," Cole snickered, trying to put his mind and his nerves at ease. "What the hell are you doing?" he asked, slamming on the brakes.

Taking a wide U-turn, Cole was heading back in the right direction once more. This time when he came upon Callie's road, he hesitated, looking all around him. There wasn't a soul in sight. Thank God there were no houses out this way. They began about half a mile down the lane, with Harve Meuller's old, weathered two-story farmhouse being the first, and Callie's modest cabin almost directly across from him. The property consisted of only two acres, with Callie's clinic and two-car garage on the eastern side, both just a short walk from the house. In the winter, she could not afford to waste precious time scraping ice and snow from her truck, and thanks to Will, her driveway was always kept clear, that being first and foremost on his list, with repeated visits. Thankfully, she had been lucky enough not to be called out during a blizzard, but if need be, her four-wheel drive truck cut through almost anything nature could throw her way. If not, there was always someone at the ready, that someone first being Will, who could plow his way down the road, if so necessary. Somehow, they always found a way.

With shaking hands, Cole pulled into her driveway, waving to the ever-watching Harve, who sat rocking on his front porch. "The entire world must know by now. I almost feel like I should be asking for his permission and what time I should have her home," he snickered, waving his greeting. "Ok, here goes nothing," Cole muttered, walking up the flower lined path to the house.

Harve craned his neck, watching with a smirk spread across his face. He, too, knew of Cole and Callie's feelings towards one another and thought that it was about time; something the entire town was probably thinking. Cole walked towards the door, with Harve's neck turning in the same direction, watching every move. Then all of a sudden, Cole smacked himself on the head and ran back to the truck. Harve scowled, watching him retreat.

"Chicken," he muttered, shaking his head in despair.

"Shit, forgot the flowers!" Cole muttered, turning and running back.

"Oh! Forgot the flowers, huh?" Harve now snickered, watching Cole retrieving the bouquet from the truck. "Ok, let's try again."

"Ok, let's get this show on the road," Cole said with new resolve, straightening his bolo once again and adjusting his hat. "Shit, sweaty hands," he cursed, rubbing them on his pants one at a time.

"Cold feet, wet hands," Harve laughed to himself.

"Well, here we go," Cole mumbled, taking a deep breath.

"Go ahead, knock. She ain't gonna bite," Harve chuckled, holding his breath.

Cole tried straightening his collar, and dropped the flowers. Harve covered his eyes, shaking his head. "Pathetic," he muttered, when Cole bent, hitting his head on the door on the way down.

His hat fell off and rolled across the porch, the flowers fell from the plastic, and Cole scrambled for both. On bended knee, he started picking everything up. Harve had a hard time watching. He held his hand to his face, looking between fanned out fingers. "Oh no, hurry up," he cheered Cole on, seeing the door opening. "Too late," he snickered, sitting back to watch the show.

Unknown to Cole, Callie stood over him, covering her mouth with her hand. She didn't want him to see her laughing, but she couldn't help herself. Instead of seeing her date greeting her, her date was crawling frantically around the deck, scrambling nervously to gather everything he dropped. He reached for his hat and Callie took a step forward.

"Evening," she said, causing Cole to jump back, falling flat onto his backside.

Harve groaned, Callie looked down in shock, and Cole just sat there, his legs splayed out in front of him, the roses falling from his arms. "Uhh, these are for you," he stammered furiously, handing her one of the errant flowers.

"Cole, what happened?" Callie smiled softly, kneeling next to him. She stared into his face, seeing the sheepish grin that spread across his crimson cheeks. Unable to help herself, Callie tossed her head back laughing at the entire situation. "I've been waiting a long time to see you get knocked on your ass!"

He laughed in spite of himself, "Well, tonight's your night! You got me where you want me!" Cole blushed even more as he realized his words.

"Care to tell me how you ended up like this?" Callie asked, leaning her elbow on one knee. Smiling haughtily, she just glared at Cole, further prolonging his predicament.

Cole saw the mischief clear in her eyes and knew he'd been had, "Yeah, do look kinda funny, huh? You see, I sort of dropped the flowers. Oh here!" he said, holding the rest out to her. "And when I bent to pick them up, I hit my head on your door and my hat fell off. And I tried picking up my hat, but ... well, you see the end result!"

"No pun intended?" she asked, causing him to burst out laughing.

Harve heard Cole's bellowing and couldn't help but smile. He raced to the phone and quickly dialed Ruth's number. While they talked, laughing until tears ran down their faces and with Ruth relating the story to Gris, Harve continued giving the play by play.

"I know! You should'a seen him go ass over teakettle after he hit his head! He's a-scrambling all over the place trying to pick up the flowers and his hat, then she comes out! Scared the bejeezus' out of him! He falls flat on his ass and she's standing over him, just staring down! He didn't know what the hell to do! You should hear them, I don't know who's laughing harder!" Harve turned red, wheezing.

* * *

"Here, let me give you a hand," Callie stood, extending hers.

Cole grinned, taking her hand in his. Once on his feet again, he held on for a moment longer as time seemed to freeze. He smiled shyly, not knowing what to say. "Oh, the flowers are for you," he stammered.

"They're beautiful; but you didn't have to do this," Callie smiled, fighting her tears.

"I wanted to. Oh, and I got Katie a flower bracelet!" he winced. One didn't go on a date and talk about their kids.

"I bet she loved that! What kind of flowers?" Callie asked, genuinely interested.

Cole brightened, remembering how much Callie truly cared about his daughter. "It's great! They're the same flowers we see when we go on our ride! All the colors are there! She was so proud of it, she had to wear it over to Ruth's to show Gris."

"I bet she's having fun," Callie smiled. "Come on, let's go in and I'll put these in water and grab my jacket and purse."

Cole followed; watching while Callie found a vase to place the roses in. She held her face to them, inhaling their scent. Cole was tongue-tied and shifted his feet nervously. Sensing this, Callie came over smiling.

"You look good ... I mean, you look ... well, you look great...." he stammered, not able to say what he really felt. He couldn't take his eyes off of her. He had thought she was beyond beautiful when he saw her at her worst last Sunday, yet tonight she sent him reeling.

"Thanks," Callie smiled back.

"No, I mean ... oh hell, I don't know what I mean. I keep on saying stupid things ... no! Not stupid! It's not stupid saying you look good!" he stammered.

"Cole, it's all right," she smiled softly.

"No, it's not all right. I've been screwing up since I got here. First I dropped your flowers all over the place and then I can't seem to say the right thing. Callie, this is all new to me. I don't mean to say anything stupid...." Cole sputtered.

"But you're as nervous as I am," Callie smiled, taking his hand.

"Yeah, cause I came to realize just how important tonight is to me. One part of me says that I'm not ready, but the biggest part is screaming for me to go ahead. See! There I go again! This is our first date and I'm talking like I'm planning our lives on it! Not that that would be a bad thing ... but it's too soon ... but a good thing ... oh shit," he muttered, turning away.

Callie came over, taking him by the arm. "Your hands are sweaty," she giggled.

"Yeah, can't help it," he said, embarrassed.

"You're not the only one," Callie replied, taking his hand.

"You too?" Cole said, his voice an octave higher.

"Yep, me too!" Callie shrugged. "Cole, do you think that you're the only one who's nervous? I'm just as nervous as you are! We both just need to calm down and just go out and have fun! That's what tonight is all about, isn't it?"

"Yeah, I just want you to have a good time," he said quietly. "And you look exquisite," he finished, finally finding the right words.

* * *

They pulled up in front of the restaurant, with Cole turning the keys over to the valet. He linked arms with Callie and proudly escorted her inside. Unknown to them, heads turned as they walked in. They made a striking couple, in spite of the nervousness plaguing both.

"I hope I don't spill anything," he whispered in her ear.

"They'll clean it up!" she shrugged nonchalantly.

"I'm not used to eating with just an adult! I mostly eat dinner with Katie and end up wearing half of what I fix!" Cole laughed.

"I know! I heard that half the time all we have to do to find out what she had for dinner is to look at you! You wear it well!" Callie replied, giggling.

"This is nice," he looked around. "Just not used to fancy."

"You know what? Neither am I!" Callie said brightly, turning in a small circle as she took in the setting of the room.

"We're a pair, aren't we?" Cole grinned, pulling her back to him.

"The best! Cole, I don't need fancy things to impress me. Those things are overrated. Not that I'm knocking tonight! I'm dying to try French food! Only, how do we know we're not ordering brains or someone's legs or anything?" Callie asked, bewildered.

"You mean frog's legs?" Cole threw his head back, laughing.

"Oooh! I can't...." Callie winced, making a face.

"Wanna know something?" Cole leaned forward, smiling as he captured her hand.

"What?" Callie asked breathlessly, leaning forward to meet him.

"My parents used to love these fancy places when we went on vacation!" Cole explained. "My dad told me that it was good to know some of the finer things in life. We didn't have to make them the focal point of our lives, but it was nice to enjoy them once in a while. He said that we didn't have to stay buried on the ranch, that it was good to get out and enjoy some of life's luxuries once in a while. Plus, my Mom said that since I didn't know what my life would bring, it was good I knew these things."

"They sound like they were wonderful," Callie said wistfully.

"They were the best. Know what else?" Cole grinned crookedly.

"No, what?" Callie asked.

"My mother made me take ballroom dancing lessons! Matt's mother too! You see, my mom and Matt's mom were best friends and they got this wild idea that it would be good for us. Mom said that I wouldn't want to go through my life just square dancing!" Cole proclaimed proudly.

"Smart woman!" Callie tossed her head back, laughing lightly.

If she was curious about Cole before, she was totally enchanted now. Callie wanted to know everything about this man. She wanted to hear what he was like as a little boy and she wanted to get to know his mother and father through him. She bet that Cole's father must have been a magnificent man, judging from the way his son had turned out. Life had not beaten Cole down, it had tried, but he had bounced back. There was so much to say and so much to do, Callie felt that their night would go on endlessly once they started. She smiled in the soft candlelight, staring intently into his eyes. To her, endless was just fine.

"So, do you like it?" she wondered, wanting to know all she could about this man.

"What? Square dancing?" Cole stammered. "Can't square dance worth a lick," he admitted sheepishly.

"No, ballroom dancing!" Callie squealed.

"Oh! Well, you'll just have to wait till dinner is over to see," he winked, staring at her through the candlelight. "So, you trust me to do the ordering?" he asked with a twinkle in his eye.

Cole didn't take his eyes off of Callie all evening. It had been so long since he had been out with a woman, he felt as if he was in another world. Everything was new, strange, and exciting. He amazed Callie with his knowledge of the French language as he read the foreign-looking menu with ease and placed their orders.

"You never told me you spoke French!" she said excitedly.

"I don't! I only know how to read the menu and what the stuff is!" Cole laughed with her, taking Callie's hand.

"Well, at least we won't starve to death in France!" Callie teased, her eyes twinkling.

Everything was magical; the food tasted better and Cole had never seen anyone looking as beautiful as she. He laughed at the way her nose crinkled when the bubbles from the champagne tickled. Their table was bathed in soft candlelight, making her skin glow radiantly in the flickering light. Cole loved the way she tossed her hair back when she laughed, then lowered her head, staring intently at him as she coyly took a sip of wine.

"I can't believe you said that!" Callie laughed, hiccuping slightly.

"I can't believe you did that!" Cole teased, mimicking her.

"I can't help it! I get the hiccups when I drink! Don't make me laugh!" she giggled uncontrollably.

"I can't help it! I love the way you sound when you laugh," Cole said, quieting down. For once in his life, he didn't care that he drew curious stares from strangers. "No one's ever laughed at my jokes before!"

"You just haven't had the right audience before! But what about Will and Brent?" Callie asked teasingly.

"What about them?" Cole shot back.

"Don't they laugh at your jokes?" she asked.

"Hell no!" Cole burst out, laughing until his face was red. "Most of the time they stare at me as if I had two heads or something!"

His hand reached out, capturing hers. Their sides ached and Callie had tears in her eyes, which she dabbed at with the corner of her napkin while she tried controlling her breathing at the same time. If she could only calm down, even just a little, she just might not get a full-fledged case of hiccups. Cole's eyes sparkled devilishly as he stared, almost making it impossible for her to still the fluttering of her heart. It felt good to laugh like this, they both needed to laugh this way as much as they needed to be together. No matter how corny their jokes were, or what came out of their mouths, they were set off in peals of laughter. One squeaky hiccup was enough to attest to that fact. There must be something to be said about love after all. Everything was a little better.

* * *

The table was cleared and before dessert was served, music played softly in the background. Cole reached down, extending his hand. Callie felt like a queen as he held her hand high, formally escorting her onto the dance floor. He then swept her into his arms, their bodies melding as they started swaying to the soft, melodic strands. They moved fluidly, their hearts racing as they tried to control their smoldering passion.

Caressing the small of her back, he gracefully dipped her low, holding her for the briefest of moments, stark desire mirrored in his eyes as Cole slowly drew Callie back up to him, his hand sliding along her waistline. He held her arm out elegantly, then ran his fingers along her bare skin, sending tingles of desire coursing through Callie's body as he pulled her hand closer, holding it to his cheek. Their eyes locked, their breath mingled.

Callie had to lean her head back; Cole was so tall, she barely reached his shoulders. That didn't matter, though, anyone watching could see that they fit perfectly and were made for one another. Cole cradled her head to his chest, resting his cheek against her hair. The music was dreamy and faraway as they slipped into a world of their own, moving seductively as one. A moment in time.

One song led to another, but neither noticed. Cole could not ever remember feeling this way before, not even with Sarah. That thought shamed him for only a second, but then he put his mind elsewhere. He had loved Sarah deeply, but their romance had been quiet. Once Cole finally admitted his feelings to her, he and Sarah dated and before they knew it, they were announcing their engagement. Once married, they settled into Cole's home, where they began their lives together.

Time seemed to slip away, and they fell into a comfortable rut, working the ranch and running their home. Sarah then became pregnant, and they awaited the baby's birth. Cole had no way of knowing if he would have felt this way with Sarah. But this ... this was different. This was something he had never experienced before. He held Callie in his arms, feeling the smooth softness of her skin under his hand.

His thumb caressed her neck, sliding down over her shoulder to the hollow of her throat. Neither realized that he was even doing this, yet both were lost in the sensation. The music ended, and it was only the clapping of the crowd that brought the blushing couple back to reality. Over an hour had passed since Cole led Callie onto the dance floor; an hour that became lost in time as they became lost in one another, something neither of them would ever forget.

* * *

"It was magical," Callie whispered quietly. "I'll never forget how tonight felt."

"The food was good!" Cole teased. "I love duck."

"Oh you! I was talking about the dancing! I could have danced all night!" Callie sang.

"Wasn't that some actress? Ginger Rogers?" Cole teased.

Callie turned, staring defiantly. "I don't think it was Ginger Rogers! It was me! I could have danced all night!"

She opened the door, and Cole suddenly didn't know what to do. He wondered if Harve was watching, but his house was dark and that gave him a bit of courage. He simply did not know how to end tonight. He knew how he felt, but he didn't know what to do next. Callie led him inside, solving the problem for him. His body was raging; he needed her so badly, he ached. Before he could chicken out or change his mind, Cole grabbed her by the arm, pulling her to him.

His lips crushed down on hers, kissing her demandingly. Callie responded just as urgently, her body rubbing wickedly against his. Cole's tongue fought for and won dominance as she parted her lips, letting him inside. She was falling fast; this was what she had dreamt about for years, never thinking it would happen. Callie knew it would be like this, she knew he would taste this good. His mouth hungrily ground down over hers, the musky taste of him taking her away. Breathlessly, they broke apart, with Callie collapsing in his arms.

"Oh God, I want this so badly," Cole gasped, his mouth seeking hers again. "Callie, you're so beautiful! I always thought you were, I was just too stupid to really see! No, I saw I just...." he gave up, only to smother her with kisses again.

Callie gasped, arching backwards as Cole's lips traveled down her neck, stopping only a moment to lightly suck on her throat. Her legs began buckling beneath her, when she felt Cole drawing away.

"I'm sorry," he gasped, pulling back.

"What are you sorry for?" Callie exclaimed, reaching for him.

"I didn't want to move so fast! I mean, I want to, but it's not right!" Cole cried out. He was confused, but had never been so sure of anything in his entire life.

"It's not right?" Callie gasped, shocked slightly. "We've wanted this for years, what's not right about this? Cole, this is more than right! It's what I've dreamed about, it's what I've always wanted! There is no shame in giving yourself to someone you love. Deep inside, you know that! No one can say that this is wrong, because it isn't! All I've ever wanted was to be in your arms like this. Just love me! The hell with anything else...." Callie spoke rapidly, only to be cut off by his kisses.

Cole kicked off his boots and swept Callie up in his arms, carrying her in the direction of her bedroom. He wasn't sure at first, but she pointed the way. His mouth hungrily sought hers, only softer this time. He wanted to savor every moment, in spite of the way his body raged. Callie pressed herself against his need, causing Cole to blush at first, and then boldly grind himself into her. She swooned, not quite believing that this was happening, yet feeling every inch of him pressing against her, she knew that this was what she wanted.

He was bold and he was shy. They were just beginning the wonder of exploring one another, revealing themselves body, heart and soul as they came together. This was a slow, exhilarating process that lasted a lifetime. Cole blushed shyly at the thought of Callie seeing him for the first time and like the teenage boy he once again felt like, stupidly hoped that he measured up. Callie stared quizzically as he tossed his head back, laughing at himself.

"What?" she quipped.

Cole looked down, gently running his thumb along her swollen lips. "Nothing," he said softly. "Nothing at all."

For as much as he was revealing himself to her, Cole knew that Callie was revealing herself to him in a fashion that would never be shared with another. They were made for one another, so there was no need for shyness. There was no need for shame. The only need that existed between them was love.

His mouth hungrily, yet seductively took hers once again, with Cole breaking the deep kiss, only to lightly place little playful nips so soft, that she was hardly aware of his mouth on hers. "Callie, you're so beautiful. I never thought that this would happen. Are you sure? Are you absolutely sure?" he asked, fearful that this was indeed a dream.

"Please don't ask me that! Don't ever ask me that! Cole, I only want you, no one else! For as long as I live, I will never be with another. I'm not asking for anything that you can't give, and I'm not looking for promises. I just want what we have right now. I want to be with you. That's all I've ever wanted," she answered huskily.

He took her mouth more urgently, deepening their kiss until he held her in his arms, breaking the kiss once again. Cole gently caressed the side of her face, his fingers entwining in her hair. His body was screaming for him to hurry, he needed Callie, he wanted Callie, yet, he wanted to woo her. He wanted to discover her and see her for the beauty she possessed. Now that beauty was being revealed to him alone, and he felt his mouth go dry as his hand reached the end of her long tresses and fell softly to her shoulder, gently brushing the back of his fingers down the nape of her neck.

Callie moaned lightly, leaning her head into his touch, drawing back only when Cole gently let her blouse fall off her shoulders. She shimmered in the moonlight, her skin a soft creamy glow from the light of a full moon cascading down on them. He leaned over, placing tiny, feather-like kisses along the curve of her shoulder as he blazed a small trail to the hollow of her neck with his tongue before settling his mouth on silken skin, giving a little nip as he suckled gently.

Callie fought the urge to toss her head back screaming. She wanted him to hurry, yet she wanted this to last forever. She needed Cole; she was tired of waiting and needed him more than he would ever know. Each touch sent waves of pure, raw pleasure coursing through her. The tingling began in the pit of her stomach and slowly spread through her entire body, until she was quivering in his arms.

Feeling her growing weaker, Cole stood back up, leaning Callie back slightly as he rocked her to and fro in his strong arms. They danced slowly in the moonlight, with Cole holding her arm out to the side, their bodies sensuously brushing against one another. His other hand wrapped around her waist, pulling Callie close while he unsnapped her bra, his breath catching at her beauty. Callie stood in the moonlight with Cole's arms wrapped around her waist, her hair billowing out in the gentle breeze through the window.

Swallowing deeply, he lowered his head to her breasts. Nuzzling each one before his mouth rested on a nipple, his eyes glazed with passion as he slowly took her into his mouth. Callie strained backwards, a strangled cry breaking from her lips as an intensity that refused to be denied built between the two. This was something stronger and greater than both, there was no longer a way to deny their feelings, and there was no sense in fighting them anymore.

She stepped back, letting her blouse slide the rest of the way to the floor. Cole swallowed deeply, staring for a moment before he ran his finger down along her cheek and over her neck to the hollow of her bosom. Callie closed her eyes, losing herself in his touch. His finger blazed a trail down her body as Cole wickedly teased her beyond all the realms of reality. The world ceased to exist as their senses mingled. His hot mouth found her nipples, his tongue dancing over their hard peaks as he sucked. Callie cried out, arching backwards as his tongue slid across her chest, only to encircle her other nipple, pulling it between his teeth. He nibbled gently, setting spasms of desire surging through her body. Callie's legs started giving away as her first orgasm roared through her, causing her entire body to shudder, her heat emanating through the remainder of her clothes.

Cole lifted his head, grinning wickedly. He rolled her nipples between his fingers as he purposely ground his manhood into her. All shyness gone, he brazenly explored her body, wanting to make their first time together last, savoring every moment. His body tingled deliciously from deep within his groin as he thought of being inside her for their first time, burying himself in Callie's sensual warmth. Yet, he used every ounce of his meager self-will to control his raging need, taking her slowly. Running his hands down her waist, he let her skirt fall to the ground. Callie stood in a pair of black panties and garters. Cole groaned at the sight, losing whatever resolve he had. He almost cried out from the pain of his need. She reached her hand under his shirt, quickly undoing the buttons, and ripping the last few off.

"Sorry, I'll fix them," she gasped, locking her mouth on his nipple.

Having never had a woman do that to him before, Cole threw his head back, jamming his fist into his mouth to keep from crying out. The minute the buttons flew through the air, Cole knew that he was in trouble. There was no sense in giving Harve another show.

"He can't hear us, can he?" Cole teased, feeling Callie undoing his zipper. "Oh God," he gasped, falling to the floor. She was now the vixen, the one in total control and Cole was at her mercy, losing any and all control he had thought he commanded.

She laughed, collapsing on top of him. Cole reached for her, but she devilishly pushed him back down, straddling his legs. One moment the lady … the next, a wicked temptress … Callie was spinning her web and catching Cole in its sticky fibers. He was a mere shell of a man, lying helplessly under this tiny slip of a woman, powerless against her will. He could no longer fight her off and regain control of the situation as he could just get up and walk off like nothing had happened at all. Cole was trapped and he looked up, drowning in a pair of blue eyes that had turned almost silver with desire. Callie was playing the role of the vixen to the hilt, arching backwards and running her hands through her long hair. Cole's eyes were glazed with desire as he watched, feeling the heat from her body through the thin material of her panties. Before he could reach out and remove them, she did the very same thing to him.

With one fell swoop, Callie pulled his boxers off, freeing his raging erection and rendering Cole paralyzed. Reaching down, she clasped him firmly in her hands, his body quaking under her touch. Callie lowered her mouth onto his, licking his lips as she broke away, kissing and suckling her way down his body. She drew him into her mouth, feeling his hips bucking upwards furiously as she took him deep, working him until he was almost mute with pleasure.

Cole let Callie have her way; he couldn't have fought if he wanted to. Every touch sent shards of icicles surging through his veins, setting his skin on fire. Rendered helpless by the way her hot mouth ravished him, all he could do was gape mutely. Reaching the end of his control, Cole had to force himself to break away and catch his breath for a moment while he lowered Callie down onto the bed.

"My turn," he grinned wickedly. "Close your eyes and just soar with me," he said softly, brushing his hand over her eyelids.

Her eyes closed and she opened up to Cole, ready for his touch. Callie shuddered uncontrollably as he kissed his way down her body, slowly running his tongue along the soft skin on the inside of her thighs. She quivered, crying out. Cole drew her closer, inhaling her scent deeply and ignoring her pleas.

"Not yet, sweetheart. Getting there is half the fun," he said, his mouth finding the very core of her.

He kissed her through her panties, causing Callie to arch violently upwards while he ripped the thin material off. Tossing them aside with one hand, his mouth took Callie savagely with her writhing beneath him. She reached her peak, unable to hold back any longer as her body spasmed under his touch.

Cole grinned, kissing his way up her body. "Callie, I need you so much. God, I need to be inside you," he moaned, his warm breath fluttering softly against her cheek.

She wanted nothing more. This was what her body had been screaming for. The mere thought of Cole loving her in such a way made Callie shudder as his manhood pressed against her. Their bodies rocked together as Cole entered her slowly, teasingly. Callie cried out in need, the fire spreading from her loins and roaring through her entire body until she was nothing but a mass of quivering desire. She felt him filling her, bringing them together as she always dreamed, their bodies fusing and their minds soaring. They ceased being of this earth as they roared above the heavens, carried on a cloud of passion that bore them away. Passion and desire outweighed carnal need, making their union more intense as their love surged through them, uniting them, bringing both to heights never before imagined, yet dreamed about.

With every thrust, they became one, unrecognizable apart, but together, creating one being that was brought into a world that they created for each other. Hot, bated breath blew across their faces. Callie opened her eyes for just a moment, afraid that her dream would vanish. But he didn't go away. Cole's brown eyes bore into hers as his body filled her totally. She drowned in those eyes, seeing nothing but his love for her hidden in their depths. With a whisper of a smile his lips came down onto hers before they slid lovingly across the soft skin of her neck, coming to a rest on her breasts. He slowly enclosed his mouth around her nipple, suckling softly as the fire inside Callie grew, spreading golden liquid throughout her loins.

They soon lost control. Cole cried out, his body arching. Using every ounce of self-control, he fought to hold back. The feeling built deep in the pit of his stomach, thundering through him and banishing every ounce of control he might have had. With every stroke the intensity built until his body reached a fevered pitch, burning into Callie. Neither wanted this to end; yet they looked to the moment they were swept away. Callie felt Cole surging through her, his body stiffening momentarily, then rocking gently as sated spasms roared from deep within. She vaulted upwards, her own climax brought on by the feel of Cole giving himself to her, shuddering in her arms as he loved her with wild abandon.

"Oh God, I can't believe that happened," he finally gasped, holding her tight.

"I don't want it to end," Callie said dreamily, still clinging to Cole.

"Honey, it won't end! Nothing as beautiful as this can end. I love you," he whispered in her ear.

Callie felt her body quivering at the words, his hands caressing her gently until she calmed again. She thought she had dreamed the entire evening, especially when she finally had Cole in her arms. She wanted to pinch herself to see if she was dreaming, but did the next best thing.

"Owww!" Cole yelped, feeling her squeezing him wickedly. "What'd you do that for?"

"I wanted to see if I was dreaming, but I didn't want to pinch myself," Callie replied teasingly.

"So you pinched me?" he whined loudly.

"Yes! And I'll do more!" Callie warned emphatically. "And I'll never let you go! It's about time you said you loved me, Cole Morgan! I've only begun to have my way with you tonight! You just wait! I finally have you the way I want you! Naked and in my control!" she cried out possessively, shoving him onto his back.

All Cole could do was utter a muffled groan as Callie worked her way down his body again, surprised that he was able to respond after what they had just shared. His eyes rolled back into his head as she kept her word. He wondered at that moment if he would be able to handle her.

* * *

"Where you going?" Callie yawned, rolling over and reaching for him.

Cole kissed her softly, then sat up on the edge of the bed. Callie laid her head across his lap, softly stroking him while they talked. It was late, he had intended on leaving earlier, not wanting Harve to see him driving away in the early morning hours. Plus, he had his horses to take care of and needed to get home. Cole knew there was no worry where Katie was concerned, she was safe in Ruth's care. But he had an endless list of chores, including their weekly grocery shopping and the meeting that night, so he had best get moving.

He never meant to fall asleep, but had drifted off, holding Callie in his arms. She slept spooned around him, their legs entwined. He woke, feeling her soft body next to his, knowing that this was what he wanted for the rest of his life. Cole felt ready more now than he ever had, yet he was still determined to take his time. The soft afterglow of a night of love was not the time or place to make a lifelong commitment.

"It's late ... or early, whatever way you look at it," Cole smiled, looking down at her. "Go back to sleep."

"Don't wanna sleep," Callie moaned, her eyes closing again.

"Are you kidding? After last night, all I want to do is sleep!" Cole groaned, yawning.

"Then sleep," she mumbled.

"Can't, it's after four and I should have left long ago," he reluctantly replied.

"Why?" Callie asked.

"I don't want Harve to see me driving away!" Cole exclaimed.

"Too late, he probably already knows you stayed," Callie said, much to his dismay. Yet, she was right.

"Well, I still have to get back home and check on the animals. Would be getting up soon anyway for them. Plus, I have to pick up Katie, go grocery shopping, come back and put things away, take care of the stock and get ready for the meeting tonight," he moaned, already tired from just thinking about his day.

"Meeting? Oh, you mean about Sinclair," Callie yawned. "I don't like him."

"Not particularly fond of him myself," Cole rose, heading down the hallway into the bathroom.

Callie sprawled across the bed, waiting for him to come back out again. She was amazed at the way they felt so comfortable with one another. Neither needed to put on airs, trying to impress the other, and both were blatantly frank and open about themselves. She had never been shy or modest, but not knowing how Cole really was in private, she worried. How do two people share the most intimate moments of their lives with one another? She found that out when Cole closed the door behind him.

"Yep, he's definitely shy," Callie giggled, burying her face in the pillow.

Minutes later Cole emerged, pulling on his boxers and then his pants. He glared cautiously at Callie, purposely staying out of her reach. The need to get home before anyone saw him leaving was the only thing on his mind right now.

"What are you doing today?" he muttered, trying to stifle a yawn.

"Sleeping!" Callie exclaimed, rolling dreamily across the bed. "And then maybe try and get some things done here. Hopefully, the phone won't ring and I can have a quiet day!"

"Sounds nice," Cole answered, coming over to the side of the bed again. "You work too hard."

"I could say the same about you, but hard work is good for a person. Besides, when you really love what you do, how can you think of that as hard?" Callie reasoned.

Cole looked down into her eyes, seeing nothing but a pure love of life and everything it held for her hidden deep within their depths. This strange, captivating woman never ceased to amaze him. She was a mystery, one which would take the rest of his life to uncover, but would never fully reveal itself. She was a hardworking veterinarian on one hand, a lady on the other and a total temptress who gave uninhibitedly of herself. Callie knew how to live and she knew how to love; she did it all with a zest for life that had been lost to Cole for so long.

He felt reborn when they came together, as if a light had come on, shedding brightness and hope into his world. Now Cole knew how it really felt to start living again; he had begun to discover that the day Katie was born, and now his journey was complete. He knew where he was and what he wanted. Softly caressing Callie's face, he looked down.

"I've never met anyone like you before," he said softly. "No one has ever loved me the way you do and no one ever will again."

"I love you more than you'll ever know; I knew that the day I saw you riding out in your pasture," Callie fondly remembered. "Cole, I know how hard everything's been on you for so long, and I just want you to know that I won't push you for anything."

"You're not pushing me, I'm right where I want to be," he gently reassured her.

"I just want us to take our time, we're loving each other, we have each other and that's what really matters. Life is too short to worry about tomorrow and what we will do, say or decide. There's something to be said for living for today and that's what I intend on doing, I'm going to live for today and not worry about anything else. I have this gorgeous man who drives me wild, and it's going to be fun getting to know him," Callie said.

"Oh, you really want to get to know me?" Cole replied, with a teasing glint in his eyes. "Then you have to come over for dinner tonight! Katie and I make a wicked spaghetti!"

"With garlic bread?" her eyes lit up.

"Of course! What's spaghetti without garlic bread?" he exclaimed. "And she makes one hell of a salad!"

"I bet she does! But let me bring dessert, ok? You may be one hell of a cook, but I'm one hell of a baker!" Callie declared.

"You bake?" Cole quipped.

"Yes, I bake! I do more than spend my days running around chasing after sick animals and pacifying nervous owners!" Callie defended herself.

"Yeah, like last Sunday!" Cole laughed in spite of himself.

"Oh God, I'll never live that one down," Callie groaned, burying her head under a pillow.

"Know what?" he teased, tickling his way up her belly.

"What?" she groaned, peeking out from behind the pillow.

"When I saw you last Sunday, I couldn't help but think how beautiful you were even then," Cole replied, kissing her softly.

"But I was a mess...."

"You could never be a mess. In my eyes, you'll always be beautiful," he whispered, kissing her fervently.

* * *

Cole should have been too tired to function, yet he felt better than he had felt in a long time. Even the nights when he was lucky enough to sleep through undisturbed, he still felt tired and sluggish when he woke. He fought that feeling off, knowing that it was something more than just not getting enough sleep. He had functioned on less before. No, Cole knew that the fatigue he felt at times had more to do with the fact that there were still days when he just did not want to be a part of things. If it had not been for Katie, Cole figured that he probably would have turned totally inward. Now, he almost felt complete.

Driving home, Cole didn't know whether to be happy or ashamed of last night. He wanted Callie to know that he didn't just take her out and into bed to use her, he would never do that. Even though he hadn't been with a woman in over four years, Cole would not take advantage of someone like that; especially Callie. No, he wanted her to know the feelings that had been suppressed and denied for too long. Something happened to him last night, something that changed him drastically. The more he thought about it, the more he wondered if it was just last night, or if it was something that had been building and just finally decided to face things for what they were.

There was something to be said for putting your fears aside and just diving right into life; when he married Sarah, Cole had never planned on spending his life alone. After her death, he not only feared for his sanity, but for his very life. If anyone could take that away, Cole knew that it would be by his own hand. He had lost too much too fast and did not want to go on. Yet, something had drawn him to Maggie. Cole was afraid of being alone, even though there was no love shared between the two. For one night, each had something to give the other. That night, Cole just needed someone.

"Then why her? Why did I hook up with Maggie so quickly but I fought my feelings for Callie?" he asked himself.

Maybe because Maggie gave you companionship without love.

What in the world do you mean by that?

What I mean is that love's the real thing, and the real thing can be scary and it hurts. It's easier to just pick up a relationship with someone based on sex, mutual need and loneliness than it is to start one based on love. Those other things draw you together, filling a primordial need in you both. But you don't love; you don't love because you know how much that love hurts when it's taken away. Yet, you're afraid to stay alone. So in order to keep one fear at bay, you turn to someone you don't love in order to try and fill a void in your life. You were just too afraid to go after the real thing.

Would have been easier to stay alone, he grimaced.

Then you wouldn't have Katie, he reminded himself.

"Yeah, she's the only thing that made all this worthwhile," Cole muttered, thinking of his daughter.

"It's about time you realized that! You should have come to your senses long ago, but I guess it's better late than never," he exclaimed, knowing that he was right.

Yet, Cole did not want to commit to Callie; at least not right away. The thought alone was too frightening, he just wasn't ready to consider that option. Besides, he reasoned that even though they had known one another for years, they had only gone out once. That was not enough to build a future on, in spite of their feelings. He needed time, yet he needed her. And now everyone would expect him to take the next step; especially since they all knew that he had been with her. No one could keep a secret in this town.

216

Even if they had not seen his truck at her house for more than half the night, they all knew about the date and one thing would inevitably lead to the other. What would everyone think of him now, knowing that he had bedded Callie, but was not willing to take things any further?

As usual, Cole had just created a new worry to mull over, as if he didn't have enough. That was his problem half the time; he had a penchant for worrying things to death, mulling them over and over until he drove himself into a frenzy. He just did not know how to sit back and let things take their course. Now he worried about what everybody expected him to do where Callie was concerned. It was only natural; it wasn't right for him to just take her out on a date and into bed afterwards, proclaiming that he loved her and then not doing anything about it.

Then he had Katie to consider. She didn't even know that he was serious about Callie. First of all, she probably would not understand, but she loved Callie and once Cole started bringing her around on a regular basis, then Katie would know that something had changed. She was only a child, but she was smart. She saw other families where they had both a mother and father and Cole knew that it would only be a matter of time before she started asking where her mother was.

"Man, now what do I do?" he moaned, pulling into his place.

What you do, asshole, is relax and take things one day at a time, he chided himself. *Who the hell says she's ready to walk down the aisle with you anyway? Awfully presumptuous, aren't you?* Cole's inner self chided.

"Yeah, but you know that she won't say no," he groaned. Leaning on the wheel, Cole just sat and fought with himself before getting out. "Listen to me! I'm talking to myself!"

Wouldn't have to if you talked to someone else, his inner voice snidely remarked.

"The scariest thing is, I'm even answering myself," Cole shook his head.

You got answers? That's news to me, the voice clucked.

"All right! So I don't have all the answers, but I'm not a total imbecile! Callie's loved me for years, I knew that even before I took her out last night. I just never admitted it. But like you said, not now! I have too many other things to do and think about today. First of all, I need to take care of the animals and then get showered and dressed. Then I have to go get Katie, have breakfast with Ruth and go shopping. God, don't even want to think about the rest of the day. It's a good thing I don't check things off and look at a list at the beginning of the day; I'd never want to get out of bed. It's easier to do one thing and then go on to the next without thinking about it," Cole shook his head, muttering to himself the entire time.

Chapter Eleven

So his day began. Soon the horses were finished, with Cole noticing how well Brent had taken care of things. He had never given that a thought, knowing how conscientious his friend was when it came to animals. The barn had been secured and all the horses were in their stalls, brushed down and fed for the night. Cole opened the barn, then walked through flinging open the doors leading out into the corral. Minutes later, horses were spilling out into the early morning sun, romping in the fields while Cole mucked out their stalls. Then they were fed and brushed down for the day.

The rest could wait; Cole desperately needed a shower and wanted to get over to Ruth's. He missed Katie more than he ever thought possible. This wasn't the first night she had spent away from him, but it never got easier. The ranch just wasn't the same without her running around, singing her silly songs and playing. His life wasn't the same without that.

It did not take long for Cole to shower and drive over to Ruth's, where they would enjoy a quick breakfast before he and Katie went off on their shopping spree. This way, they could be home by noon, which would be a blessing compared to last Saturday. Slapping his forehead, he remembered the necessity for a babysitter later that night. Cole hated asking Ruth again; she would do it with no problem, but she had been taking care of Katie almost nonstop all week long and then kept her for the entire night last night. In his mind, Ruth needed a break.

"Ahh, will think about it later," he grumped. "Hey punkin'!" Cole cried out, gathering Katie in his arms.

She had heard her daddy pulling in and ran down the front walk, dragging Bunny behind her and wearing her bracelet on her wrist.

"Hi Daddy! Did you go someplace fun?" she asked, tickling his face with her fingers.

"Yes, Daddy went someplace fun for grown-ups, but I don't think you would have liked it. Did you have fun here?" he grinned, nipping at her fingertips.

"Papa and Uncle Brent were here! We drew pictures and had ice cream. I showed Papa my flowers!" Katie proudly stated, holding up her wrist.

"Did you sleep with them on?" Cole asked, his eyes narrowing teasingly.

Katie nodded her answer and wriggled out of his arms, running back up the flagstone walkway with Bunny bouncing along behind her. Cole followed, shaking his head at her exuberant energy as he greeted Ruth on his way in.

"Did you have fun?" Ruth asked, trying not to smirk.

"Did you talk with Harve?" Cole demanded teasingly.

"Why, yes I did! As a matter of fact, we had a nice long talk!"

"I bet you did," Cole glared sideways.

"Are you going to answer my question?" Ruth asked again, relentless in her quest for the truth.

"Give me a cup of coffee and I just might tell you," Cole bribed, following her into the kitchen.

"Daddy, did you eat frogs?" Katie asked, skipping over.

Cole sputtered, almost choking on his coffee. He felt some of the hot liquid going up his nose and wiped it on his sleeve. Ruth handed him a napkin and a look of reproach.

"Sorry," he smirked, seeing her soften. No matter what, Ruth simply couldn't seem to get mad at or stay mad at him. "Now, where did you get the idea that I ate frogs? Or need I ask?" he addressed Katie, knowing that Brent had paid her a visit the previous night.

"Uncle Brent," Katie answered innocently.

"What does a bug eater know?" Cole groaned, casting another apologetic look at Ruth.

"Then what did you eat?" Katie asked, still not giving up.

Cole couldn't help himself; thoroughly delighting in the look on his daughter's face when he rattled off the menu. Seeing the shocked surprise in Ruth's eyes was an added bonus.

"Well, we had *les feuilletés d'asperge, salade verte, magret de canard au poivre vert, haricots verts au naturel* and then for dessert we had *gateau glacé aux noix*."

Sitting back, Cole stared at the two; this time it was his turn to smirk.

"Did you eat that?" Katie asked, her eyes growing wide. "What is it?"

Cole almost fell out of his seat laughing at that remark. "So, you want to know what it is, huh Katie bug?"

"I would too! Lord, I had no idea you could speak French!" Ruth said, still amazed.

"I don't speak French! I can only read the menus!" he laughed with her. "You should have seen the look on Callie's face! She looked like you two do now!"

"What was it, Daddy?" Katie persisted.

"Honey, it's French," Cole answered, seeing the look of confusion still in her eyes. "Honey, that means it's from a country named France. Never mind, one day you'll understand. Anyway, it's the type of food that they eat and all it is was asparagus with chives and butter sauce, then we had a green salad. After we finished with that, we had roast duck with green peppercorn sauce and boiled green beans. Oh, and for dessert we had frozen walnut cake!"

"We had hamburgers," Katie answered, still trying to make heads and tails out of what Cole had told her.

"Well, hamburgers sound fine. They're almost my favorite food! Did Papa come for dinner?" he asked, winking at Ruth.

"He brought the hamburgers," Katie replied between mouthfuls of cereal.

"That sounds like fun! Hamburgers and ice cream!" Cole exclaimed brightly.

"It was a nice night, honey," Ruth beamed. "One of the nicest I've had in a long time. Gris and Brent decided that I needed a break from cooking so they brought over burgers and fries for all of us and then we had a quiet evening coloring and just visiting. And I can't forget the ice cream!"

"Chocolate!" Katie announced.

Cole dug into the plate of bacon and eggs Ruth prepared, listening intently to his daughter's evening. Soon Katie finished and ran off into the living room to watch her morning cartoons. She was as comfortable here as in her own home; for that, Cole was forever grateful, he could at least provide a grandmother figure. Ruth smiled as she watched Katie through the doorway, seeing her settling down on the floor.

"She was such a good girl! And good company! It was so nice having her here," Ruth said softly, wishing that last night had never ended.

Her home now had the love and laughter of a child, something that was more than long overdue. Ruth felt that her house had ached for the kind of companionship that she, herself, had always yearned for. A home needed a child running through, and while other women complained about the fingerprints on their walls, Ruth treasured them. She also treasured the night she and Katie had just spent together, watching television quietly after the men left. Katie didn't stay awake much longer, but Ruth didn't have the heart to put her in bed. She just picked Katie up and held her close while they rocked. Ruth's rocking chair was another thing that was no longer lonely. It, too, now had a baby to hold.

Cole saw how quiet Ruth became for a moment, almost laughing at the faraway look that shone into her eyes. But he didn't. No one knew that feeling better than he; Katie gave both him and Ruth something they needed, without even realizing it. She was just a little girl, doing what little girls did best ... spreading that love to whomever she touched.

"I'm glad," Cole smiled back. "And I'm glad that Gris and Brent brought dinner over! I never expected that!"

"I didn't either, to tell you the truth!" Ruth laughed with him. "I was going to cook, but he called and told me that I better not! Now, what about you? Did you really have a great night?"

Cole leaned forward, talking quietly. "Well, at first I almost chickened out. I drove right past her road!"

"Oh Cole," Ruth clucked.

"Now, you know from Harve that I ended up there eventually," he reminded her. "Anyway, we had a really good time."

"Is that all?" she raised her eyebrows.

"Well, dinner was good and we had some wine and we danced," he answered back, still eating.

"And?" Ruth queried.

"And we finished dinner and I drove her home," Cole shrugged.

"You drove her home...." Ruth smiled teasingly.

Cole put his fork down and took her hand, "All right, I can't and won't lie to you. But please don't go reading anything into it, ok? You and I both know that I have feelings for Callie...." he began, seeing her knowing stare. "All right, I ... I love her," he finished softly.

"I know," Ruth replied, squeezing his hand. "I know you do, honey," she smiled back at him.

They finished their breakfast in silence.

* * *

Cole and Katie finally pulled into their driveway, tired and hungry. She ran up onto the porch while he walked over to the barn. Brent's truck was in their driveway and Cole met his friend as Brent made his way out of the building.

"Hey, what brings you over?" Cole greeted him with a handshake and a smile.

"Dropped off that liniment I borrowed last week," Brent smiled back. "Was hoping to find you home, but you weren't here so I just put it in the cabinet. Thanks for letting me borrow it."

"Cow better?" Cole asked.

"Yeah, was just a pulled, sore muscle like we thought. Thank God, would have hated to have another vet bill on our hands," Brent said, wiping the sweat from his brow. "Need a hand?"

"You offering?" Cole grinned.

"Only if you bought something good for lunch," Brent grinned, evading a straight answer.

"Ham and cheese sandwiches and chips is about it," Cole answered.

"Sounds good to me!" Brent brightened, grabbing three of the bags.

Katie ran over and opened the door for the men, who staggered onto the porch, trying not to spill their contents.

"And I wanna thank you for taking care of things last night," Cole turned to Brent again.

"Glad to do it. So, did you two have a good time?" Brent couldn't help but ask.

"Daddy ate funny stuff," Katie wrinkled her nose.

"What kind of funny stuff?" Brent wanted to know.

"Ducks and other things I can't say," Katie shrugged.

"Ducks! Daddy went out and ate ducks?" Brent teased.

"Yep, and a frozen cake," Katie suddenly remembered. "And something green!"

"See! I told you he ate frogs! Frogs are green!" Brent triumphantly announced.

"Daddy! You said you didn't eat frogs!" Katie squealed.

"Honey, I didn't eat frogs! I told you it was a green sauce!" Cole exclaimed.

"Yeah, made of frogs," Brent quipped.

"It was a frog sauce!" Katie joined in.

"It was a peppercorn sauce!" Cole defended himself. "And it was good! I didn't eat anything that had to do with frogs!"

"Hey, did you have any of that escar stuff?" Brent cringed.

"You mean *escargot*?" Cole asked.

"Yeah! That's the stuff!" Brent burst out.

"What is that, Uncle Brent?" Katie asked, tugging on his sleeve.

"Honey, it's snails!" Brent replied.

"Ewwwww! Daddy, you ate snails!" Katie shrieked, clamping her hand over her mouth.

"Honey, first of all they're really supposed to be a good dish," Cole tried explaining, but seeing the look in her eyes, he knew that she had already made up her mind. "No, I didn't eat snails."

"They're gooey! And dirty!" she declared.

"Honey, I didn't eat any snails and if we don't get this stuff put away, we won't be eating any lunch either," Cole stated. "Thanks a lot," he grumbled, pushing past Brent, who shrugged slightly, feigning innocence.

As soon as they finished eating, Cole cleared the table and put Katie down for her nap. Tossing a cold beer over to Brent, they went out to sit on the porch. "You gonna tell me about last night?"

"Nope!" Cole stated.

"That's ok. It's already all over town that your car was there till almost dawn," Brent laughed, seeing the way Cole seemed to sink lower in his chair.

"You gonna be at the meeting tonight?" he asked, quickly changing the subject.

"Oh yeah, the meeting," Brent quickly sobered. By the way, you seen Sinclair around lately?"

"Come to think of it, I haven't. But I haven't been to town either, so who knows! Has anyone spoken with Ed about the argument he had with Sinclair in his office that day?" Cole wondered.

"Yeah, last night Gris said that all Ed would tell him was that it was just a conflict of interests," Brent shrugged.

"That's it?" Cole asked, his curiosity piqued.

"So he says," Brent shrugged. "You know, I feel like Sinclair is a vulture, hovering and waiting to pick us clean."

"He ain't gonna find it that easy to pick me clean and if I have my way, he won't be doing anything to anyone else around here either. Can't help but wonder who he works with though. I mean, first Walt's place and then mine? Gotta have bucks and a plan to want land like this," Cole said.

"Yeah, but what?" Brent asked. "And why don't they just take no for an answer? It's not like any of us are going to sell. Besides, there's plenty of places where folks want to sell, so why not go there?"

"I have no idea, I can't see bringing any type of industry into the area. The population just isn't that great. Anyway, I'm gonna go take a nap and do some thinking on the subject. I'll see you later, ok?" Cole rose, stretching and yawning.

"Yeah, you look a little peaked," Brent laughed under his breath. "Night Sleeping Beauty!"

* * *

Everyone was gathered by the time Cole drove in. Brent and Will strode over to his truck, greeting him heartily. He felt bad that he held things up by being the last one to arrive, but it couldn't be helped. Katie had taken a longer than usual nap, and so had he. Cole simply wasn't used to late nights like the one he'd had, and avoided the teasing looks tossed his way as he walked up to the porch, blushing from head to toe.

It had been almost four o'clock when he and Katie woke up and Cole still hadn't made any arrangements where she was concerned. To his surprise, both Callie and Ruth showed up at his door.

"I wasn't expecting you!" he exclaimed, giving Ruth a peck on the cheek. "Oh no! Dinner! Callie, I forgot all about dinner!" Cole suddenly exclaimed, running his hand through his tangled hair.

"Looks like we woke you," she giggled.

"No, I woke up a few minutes ago," he said apologetically, "but I didn't get anything started yet!"

"We figured as much, that's why I came over with Ruth," Callie smiled, breezing into the kitchen.

"What did you two do?" Cole asked, following close behind.

"Honey, we knew that you had a busy day today, so we decided to surprise you," Ruth explained. "We're just glad that you didn't start cooking yet!"

"If I did, then we could have put it away for tomorrow, cause what you guys brought smells a heck of a lot better than anything that I could have done," he sniffed appreciatively. "But neither of you had to go through so much trouble," Cole winked at them.

"You have that meeting tonight, don't you?" Ruth said.

"Yeah, but—" Cole hedged.

"No buts! We have business to take care of and I thought from the get go that I'd be watching Katie and asked Callie to come over so we could keep each other company. Don't you worry, Gris dropped me off and he's going to bring me home so you don't have to argue about me walking back in the dark," Ruth said, putting an end to any arguments before they could start.

"I don't want you walking home in the dark! And thank you," Cole said, kissing Ruth soundly on the cheek.

He went in to shower while she and Callie got their dinner heated up. Ruth had known of his busy day and spent the afternoon making a chicken casserole and a salad. Callie set her blackberry cobbler on the counter and went about brewing a fresh pot of coffee and setting the table, humming to herself as she worked. A loaf of fresh-baked bread was sitting on the table and Katie stumbled from her bed, rubbing her eyes.

"Come to Nanny, honey," Ruth cooed, taking the small child in her arms.

Taking Katie to the front porch, Ruth rocked her while Cole went into the barn. After a few minutes, she woke fully and was anxious to climb down and play. The horses were soon tended and before leaving, he would bring them in. With a wink as he jogged back into the house, Cole headed straight for the shower.

Finally dressed and ready, he came into the kitchen, where the women and a table laden with food greeted him. The meal was thoroughly enjoyed by all, as was everything Ruth made. Then Katie got ready for her bath, Cole closed the horses up in the barn and kissed the women goodbye, blushing and staring defiantly at Ruth after the kiss he gave Callie. She clucked her tongue knowingly as she turned to watch Katie, who was too busy running in the yard to have seen. They waved goodbye and sat back down with their coffee, while he drove off.

Cole arrived at the meeting late and anxious to get started. The problem was, no one knew where things stood. They were worked up, but with no good reason. Sinclair had done nothing wrong except to rattle their cages. He had made an offer on Walt's land, which was refused, he then made an offer on Cole's land but was driven off, and he had a fight with Ed. Was that enough to warrant all this strife?

"Yeah, but did anybody actually see him leaving town?" Cole asked, looking around. The familiar unexplainable dread began in the pit of his stomach, leaving him troubled.

"No, not that we can say," Walt shrugged.

"I know that he didn't check out of the motel," Jared Beams informed them. "I'd know! My brother-in-law would have told me. Lars said that Sinclair's been paying his bill day by day, but he left very early Thursday and hasn't been seen since. He also didn't formally check out, so Lars has no idea whether to hold the room or not. Seems like Sinclair stuck him for a night."

"Could be he just gave up and is out preying on someone else," Cole shrugged.

They eventually drifted into Walt's spacious dining room. Walt had taken his usual seat at the head of the table, with Zach to his right. Cole sat on the left, with Will next to him. In his usual manner, Brent was too wired to sit, so he mostly stood on the other side of Zach, pacing the floor or leaning over his chair. Everyone else gathered around the table, with Gris taking the seat at the other end, watching over them all. A pot of coffee and a platter of homemade pastries sat in the middle, but for the time being, beer was the drink of choice. Once the meeting was over, then they would share a hot cup of the steamy brew and tackle the baked treats. Right now, they had other things on their mind. Everyone was quiet for a moment as they contemplated Cole's words.

"I'd like to think he's gone, but what if he isn't?" Brent shot back. "I mean, no one's seen him and he hasn't been back to the hotel since Thursday, but does that mean he's gone? And it doesn't mean that he won't come back!"

"Why do you think that?" Gris asked.

"Cause nothing like this has ever happened here before, that's why!" Brent replied. "No one has ever come nosing around like he did and even though he left peacefully, I still don't like or trust the man!"

"You haven't dealt with him," Will reminded Brent.

"No, but just seeing him was enough to set me on edge. I can tell by looking at the fellow that I don't like the looks of him...."

"I should have thought of that the first time I laid eyes on you," Will snickered with Cole.

"Very funny! Now he makes jokes!" Brent exclaimed.

"Boys, can we manage to convene this meeting in a civil manner?" Gris groaned.

"Sorry, Gris, he just don't have any manners," Brent grumbled.

It was on the tip of Cole's tongue to correct his wayward friend's grammar, but he thought better of it, knowing that would only set off another argument. If there was one thing about Brent they had all learned over the years, it was that when he became upset or nervous, he always shot off his mouth. It was a given. He just couldn't help himself. Starting an argument with his friends was just his way of letting off steam.

"All right," Cole stepped in. "We've all been on edge since he came to town and we don't like the fact that he came nosing around asking questions that were none of his business. But does that make what he did so bad?" he asked, looking around the room. "Anyway, like Gris pointed out, he didn't push the issue and he left both mine and Walt's place peacefully. But does that mean he won't come back? Maybe he had other business elsewhere that he had to attend to and he'll be back. I don't know. It seems funny that he paid his bill every day and then stiffed Lars for the one last night. But maybe the bastard ran out of money...."

"Or maybe he drove into one of the mud bogs," Brent snickered. "Dumb shit was out scouting the area!" he scoffed, snickering with Will.

"Could be, but we'll never know. I just have this sinking feeling...."

"So did he!" Brent blurted out, unable to help himself as both he and Will broke out in raucous laughter.

Glaring impatiently, Cole cleared his throat and continued. "Like I said, since he came with offers for our land, I doubt if he would have left so quickly. I mean, it takes a while to get familiar with these areas. And why did he come to Walt first? Then me? Our ranches are the furthest from town, so why did he choose us? Everyone else is in the other direction, but he came here. It seems funny to me. If he were to bring some malls or industry to the area, one would think he would stick closer to town, not out in the middle of nowhere!" Cole pointed out.

"Maybe he doesn't have a mall in mind," Will pointed out.

"Well, he had something in mind and even though he seems to have left, I'd like to know what he wanted," Cole nodded.

"You and me both," Brent grumbled. "Wonder what the hell he's doing with his time."

"That's what I'd like to know," Zeke replied. "But I'd also like to know the reason for all the panic. Someone comes and makes an offer on two places, is told no and then leaves? Why this meeting and why all they worry?"

This time, it was Cole who stepped in. "Not panic in a sense, just being wary, I suppose is the way to put it. Zeke, I've seen this type of thing before. Some guy comes along representing a business or developer or just a person with a lot of money and starts making offers and buying up people's homes. Nothing wrong with that. The only way for some industries, developments or malls and such to be built is done that way. I've seen lots of places that used to be farms or ranches that are now large developments. The owner sells his land and leaves with the money; it's done all the time. But the thing is, we don't want that here, at least I don't."

"Me neither," Brent jumped in.

"I can do without it," Walt agreed.

"Zeke, the real reason for this meeting is to see where we all stand," Cole explained. "I know our feelings border on paranoia, and I'm sorry to get everyone so worked up, all I want to do is discuss what happened. Now, I know that everyone here except me has been in their homes their entire life. But I love my place just as much and can't ever imagine living anywhere else. My daughter was born here and this is all she knows. I want to raise her here, giving her a sense of security, a place to call home where she knows and loves everybody. I guess what I'm trying to say is that I plan on staying and just wanted to know how everyone felt."

"Why would you even think we'd leave, Cole?" Zeke asked of him.

"Cause I've seen people who have been in their homes all their lives and have sold. And when you're dealing with a developer who's buying the land for a specific reason, it only creates problems for all. He needs all the land from the folks he's made offers to and if only one sells, then it makes a hardship for the buyer and for those left behind. Hard feelings all around, you know? He needs the rest of the land and sometimes goes ahead with his plans anyway. There's this guy in Wyoming who did that, name was Culver. He bought some land and started putting up this strip mall. One of the other ranchers held out and only suffered cause of it," Cole replied.

"How so?" Brent leaned forward.

"First of all, the traffic to the mall cut right in front of his place. It just wasn't safe for him to ride on what used to be a quiet country road anymore, there was always garbage thrown all over the place where there never was before and the noise from the cars was overwhelming. Before the mall, the only cars that passed by his place were the former owners of the property. Then, he was bombarded. Not only that, people began screwing around on his land, especially teenagers who loved to scare and torment the animals," Cole answered.

"See?" Brent proclaimed, looking around. "It starts that way! You get one person caving in to these guys and then once people start coming around, everything goes to shit! Cole, did this happen where you lived?"

"Yeah, but it wasn't Sinclair," Cole shrugged. "This guy named Culver came along and bought up some of the land. He sent out his so-called spokesperson to all the ranches, but like here, he didn't have it easy. Two of our neighbors sold. One was one step away from having his farm taken over by the bank and the other was an easy buy. It was the Hendershots' place and Sam Hendershot just inherited the land from his father. Sam was young and impressionable and when he got the offer from Culver, he took the money and ran. Culver sure knew how to play people! That's where the mall went up, choking the life out of Ted Raines, the rancher I told you about."

"Is he still there?" Walt wondered.

"I have no idea," Cole shuddered, growing quiet for a moment.

"What's wrong?" Will asked.

"Well … God that time is a blur to me! I know that this guy started coming around asking about the same things as Sinclair, but none of us wanted to sell. He came to me first. I refused. Then he went to Matt's place and he refused. But for some reason, he came to my place a few times," Cole said brokenly.

"He do anything?" Brent wondered out loud.

Cole was quiet for a few minutes while they quietly waited for his answer. "You know, I haven't given that time much thought, it was right before … anyway I haven't given it much thought lately, cause what happened just didn't matter anymore. But this guy who made the original offer came back a few more times, pleading for me to sell. I refused and then had a visit from a two other 'gentlemen' who worked for the buyer. We got into it a few times, but it never went further than that. Their boss wanted my land, I wouldn't sell, then Sarah died. After that, I didn't give a damn about them or what they wanted. Everything else sort of fell apart and I just sold the place and left. Just didn't care anymore."

"Who did you sell it to?" Brent asked.

"Don't really know, I just went to the real estate in town told them that the place was for sale and signed the papers; then I was gone. I didn't care who bought it and I never looked back or asked. Nothing else mattered; I never checked back to see what happened with the offers or anything. For all I know, it could have been the same guy who made the first offer, cause that's the only thing that makes sense now as to why it sold so fast. My broker knew of the offer and probably went to them, saying they could have it. That's about all I know. Everything from that time is so jumbled in my mind, I can't make heads or tails of it," Cole frowned, more confused and unsettled when he finished.

"That's ok, Cole, no one can be expected to think straight and pay attention to such matters at a time like that," Walt comforted the man. "What do you want of us here?"

"Walt, all I can remember about that time is that none of us united. Matt and I bitched about this guy coming around, but that's all we did. We didn't get together and talk about it. We didn't know if any of our neighbors would sell or not. I knew that a few might have been persuaded and I knew of others who wouldn't leave for anything. What we need to do here is let one another know of our intentions. This way, we know where we stand. Me, I won't sell no matter what. I'm not uprooting my daughter and I'm not starting over somewhere else. I've already done that and don't have the energy or the desire to do it again. I love it here, this is my home. I just want to know who's making these offers, what they want with the land, and where all of you stand," Cole finished, looking around at their faces.

"Well, you know where I stand," Brent replied. "Dad and I aren't going anywhere. I plan on running the place long after he's gone and hope that my kids do the same."

"That's right," Cal agreed with his son. "I'm passing the place on to my son here and no one can change my mind."

"I was born in this house," Walt said quietly. "It's the only thing I know. I wouldn't know how to live anywhere else. My next home will be a pine box when the good Lord calls me home."

"And when I'm grown I ain't selling either," Zach insisted, looking at his father. "I'm going to run the place just like Dad here and then pass it down!"

"You know my answer," Will nodded, not needing to say anything else.

"And mine," Jared stepped in.

Everybody became quiet, noticing the upset Zeke was experiencing. Shaking his head futilely, he stared questioningly at Cole. "What are we doing here, again?" he asked, his voice trembling.

Expecting such confusion due to his injury, yet unwilling to leave Zeke out of tonight's meeting, Will placed his hand reassuringly on the man's shoulder and, once again, explained the reason for their gathering. "It's all right, Zeke, we're just discussing this Sinclair fella. Wants to buy our land, remember?"

"That's right," Cole interjected. "No trouble, we're just seeing where everyone stands. He hasn't caused any trouble, and all we want to know is whether the other will sell," he explained, just as patiently as the others.

"That's right, Zeke, and don't you go worrying any, remember, we all watch out for one another, right?" Walt asked, looking around.

"No other way to be," Brent nodded reassuringly.

"Just wish that Kaitlin could've been here," Zeke replied. "Sometimes I get lost," he finished sadly.

"Hell, Brent's been lost for years!" Will snorted, in spite of himself.

His remark might have gotten a look of reproach from his friend, but it brought a smile to Zeke's face. Sometimes the man remembered everything like it had been yesterday. He never forgot his past, remembered every little detail of his life from the time he was old enough for recognition to set in, his marriage, and the birth of his daughter, Kaitlin, but the here and now sometimes became muddled. No one minded, and everyone sought to put him at ease.

"You know, I'm too old, stubborn and set in my ways to start over somewhere else. Besides, where would I go? Don't know anywhere else and don't want to know," Zeke replied, now pacified and more confident. "Nope, this is my home and no one can take that away. Don't give a damn how much money they got. This place gets in your blood, no place on earth can make me as happy as living here. At 49, am too damned old for changes! My daddy started our ranch and by God, I'm gonna keep it going. Only difference being is that my place will be passed down to Kaitlin. But don't go selling her short! She'd be here tonight, but there was too much work back at the ranch, so she sent me along," he chuckled, grateful for a moment of remembrance.

If anything, 26-year-old Kaitlin was as headstrong and set in her ways as her father. She resembled him in every way, except stature. For that, she could thank her mother, who stood only five-foot six inches tall, and weighed no more than 120 pounds. Her face was tanned to a deep bronze and her deep brown hair shone red from a lifetime spent outdoors, working from sunup until sundown. She could ride, rope and brand cattle just as well as any man sitting there, and was taken just as seriously.

Every chore involved with a ranch, from keeping the books, tending the animals and stacking bales of hay, was handled as capably as any man.

Everyone knew that Kaitlin was also as stubborn as her father and there was no way she would ever sell. Their property was sandwiched in between Brent's ranch and the mountains. If one or the other of them ever sold, then it would cause problems; everyone could easily see that and no one wanted such a thing to happen. Now that they knew of each other's intentions, it was time to band together.

"Well, now that we know where everyone really stands, all we have to do is run this Sinclair guy out of town," Brent replied.

Gris, who had been sitting quietly taking everything in, decided that it was his turn to talk. "I've been listening and I agree with all of you. The thing to remember here is that we shouldn't lose sight of our tempers. I've seen it happen with things like this, we're defending our homes and feel no one has the right to come in and take it over."

"No one does!" Brent argued back quickly.

"Easy there, Brent! I wasn't implying anything," Gris interceded, holding up his hand. "All I'm saying is that the basic question here seems to be who this Sinclair guy is and who is he working for. I'll have my office do a little checking. You know, I've heard of where things like this go bad, yet not all the folks who come out looking for land to start building something are that way. Most of the time it's something simple as a businessman who wants to expand or a developer who sees a lot of land for a lot of houses and the dollar signs start blinking in front of him. It's only natural that they ask. They know we're not going to come to them, so they come to us. We say yes, we say no, and they accept our answers and try elsewhere."

"I suppose you're right, Gris, since this Sinclair guy has done nothing more than go to Walt and come to me, I don't mean to get everyone worked up," Cole apologized.

"Cole, you're not getting anyone worked up," Gris reassured him. "We need to talk this out! We don't know Sinclair, he drives into town and it's only natural we want to know the answer to those questions. It's also only right for all of us to get together and talk about what one's intentions might be; especially considering that the decision they'll make will impact on all of us. It's only natural to want to know where we all stand. I just say let's not panic, ok?"

"Gris, I know you're right and all, but this is just unsettling to me," Brent shuddered. "We're just not used to strangers poking around!"

"No, we're not," Gris agreed. "But let's not jump to conclusions and get out the lynching rope yet, ok? He's probably just someone trying to make a living like we are. Not everyone lives on a ranch making their way in that manner! Some folks get out there and see what they can scrounge up. There's all types of walks of life and all out there, let's not go flying off simply cause one comes to us."

"Let's not bury our heads in the sand, either," Brent continued to argue. "Look, Gris, we're not going off on this guy and skinning him alive or anything, we just want to know what he wants with us!"

"I'd still like to know where the hell he is," Will worried.

"Been thinking about that," Cole answered between sips of beer. "Maybe he's just out scouting around other areas; you know, he's probably driving around someplace else since we said no. Lord knows there's plenty of open land around the entire area; could be he's out looking at some other places for his boss."

"You think so?" Will asked.

"Only thing that makes sense," Cole shrugged. "What else would he do?"

They stared quietly at Cole for a moment, absorbing his words. What else could they do? Something still didn't feel right, yet he was unable to zero in on his feelings. Nothing about Sinclair felt right, but since the only thing the man was guilty of was asking a few questions, Cole had nothing to go on. Yet the nagging suspicions were back, trying to beckon something deeper and more sinister hidden deep inside that he was just not willing to let surface. He even kept that from himself, claiming that the dead were better off buried; and that's what his past was ... dead.

Having no answers and accomplishing very little other than to reassure one another that no one was about to bail, everyone spoke quietly about their feelings for another hour before deciding enough was enough. Coffee was poured, the pastries disappeared in a flurry, and they left feeling stronger in the knowledge that not a one of them was in this alone.

* * *

The house was locked, but there were still lights on inside. Through the front window, Sinclair could see Ruth watching television while quietly sewing. There was no sign of Katie, but since the hour was growing late, Sinclair figured that she was probably in bed and fast asleep by now. Much to his relief, the lady veterinarian had gotten into her truck and left, probably going on a late night call. Cole was off again, and Sinclair knew just where he had gone.

"What the hell do those stupid cowboys think they're going to accomplish anyway?" he sneered. "They won't stand a snowball's chance in hell by the time we're through with them."

He knew of the meeting and knew that they were probably banding together. But he also knew that it was early yet. None of them had anything to lose right now, and they didn't see the stakes as being too high. That was only because he hadn't really gotten to any of them yet, but he was slowly starting. And that was because they were too naïve and trusting; not one single rancher had the tiniest inkling of what he was really capable of.

What he had done so far was a drop in the bucket compared to what he was capable of. They had written it off as just one of those hundreds of little accidents that occur while running a ranch. As far as Sinclair knew, no one suspected him at all. Bremmer's cattle had gotten loose due to the carelessness of a teenage boy, and everyone knew how careless kids could be these days. Sinclair snickered. Everything was falling into place.

As long as he kept a low profile, by the time anyone realized what had really happened to them, they would be long gone, Sinclair would be nowhere to be found, and Culver would have his land. He had told Culver of his plans, buying time and getting his boss to settle down and wait for things to happen naturally.

"Push a little and you get back tenfold," Sinclair snickered as he snuck into the back of the barn. "Now, where's that liniment? Ahhh, here it is. Heard how Williams said he returned it earlier, but too bad he was lying," he sneered, putting the jar in his pocket. "Make Cole wonder just what his friend was doing in his barn when he wasn't home. Especially when his horses turn up sick, which won't take long now."

For the second night in a row, Sinclair snuck into the horses' stalls, hand-feeding the alfalfa cubes to the three horses slated for sale, and quickly giving some to a few others. Most of the horses chose to ignore the unwelcome treat, perhaps sensing that Sinclair was up to no good. One of the younger horses of Cole's, however, chose to eat quite a few, which only heightened Sinclair's excitement. With any luck, by morning, the animals should be feeling a little under the weather.

Not wanting to leave any traces of the alfalfa behind, Sinclair carefully brushed his hands off and looked around the barn. He didn't care if Cole knew about the alfalfa or not, but he also knew that Cole's paranoia would take over. Also, not knowing how his animals had gotten ill would only add to his upset. Sinclair could see Cole driving himself crazy trying to figure this one out. If he didn't start doubting himself, then he would surely look somewhere else, or to someone else. Brent would be just the perfect person to begin with. Other than Cole, he was the only other person who had access to the animals of late, and it wouldn't take long for him to figure that out. All Sinclair had to do was sit back and watch the show.

He thought that he should be feeling some kind of remorse for what he was doing to the horses; after all, they were magnificent animals. Colic could be fatal, but that wasn't his problem. If Cole had only cooperated in the beginning, then none of this would have happened. This was just a necessary step, nothing more. It would cause complications where the buyers were concerned, with the date looming just a few days away. That, Sinclair knew, would impact greatly on Cole, who was just barely holding on. When the people found out that their animals were sick and pulled out of the deal, he would be left hanging with no money coming in.

Everything was falling into place nicely. Sinclair made his first move easily Friday night after Brent finished with the animals and drove away. Having him show up unexpectedly that afternoon and be seen coming from the barn by Cole was an added bonus.

"Nothing like a little friendly persuasion, huh, cowboy?" Sinclair grinned, looking around the barn one last time.

The one thing he failed to notice, however, was the cubes that had fallen from his pocket when the first, excited horse nudged him. Without a second thought, Sinclair left as quietly as he arrived.

Chapter Twelve

"Come on, Katie bug, let's get outside and get some things done," Cole called out to his daughter.

It was a bright, sunny morning and both father and daughter were eager to get out into the warm sunshine. Cole led the way to the barn, with Katie skipping along behind him. Their breakfast was finished, which Katie had decided they should eat outside on the porch, and the kitchen was clean. It was going to be a fairly quiet day, which was what Cole needed. Last night's meeting had gone well, but it brought up a lot of questions. It had also brought up a lot of memories, most of which were foggy.

Wish I could remember more about Culver, Cole thought again for about the hundredth time.

Why would Culver bother him now? All he had done was make an offer on Cole's ranch back in Wyoming. Cole had refused, his wife died, and he left Broken Arrow. It was as simple as that. Yet, it still nagged at the corners of his mind, heartlessly driving Cole into a quandary of feelings he did not want to relive.

"Just wish that everything about that time wasn't so jumbled. I know that they weren't too happy with me not wanting to sell, but what the hell! We had a few scrapes, but I've been in fights before. He probably thought he could strong-arm me into leaving, but when he found out that was not to be, he left us alone," Cole muttered to himself.

As usual, he had tossed and turned all night long; the meeting set his mind into overdrive and it refused to quit. Bits and pieces of that time came back, especially the night Sarah died. He tried shoving those disturbing thoughts aside, but they refused to be vanquished. He lay in bed wondering, why now? Was it because he was subconsciously feeling guilty for being with Callie? Or did the meeting dredge up things from the past that he simply chose not to think about anymore?

He missed Callie upon his return home, hearing how she had been called out to the Johnsons' farm shortly after he left for the meeting. "No wonder Dave wasn't able to show up," he replied to Ruth after hearing the trouble Dave had with a mare that was ready to foal. Everything had turned out fine, as Cole learned later that night when he lay in bed talking to Callie on the phone. He missed her, hearing her voice only prolonged the agony of their separation, making both yearn for when they could be together again.

No, it wasn't his relationship with Callie that had Cole bothered, neither had done anything to be ashamed of and he wasn't the least bit sorry. Lying there, it felt good talking to her; if they couldn't be together then they could at least hear each other's voices. Cole wasn't fighting any guilt there. He just wished that he could keep the past in the past, especially now that he had finally decided to try and get on with his life. Yet, it kept on coming back to him. Only he wasn't sinking into the dark pit of depression that so often claimed him. Instead, it was more like fighting a repressed memory that was struggling to break through. One part of him wanted to remember and strove towards that goal, but the other part kept things locked up tightly in the confines of his mind.

"You sure you don't mind me going to the rodeo?" Cole had asked, feeling that he should stay home.

"Honey, go on! It's about time you relaxed and had some fun," Sarah had smiled, kissing him goodbye.

"But it means an overnight trip!" Cole argued. "You know, I never should have let that brother of yours talk me into it."

"Give Matt a break! He's right! You need to get out and have some fun, it's been a long time since the two of you did anything but work, and besides, it's a girls' night out for me and Mom! She's going to come over and stay with me," Sarah reassured him.

"At least I know you won't be alone," Cole smiled, holding her close. "And remember, the doctor said no heavy lifting or no bending! Anything that needs to be done, I'll do when I get home. Oh damn, I forgot to go into town to get that special feed for the colts," he winced, knowing that they only had enough for a few days.

"I'll go get it," Sarah had volunteered.

"No you won't! There's enough for Dave to use till I get back. I'll have Matt stop on the way home and we'll pick it up. After all, he's the one who's been pestering the hell out of me to go, it'll serve him right."

"You worry too much," Sarah chided him.

"You don't listen," Cole replied crisply.

"Just go and have fun, ok?" Sarah pleaded.

"You promise not to do anything you're not supposed to?" Cole asked, knowing that it was useless.

"Please! Mom will be here! The only one who's worse than you about not letting me do anything is her!" Sarah exclaimed.

"Then I know you'll behave," Cole laughed, kissing her soundly on the lips.

He climbed into his truck and with one last kiss, drove off waving. Sarah stood, waving back until he drove out of sight. Sighing, she went inside to start her daily chores. She did not have to worry about the horses, but she wanted to go into town later that night. She thought that she and her mother could possibly get something to eat and maybe catch a movie or two.

Maybe I can pick up the feed he needs, Sarah thought, starting her own work.

She finished a little before dinnertime and took a shower. Just as she finished dressing, Sarah called her mother and they made plans to go to the diner for their dinner. "Dad can fend for himself, there's enough chicken and potato salad left over," her mother had laughed, anxious to begin their night out. "I hope there's a good movie playing."

"Even if there isn't, we're getting out," Sarah laughed back, feeling free.

It had been a long time since they were able to spend time together. Tonight, there would be no cooking; only relaxing over a quiet meal and maybe a movie afterwards. Sarah grabbed her keys and went out the door to pick up her mother. ...

"It's over; it was a long time ago and it's over," Cole admonished himself as he lay back trying to sleep.

Last night sleep was denied again. This time, it was because of things best left forgotten. Now he and Katie were ready to begin their day. The stalls had been mucked out earlier that morning, and the horses were fed, but Cole had waited until now to begin the actual grooming. After making sure that Katie was occupied by playing with the kittens romping in the nearby hay pile, the long process began. Special attention needed to be paid to those slated for sale, but all the horses would be getting the same treatment.

One by one Cole pulled the horses over to the side of the barn, where he would begin by brushing them down. Their ears needed to be cleaned, teeth needed to be checked and cleaned, and then he would recheck their hooves. Two of the buyers wanted their horses shoed and one did not. Cole would make sure that everything was finished to their specifications, with the smithy coming out on Monday for the shoeing. He bent over concentrating on a small pebble, which was popped loose from one of the animal's hooves, when he heard Katie calling to him.

"Daddy, how come the horses are tired?" she asked innocently.

Cole's head sprang up, alarmed at her words. Horses just didn't tire like that; even Katie knew when something was wrong. Cursing his own lack of attentiveness, he ran over, finding one of his own horses and two of the newer ones standing by the fence. Their heads hung low and they did not seem to have any energy. One of them was kicking at his abdomen and another just stood listlessly. Seeing how lethargic they had become, Cole immediately checked their gums, which had become white and dry.

"Shit, colic," he swore. "Katie, come on," Cole cried out, grabbing her by the hand and scooping her up into his arms.

Her cries rang out as he ran into the house, dumping her onto the couch. He wanted to comfort his daughter, but that would have to come later. Cole had a real emergency on his hands and if not taken care of immediately, it could prove fatal.

"CALLIE!" he shouted, his hands shaking violently.

"Cole, what—" she burst out.

"Colic! Three down so far and I'm looking at the rest...." was all he said before he hung up the phone, picked up Katie, and immediately ran back outside.

It would take Callie only a few minutes to drive over, so he placed Katie on a pile of hay near the back of the barn. "Honey, don't move from there," Cole ordered, not meaning to sound so firm but unable to take the time to explain things.

Cole hated leaving her there like that, the way her eyes filled with tears and the quivering of her lips broke his heart, but he had no choice. He had to separate the stricken horses from the herd and begin checking the others. As he sprang into action, Callie jumped into her truck, needing no further urging. She drove by Ruth's, finding her on the front porch. Blaring the horn as she skidded to a stop, Callie flung the passenger door open.

"Honey...." Ruth asked, her eyes wide with fright as she ran over.

"Colic! Cole's got three down and maybe more. Thought you could watch Katie for him," Callie explained as she gunned the engine.

Cole's call was one of Callie's worst fears. Colic might not seem like much, but it posed a great danger for the animals, who succumbed quickly. She only hoped that they had caught it in time for the medicine to work, and hoped that they would not have to resort to other treatments. Disgusting or not, it was a job done willingly. However, she feared that once the disease had advanced to the stage where that treatment was required, the chances of a full recovery were lessened. She had been lucky with Patches, they had caught the disease before it had the chance to progress further; she could only hope that Cole would fare as well.

Callie found Cole with four horses, which he had led into the smaller corral. The fourth animal was found standing behind the bales of hay stacked just inside the barn. He hopped over the fence and continued checking the other animals, while Callie grabbed her bag. Frowning at the way one of the horses started leaning against the fence, she knew that he would soon be cramping and lying down to try and ease the pain. Time was running out. When they squirmed in such a manner, they ran the risk of twisting their intestines, which could rupture.

"Shit, four horses and only one of me," she cursed, running over with Ruth close behind.

"Callie!" Cole called out breathlessly, taking her hand. "I think it's only these four, but I'm still checking. Ruth?"

"I swung by her place so she could watch Katie for us. I'm going to need your help," Callie quickly explained on her way into the corral.

"Thanks," Cole smiled, squeezing her arm.

She felt the way he trembled and prayed she could be of help. "Gonna be a long night," Callie said to both Ruth and Cole.

"Ruth, she's scared! I dragged her into the house and then back out here and didn't say a word! She told me the horses were tired, and I found them like this. Poor kid, probably thinks she did something wrong!" Cole frantically explained.

Ruth could see the trembling of his hand as he ran it through his hair; his eyes were dilated, wild with fright and worry for both his animals and daughter. Without hesitation, she ran out back and scooped the weeping child into her arms. Katie's eyes were swollen from crying, her face smeared with dirt and tears. She sobbed pitifully as Ruth bent over her, her heart breaking at the sound.

"Honey, it's all right! Don't cry now, Nanny's here," she soothed, carrying Katie back towards the house.

"I was bad and Daddy's mad at me," she sobbed her heart out.

"Sweet baby, Daddy's not mad at you. You found the horses sick and saved them! But he's so scared for them right now that he had to call Callie to come and make them better and I came to watch you. He's not mad at you, sweetie, he just needs to concentrate on the horses right now," Ruth soothed.

"Daddy's not mad?" Katie sobbed brokenly.

"No, sweetie, he told me to tell you that he's not mad," Ruth reassured the small girl, whose tears began to dry and a fleeting smile crossed her face. "Come on, why don't you and I go inside and make some coffee and sandwiches for dinner later on? I think that Daddy and Callie are going to be working for a long time.

Ruth winked as she walked by Cole, who winked back at his now smiling daughter. He waved and blew a quick kiss in Katie's direction, which caused her smile to become even brighter. That was one burden lifted; leave it to

241

Ruth to fix things. She could always make things right again, that he never doubted.

* * *

Cole watched as Callie listened for any kind of bowel sounds from the horses. She ran the stethoscope down the underbelly of one, and smiled, standing back up. She had given them all 10cc of Dyperone on each side of the neck and the medicine seemed to be working. They both noticed that the afternoon had slipped by and darkness was just beginning to creep in. Neither had even been aware of that happening. Once they brought the animals into the barn, they kept the stricken ones isolated in another section, and kept a close eye on them all.

"I think we caught it early," Callie smiled reassuringly. The relief in Cole's eyes was more than evident.

"Thank God, I was really scared," he said, taking her in his arms.

Shadows lengthened across the barn, giving a dim, almost cozy glow to the atmosphere. Callie felt the beating of his heart against her cheek and could almost feel the tension draining from his body. The barn was hushed, with the horses standing quietly now that they felt a little better. They no longer kicked at their stomachs or tried lying down to ease the pain. The rest of the horses were in need of their grain, which Cole was reluctant to give without checking. Walking over to the bin, he looked inside.

"Four sick horses," Cole said quietly, staring idly into the bin. "And to make it worse, I have no answer as to how they got sick!"

"Honey, we might never know! These animals get into everything! Look at Patches! God only knows what he had eaten to cause his colic! We might never know. I just thank God that we were able to get results so quickly," Callie said, trying to reassure an obviously shaken Cole.

"It can't be the feed!" Cole exclaimed.

"You wouldn't think so," Callie agreed. "This is the same mix you've always used, isn't it?"

"Yeah! I haven't changed a thing! God, I'm so careful with them!" Cole declared.

The only thing that made sense right now was to go inside the horses' stalls and look around. They needed to be mucked out and their bins needed refilling, but all were empty; not a bin held anything suspicious. Cole saw how some of the animals had spilled some grain from their bins and scattered it around the floor. Taking his foot, he shoved the mess aside, finding nothing out of the ordinary. However, once he reached the stall of one of the newer

242

animals, he frowned, bending down.

"Callie, what do you make of this?" he asked, standing up and holding out a strange-looking, green cube.

"That looks like an alfalfa cube! Cole, did you start giving alfalfa to your horses?"

"I didn't change a thing!" Cole exclaimed, shocked at the discovery. "I know that a sudden change in diet isn't good and I know that alfalfa, especially, can cause this kind of problem. How the hell did that get in here?" he asked, finding two more as he swept the floor clean. "I'm gonna go check the others."

"I'll help," Callie said, entering the dim interior of the next stall. "Well, I don't see any more on the floors, but we won't be able to really be sure until we get the stalls mucked out completely," she said, coming back out into the main section of the barn.

"Me neither," Cole shrugged. "Just this one that I found on the floor of the corner stall. But the question is, how the hell did it get in here? I don't buy this shit! And it's obvious that my horses ate it, so it had to have been put in their feed!"

A thorough check of the stalls and bins were made, with Cole mucking them out entirely and then giving them a thorough sweeping. Having no idea of how such cubes could have gotten into his barn to begin with, there was no way of telling how many of his horses had eaten them. It was obvious that the four stricken animals had eaten some alfalfa, but the remaining horses seemed to be doing fine. Nevertheless, Cole was alarmed; it was bad enough that he would have to dump the grain in the larger bin, and there was no guarantee that his other horses wouldn't succumb to the disease.

"Callie, how do I know the others won't get colic?" Cole worried, his face pale, his hands shaky.

"Cole, try not to worry! I know how futile that sounds, but I don't think any of the others are in any kind of danger! I've checked them thoroughly, and they have good, strong bowel sounds. I'll also keep a close eye on them tonight and tomorrow, but I think that we're through the worst of this!"

"You think so? Callie, I think it's only beginning! Do you know what this would have done to me? Do you know what this did to me?" Cole said, pulling away.

Not one to withhold information, Cole knew that he would have to call the buyers and inform them of the setback. The animals were fine and after a few days, should still be ready for shipping. Callie had promised to come by each day to make sure of that. Yet, he hated making the call. Just when things were up and running, his first shipment of the year was hit with problems. That didn't bode well; one might misconstrue that with shoddy care where the animals were concerned, and think the animal inferior. If that happened, if word got around, the setback would be devastating. His name would be ruined.

"Cole, do you think Brent might have mistakenly thought that he could give the horses this?" she asked, feeling him stiffen and pull away.

"No, I don't think so. Brent wouldn't do that, he knows better! Callie, I don't have a good feeling about this. Why the hell did this happen and why now? I mean, everything hinges on their sale! It just doesn't make any sense!" Cole said.

"I know that it doesn't make any sense," Callie sought to reassure him.

The one thought on her mind was inconceivable, yet it nagged endlessly. Such a subject was too fearful to even broach. It was just too cold, heartless, and calculating. It brooked on someone giving the cubes to the horses on purpose. She shuddered, not wanting to think of one of their neighbors even considering doing something this heinous. Callie was ashamed of herself then, because no one she knew would do anything like this. It just wasn't in their nature and no one had a motive. All of their friends and neighbors banded together helping one another out; they would not hurt one of their own.

Yet, who would? As much as Callie leaned towards someone attacking Cole where it would hurt, she shoved that thought from her mind. No good would come of broaching a subject that would only cause accusations and trouble where none were afforded. It could have simply been a fluke. Maybe it was a packaging error on the part of the shipper and only a few cubes of alfalfa slipped into the grain, ultimately going into the horses' bins. It sounded flimsy, it was far from plausible, but Callie did not want to think of the alternative.

It was just plain odd, so with no explanation, it was just best to make sure that the horses were no longer in danger and to just go on from there. Sometimes, life brings things that are beyond explanation. Neither Callie nor Cole gave Sinclair a thought. Whether consciously or subconsciously, they refused to let their minds wander there. As far as they were concerned, the odd man had simply given up on them and was looking elsewhere. The thought of him doing something like this was just too horrifying to put into words, so no one did.

Callie went over to Cole, but he was beyond comfort. In his usual fashion, he pulled away from her and paced about the barn. The stalls were ready for the horses to be brought in, and Cole went ahead, dumping the grain bin and refilling it with new. Not knowing where the alfalfa had come from, he felt there was simply no choice. He could already feel the pinch this loss made. It didn't make sense, and that's what bothered him the most. The only comfort Cole had at the moment was that none of the other horses were suffering. Callie was keeping a close eye on them, but it looked like they would be fine. Still, he couldn't afford this.

"Cole, it will be all right," Callie tried soothing him.

"It will? How can you say that? We don't know how this happened, and I can't afford to go around dumping grain! Shit, I might as well toss my money down the drain!" he shouted angrily, flinging his arm up in the air.

It was on the tip of her tongue to tell him to go speak with Mel at the feed 'n seed, but thought better of it. There was no sense in casting accusations, yet she still felt that Mel should know. She would talk to him herself, on the sly. This way it would only be between the two of them and no one else would have to know. Besides, it was her duty. If there was inferior grain from one of the manufacturers, more animals could be threatened and that was a chance Callie could not take. It would be hard, but she and Mel might be able to check the feed that was open, or he could at least warn others to be on the lookout for the suspicious green cubes. After all, they were easy to spot if one was looking for them; they stuck out like a sore thumb amid the tiny bits of grain.

Brent could have unwittingly given them to the horses the other night, not even thinking that something could have been wrong with the feed. He had no reason to suspect something was amiss. The interior of the barn was probably dim by the time he fed the animals, in spite of the overhead lights. It would have been very easy for anyone to miss the few cubes that had gotten into the animals' bins and go on about his business. Cole had fed the horses last night, and the same could have happened to him. To mention that now would have been detrimental. Callie thought it best to keep quiet and handle things on her own; Cole simply wasn't in a mood to be dealt with. If there were answers to get, then she would get them.

Shadows stretched long and dark across the interior of the barn. The remaining sliver of sunlight streaked in through the window, sending bright golden hues over the pile of hay in the corner. What caught Cole's attention was the way the cabinet door hung open. Remembering how Brent had returned the liniment, he went over and looked inside The cabinet held only a few rags, a hoof pick, and a currycomb. There was no liniment. Without a word, Cole closed the door and strode out of the barn.

* * *

"Honey how are—" Ruth asked, as Cole passed her by.

She stood back watching while he went straight to the phone. She had seen him upset before, but had never seen this angry, dark side. Katie was asleep, for which Ruth was grateful. The child had been upset enough and seeing her father this way would not have helped. Fearing the worst, Ruth moved closer.

"Brent, it's me," Cole said, trying to control his anger.

"Hey! What's—"

"Do you know what this is gonna cost me?" Cole burst out. "Don't you know the difference between feeding cows and feeding horses? They don't eat the same shit that your cows do!" he yelled, feeling the vein on the side of his head throbbing.

"Cole! What the fuck are you talking about? Of course I—" Brent sputtered.

"Then how come four of my horses are sick with colic?" Cole challenged.

"I don't—" Brent began, only to be cut off again.

"Alfalfa, Brent! That's what my horses ate! Alfalfa! Can you explain that? I thought you knew only to give them—" Cole started, this time being the one cut off.

"Now, you just hold on there, I'm coming right over," Brent yelled back, breaking off before he said something they would all regret later.

He and Cole had been friends for too long to try and settle something like this over the phone. Brent could feel his own anger rising and fought hard to control his mouth. This was Cole! The entire call was much too confusing. Hearing Cole's voice on the other end, Brent had not expected to be attacked in such a manner. Caught off guard, his own anger flared for a moment, but was quickly quelled. He couldn't believe the accusations flung at him over the phone and was confused as to why Cole was angry with him. Brent had picked up on the world colic, but he knew nothing about that. Cole surely couldn't blame him for that.

Brent had to control his own temper so that he wouldn't say the wrong thing, thereby making things worse. It was clear that Cole wasn't thinking straight right now, and he vowed to do his best to not only keep a lid on the situation, but not to lose sight of what Cole meant to him. They had been through a lot over the years, and now this?

All Brent did was feed the horses according to his instructions. Nothing was ever said about alfalfa and Brent didn't even have access to the stuff. Both he and his father were as picky with their cows as Cole was with his horses. Not only that, Brent was no stranger at taking care of horses; he had spent his entire life around the animals and knew how to handle and feed them. It waas nothing new, and it wasn't the first time he had taken care of Cole's stock. Pulling into the ranch, he found his friend storming out of the barn.

"Now Cole, you better settle down before we both say and do something we'll regret later!" Brent held up his hands.

"Brent, I'm trying very hard to hold myself together right now, but am not doing a good job of it. I found this in the barn! Can you explain how that got in there? Did you think that it would make a nice treat for the horses?" Cole shouted, holding out the cubes.

Brent never wavered. "Cole, I swear to you on my life that I never did anything like this. I know what your horses mean to you. I would never do anything to undermine you or jeopardize your stock! You got to believe me!"

"And the liniment! Where's the liniment?" Cole asked, staring intently.

"In the cabinet," Brent shrugged.

Cole reached out, grabbing Brent's arm as his friend moved to enter the barn. "I leave you to take care of my horses, and I come home earlier today, finding you coming out of my barn. You said you were returning the stuff, but it's gone. It's not there! And some of my stock is sick."

Callie and Ruth hung back, shoved aside by Cole, who was beyond reason. They couldn't believe their ears at the words he threw at Brent.

"So it's my fault? I returned the stuff! I do you a favor and this is the way you act? What the hell's wrong with you?" Brent cried out, still not knowing what had really happened.

"What's wrong with me is I'm trying to figure out why a friend of mine would do something like this to me! Can you explain it?" Cole fought back.

Brent's eyes narrowed. Both men moved closer, staring unwaveringly. Neither moved for a moment, but their anger ripped through the air. Tension charged the atmosphere as they faced one another down. No one knew what was happening; Cole was a stranger in their eyes. He was a stranger in his own eyes and that scared him even more than the sick horses did.

Something was happening ... something that instilled a fear so deeply ingrained, Cole couldn't fight it. He was confusing the past with the present, not realizing that it wasn't some unseen and long forgotten enemy he was fighting, it was Brent. A cold face and strange voice from another time and place had replaced his friend, coming in flashes that made any kind of coherent thought on his part impossible. Licking his lips, Cole ran a shaky hand through his hair while waiting for Brent's answer.

"I have nothing to explain. You either take my word for it, or you don't," Brent said, turning to leave.

"Where the hell do you think you're going? You have a lot of explaining to do!" Cole cried out, spinning Brent back towards him. His face red with rage, he grasped the front of Brent's shirt and shoved him back against the truck. "Why? Can you tell me why?"

"God, Cole! What's happening to you? What are you—" Callie cried out, running over with Ruth.

"Honey! Stop! PLEASE STOP!" Ruth's cries went unheeded.

Both women came running over in an attempt to restrain Cole, yet they were shoved aside, ignored. Brent broke Cole's grasp, pushing him back.

"I can't tell you a damned thing! You want explanations? Well, so do I! I want to know why someone I consider a friend and love like a brother is standing here accusing me of something so unthinkable, I can't believe what I'm hearing! And then he attacks me? I don't have any explanations because I didn't do anything. If your horses got alfalfa, they didn't get it from me! It had to have been in the grain to begin with, I didn't do anything but feed them from there," Brent desperately defended himself.

He didn't want to fight.... Brent couldn't strike out against Cole. Yet he felt that Cole was fighting, only it wasn't him that he was angry with. Cole was angry and he was confused, but the glassy eyes that stared coldly back weren't Cole's. They belonged to someone else and Brent had the eerie feeling that they were staring at somebody else.

"Then why just the four? And where's the liniment? Can you tell me that?" Cole demanded to know.

"I can't tell you a thing! I returned the liniment. What? Did you think that I came back to the scene of the crime? You think I brought in some more stuff to add to their feed and used the liniment as a cover story? Hell, if I was guilty, then I'd make a cover story that stood up. And since the liniment is gone, it obviously wouldn't have worked. And if you know me, if you really know me, then you would know that I would never do anything to hurt a friend like this. I'd rather die first," he said, staring deeply into Cole's eyes.

"Brent..." Cole managed to choke out, sparking a glimmer of recognition as he stared at Brent's face.

Brent continued shaking Cole, hoping to instill some sense into his friend. "And you would also know that I have nothing to gain from you losing money or your stock. What the hell good would it do me? Can you tell me that? How could you even think that of me?"

The minute Brent's words were out, he was sorry. Cole's head snapped up. The anger drained from his eyes, only to be replaced with a deep sorrow that reached down into his soul. Brent was right and he knew it. He was standing here blaming a friend for something he did not understand; something that he knew in his heart was wrong, but something that he had been unable to stop. The words were out before he could even think them over. Cole had been scared and upset, and had struck out in the only way he knew, but he had struck out at a person who had been nothing but a good friend ever since his arrival.

Just because Brent was the one to take care of the animals did not mean that he was the one who had harmed them. Cole immediately knew how wrong he was, Brent just wouldn't do that. He had nothing to gain from it and he had everything to lose. Brent was Cole's best friend and an uncle to his daughter. He loved Katie with all his heart and had more than proven that over the years. And this was how Cole repaid him. He stood before Callie and Ruth and ripped apart a friend he cherished deeply. Instantly sorry and thoroughly ashamed, Cole couldn't face them any longer.

"I don't know how or why I could have even thought of blaming you. And there's nothing I can say to excuse myself or ever take the words away. I hurt you only cause I was faced with something I couldn't handle, but that doesn't make it right. You've offered me nothing but friendship since I arrived and I threw it back in your face. I'm more than ashamed of myself. Right now I can't fucking stand myself. Like in the past, I always turn and hurt those I claim to care about the most," he snorted.

"Hey Cole, don't—" Brent reached out, only to have Cole pull back.

"Brent, I know you had nothing to do with any of this. I don't give a damn about the liniment, it could have fallen and rolled somewhere. You're always welcome here and I know you didn't do anything! You can't! I'm the one who's screwed everything up for years now and this is no different. It's inevitable, I do it all the time and I'm doing it again. Guess I'm just not fit to be around. I'm just a frigging outsider who came here and all of you would have been better off if I'd never arrived," Cole said brokenly, unable to even lift his eyes and look at any of them.

"Cole, no," Callie cried out, running over.

Ignoring her, Cole spun on his heels and strode to his truck. Brent stood in shock before he could even think of moving. He knew that Cole was hurt, but how much and how deep, he simply couldn't fathom. He also knew that something else had happened here. It was as if someone had stepped into Cole's body and was playing out a role that had been done years ago. Shivering, Brent tried making sense of the scene between him and Cole, but there was no sense to it. There was still a lot about Cole and his past that they knew nothing about and Brent had the unsettling feeling that Cole didn't know, either. Yet, somehow, a tiny memory had played out tonight. Brent also knew that Cole was not only scared, but that he would never forgive himself. The slamming of the truck door jarred him to his senses.

Brent heard Callie crying out for Cole, and the engine as it was kicked it into gear. She ran over, only to have the truck slammed into reverse, kicking up gravel as he spun it around, racing out onto the road. Ruth cried, heavy tears coursing down her face.

"Oh Brent, go after him! He didn't mean it, and he knows that!" she begged.

"I know! I know Cole, and I know he didn't. I'll go after him," Brent said, jumping into his own truck. As he drove away, Callie turned to Ruth.

"What the hell is going on here? Ruth, I've never seen him like this!" she cried, trembling violently.

Ruth pulled Callie close, trying her best to offer what little comfort she could. "Honey, he's scared! A part of Cole will always run scared. He just doesn't know how to deal with love or deal with hurt. He runs on fear, fear of having love in his life again because it hurts too much when it's taken away, and the fear of being alone. He's been alone and doesn't like it one bit."

* * *

"Boy, am I glad to see you," Mack exclaimed, nodding towards the end of the bar. "He's been belting 'em down pretty good."

"Thanks, Mack. I had a feeling he'd come to one of these places," Brent replied, clapping him on the shoulder.

Walking towards the end of the bar, he stood silently next to Cole and ordered a drink. Mack poured, then stepped away. Neither said a word. Cole turned his head, too ashamed to face Brent after what was said and done. Brent felt that shame and wished he could take it away. Sometimes Cole was just too hard on himself.

After leaving the house, Cole had driven straight to the bar. Brent had the feeling that he intended on getting very drunk, but there were four places to try. He decided on looking at the closest ones first, and was kicking himself for wasting the time. He should have known that Cole would go to the one furthest out, hoping he wouldn't be found.

"Hitting that shit pretty good," Brent said, looking as Cole downed yet another.

"Just don't give a fuck about things anymore," Cole replied. "No matter what I do, no matter where I go or who I turn to, I ruin it all. Always have and always will. Look what I did to Sarah. And then Maggie! All it took was one night with me to screw her life up! Now tonight I turned on you, accusing you of something you would never do in a million years. Wonder

250

just how long it will be till I fuck up something where Katie and Callie are concerned."

"Will you quit it? You've done nothing tonight but react to sheer fear. Hell, you were upset about what happened, and what makes it worse is that neither of us can explain it. I get pissed over things that go wrong that I can't explain! Especially something this wrong! Cole, we lose our stock, we lose everything! That's enough to strike the fear of God into any one of us! And it does look and seem odd, I mean, I did feed your stock the other night and I was in your barn yesterday when you weren't home," Brent said adamantly.

"You have every right to be in my barn and my home when I'm not around. Brent, you're family. My place is yours. But tonight, I forgot that. Just not good for anyone lately, and haven't been for years. And the other night with Callie never should have happened, she doesn't need my brand of poison," Cole slurred, raising another shot.

"Damn it, now that's it! This is just the whiskey talking," Brent reached for the glass.

"Hell, no! It's me! Look at me, Brent! It's me talking! The one who killed his wife! And—"

"Will you shut the fuck up?" Brent yelled, finally losing his temper as he smashed the glass against the wall, Cole's words chilling him to the soul.

"HEY! Watch what the hell you're doing, Brent!" Mack cried out.

"Sorry, Mack, won't happen again," he answered, ripping Cole out of the chair. "You got some coffee?"

"Coming right up," Mack said.

Never had Brent heard Cole refer to Sarah's death in such a way, and he worried, wondering what really happened. Sarah had been killed in a fire. One night when Cole wasn't home, Sarah, who was 5 months pregnant at the time, and her mother, Myra, were killed when Cole's home burned. How he could possibly think himself responsible, let alone sit there and say that he killed her, was beyond him. Whatever it was, Brent was sure that it was the crux of the problem still bothering Cole to this day. If he only understood, he could help.

Mack quickly poured two cups and carried them over to where Brent forced Cole into a chair. He set them on the table, but Cole turned away. "Don't want that shit."

"You're gonna get this shit if I have to pry your mouth open and pour it in!" Brent declared, shooting a fiery glare in Cole's direction. "You gonna sit here and get stinking drunk all night long cause you're feeling sorry for yourself?"

"What the fuck do you know?" Cole cried out.

"I know plenty!" Brent shot back. "I know what happened to you and it's about time you stopped living it! It's also time you really trusted the people around you, and more importantly, it's about time you learned how to trust yourself. But you're so damned stubborn that when faced with the truth, you refuse to hear a word of it! Cole, you like living on lies or something? You really don't think much of yourself!"

"Are they really lies? I can't stop living them. They're everywhere I turn, slapping me in the face," Cole said, his voice hushed. "It wasn't you," he began, then stopped himself.

"Then who was it, Cole? Who were you fighting? And why?" Brent asked, becoming more worried than ever.

"I ... it was nothing," Cole stopped, dropping his hands onto the table. He tried a sip of the coffee, only to feel it hit his stomach violently. Yet, Brent wouldn't let him be.

"Drink that shit before I pour it down you," he warned as he stared at Cole, showing that he truly meant business. He was going to sober him up or die trying. Either way, they were not leaving until Cole started making sense again.

"Cole, you ok?" Brent asked softly. "I mean, are you really ok?"

"Matt...."

"Matt? You mean Brent, don't you?" Brent asked, startling Cole.

He looked at Brent, his face finally focusing. All night long flashes of Matt's face and someone else that he couldn't make out had been confusing him. Now, they were gone. Cole took a deep breath, seeing Brent sitting there. It really was Brent.

"That was stupid," Cole snorted. "Of course I mean you, Brent! Who else would I mean? God, you won't ever know how sorry I am. To be accused of something like I accused you of can destroy a man. Brent, I don't know how you can forgive me."

"Me neither! But I'll try!" Brent quipped, trying to shake Cole up a bit. He almost succeeded, seeing a fleeting grin flash across Cole's face for the briefest of moments. Casting a lopsided grin in Cole's direction, Brent nudged his friend.

"Forgive you? What the hell are you thinking of?" Brent teased. "There's nothing to forgive!"

"Brent, I think of a lot of things, and then I don't think at all," Cole hedged, catching himself.

"Cole, what do you mean?" Brent asked of him.

"Nothing ... not important," Cole repeated, trying to change the subject.

"Come on, there's something bothering you," Brent continued trying to get Cole to really open up.

Like Ruth and Gris, Brent always had the feeling that there was something else regarding Sarah's death ... something that Cole refused to speak about for some reason. That something was still a source of torment to this day. Brent felt that if he could get Cole to really open up to him, then maybe the torment could end. Seeing Cole hurting like this tore him apart, yet he refused to say a word.

"Come on, Cole, what gives?" Brent continued, trying to urge Cole to talk.

"Nothing," Cole shook his head. "Besides, you don't want to know," he finished, shoving his coffee back.

A long, unexpected night was getting longer by the minute as Cole abruptly rose and stormed out, leaving Brent with more questions than answers. What Cole refused to talk about had him on edge. Did it have something to do with Sinclair? And where was the odd, little man anyway? And what had really happened to Sarah?

Look what I did to Sarah, rang morbidly through Brent's mind.

He shuddered at the words, something had happened that Cole refused to speak about. From what Brent knew, Sarah's death had been an accident. How could Cole blame himself for that? He wasn't even home the night Sarah had been killed. Brent's head snapped up, wondering if the guilt Cole had been carrying around all these years had something to do with him going away for the weekend with Matt. He left Sarah alone.... No, he left Sarah with her mother. There was nothing wrong with that. People did things like that all the time. Did Cole blame himself so deeply that he would never forgive himself for going away?

Was it her death that caused him to leave Broken Arrow? Cole had already shown Brent that he was stronger than he thought himself to be, and Brent doubted if he would just leave the only home he'd ever known his entire life because of his wife's death, no matter how devastating. And Cole did have a falling out with Matt, but in his heart, Brent doubted if that was the reason for Cole closing down and leaving like he did.

"And ... and ... and ... you can sit here all night long running scenarios through your mind and asking questions. Maybe he was just scared and still is," Brent shuddered, remembering the night after the funeral that Cole had sat in the barn contemplating taking his own life. "Maybe it was all those things rolled into one that drove him to leave. Maybe if he had stayed, he would have killed himself. Oh well, guess I'll never know unless Cole tells me," Brent muttered, talking to himself as he jumped up, running out the door.

In his present state, Cole didn't get very far. Brent was surprised that he had managed to make it through the door and out into the parking lot. Looking at Brent through bleary, bloodshot eyes, Cole was unable to hold back any longer; he held his face in his hands and totally broke down. Worried, but understanding completely, Brent hooked his arms under Cole's shoulders and dragged him over to their trucks.

Mack worried as he watched the two through the window, knowing that something was going on. There seemed to be some kind of undercurrent running through town that had people on edge, yet no one could quite explain it or why it was there. It was as if a foreboding of things to come was hanging over them, yet no one could prepare for it. Shaking his head, Mack turned back to wiping down the bar.

Once at the truck, Brent lowered the tailgate and sat Cole down. "Hey," he said, softly, seeing his friend collapsing forward, resting his elbows on his knees.

"God, I'm sorry! Brent, I'm so sorry I said and thought all those things! I can't lose any more! I lost everyone I cared about once; it would kill me if it happened again! And this time I have Katie to think about! If I go fucking things up again, then she hurts too!" he sobbed, speaking the truth, but losing his control due to the drinks that had loosened him up.

"I'm still here, aren't I?" Brent nudged him.

He had taken a seat on the back of the tailgate next to Cole, letting his friend get things out. That was the best he could do. Cole needed to find the release to work past his torment. There was no reason to carry things any further; to Brent, this was nothing more than one of life's little quirks, and had not impacted their friendship in any way.

"It would take a hell of a lot more than you giving me hell to make me turn my back on you. Cole, I don't hold a grudge against you and I know you didn't mean what you said. Like I said before, it does look suspicious; even I would have blown up like that. But the thing is, I didn't do anything and you were running scared. God, we're friends! That didn't change and I don't think any less of you," Brent said, his eyes dark and imploring.

"How can you not?" Cole replied, aghast at that disclosure.

Brent leaned closer for a moment, "Cole, something happened to you back there at the ranch. Can you tell me what happened?"

"I ... Brent, nothing happened," Cole shrugged, turning his head and refusing to say any more.

Brent took a deep breath; it was useless to push him any further tonight. If Cole wanted to talk, then that was fine; he was there to listen. It wasn't the best time to seek answers and even if he did, most of Cole's thinking might have just been the booze.

"You know, that was a bad time in your life, Cole. Tonight wasn't the same at all! What happened tonight has no bearing on what happened back then...."

"It was the same thing. Things happened that we couldn't understand tonight; it's just like ... well, it was just wrong," Cole argued.

"All right, so I'll kick your ass around the barn a few times tomorrow. But only after you're sober so you can remember what happened! In the meantime, you didn't mean what you said, cause if I really thought you did, I would have already kicked your ass then!" Brent grinned, looking sideways.

Cole lifted his head, looking through blurry eyes, "I guess I really made an ass out of myself. And in front of Callie and Ruth. What the hell's wrong with me?"

"Nuthin's wrong with you. Cole, let yourself be human for once! We blow up at things that scare us and we don't understand! That's what you did. Is that so bad?" Brent shrugged.

"It is when you blame a friend," Cole said sorrowfully.

"It is when you accuse a friend and refuse to see the truth and continue to act on that," Brent pointed out. "You said a few things in the heat of anger and you knew right away that you were wrong. The truth was there and you saw it. You ran cause you wanted to escape yourself, not cause you wanted to run from me, Ruth, or Callie. And as for what you said earlier, you don't hurt those you love. Life has hurt you; there's a difference. It wasn't wrong for you to get together with Callie, you two deserve happiness; and Ruth's life is richer and better for having you in it."

"You mean that?" Cole tried smiling.

"I don't say what I don't mean, I think you know that by now," Brent stated. "Cole, I watched Ruth for years after Gerald died. She tried bravely to carry on. She threw herself into work as a volunteer at the clinic, did some bookkeeping and sewed her quilts for extra income. She tried her best to fill her life with friends, hoping to fill the void, but we knew how lonely she really was. All she ever wanted was to be surrounded by kids and grandchildren; but she had lost everything. She lost her babies before any of them had the chance to live," he said, cringing as soon as the words were out.

Looking over, Brent saw a fresh onslaught of tears and noticed the way Cole buried his face in his hands. "I know the feeling," he said after taking a few minutes to compose himself.

These were the times Brent truly detested. Falling back on jokes and endless torment in his quest to comfort a friend had no place here. Neither did his empty words. He sat tongue-tied, kicking himself, his own emotions held barely in check. Cole knew full well how that felt, perhaps that was what had drawn him and Ruth together in the first place. They had both lost babies before they had a chance at life. Brent threw his arm around his friend's shoulder.

"I'm sorry," he managed to choke out.

Nothing was said for a while; Cole sat sullenly, remembering all that was gone. Images of a baby lost filled his head. He wondered if it would have been a boy or a girl; Cole never had the courage to ask the doctors that question. At the time, he thought it easier not knowing. He had always wondered what the baby would have looked like.

Would he have had Katie's free spirit and imagination? Or would she have had Katie's eyes and long hair with loose curls that hung down over her shoulders? Cole wondered if she would have run through the yard, singing as she played in the sunshine, or if he would be like him and possess a restless streak, always wanting to be outside working the ranch. Those thoughts never quit. He had lost a real child and sometimes Katie was a reminder of that loss. Brent was right; he was just plain scared. Now, he loved again. He loved so many. He couldn't lose a one of them. It took a few minutes for him to fully compose himself. Sitting up, Cole took a ragged breath and drew his arm across his eyes and nose.

"Am a fucking mess," he tried joking, wiping the snot from his face.

"Yeah, have definitely seen you looking better," Brent joked back. "But Cole, you have to know what you mean to all of us here. Ruth loves you; you've given her what she needed most. She now has a family and Katie is a grandchild to her. I can't even say, 'like a grandchild,' cause it goes deeper than that. We all can see how Ruth looks on you as a son and Katie as her grandchild. The love is that deep and intense. How can you think you hurt her by giving her all that? She now has someone to go on for!"

"Guess I'm just afraid to see things that way. I run from things. I ran from Wyoming and never looked back after Sarah's death, it just seemed easier that way. I thought that if I didn't have to live where everything happened, that somehow it would all just disappear, almost as if it had happened to somebody else. Thinking of it happening to me was just too hard; everything fell apart so fast after the accident. Life is so fragile. And tonight made me see how quickly everything can fall apart, so I ran again. I'm sick to death of being scared and sick to death of hurting and running. I love everyone here, I love my life now and I was finally smart enough to realize how much I love Callie."

"And it's about time you realized that, too," Brent nudged him with his elbow.

"So, I'm a slow learner," Cole smirked.

"Better slow than never! But I won't ask Callie that," Brent laughed, especially seeing the way Cole blushed, groaning as he hid his face again.

"You never let up, do you?" Cole moaned.

"When it comes to the people I love and care about, I don't," Brent replied seriously.

"Good for me, cause I can be an ass at times," Cole sighed heavily.

"You think?" Brent continued with his torment. Things had gotten entirely too serious, and he needed to lighten them up and bring Cole back to himself.

"Yeah, can be a dumb ass at times," Cole sheepishly admitted.

"We all do a good job at that! But Cole, what happened today would rattle anyone. We don't know how that stuff got in there, maybe it was a fluke and some of that shit spilled into the grain when packaged, or something. It could have been in the top and only got to a few horses. I guess it was just the luck of the draw, for lack of a better explanation," Brent shrugged helplessly. "For the life of me, I just can't figure it out. I mean, I was careful and didn't see anything out of the ordinary, but I've been known to have my head up my ass at times and probably just went along feeding the animals without paying much attention."

"Who would?" Cole exclaimed. "Hell, I'm like that almost every night! I feed the horses the same grain and I don't examine every single kernel! We just go about the business of feeding our animals! Why would we act or think differently? And don't forget, I fed them last night! It could have been then, too!"

"Who knows what the hell it could have been. Let's just be thankful that things aren't any worse and go on from there. The most important thing is we gotta stick together," Brent replied.

Cole's head shot up as if slapped, "Brent, you think someone could have done that on purpose?"

"Yeah, but who?" Brent asked, his blood running cold at the thought.

"Come on! You really think that shit got in there by accident? Can you explain how an 'accident' like that can happen? Brent, I never had any of that shit, so there's no rational explanation for why I found those cubes on the floor of my barn! Don't you think we're skirting around the issue here? Tiptoeing with stupid innuendos so we don't have to face what's really on our minds? We both know that shit didn't get into the feed by accident! In all our years of ranching, did you ever hear of something like that?" Cole asked, staring intently.

"No, can't say that I have," Brent answered slowly, just as reluctant to put his thoughts into words. "But I fear you're right. Not accidental, but deliberate? Maybe a mistake?"

"A mistake?" Cole asked.

"Zach?" Brent asked, his voice breaking.

"Zach! Why the hell would you say Zach?" Cole exclaimed.

"Cause I don't want to think anything else!" Brent cried out. "Cole, he did feed the horses that one night—"

"He fed them according to my directions!" Cole argued back.

"Yeah, but what if he had the shit in his pockets or something? Maybe he innocently fed it to the horses, thinking it was a treat. He's only a kid, he probably didn't know that it could hurt them. And their gate was left open...." Brent still argued.

Cole stared intently for a moment, "Brent, you really want to blame the kid? I don't! It's like me blaming you! It's an easy answer, but one I don't want to consider."

Brent blanched; jumping from the tailgate, he paced slowly. He had the sickening feeling that Cole was right. All night long he'd had that feeling, and it scared him to death. If someone was low enough to do this to Cole, what else would they stoop to? And why? He had no enemies here in town, so why would anyone even think of doing something like this? Yet, like Cole, Brent chose not to think about that. But not thinking about something didn't make it any easier and it didn't make it go away.

Turning, he faced Cole, trying to still the shaking of his hands. "Cole, what the fuck are you saying? Do you know what you're saying? Who the hell!"

"Someone who wants me to give in and sell, maybe," Cole stared coldly into Brent's eyes.

Brent stared back at the steely anger he saw in their dark depths, "Oh shit, you don't think...?"

"Brent, who the hell else could it be? Can you name one person who would do something like this? Anyone around here capable of that?" Cole asked.

"No, but I think I liked it better before the booze started wearing off," Brent said, a sick feeling in the pit of his stomach. "But you may be right. Nothing bad's happened here till Sinclair came along!"

"Yeah, and I've had a bad feeling ever since. Zach said he closed the gates that night, yet some of the cows got out and we had a 15-year-old kid wandering around the bog. What if he'd fallen in? I just thank God I was there to help! He could have panicked and tried getting the cow out himself instead of running for home!" Cole cringed.

"And he's also not one to be careless. I've seen him working with Walt, kid's not a goof. But he is a kid and they do make mistakes," he reminded Cole.

"Yeah, guess it could happen that way. Since we have no proof, then we got nothing to go on anyway. The only thing is, I can't explain what happened to my horses," Cole shrugged.

"Fluke? Who would do this?" Brent choked out.

Cole turned to look at Brent again, "Could be someone who thinks he has something to gain from my misfortune, or maybe it's someone who wants to drive a wedge between us."

"Oh fuck," Brent shuddered, not wanting to have to think that way. "Do you think?"

"Right now, I don't know what the hell to think. But you know, maybe it's been nagging in the back of both our minds all night, only neither of us was wanting to put it into words," Cole said, seeing the way Brent looked quickly away. "Yeah, me too. Well, it's been one a hell of a day. I'm worried sick about my horses and I feel like shit. My head's pounding and I'm thinking things I don't want to think. All I know is that we shouldn't jump to conclusions that would start trouble and cause folks to start getting hurt. So Sinclair asked a few questions. He hasn't done anything we know of, and we certainly have no proof."

"And we have no way of getting any proof. Guess we're back to square one; we have to keep our eyes and ears open and we have to just try and not fly off the handle. Can't go stirring up anything where there's nothing to be stirred."

"That's about all we can do. Let's face it, Ruth feels uneasy about this and I don't like it either; something just doesn't feel right, yet I can't even begin to explain things. All I know is that we gotta stick together, you know?" Cole turned to him again.

"Yeah, I know. Cole, you gotta know I'd never do anything to hurt you," Brent answered solemnly.

"I know that, but I hurt you," Cole solemnly replied.

"Nah, you were just scared. I don't blame you," Brent said quietly.

"No excuse," Cole shrugged.

"There's never been an excuse for you," Brent replied so dryly that it took a moment for the words to sink in.

Either that or Cole's brain was still fuzzy from the whiskey he had downed earlier. He looked at his friend for a minute, then doubled over, laughing so hard he almost fell from the tailgate.

"Shit! Let's get the hell outta here," Cole gasped, stumbling to his feet.

"Yeah, but I'm driving," Brent called out, flashing a toothy grin.

"But ... my truck!" Cole stammered, looking at his vehicle.

"Your truck will be here in the morning," Brent said, shoving Cole towards the door. "Besides, Ruth and Callie are waiting and they're already gonna skin us both alive. Especially you when they smell the booze! You gonna give them more of a reason by driving in the shape you're in?"

Cole groaned, not wanting to go home and face the music. "Life used to be so simple," he mumbled, thinking of confronting the women.

"Yeah, wouldn't want to be in your shoes right now," Brent shot back, knowing that deep down neither woman was mad. Like he and Cole, they were just scared.

Chapter Thirteen

The bright afternoon sun blazed down upon the land, teasing them with the promise of a long, hot summer. Cole took his hat off and wiped his brow. It was already Monday afternoon and the horses were doing fine. Only one of the buyers had been livid, stating that he would go elsewhere, but after talking calmly and considering Cole's honesty, he eventually changed his mind. This setback was something Cole could have kept to himself; just the fact that he came forward, open and honest about what had happened, was enough to bring the man around.

Cole then sat back, letting out a sigh of relief; he had come so close to losing his buyers that it made his stomach churn. Even losing one would have hurt. He owed Callie more than he could say; it was only because of her knowledge and quick action that Cole was able to save the animals at all. Just thinking about what could have happened was enough of a scare for a while. His entire livelihood rested on the sale of those three horses, which would enable him to make it through most of the summer when another batch of the younger horses would be trained and ready to go. That shipment was due the last week of July, with another shipment planned in the middle of October. If all were successful, then Cole could relax over the winter, knowing that he had enough money put away to pay the bills, put food on the table and maybe even add to his stock in the spring.

Things were definitely looking better; Katie was getting older so it would soon be easier to devote more time to the ranch. Right now, Cole had all that he could handle. The horses were prancing around the lush, green field, and the deep colors of spring were settling in, shining across the land before the summer sun had the chance to burn it brown. There wasn't a cloud in the sky, but the shadows from the mountains in the background stretched across the plains, lending a quiet sense of darkness to the day.

The past few days had been tiring, and Cole had no desire to repeat them. He returned home Sunday night looking and feeling like hell. Brent had insisted on driving him home, and refused to take no for an answer. It had been an interesting ride, with Cole almost falling out of the truck in his quest to open the door before he got sick all over the interior.

261

"Brent...." he had gagged, clamping his hand over his mouth.

"SHIT! Hold on!" Brent cried out, swerving onto the shoulder. "OPEN THE DOOR! Open the door! I'll never get that smell out!" he exclaimed, shoving Cole out onto the ground.

"Gee, than—" Cole heaved, vomiting in the field.

"You ok?" Brent shouted out, jumping out of the truck and kneeling alongside him.

"Fu—" Cole gasped, gagging again. After he finished heaving, he sat back on his haunches, wiping his mouth. "Man, remind me not to do this shit again," he groaned, falling back onto the ground.

He lay on the hard earth for what seemed like an eternity before things stopped spinning. "You believe in flying saucers?" Cole asked out of nowhere.

"Flying saucers? Hell no!" Brent exclaimed, lying back himself. It was growing late and the women would be worried, but they needed time by themselves. "Why would you ask that?"

"Cause it would explain how that shit got into my feed! Maybe little green men did it!" Cole chuckled.

"Maybe Sinclair's one of those little green men," Brent snickered.

"Yeah, he's freaky-looking enough," Cole broke down laughing, leaving both him and Brent wheezing for air. "You ever read all those newspaper clippings about ranchers who come out finding their cattle mutilated in the fields?" he asked, turning sideways.

"Yeah! Years ago! They had no idea of what happened," Brent shook his head.

"See? They couldn't explain it either! So it had to be little green men!" Cole said, proud that he had everything all figured out.

"I read something like that once when I was about ten, scared the shit outta me," Brent explained. "I was afraid to go out at night, cause our area was like what they described in the article. We're stuck out here all alone. No one would ever know if aliens swooped down and took us over! We'd be toast before word ever got out! One day, some rare tourist would happen by and find all our bones all bleached and drying in the sun...."

"You know, you're a sick fuck!" Cole exclaimed, sitting up on his elbows. Looking at his friend, he tried deciding if he was serious or not. "Where the hell do you come up with this shit?"

"From those articles! No one saw or heard anything, yet the next day, the cattle were dead! Hell, we haven't had any modern-day rustlers in years, that all stopped back in the fifties. Since then, things have been pretty quiet," Brent replied.

"Ahhh, the good old days. Those really were the days, you know?" Cole asked, a wide grin plastered across his face.

"How so?" Brent asked of him.

"I mean, it was great! That's when a cowboy was a cowboy! We'd ride the range wearing our six guns and anyone who pissed us off or tried anything, like stealing our herd or our women, faced a good ole' taste of Montana justice!" Cole replied.

"Yeah! Montana justice! Now that's the way to live! Ride the range and create your own justice when wronged!" Brent whooped.

Cole turned serious and was quiet for a moment before he sat up, facing Brent. "You know, if push comes to shove, I'll make my own justice," he stated flatly.

Concerned, but more intrigued than alarmed, Brent sat up himself. "What do you mean?"

"Brent, this doesn't go past you and me. Not even Will for now, ok?" Cole pleaded.

"Yeah sure, but—"

"But what I'm saying is that I've been pushed around enough. I've had enough people screwing me over in my life and I won't let it happen again," Cole stated, cutting Brent off.

Brent stared, seeing a side of Cole he never thought possible.

"Don't look so shocked!" Cole cried out. "Fifty years ago if a man fought for his rights and what was his, he was looked upon as a hero. Nowadays, he's looked down on. When someone wrongs you, turn the other cheek. When someone hurts you, smile in their face and forgive them. When someone threatens your way of life, you turn to the law. When someone hurts you or someone you love, then you turn to the law there, too."

"I'm not shocked at what you said, Cole," Brent said apprehensively. "I'm shocked because now I know you feel the same way I do. It's not very easy to admit and it usually doesn't come up in normal conversation, but now's the right time."

"It's more than the right time! I've been pissed for a long time now and it's about time I stopped feeling that way! The hell with turning the other cheek, you only get slugged again! And the hell with smiling in their faces when they fuck you over and then turning to forgive them! That only leaves you open to be screwed over again and again! It doesn't stop! And the hell with the law! All it does is let bleeding heart liberals scream for the rights of those who don't deserve any rights! When I see someone who commits a grave crime getting off with a slap on the wrist, where's the justice in that?"

"There is no justice in that. Whole country's gone to shit since they got rid of the death penalty. A hundred years ago, the town gathered in the square with picnic baskets and let their kids run and play while they walked a murdering bastard to the gallows. Nowadays, we're lucky they're even convicted!" Brent replied.

"No one seems to get convicted anymore. Brent, the world stopped making sense a long time ago," Cole said tiredly.

"You talking about Matt and Sarah now?" Brent asked.

"I dunno, maybe ... yeah, I guess," Cole shrugged.

"Cole? What's wrong?" Brent urged, hoping that Cole was finally calm enough to talk.

"Nothing! Just feeling everything at once! I tend to get a bit loony when tired, and the booze sure didn't help any!" Cole said, looking quickly away.

"We all know you're a bit touched! That's nothing new!" Brent shot back, seeing all Cole could do was nod his head in agreement.

That was the moment Brent realized that he had been right all along, he would bet his life on it. They hadn't heard the entire story. Then he chastised himself as he so often did. Cole's wife had been killed. What more was there to the story? If Cole hesitated and held back when speaking of her, it was only because even after six years, he was still traumatized. One doesn't get over something like that easily, if they get over it at all. After a while, they learn to live again, but they never forget. Yet Brent couldn't help but wonder where all this talk about not being pushed around anymore came from. And who did Cole mean when he talked about being screwed over? The more they talked, the more questions loomed.

"Cole, we all know that you're still blaming yourself on some level. What happened wasn't your fault," Brent strove to reassure his friend.

"Maybe, maybe not," Cole answered glumly. "All I know is that everyone probably thought Sarah wouldn't have died if ... if I had stayed home with her," he said, wishing that Brent would leave the subject alone. He was going somewhere Cole didn't want to go.

"How do you know? How do you know what everybody thought?" Brent challenged.

"Brent, I can't even answer that now, cause you see, right now I'm sitting here thinking clearly...."

"Wanna bet?" Brent smirked.

"As clearly as I can," Cole glared back. "Oh, what the hell. I can sit here and say maybe this, or maybe that, until I turn blue in the face. I don't have any answers for anything, especially for—" Cole abruptly stopped.

"For what, Cole?" Brent gently prodded.

"Nothing," Cole quickly changed the subject. "Nothing, Brent. It was just a bad time, that's all. I really don't want to talk about it anymore. Maybe if I'd stayed home that night, everything would have been different."

"And maybe if the good Lord had given frogs wings they'd fly instead of hop," Brent shook his head.

"All right! I can't change the past, but we can change the way we handle the future! You know, maybe if some of my decisions had been different, then...." Cole spoke, hesitating once again.

"What decisions, Cole?" Brent asked, growing bewildered.

As usual, just as Cole was on the brink of something, he expertly skirted around the subject, alluding to his guilt and his loss, but not giving any specific reason for either one.

"Nothing; no decisions," Cole sighed deeply. "I meant that if only ... well, if only things didn't happen like they did. Hell! It seems that we always run our lives on 'if only'. If only I had left yesterday instead of today. If only I had chosen this instead of that, or if only I had said yes instead of no. Don't you see? If only we change one of the decisions we've made in our lives, then everything would be different! I still can't make sense out of what happened back then. And afterwards, I was so damned depressed about the entire thing that I wanted to end my own life. I just didn't have the courage!"

"Amen," Brent whispered. "You see, that was one 'if only' that worked out right," he finished, staring over at Cole.

"Anyway, I'm here and I've started my life over for what it's worth and no one, and I mean no one, is going to take that away! Brent, if this upsets you or you think any less of me for saying this, then I understand. But if someone even tries or does me and mine wrong again, I'll make them pay. The more wrong they do us, the more they'll pay."

"How wrong are you talking?" Brent asked, almost afraid to put his words into a sentence.

Cole leaned forward, quietly talking. His eyes never wavered, he never flinched and he never winked. "I'm talking about a man standing up for what's his. If that means I have to kill to do that, then so be it. Anyone comes across me and threatens those I love, or worse, is a dead man. There are plenty of ways to dispose of a body here. Drag them so far into the woods or mountains that they won't be discovered for months or years, if they're found at all. By the time that happens, all that'll be left is their bleached white bones."

"Or you could simply drag them to the mud bog and let that do the job," Brent said just as steadily and deadly.

Their eyes locked for a moment, with two friends seeing another side of one another; a side that they both had kept hidden from the world, but a side that they agreed on one hundred percent.

"It sounds like that was done before," Cole said quietly.

"Not by me, but it's been done. Heard tell of a story around my great-granddaddy's time where this fella came into town causing trouble. Little by little, folk's herd started disappearing. Then one night, my great-granddaddy's herd was hit. In the process, the bastard shot and wounded my great-uncle, who died 'bout a week later. He was only 13, and my great-granddaddy took matters into his own hands," Brent said flatly.

"And?" Cole asked, barely above a whisper.

"He never said what he did, but that fella simply vanished. They looked high and low, but there was no sign of him. The only thing I can tell you is that my granddaddy told me how he came out to the barn one night. He was about 15 at the time and saw my great-granddaddy cleaning a coating of mud off of his horse and his self. My granddaddy quietly got some rags and helped. They then burned those clothes and rags so no one would know the better. He never did say what he did; but if you ask me, he had himself a taste of Montana justice," Brent finished, staring unblinking.

"Sounds like your great-granddaddy was a smart man. We can learn from him," Cole stared back.

"Cole, let's make a pact," Brent suggested.

"Go ahead," he nodded.

"We keep our eyes and ears open. We come up with whatever we can, and don't let anyone ride shod over us," Brent replied.

"You sound like something's cooking," Cole stated.

"Somethin's in the wind," Brent said.

"I know, I can feel it in my bones, too," Cole shuddered.

"Me too," Brent nodded. "Have for days. No rhyme or reason for it, but I feel it. Cole, we watch each other's backs and we keep this from the women. No sense in scaring them."

"Can't keep it from Ruth, she knows. She slammed and locked the door in Sinclair's face the first day," Cole reminded him.

"See! He even got to her!" Brent exclaimed. "But you're right, there's no fooling her. Let's just keep our eyes and ears open like I said, and try and get a handle on this Sinclair fella. I want to know where he goes and what he's doing. I don't trust the little bastard and I'll be dipped in shit if I'll let him take us by surprise. No, like you, nobody's gonna take me by surprise. I refuse to let something like what happened to my great-uncle happen again."

"I agree," Cole nodded. "Out here, we have to take care of ourselves. In many ways, nothing's changed since the old days. We're still as isolated and still as rugged. We live hard, we work hard, and we love hard. When any of that is threatened, there's no one who cares to come in and help us. We're on our own and have to take care of our own."

"That's what I'm gonna do," Brent declared.

"I'm with ya. And if either one of us, or any of our neighbors, falls prey to anyone coming around looking for trouble, I say we take matters into our own hands. No matter what that means," Cole replied.

Brent stared so intently, neither blinked or even breathed for a moment. "I couldn't agree more. From now on, we take care of things ourselves."

They made their pact and Cole felt a little better for it. He didn't know if it was the fallout from their misunderstanding, the booze, or the tension of the past few days coming to a head, but he and Brent had reached an impasse and came out realizing that they both wanted the same thing. They were willing to fight, and ready to take matters into their own hands if need be.

Looking out over the ranch now, Cole was hard-pressed to believe that he could have even had such dark thoughts. Nothing bad could happen on a day like today. The sky was blue, the birds were singing, and so was Katie. Ruth was cooking their dinner, the blacksmith just left, and his horses were better.

Once again, Cole's mind wandered back to the previous night. He and Callie had spent the entire night in the barn while Ruth slept in the spare room. Katie had been asleep for hours and it seemed as if the worst of the emergency was over. Cole was tired, but more than that, he was ashamed of his behavior. Looking at Callie, he wondered how she still had the energy to go on.

"Why don't you go home and rest?" Cole had asked, his mouth dry and sour, his hair unkempt and greasy, and his face caked with sweat.

Getting drunk and lying in the dirt talking the first half of the night away with Brent hadn't helped. Neither did the fact that he had been sicker than a dog; something he deserved for his earlier bout with the bottle. Now, though, he stood with Callie, embarrassed at himself and his earlier actions, yet she didn't care.

"No, I'm here for the night. The horses need me and so do you. Cole, come here," she urged, holding out her arms.

"I'm a mess," he cringed, pulling back.

"I don't care. Come here," Callie said, drawing him into her arms.

The barn door was closed and the house was dark. Cole needed her more than he could ever put into words. He fell into her arms, feeling her love engulf him. She rocked her body back and forth slowly, holding him as best she could, considering her size. Yet, it was all Cole needed. He needed to feel her love ... needed to know that they were more than just what they had shared the other night when they first reached out to one another.

Cole had loved her then, and he loved her even more now, because this was real. The other night had been magical. Tonight, though, tonight was real life. It was two people coming together as more than lovers. They didn't need fancy suits, ritzy restaurants or perfumes and colognes to be together. They accepted each other for what they were and this was it. Callie's face was streaked with dirt, but she looked as beautiful to him now as she had the other night. Her hair stuck out from her ponytail, with pieces of hay and grain embedded. To Cole, they were more striking than any jeweled comb she could wear.

She smelled of horses and the barn, intoxicating him, making his senses reel. Callie was real, she reached out to life truthfully and honestly with no false pretenses and she loved him the same way. She didn't need to put up phony fronts or fancy window dressing, this was what she was and this was what Cole wanted. He loved every inch of this woman, whether she was in the barn mucking around with his horses or if she was sitting across the table bathed in candlelight. This woman was real, her love was real and her body fit his perfectly. They gave of one another more than either had ever given to anyone else in their lives. For as long as they lived, neither would ever go to another.

Cole reached out, slowly pulling Callie down onto a bed of hay. The other night they had loved on satin sheets and tonight they came to each other's arms in a pile of hay, lying on a scratchy old blanket. Little by little, their clothes fell away and they wordlessly fell onto the hay with Cole coming down on top of her. His need was great, his erection raged, and his blood boiled.

Callie's need was just as urgent. Little moans of desire escaped as she whimpered, pressing her body close, needing to feel this man inside her. She lived for his touch, she longed for him to fully enter her, driving himself so deep that it would be impossible to tell where one ended and the other began.

They came together naturally. Cole's mouth sensuously took hers, gently at first, yet more demandingly as he sucked on her lower lip, tracing his tongue along the line of her mouth. Callie gasped, shooting upwards as he suckled on her bottom lip, blazing a hot, wet trail down the hollow of her neck to her breasts. Her nipples formed hard peaks of desire, which he let slip between his teeth one at a time, sucking until her body melted with passion and burned with need. Callie felt the flames shooting up from her toes as a golden, hot liquidy fire built within her loins, exploding throughout her body. Shuddering, she cried out desperately when Cole finally met her need, penetrating her womanhood and pushing deep inside her body, burying himself in her very core.

Lost in the throes of passion, they grappled, moving in sync. Pumping furiously, Cole totally surrendered himself to Callie as their bodies exploded as one, soaring as spasms worked through them. Finally, they rocked quietly as they came back down, with Cole slowly sliding in and out of her until he stopped throbbing, sated from their union. Collapsing onto the hay, he held her, not saying a word. He lay on his back, feeling Callie wrapping her arms and legs around him. They slept that way until the first rays of the early morning light streaked in through the windows.

* * *

"You saved me again," Cole whispered to himself as he stood on the fence, staring out over the horizon. "You saved me when I didn't know I needed saving and you did it again that night. You saved my horses and brought me out of myself. I don't know where I'd be today if it weren't for you. I know I wouldn't be as far as I am or as well off. My life would be so empty if you weren't in it," he said, thinking of Callie.

"Hey handsome," she whispered, snaking her arms around his waist.

So lost in thought, he hadn't even heard Callie driving in. Jumping, he let himself settle back into her embrace, feeling the warmth of her inviting body.

"Hey, when did you get here? I didn't hear you coming!"

"That's because you were in outer space," she giggled, nestling herself next to him. "I feel like taking you into the barn and having my way with you," she whispered, her soft breath blowing against his skin. Her fingers danced teasingly on his belt buckle, causing an involuntary moan to escape his lips.

"God, what you do to me," he moaned.

"No, what I want to do to you," Callie giggled, turning to lean back on the fence. Smiling, she stared up at him.

Cole turned to the side, resting his arm on the top of the fence as they talked. "I know what you'd like to do to me now, but I don't think Ruth'd want to see it. So, not that I'm complaining, but I didn't expect you today!"

"I know, but I'm sort of making my rounds and thought I'd stop by for a few minutes! It seems that spring has sprung and all the mares are about ready to pop!" Callie laughed heartily with Cole.

"Oh, the wonders of spring!" he laughed. "I think I have a few more weeks for my two, guess they're late bloomers!"

"Oh, I wouldn't worry about that! They just want to be the center of attention when their time comes! I just thank God that they weren't the ones to get ... well," Callie cleared her throat.

"I was thinking the same thing over breakfast," Cole replied softly. "It was bad enough that the others got sick, but if it had been any of the expectant mares, then they might not have been so lucky! You know, the only reason everything turned out so well was because you were there. I don't know what I would have done without you," he finished with a smile.

"I'm just glad that everything worked out as it did. The horses look good!" she beamed, looking over the herd.

"Callie, I'm really sorry about the way I acted, taking off and drinking like that," he blushed, averting his eyes for a second.

"You gonna beat yourself over the head for that the rest of your life? Cole, you have nothing to apologize to me for! You know, just because we're together doesn't mean we own one another. You still have your life and you're free to come and go as you want. You don't owe me any explanations for what you do!"

"When I upset you and leave like that, I do," he corrected her.

"All right, that I'll accept the apology for. But for anything else, what I just said goes. We still need to be our own person. I guess that's one of the reasons I'm still single," she replied.

"And I thought that it was cause you were waiting for me," Cole grinned devilishly, running his finger along her arm.

"You're so full of yourself, you know?" she leered, playfully shoving him away.

"But you love me anyway," he drawled, turning his grin on her.

"I'm not even going to dignify that with an answer!" Callie turned away, leaning on the fence. "They look good," she said, staring out over the pasture.

"Yep, and they're ready to go," Cole answered proudly.

"That's right! The buyers are coming the day after tomorrow! You must be excited!" Callie exclaimed.

"I doubt if I'll sleep the next two nights!" Cole chuckled.

"I know! You never sleep when you're nervous or excited! And just think, the next day is Katie's birthday and you probably won't sleep again Wednesday night!" she teased. "You still having her party?"

"Are you kidding? Ruth's already started cooking! She, Helen and Irma are cooking and baking up a storm! I tell you, you'd think they were expecting to feed an army!"

"They are! You, Brent and Will are gonna be there!" Callie giggled, snuggling closer.

Both leaned on the fence, staring out at the mountains. "I just wish we could stay like this forever," he said wistfully.

270

"Like how?" she squinted her eyes against the sun as she looked over at him.

"Like we are right now," he explained. "Everything is going good; Katie's happy, I finally have you in my life, I have Ruth and my friends, and my horses are being shipped Wednesday and more later in the summer. Everything's going good, you know what I mean? I just don't want it to end," he finished, staring down at her.

Callie quietly leaned against Cole's arm, feeling him kiss her softly on the top of her head. If she had her way, they would stay like this forever, together and loving one another with no interference from the outside world. Yet, in the back of Callie's mind, someone was already interfering. Even though she never broached the subject, Maggie still lurked. Cole might not see it for himself, but he shared a child with another woman and even though that woman had been gone for years and had never made an attempt to know that child, there was always the chance that she might show up one day. As much as Callie hated to admit it, she would always see Maggie as a threat and a part of Cole's life.

* * *

There was only one more day in which to make final preparations. As expected, Cole had difficulty sleeping the night before, but was too busy with the horses to give it another thought. Having caught on to her father's mood, Katie had been a livewire, with it taking three extra stories before she was willing to give in to sleep. He expected much of the same behavior tonight, with the excitement of her birthday looming just around the corner. There was a long list of chores facing him. Most of them were unnecessary, but he was taking them on anyway. The horses were ready, but that was not good enough for Cole.

Being a perfectionist at heart wasn't always the best thing for a person, something Cole knew well. Not only did he drive himself relentlessly at times; he was also his own worst critic. Nothing ever seemed good enough. In what had turned into a never-ending, self-imposed process, the horses were washed and brushed, their hooves were picked and cleaned once more, and Cole planned on brushing a fresh coat of turp on them. That was the only thing he had forgotten to do the other day and was finally getting around to it. He was cleaning each and every animal from the tips of their ears to the bottom of their feet, wanting his own horses to look as good as the ones he was selling. First impressions meant everything and Cole was determined to have his ranch known for the quality of its animals.

271

The fence had been repaired, with a fresh coat of paint splashed on the rails. The front porch had been cleaned thoroughly, new baskets of flowers hung along the entire length, windows were washed, and the flower beds were weeded. Even the flower boxes under the windows were given a fresh coat of paint and stood grandly, their colors in full bloom. And that was only the beginning. Between him and Ruth, the house fairly shone. Ruth was busy hanging newly washed white muslin curtains in the front windows, and the yard was mowed, the tack room cleaned and the barn was given the once-over.

"Hey, you want a brush and rag so you can spit-shine their feet?" Brent had teased as he and Will dropped in for a quick visit after lunch.

"Yeah, thought that a ribbon in this one's mane and a top hat and bowtie for the other two would be just the ticket," Cole snickered, trying desperately to ignore the two. It never failed, whenever he needed to concentrate on something, they seemed to show up out of nowhere. "You two have a reason for being here or did you just come to torment me?"

"Hey, come here," Will grabbed Cole while Brent kept Katie amused. "We're finished! Can you believe it? What do you think?" he said as he took Cole off to the shed.

"They're great and they're gonna be perfect," Cole exclaimed, admiring the tiny horses that Will had made to go along with the dollhouse. "You said that you had something going, but wouldn't say what. We have a house, but people don't live with horses in their houses! You finally going to show me what you were talking about?"

"Come on, carry this over while Brent keeps her busy," Will said, shoving a cloth-covered box into Cole's hands.

"What is this?" Cole queried, stalling.

"Will you just come on?" Will hissed, shoving Cole along.

They came to the shed with Will looking around conspiratorially. No one had followed; Ruth was still inside the house and Katie was playing on the front porch with Brent, who was a master at keeping the small child busy. Will then kicked the door shut and shoved Cole over to the table.

"Come on, put it here," he said, almost bouncing with excitement.

Will stood, clearing his throat as he made a big production of things. Cole shook his head, no one but he or Brent could make such a big deal over the smallest things. Yet, Cole had the feeling that both had been keeping something from him since this entire project had begun. Everybody had pitched in with the house, working it out to the tiniest little detail. Cole had wanted it to be perfect and now wondered what these two had gone and done. The door opened, and Brent entered with a huge grin spread across his face.

272

"I couldn't miss this," he grinned widely.

"Oh no, this can't be good," Cole groaned. These two standing there staring like the cat that had the rat cornered couldn't be good for anyone, especially if that someone was him. Cole felt like the rat and Will and Brent had him trapped. "What did you two do?"

"What did we do, he asks," Brent elbowed Will. "Why does he always think we did something?"

"Cause it usually is that way," Cole reminded them. "And because I know you two and don't trust you for about as far as I can throw either of you."

"Oh, now that hurts," Will feigned wounded pride. "Katie with Ruth?"

"Yeah, I made sure that she was in the kitchen. Ruth promised to keep her there until after the unveiling," Brent snickered.

"You mean Ruth knows?" Cole gasped.

"Heck, we think you're about the only one besides Katie who doesn't know," Brent chuckled. "Come on now, just relax and trust us!"

Cole took a deep breath, knowing that he had no choice. For the life of him he wouldn't let them see how excited he really was, but they knew. He tried hiding his feelings, preferring to give both a hard time instead, yet he was so caught up with the preparations for the party that he simply couldn't help himself.

"Looks cute when he bounces like that, huh?" Brent snickered.

"Beats me, ask Callie," Will shrugged.

"Will you two just get on with it? What's in the box?" Cole exclaimed, knowing that even Katie had more restraint than he did at the moment.

"Who's the kid, him or Katie? Even she has more self-control than this," Brent continued teasing.

"Yeah, maybe we'll make him wait," Will decided.

"Like hell you will! What's in the box?" Cole whined pitifully.

Brent placed his hand on Cole's shoulder and started talking, "This is something Will and I did for Katie on our own, we really wanted her birthday to be special," he smiled at his friend.

"It already is, even without all this," Cole answered, feeling his eyes growing wet. "Will you two hurry up?" he said, his voice getting gruff.

For all the pretenses Brent hid behind each and every day, he, too, wasn't unaffected by the moment. His own eyes grew misty and he had to turn away, clearing his throat. Will had gone over to the box and waited until both men were ready.

"Hey, we got to talking one night and decided that Katie needed something to go along with the house. And what's more appropriate in Montana than a house with a barn and outbuildings?" he asked, unveiling

273

their little surprise.

"Oh, shit," was about all Cole could say without going mushy on his friends.

He had to blink furiously, hoping not to make a damned fool of himself, but it was too late. This was just too precious to let go without showing how much he not only appreciated their efforts, but how very much it all meant to him. Cole just stood staring at a duplicate they had built of his ranch, including his shed, tack room and corrals. All of this was then mounted and set on a wooden platform, which was painted and decorated to resemble his land. They even made a replica of the stream that ran behind his property. If Katie filled it with water she could lead her horses from their corral and let them graze and enjoy a cool drink.

"I can't believe you guys did this," Cole said softly, finally regaining full use and control of his voice.

"Why not? It's perfect!" Brent exclaimed. "Look! Looks like real grass!"

"I'm afraid to ask," Cole shook his head.

"Well, dummy here said to get real grass and paste it to the wood, but I told him it would only die. Then he wanted to use coconut died green, and I said that we weren't building something for the frigging Easter bunny, we were making something for Katie. Plus, it would have rotted," Will explained.

"Who you calling a dummy?" Brent shot back, leaving Cole shaking his head and wondering just how many arguments had ensued between the two while working on the project. "It was your idea to use cotton balls died green! Cotton balls, Cole! You stick them things in your ear or whatever else you want to clean out!" he spat out, looking triumphantly at Will.

"You know, I'm sort of glad I wasn't there to hear all of that," Cole had to laugh, shaking his head at the two. "So, who finally came up with the solution and what is this?"

"Ruth did!" Brent exclaimed, his face red and cheery.

"Yeah! She solved the whole problem!" Will joined in.

"I should have known," Cole found himself snickering. "What would any of us do without that woman? She's the center of all we need, holding things together and always coming up with the right answers to everything."

"She sure is one of a kind," Brent said wistfully. "Anyway, she went to town and bought a little piece of this indoor outdoor carpeting and after we got it all cut to size and placed where needed, she had strips of green ribbon which she cut into thin slivers and curled them with her scissors. She then cut them small and attached them with a hot glue gun, one piece at a time."

"One piece at a time!" Cole exclaimed, not quite believing his eyes.

274

"There must be a million pieces here!"

"A million and one, I counted," Will snickered. "Well, think she'll like it?"

"You know, one thing I know is not only will she like it, but she'll love it. This is something she'll treasure her entire life, and will never forget what all of you did for her. She'll think of you every time she looks at this," he replied wistfully, admiring Gris' telltale workmanship.

"Another part of the legacy, huh?" Brent asked, quietly.

"Yeah, one I'm glad to be a part of. I never knew that my life would turn out like this when I first arrived here. I never thought that I'd care about anyone again or that anyone would care about me. But I not only found people I love deeply; I found a family and a home to raise my daughter in. I can't think of a better place on this earth to live or better people to call my family," Cole said softly.

"Hey, listen to who's getting mushy," Brent cleared his throat just so he could speak.

"We loved every minute of it," Will smiled back.

"Thanks, guys, you just made her birthday complete and special," Cole replied.

They spent a few more minutes admiring everything down to the tiniest detail. Cole laughed at the tack room and all the little saddles, blankets, and bits hanging inside. The saddles were fashioned from rawhide, which was cut, shaped and dried. They were then painted and had real leather stirrups attached. The bits, harnesses and reins were made of real leather, with tiny pieces of metal soldered into them. Ruth made the blankets, something Cole had known immediately.

He couldn't believe his eyes. The dollhouse they had made was different than his own home; Cole had just gone too elaborate, yet the land was the same. It was as if he was looking at his place in a different time, maybe from a time in the future, where Katie might live in a new home with a family of her own. The entire thing was just too overwhelming for him, and he spent the rest of the afternoon just thinking about it.

Cole also couldn't thank his friends enough, or get their efforts off of his mind. He now had a real home, something he thanked God for each and every day. The loneliness and heartache was still there, but it was quickly fading into the back of his mind where it belonged. He now lived fully, and loved totally and unconditionally. After Brent and Will left, Cole went into the house, where he cornered Ruth in the kitchen. Katie was down for her nap, so he knew that she would not hear.

"You knew all along, didn't you?" he asked, taking Ruth by the hand and pulling her away from the sink.

"My, what are we talking about?" she asked innocently.

"Uh huh, like you don't know! Ruth, you are the eyes and ears of this entire community! You're also the heart of it, too. I know that you're one of the most important people in my life," Cole said softly, bringing tears to her eyes.

"Honey, what I do, I do out of love for you and that little girl. That's what family is for, isn't it?" she sniffed.

"Yes, that's what family's for and that's what we are. We're an odd sort, but we're family," Cole smiled, taking Ruth into his arms. "Thanks for showing me how to live again," he said softly, causing a fresh onslaught of tears to flow.

* * *

Before Cole knew it, the afternoon slipped away and the horses were bedded down, waiting for their big day. He could hardly eat his dinner and listened to Katie chatting up a storm. Ruth kept an eye on him, silently willing him to eat, which he finally did. They cleared the dishes and went out to sit on the porch for a short while. Cole had spoken with Callie earlier, wishing that she could join them, but she had been called out once again.

That was going to take some getting used to; Sarah never worked, and had preferred remaining home. Cole tried not to be archaic, he was just used to a certain way of life. His grandmother had been home, his mother had been home, and Sarah had been home. But Callie was a different person and he was not going to let this become an issue between them. He loved her just the way she was. To change that would be to change her, and she was perfect in his eyes. Yet, he still missed her, but they at least had their late-night phone calls.

Both Ruth and Cole knew that the next few days promised to be busy ones, and they sat relaxing before the frenzy of activity began in earnest. The ranch had never looked better, the horses were more than ready, and in the morning, the real fun would begin. Cole was already a nervous wreck; once he managed to make it through tomorrow, he would be fine. The sales made him nervous and the party had him excited; right now, Cole just wasn't sure how he should be feeling, so he decided to simply take things in stride.

At first he thought it a mistake to plan Katie's party so soon after the buyers came and had considered Saturday, instead. But after speaking with Ruth, Cole knew that Thursday was just as good a day as any. It actually made little difference in the realm of things. Life went on much in the same way on the neighboring ranches. They all faced the same chores day in and day out, making one day no different than another.

"Plus, it will make it even more special if we have the party on her actual birthday," Ruth had finally talked him into it.

"Not to mention the break in the middle of the workweek," Brent snickered.

"Our workweek never ends," Will grumped, reminding him. "We work seven days a week and don't get weekends off like everyone else does!"

"All the more reason to look forward to the party! We can eat all we want, party, raise hell, and be as loud as we can be! Gonna feel good to really let loose!" Brent exclaimed.

So, Thursday it was, and Thursday was quickly approaching. Another factor in deciding on Thursday was the fact that Brent and his father had just finalized the plans for the shipment of their cattle, which would take place on Saturday. Cole had promised to arrive early and help herd the animals into the large trucks, which were commonly referred to by truckers as 'bull haulers." In all actuality they were regular tractor-trailers that had specially ventilated trailers in which the animals were then hauled to the stockyard. There they would be put into special holding pens until they were then loaded onto boxcars and shipped by rail to various auctions and slaughterhouses across the country.

Cole groaned just thinking about all they had to do the rest of the week, especially with the coming of the two big days he and Brent had worked towards for months. The fruits of their labors were finally in sight, nothing could be better.

"Yeah, nothing but getting you into bed," Cole giggled with Katie later that night as she happily splashed in the tub. Her bright smile could always melt his heart, even when she splashed him with soapy water. "Hey! I don't need the bath!" he exclaimed brightly. "Time for bed."

"No bed, Daddy!" Katie mischievously replied.

"Yes, bed," he groaned, knowing that he was in for a time.

After a long day of grooming horses, cleaning the barn and around the yard, Cole's back ached almost to the point of making him nauseous. Leaning over the side of the tub didn't help any either; all he wanted was get her bath over with, sit in the rocker with their book, and eventually go to bed once he had the chance to relax for a little while. However, Katie wasn't having anything to do with his plans, as Cole had expected earlier.

"No! Play!" she giggled, splashing him again.

"Katie bug, stop that, please?" he pleaded, seeing the mischief in her eyes as his answer. "Oh no, you're not tired, are you?" he asked, resigning himself to the fact that tonight was just going to be one of those nights.

"I want to play with my dollies!" she stated.

"Your dollies are asleep," Cole groaned.

"No, they're waiting for me!" Katie informed him.

"Honey, Daddy's tired," he pleaded.

"Then go to bed," she shrugged, not seeing anything wrong with being left on her own while he slept.

After being splashed a few more times, Cole managed to get his squirming child from the water, wrapped in a thick towel, and into her pajamas. He ended up reading four stories before Katie finally relented and fell asleep. Sighing deeply, Cole looked up and mouthed a simple thank you for the moment. He could now put her down, safe in the knowledge that she would not be running through the house while he slept. Once Katie fell asleep, she stayed that way until morning.

Now the problem was getting himself to sleep, "Wish I had someone to read me four stories," Cole laughed to himself. "But that wouldn't help cause all you want to do is go outside and get your horses ready, but they are ready! You're just never satisfied!"

He finally locked the front door and tried going to bed. For more than two hours Cole tossed and turned, falling into a fitful sleep. His dreams were back, something he did not need that night.

"Hold on to it while you can," Matt snickered, waving his future in his face.

All around him, Cole could see everyone disappearing one by one, whisked away by a woman shrouded in black. She never showed her face, but her bony fingers wrapped around each and every person Cole held dear. Dry strands of straggly gray hair stuck out from under the black hood she wore, hiding everything but the yellow eyes that burned through him. She came closer, holding a finger up in front of his face.

Cole paled, slowly walking backwards. He backed up against the wall of the barn, trapped as she approached. He swallowed deeply, trying to quell the screams that started roaring from deep inside his very soul. The finger reached out, scratching across the right side of his cheek, breaking the skin and causing a steady stream of blood to flow. She cackled, running her finger through the sticky liquid, which she drew to her mouth, licking his essence from her fingers. Holding them back up, she laughed again as droplets fell from her fingertips, drying instantly in the dusty earth as each clot was absorbed.

"It was you," she whispered menacingly as she started backing away. "Soon they'll all know what you did!" she threw her hooded head back,

screeching into the night sky. Shrieking, Katie ran into the darkness, her screams resounding through the nigh air.

"Katie! KATIE!" Cole screamed, struggling to run after her.

But his feet were paralyzed, frozen in place. The figure continued her dark torment, shrieking until he covered his ears against the sound, screaming as his own insanity started taking over.

"My baby! Where's my baby? What have you done with my baby?" Cole sobbed, falling to his knees.

"She's where you put her," the figure backed away, casting a menacing glare. "You know what happened! You know, but you won't admit it, not even to yourself! And now, you're going to let it happen again!" she shrieked.

"Nothing happened! It was an accident and I didn't cause it!"

"It was more than an accident and you know that! You never told anyone, did you? You never told them what really happened, did you? You pushed it into the back of your mind so deeply that you can't even remember it yourself. It's like you've forgotten what happened. By shoving it aside, you can erase it from your heart and from your mind. You don't have to tell anyone about it and you don't have to think about it anymore."

"I don't know what you mean!" he cried out desperately.

"Oh, you know! You only think you forgot, but somewhere, you know! Did you think it would all go away if you just pretended that nothing happened? Or worse, do you really think everyone here believes you? You're lucky, you know. You're lucky that they're so open and willing to believe what you say, and that we are so far from Broken Arrow."

"Will you just stop it! That has nothing to do with things!" Cole screamed in desperation, squeezing his head between his hands.

"It has everything to do with things and you know it! It's happening all over again. They caught you by surprise in Broken Arrow, and they'll do it again here. He'll do it again here! And they believe you! What would you do if Gris decided to check into things? All he has to do is make a few calls, pull in a few favors—"

"SHUT UP!" Cole screeched.

"That's all it would take, and everything will be all over. I can't believe that you've been so lucky. You think that you can forget! That by forgetting, nothing happened. But it happened, Cole! And the sooner you face it, the better off you will be! You want it to happen again? You want to come home one day and find everything gone? You want to find your home—"

"MY HOME IS FINE! Nothing will happen to my home! Why are you doing this to me? I didn't do it! It wasn't me! Nothing happened, I tell you! Nothing! Why can't you believe me?" Cole cried out. His heart hammered,

his skin grew icy cold and his wobbly legs barely held him upright.

"Go ahead! Keep on lying to yourself! You'll be found out eventually! Liars always are! Nothing stays secret forever! The truth always has a way of coming out and we can't stop it! Are you so blind that you're going to let it happen again? You've always had your head buried in the sand and you're doing the same thing now. Think, Cole! Think about—"

"I don't want to think! I'm not ever going to think about that time again! I don't want to know anyone or anything from back then! That was another life that happened to another Cole Morgan. I'm not the same man anymore! I have a new life and I'm different!"

"Fate, Cole! Fate always has a way of stepping in when we turn our backs on ourselves. One day, fate will get you again," she threatened, laughing shrilly as she slowly vanished into the mist rolling down from the mountains.

Cole woke, vaulting up in bed. The dreams were back, as they often were when he worked himself up into a frenzied state. Yet, this time the dream was different. In the past it was everyone gathering around him, blaming him, stoning him, and sending him out of town to live in the wilds, alone and defenseless. She never came to him. No matter how much he longed for her, or no matter how many times he prayed to see her face just once, she never came. Only the details of her death came to him over and over in sickening clarity. Details he no longer admitted to himself, and had almost totally blocked from his conscious mind. He had never told anyone and he never would; as far as Cole was concerned, nothing happened.

There had been a fire, that was all he had willingly admitted to, and never spoke of again. But it wasn't the fire that killed Sarah, and that was what he couldn't live with. He had been the one who killed Sarah. He knew that in his heart and he knew that the minute he walked out of the hospital that day. Everyone knew it. That is, everyone back in Broken Arrow. Guilt and grief had been the reason Cole left; he could not stand the stares from everyone in town, for they knew the truth.

He sat alone during the church service and he stood alone at the cemetery, distancing himself from everyone. Cole endured their stares, and never once lifted his eyes to meet theirs. He couldn't meet theirs. Empty and void of emotion, Matt's eyes already haunted him. Not a word was said, Cole's actions had spoken volumes. He simply could not stand seeing that look in their eyes as they stared. And he would not be able to endure the looks on everyone's faces here if they knew. If that happened, then he really would have nothing left. He couldn't let that happen, there was just no way of understanding what he had done. The only thing to do was wipe everything from his mind like it had never happened.

That was what Cole did best. Shutting out life. You shut out life, you shut out memories best left forgotten, and dreams once thought to be conquered. They were held at bay for a short while, but had returned with a vengeance. When they started to peek out from beneath the ragged edges of his mind, he would shut down, shoving them back. He had vowed to never talk about that time to anyone, and he never did. He had also vowed to no longer remember the details, and had almost succeeded. Bits and pieces came from his jumbled mind, not making any sense and only acting to muddle an already tangled memory.

No one had any idea of the real burden Cole carried around deep inside and he wanted to keep it that way. He was a master at shutting things out, doing such a complete job of it that it seemed as if the memories came from an old movie or were told to him as happening to someone else. As far as Cole was concerned, it had happened to someone else.

When he left Wyoming, he left everything behind; it had no place in his life now. The only thing he wanted from the past was to see her face. If she would only come to him in his dreams, then he would know that she didn't blame him too. Yet, her face was always absent as was the face of her mother. Neither woman came to him. Neither woman would ever forgive him, even throughout eternity. Sarah and Myra had loved him on this earth, but he had let them down. Now, they were finally back and tormenting him in his dreams.

"Why now? Why do you come now and torture me like this? I'd rather you leave me alone than to come to me the way you are now. It's easier to only wonder if you hated and blamed me. I didn't want to really know! Is it cause I now have Callie in my life and that's wrong? Or is it because I haven't changed and will only repeat the mistakes of the past, and you are reminding me of that? Maybe I haven't changed, maybe I never will change," Cole whispered, falling back against the pillows.

* * *

With the exception of the surprise visit by Will and Brent, Tuesday had been quiet and uneventful, in spite of the workload Cole had carried. Ruth dominated the kitchen like a whirlwind, baking up a storm and never happier. Cole couldn't help but laugh at the way she bustled about, with a dab of flour on her cheeks.

"Love your powder," he had teased, brushing the flecks away.

Laughing heartily, Ruth turned back to the counter, where another batch of cookies waited to be tended. Katie helped, and even came out announcing that she had cleaned her room. To Cole's surprise, she had done that very thing. She suddenly realized that her room was her domain, and put her mark on it. New artwork hung on the walls and the blankets were pulled up crookedly on her bed. Katie had also taken an old pink scarf, which she used to cover her dresser, and arranged her stuffed animals on the bed, table and windowsill. Some were dressed, one dog wore a pair of sunglasses and a lace scarf, and others were not touched at all.

She stood proudly while he and Ruth examined her efforts, paying special attention to the new pictures. With his foot, Cole slid the area rug by the side of Katie's bed over, covering the new paint stain she had managed to make. There would be time enough later to scrub the stain out; in the meantime, rugs did wonders.

Frayed nerves had kept sleep at bay, and Katie had been harder to get settled than usual, but all of that was forgotten in the light of day. Cole bounced out of bed, anxious to get started with his chores. Not only did he want the horses and the ranch to look perfect, he wanted the house to look good. He quickly dressed, poured a cup of coffee and went out to the barn.

Soon everything was in full swing. Ruth arrived and began their breakfast. Katie was up and dressed, the horses were out running through the fields, and the stalls were mucked clean. Cole ran ragged for the next few hours making sure everything was in place.

Ruth had vacuumed the house thoroughly just the day before, but Cole gave the small foyer and living room another quick sweep. He rearranged the vase of freshly picked flowers that Ruth had brought over that morning, then stood back examining them. Taking a few steps forward, he fixed a few more blooms and nodded, appeased for now. He swiped at the surfaces of the wooden furniture with a dustrag and adjusted the curtains. The windows were gleaming in the bright sunshine, sending a stream of golden rays into the room. Instead of appearing brighter, the light from outside only enhanced the dark, wooden beauty Cole's home.

He fussed and clucked his way through the living room, into the kitchen, and then back out again. Even the pictures hanging on the walls were quickly straightened for what had to have been the hundredth time, and he bumped into Ruth, who was flitting around just as much. After one last quick inspection of the house, Cole went out onto the porch and swept it again. It had been an entire hour since he had first done that very thing, and with the slight breeze that caressed them that morning, Cole had himself convinced that it needed another going over.

Ruth set up a small, wooden table on the corner of the porch, on which

282

she covered with a lace cloth made by her mother, and placed a vase of flowers in the middle. They were finished; everything was in place and the horses were waiting. When Cole finally stood on the front porch dressed in clean clothes and slicking back his still damp hair, he saw the first car approaching. With his heart in his throat, he stood waiting. Not seeing any trailer for the horse to be carried in, he became puzzled.

"Maybe it's the buyer coming to check things out and the trailer's on the way," he said to Ruth as she came out, joining him.

They both stood in shocked silence as a figure clad in black climbed from the car, slinging her perfectly coifed hair from her shoulders. Standing with her nose in the air and peering out from behind a pair of dark glasses, the woman in spiked heels carefully picked her way over the uneven ground until she finally reached the house.

"Hello Cole," Danielle Sterling greeted him stiffly. "It's nice to meet you."

Chapter Fourteen

Cole stood staring, the breath knocked from his body. His worst fear playing out. Next to Maggie showing back up on his doorstep unannounced, this woman was his second-biggest fear. Danielle hovered, ready to snatch his life away. Cole had always expected this day, with a part of him praying it would never come to be. It had been four years. He thought that with that much time passing, he and Katie would have been forgotten by now. At least, he wished that they were forgotten.

Maggie had no place in his or Katie's life and Danielle had no right being here at all. They had never recognized Katie or her birthday before, and Cole wondered what Danielle was doing here now. Looking back at the car, he was relieved to see that Maggie had not accompanied her sister.

Katie did not need this interference in her life. She knew nothing about her mother; as far as she was concerned, her life consisted of Daddy, Nanny, Papa, and a special set of uncles who adored her deeply. Katie never had a mother and Cole was determined she didn't have one now. She also did not need the aunt that stood before him. It may have been cold-hearted on his part, but the only thing that had been his doing was Katie, herself. Anything else that conspired afterwards was totally fabricated by Maggie and Danielle.

They deemed how things were to be and Cole went along with their demands, never questioning and never arguing. He simply accepted their will and carried on with his life. If he had done that, then they should live by what they had set forth. They walked out of Katie's life and had no right or reason to walk back in. If they came to claim Katie, they had another thing coming. Cole would die before he gave his daughter back.

"Just what the hell are you doing here?" he hissed.

"My, that's no way to greet a lady," Danielle sniffed haughtily.

"When I'm greeting a lady, I'll change my tune," Cole shot back. "Katie's here and she doesn't need to see you. She doesn't need to see any of you! What the hell do you want? Or should I ask what does Maggie want?"

"It's plain to see that you've not explained anything to that child about her mother. Just what did you tell her, Cole? I sure hope you didn't tell her that age-old story about a big white bird dropping her off," Danielle sneered.

"You never mind what I tell my daughter!" Cole said, trying to keep his voice down.

"As her aunt, I do have some—"

"Don't! Don't you dare have the nerve to say you have any rights to my daughter! Because that's what she is. She's my daughter! You will never be known as her aunt! She has a life here and she has a family here, she doesn't need to be confused with another, especially one that tossed her aside! It wasn't my idea to walk away from her!" Cole said vehemently.

"Oh, was it your idea to impregnate my sister?" Danielle said maliciously.

Cole advanced, his eyes cold. "You know, I've always regretted being with Maggie. But you seem to forget one thing. Maggie walked into that bar on her own. I didn't ask her to come. Things just happened, that's all it was. It was wrong, but both of us were wrong. We have to live with that. And now you have to live with the outcome of your doings, just as I do. And I've been doing just that! You were the one who strove to protect your sister! You were the one who never wanted anyone in your family to find out. Did that change? Is Maggie ready to come clean?"

"Maggie is ready to know her daughter. She just wants to see her daughter," Danielle said tiredly.

"That's too damned bad! Maggie left her daughter for another life. Katie doesn't need her now. She'll never need her!" Cole fought back.

"Look, Katie's young, she is still young enough to understand. I've sat by the past four years watching Maggie sink into a depression. Her marriage suffered for it—"

"And I'm supposed to feel sorry for her? I don't give a damn! Her marriage was suffering before, that's nothing new! She'll have to deal with it now without me and without Katie. She used me once to forget about her bad marriage, I won't let her use Katie for the same reasons!" Cole shouted, thankful that Ruth had whisked Katie out the back.

"You think you're so high and mighty, don't you?" Danielle hissed. "You think that you're the only one with rights to Katie?"

"YES!" Cole shouted, pounding the wall. Danielle jumped, but remained undaunted. "I am the only one with rights to her! I'll always be the only one with rights to her! Maggie gave up her rights the day she walked out on us! She could have been a part of Katie's life back then! I begged her then, but it's too late now! I'm the one who has been here for Katie since the day she was born! Not Maggie! ME! I'm the one who has fed her, clothed her, and rocked her nights. I'm the one who walked the floors when she was sick and I'm the one who runs to her at night if she has a bad dream! I'm the one she runs to when she's happy and comes crying to when she's hurt. I'm the one she expects to make things better! Not Maggie! It will never be Maggie!" Cole shouted.

Cole fought very hard to control his temper. It wouldn't serve any purpose to lose control now. He was literally fighting for his life. He stood, staring into the cold eyes of Danielle, seeing a formidable enemy hidden within. Why she was here now, after all these years, still made no sense.

"You were the one who crafted this entire scenario," Cole reminded her. "It was so important to protect Maggie's dirty little secret. But that's where we differ; where you two thought of Katie as a dirty secret, I thought of her as a child that I would spend my life loving. I didn't care who found out. You strove to hide your secret, and now you have to live with that. It's too late to change things now."

"It is not too late," Danielle shook her head. "Cole, Maggie has a right to see her daughter—"

"She has no rights and Katie isn't her daughter!" Cole shouted angrily.

"She is her daughter! Nothing you say or do will change that! Tell me, what are you going to tell Katie one day when she asks?" Danielle challenged.

"That is none of your business!" Cole answered gruffly.

"It is my business! It will always be my business, whether you like it or not! One day Katie will want to know. One day, Katie will be old enough to search for the answers on her own. What are you going to tell her then? Are you going to tell her how her mother made a mistake and when she tried to rectify things, you turned her away?" Danielle asked.

"There you go again. Katie is nothing but a mistake to you. You can't even refer to her as a child. She'll always be Maggie's mistake," Cole sighed. "I feel sorry for you. I never thought of her as that, and how things turn out in the future is none of your business. I'll tell my daughter what she needs to know when she needs to know it. I'll deal with the fallout and I'll deal with anything that comes along. Even if she decides to go off on her own, as you put it, I'll be the one to deal with that, also! So, if you came today to bond with your sister's mistake, then you can forget it," Cole replied.

Danielle sighed, holding out her hand. "I came to give my niece this. It's from her mother. Maggie thought it best I come and talk with you. She means you no trouble; she just wants to know about her daughter. Cole, whether you believe it or not, she never meant you any trouble. Can't you find some compassion for her?"

Cole unwittingly took the brightly wrapped box, immediately sorry that he had. "Here, I won't give this to Katie. Give it back to Maggie," he said coldly.

Danielle stepped back, refusing the package. "No, I won't bring it back to her. My sister wants her daughter to have a present on her birthday."

"What? You finally ready to let your *dirty* little secret out?" Cole hissed, his anger building. "She's mine! You'll never know her. I have no intentions of introducing my daughter to her long-lost, loving mother!"

"When did you become so cold?" Danielle asked, her tone hushed and urgent.

"Honey, I've always been this way when it comes to what's mine. You and Maggie just haven't seen this side of me," Cole stated flatly. "Your sister can't do her math. This is Katie's fourth birthday and this is her mother's first present. Too little, too late," Cole retorted.

"You are a cold man," Danielle met his gaze, their eyes locking. "I've watched my sister struggle through her depression all these years. She's not the woman you remember. She's so closed up and hurt that she needs this. She needs to know her daughter."

"Did you expect me to welcome you with open arms? When you decided to sweep Maggie's little problem under the carpet years ago, there were no conditions giving any of you the right to come back. You can't come back and change things on a whim. Like the old saying goes, you made your bed, lie in it," Cole replied coldly.

"This is getting us nowhere. Just what are you afraid of, Cole?" Danielle said, her eyes steely and cold.

"Who said that I'm afraid of anything?" he said, his back stiffening.

"Oh, I can see it in your eyes, darling. You're afraid. You're so afraid of losing your daughter that you won't even let her mother back in," Danielle noted.

"Her mother walked out! She did that! I didn't force her, in case you don't remember!" Cole shouted.

"Her mother has paid for that every second since then," Danielle replied.

"I don't give a damn. I haven't given a damn about Maggie since the day she left. I tell you, if she tries to take Katie from me, if any of you try to take Katie from me, you'll be in for the fight of your lives. I won't let my daughter go. I'll never let any of you near her and I'll never let you take her. You'll have to kill me first. And if you don't do that, you'll wish that you had. I'll destroy Maggie and everything she has before I let any of you near my daughter," Cole said, his eyes so cold and deadly that Danielle backed away from him for the first time since their encounter.

"Maggie never told me how cold you could be," she said flatly.

"Maggie never threatened me before," Cole replied just as adamantly.

"She isn't threatening you now," Danielle reminded him.

"Just sending you is enough of a threat. But it stops here. You go and tell Maggie that my daughter is fine and is happy. And she's doing well just the way things are. I will not shake up her life like this. I refuse to upset and confuse her. She's only four. Ask Maggie one thing, you say that I might have to answer to things one day? What will Maggie say if Katie ever asked her how come she walked out on us? She never even held her. She just gave birth and left. She's the one who did that, not me. Do you really think she can come up with an answer that warranted walking out on a baby and not bothering with her all these years? If I were Maggie, I'd worry about myself and live with what I've done, instead of trying to rip everyone else's lives away," Cole said.

"She's not out to destroy anyone. I could give you the same answer you gave me. Maggie will just have to face that one day, just as you will," Danielle replied.

Cole took a step forward, shaking his head. "No, that's where you're wrong. You see, neither of you will ever face that day because I'll never allow it. I won't let either of you have anything to do with my daughter."

"Like I said, what the hell are you afraid of?" Danielle said, leaving in a huff.

There were no hugs and tears, and neither spent time on fancy goodbyes. As effortlessly as Danielle swooped down on him with her arrival, was as quickly as she spread her wings and left, leaving Cole in the dust. With one final look back, Danielle stared coldly for a moment before she climbed into her car and drove off. Cole walked into the house, shoving the small box in the back of his desk. He would get rid of it tomorrow. Right now, it was all he could do to keep from screaming. He refused to give in to his fears. He refused to let them win. But they had already won. Cole shook violently as he looked back out the door, afraid to see who would be coming next.

* * *

Ruth found him standing on the porch almost ten minutes later. Cole had not moved a muscle since Danielle drove away. He stood dejectedly, almost stupefied, as she slowly approached. She could see how the color had drained from his face and her heart began to race. They did not need this today; Danielle's visit could not have been more ill timed if she had planned it that way. In less than fifteen minutes the first buyer was due to arrive.

Everything was at the ready, including the table on the corner of the porch, set with the linen tablecloth and Ruth's best china service. For the occasion, she had baked a batch of her special jelly cookies, which looked like tiny sandwiches with a squeeze of jelly in the middle. Dusted with confectioner's sugar and placed on a dish on top a paper doily, they looked like a treat fit for royalty. And that was how Cole felt, Ruth knew that. She had seen how hard he had worked from the beginning and especially the last few days, just making sure that everything went as planned.

Now it seemed as if Danielle's visit had destroyed everything. Ruth had to put her own fears aside, their worst nightmare had played out. After all these years, they came asking for Katie. They had no rights to her and Ruth was determined to see they never did. Right now, though, she had to reach Cole. Her boy had worked too long and too hard to get where he was today, and he needed this. She was not about to let anyone, especially Danielle, destroy everything he had worked for. Ruth stepped in, taking control once again.

"Come on, honey, we have a few things to do yet," she said, guiding him back inside.

"I can't," Cole replied, his voice raspy.

Ruth could feel just how hard his hands were shaking; she also knew his thoughts. She had seen him like this once before when he needed her dearly, now he needed her again.

"Yes you can. Katie's in the kitchen eating a snack and you have to get ready. Come on, we'll talk about it later," she said adamantly.

"Nothing to talk about. She wanted to see Katie and I said no. They have to stand by their decisions. They don't have any rights to Katie now and they never will. That's all there is to it," Cole said, pulling away.

Standing her ground firmly, yet lovingly, Ruth fought back, "Don't pull away from me," she said softly. "Don't let them ruin today for you. We always knew that one of them would show up sooner or later, but they know where things stand. They won't get Katie and there's no sense borrowing trouble. You have other things to concentrate on now," she gently coaxed

"Other things? Katie is the only thing," Cole shuddered.

"And Katie is the one you're doing this for. Honey, don't go borrowing trouble. As dark as things look right now, in the light of a new day, our lives always look brighter. You just have to believe in that," Ruth said, seeing how Cole turned away.

He had lost his faith and was basing his life on fear. That broke her heart. As much as she refused to push her beliefs on him, was as deeply as she wished that he would let some faith back into his life. If he could only base his life on belief instead of darkness, the suffering and worry would diminish. His fears would be cast aside. Yet, even she was shaken up today; for as deeply as her faith went, Ruth's own worries surfaced.

"I'll leave the believing for you," Cole said darkly, averting his eyes.

She took no offense. Ruth never took offense; she only sought to comfort her boy. "Honey, they can't take Katie from you, she's been yours from the beginning. I doubt if Maggie even told her husband. She just wanted to know about Katie, that's all. If Maggie wanted to see her daughter, she would have come instead of sending her sister," Ruth reminded him.

"You weren't here, you don't know—"

"I do know what she said," Ruth cut him off. "I don't have to hear it, I just know. I can see it in your eyes. She used your past like a dagger, sinking it into your heart."

"No, it's not her, that's already happened. And I have no heart," he said, turning away.

Ruth reached out, grabbing him and spinning him back around, "You look at me, Cole Morgan! You may think you have no heart, but you try telling that to me! You try telling that to that little girl in there! I don't know why you think of yourself in such a way. Maybe it's because the past has been so cruel that it's jaded your image of yourself. Or maybe it's because you still haven't forgiven yourself and you're questioning everything you've done. Honey, believe in yourself! You can do it! Now, you straighten up and look sharp! It's almost time!"

She smoothed his shirt down and ran her hand through his hair. Standing back, Ruth saw a little bit of Cole shining through, yet knew she hadn't fully reached him this time. He was only putting up a front for her sake. She saw through that front, however, knowing that Cole was scared to death. His worst fears had played out. His past had reared its ugly head, threatening to claim what he held most dear.

No one knew better than she how petrified he was at the thought of losing his daughter; and no matter what she said, nothing would help. She had always expected this day and now that it had arrived, there were no words. Cole just had to try and have faith. If he could only believe in himself and have faith, then he could make it through. Now was not the time to dwell on that, however, for the first car was driving in. Taking Cole firmly by the arms, Ruth shoved him out the door.

"You did good, honey," she said, softly kissing him on the cheek as he went out, pasting a smile on his face and greeting his guests.

* * *

"Well, Cole, that's one fine animal you got here ... or should I say that I now got here?" Sam Beaureguard laughed, extending his hand. "I have to admit that I was a bit skeptical after your phone call the other night, but after talking things over with you, I'm glad I changed my mind."

"Mr. Beau—"

"Now, what did I tell you?" he laughed at the way Cole blushed.

"I'm sorry! Sam! As I explained to you earlier, they're on a special feed. I only use this one blend of grains for my horses and the instructions are in the booklet I've written up for you. It shows the amount and the times, both are important. Horses are creatures of habit and they like to be fed at the right times," Cole replied.

"Don't we all! Your Ruth sure put on a good feedbag!" Sam laughed contentedly, rubbing his stomach. "But I know what you're saying, it's good for them to be on a schedule. Don't you worry, I have a very reliable stable hand and since your phone calls, I've already made sure that everything is as stated."

"And again, I'm very sorry about the bout with colic. I have no idea how those alfalfa cubes got into the grain in the first place, except that it had to have been a mistake on the part of the maker. Perhaps a small amount accidentally fell into the bag of grain and was so minor that it only affected a few horses."

"Well, that's water under the bridge, son," Sam clapped him on the back. "My boys have Sir Gallahad already loaded and he's off to home!"

"Sir Gallahad?" Cole quipped, unable to hide his smile.

"What can I say, except that my 14-year-old daughter is on a knight in shining armor kick! You wait until that little beauty of yours grows a bit older, son! You'll be in for the ride of your life!" Sam bellowed.

"I can see that already, cause she sure keeps me moving now," Cole, laughed, shaking his head. "But I wouldn't have it any other way."

"Nope, neither would I, son. Neither would I. They work their way into your heart the minute you lay eyes on them and they never let up. I have a lot of money, but even without all my wealth and power, as long as I have my little girl, I'm a rich man," Sam said. "Well, speaking of little angels, mine is probably sitting at home pestering her mother to no end! She hasn't been able to sit still for days! The closer it got to the time to pick this fella up, the more she climbed the walls! The one thing you don't have to worry about is the welfare of this animal. Shelby's already bustling around like a mother hen getting things all set up for him. I just know that we're gonna have a hard time getting her to sleep in her own room once I get this fella home!" he laughed.

"I've done that a time or two myself," Cole admitted.

"You and me both, but you're only a kid once, so what the hell!" Sam's booming laughter rang out. "Well, I better get a move on. I thank you and I'll be sure to spread the word," Sam beamed, shaking Cole's hand one more time.

"I thank you," Cole replied. "And you all have a safe trip home," he smiled, watching them close Sir Gallahad up and drive away slowly.

* * *

The sun was just setting below the mountains. The day had been long and tiring. A myriad of feelings coursed through Cole. He was elated, the sales had been successful and more; the setback with colic had not done the damage it could have, for that Cole was grateful. His name was slowly gaining in popularity, something that had always been a lifelong dream. Each buyer had been so pleased, they had promised to pass his name along to their friends. Next year looked promising, and Cole knew that he would have to find a way to extend his stock. As small as his herd was right now, he stood with his chest puffed out.

"I feel like the king of the world," he laughed with Ruth.

"I dub thee King Cole!" Ruth laughed.

"No pun intended?" Cole wheezed, his face red with laughter.

"Oh, you!" she laughed in reply.

"You know, this is gonna be great!" Cole spoke excitedly. "Next year more buyers might be coming! I feel like I'm the largest, richest rancher in the whole wide world" he whooped, scooping Katie up into his arms, hugging Ruth at the same time.

He did feel like a king, but a tired king. Yet, the tired king doubted if he would be able to shut his whirling mind down and sleep much that night, for his little princess had her party the very next day. Plus, they had their special ride to take in the morning. Their flowers were in full, glorious bloom right now, and the lush, green foliage was at its peak. Riding out into the open range would be a journey into another realm.

Nature was special in her own way, sharing her glory and spreading her warmth around them while they reveled in her quiet beauty. Even at her young age, Katie already realized the wonder of nature, and looked forward to their ride. One year soon, Cole knew that she would be riding alongside him on her own mount, but for now, father and daughter would ride together.

He still had to get through tonight first, though. Knowing that tomorrow promised to begin early and be a busy day, Ruth was staying over. The house was still and she sat sewing while he read to Katie. The smile never left her lips as she raised her eyes every once in a while, watching her family rocking in front of the unlit fireplace. The house was quiet and cozy, with Ruth wishing the moment would never end. For now, the world was held at bay.

Every moment has its time, however, and soon theirs was over. Ruth packed up her sewing and after helping Cole tuck Katie into bed, went into her own room. Now he had the distinct pleasure of allowing himself the luxury of falling apart. All day long he had put up a brave façade and shoved his torment to the back of his mind. He was getting good at that; either that, or he was the world's most polished liar.

Not wanting to upset Ruth any more than she already was due to Danielle's visit, Cole kept the smile pasted on his face all day long and had done what was expected of him. He did well; he had been successful, polite, witty and charming, everything that was expected of him. Now, he could be himself.

There was no sense in trying to sleep, Cole knew that he needed to exorcize his demons and he knew where he had to go in order to do so. The barn door creaked slightly as he went inside, breathing deeply of the mingled scents of horseflesh and hay as he walked into the darkened interior. The horses snorted slightly at his intrusion, but settled down immediately. The moon was high, casting a soft glow over the ranch. The stars were out and the crickets were singing. Yet, the land was hushed. Night brought its own tranquility as it settled down over everyone, blanketing them in a soft, twinkling darkness. The air smelled of fresh flowers, soft green grass and sweet hay. A whisper of a breeze blew through the open window of the barn.

Once again, Cole's mind was in turmoil and he sought sanctuary. He found that with the animals who welcomed him into their world. Their soft, trusting eyes greeted him. Their gentle nature soothed him, and their wisdom comforted him. They were wise beyond their years, seeming to see into a world only they were privy too. A horse loved unconditionally, he never doubted that love and he never had to question it. He just felt it. He was happy with what life had given him and he never wasted time 'finding himself'. He knew who he was.

Cole looked into their eyes, wondering how they had acquired that nature. "If only people could learn to live by your ways. We think too much, we do too much and we want too much. Where you are always satisfied with what you have, we seek more. Why can't we just be happy and content with our own lot in life instead of always looking? And what are we looking for? Seems to me it should be so simple. Aren't the answers right in front of our eyes? If so, I wished that I knew how to look," he sighed, sitting upon a bale of hay.

"Know what I think it is?" he spoke softly, lifting his head and turning towards the animals once again. "We're afraid to live and you're not. Where you just take life as it comes and enjoy each and every given moment, we're afraid to grasp true happiness when we have it. We're so afraid of losing it, knowing how much it hurts, that we miss out on so much by not letting ourselves enjoy it. So either way, we lose. You, you don't lose. You aren't afraid to be happy today because you might lose it tomorrow. You just live."

This was not the way Cole wanted to end today, yet he had no choice. His demons had returned. He should have known better. The dream suffered last night had not been a dream, but a premonition of things to come … things that terrified him beyond comprehension. Just the thought of Maggie walking in and claiming Katie as her own was enough to make his heart freeze. His stomach lurched sickeningly as he jammed his fist in his mouth, trying to still the fear coursing through him.

Danielle was right. He was scared. He was scared to death. Other than the night Sarah and Myra perished in the flames of what once was their home, he had never been so debilitated with fright. Cole could not stand any more losses. He couldn't lose Katie; from that, he would never recover. He couldn't help but wonder what he had done wrong in this life to warrant such suffering. He had always done right, his parents had taught him to think of others, treating them as he would want to be treated. Perhaps it was because he had forgotten their teachings. He tried, he always tried, but every time Cole let himself free to love, that love was inevitably yanked from him. Fate intervened. Fate always intervened. Last night fate had come to him while he slept, telling him that someone from his past was going to arrive, only he had been too blind to heed the message.

That someone turned out to be Danielle. In his dream, Cole saw a woman shrouded in black taking Katie from him. She had no face, he couldn't see her face, but she came, whisking Katie away. Then Danielle showed up. He couldn't fathom whether the woman in black was Danielle or Maggie. Maybe it was a manifestation of both, for both had the power to destroy his life. They had the power to take Katie from him.

Then Cole stopped shuddering, his hand falling limply from his mouth. His eyes growing wide as a thought came. The woman in black wasn't Danielle or Maggie. He knew that now, her words rang through his mind.

"You know what happened! You know but you won't admit it; not even to yourself! And now, you're going to let it happen again!" she shrieked.

"No, no, it can't be," he gasped, clutching at his chest as sheer ice pumped through his veins. "She does know! She's always known! That's why she never came to me! For years I begged her to come to me and she did! Only I didn't know it then! She came to me last night! It's her and she blames me! She knows what I did to her. If it weren't for me, she'd be alive today. No wonder she won't let me see her face! As repulsed as she is by me and what I've done, she's still sparing me the shame and loathing in her eyes! Sarah won't let me see her face! She's right, I haven't changed, and I'm going to let the same thing happen again. I never learned!" he shuddered, dark, heavy tears streaming down his face.

Cole hated to think of the woman in black as being Sarah. Such a thought was too menacing to even consider. But it had to be her. It was Sarah, and Cole had his answer. Sarah had never forgiven him. She blamed him for her death, which he sent her to. In his dreams, she held on to every person he now cared for and he was just as powerless to stop her as he was with Danielle and Maggie. All three had the power to destroy him. Cole knew that he could never fight any of them off. He was at their mercy.

He would never forget the words that faceless image spoke to him. He now had his answers. He also knew that his fears were founded, he did not deserve to be loved. He was loved once before and he had turned away from that love. No wonder he was being punished in such a cruel manner. He brought it all about by himself. A day Cole had looked forward to with abandon left him shattered at its end. He could put everything from his mind, but Sarah would never let him forget.

Danielle couldn't have picked a better day to come to him. It was as if she were willed. If so, then Cole knew who had brought her to him. He had robbed Sarah of her life and now it was his turn to pay. He could deny the fact all he wanted, but the truth of the matter was, Katie did have a mother, and she would want to know about her mother one day. It was only natural. A child needed to know where they came from. They needed to know what made them who they were. They were spun from a long line of people, with roots that went back to the beginning of time. A child needed to know those roots. In knowing, they learned about themselves. To be denied that knowledge, tore a part of that child away.

'Why don't I have a Mommy?' Cole imagined Katie saying to him.

He sighed deeply, sinking back into the hay as that very question tormented him. "Katie bug, I wish I had an easy answer for you, but I don't. You do have a mommy, honey. You have a mommy, but your daddy was always too scared to let you know that. He didn't want to hurt you. My heart breaks every time I envision your face, wondering why your mommy left. In trying to protect you, I know that I'll only end up hurting you worse. For no one knows better than I do that the truth always comes out, whether we want it to or not. We're only fooling ourselves if we believe anything else."

Cole sobbed slightly, grinding his palms into his already bloodshot, tired eyes. There were no answers, there were only threats and nagging torment hanging over his head. Katie was such a loving, trusting child; she simply wouldn't understand her mother not loving her enough to stay. No child would, and then Cole feared her doubting everyone's love. Plus, if she found out about his lies, would her trust and faith in him be lost forever? In Cole's mind, withholding the truth ranked the same as lying. The truth was kept from them. If that happened, then trust flew out the window. If a child didn't have trust in their parents, they had nothing. So far, Katie had nothing. Her father was a weak-willed liar who imposed his sins on her, and her mother had walked out of her life.

"You sure hit the jackpot, didn't you?" Cole sobbed painfully. "You're only a little girl who'll want to know everything about her life one day, but the only thing I have to offer is a batch of lies. Everyone wants to know all they can about themselves and the world around them. It's part of the joy of discovery. But when your world and life is based on lies, what do you have to be proud of? What kind of legacy am I passing down to you?"

"Oh Katie bug, what a frigging mess this is," Cole shuddered. "Daddy loves you so very much. What you might see as lies one day is really only my attempt to make your life a good one. I just want you to be happy, baby. I don't want you to know the pain I've experienced. I never want you to feel that kind of pain. I've made mistakes, darling, but they're my mistakes, not yours. You were never a mistake. Will you believe that when I tell you one day? Will you be able to understand? I'm sure passing down one hell of a legacy to you.

"God, I can't take this," Cole sighed, closing his eyes.

If he could only find peace, if he could only let himself feel the happiness he knew was surrounding him, yet Cole held back. Either that, or he was just too blind to know what was good for him. Everything in his life was fleeting. Cole had seen firsthand how very fragile life was. He hated that fragility. You loved and then you lost. Did the two always walk hand in hand? Did one get punished for letting themselves have too much? Was it wrong to have love in one's life? Cole had loved so many, but so many had left him. First his parent's died. Parents always pass on, that was something a person accepts as the natural order of life. What one doesn't accept is when they are taken away too soon. Then Cole lost Sarah, their baby, and Myra. He would never stop missing any of them.

If Ruth could hear you know, she'd wring your neck, Cole's inner self fought.

"I'd deserve it," Cole shivered. "After what I've done—"

Oh please! Not that sorry song and dance! Suck it up! You've been feeling so damned sorry for yourself for years. It's about time you got over it! You think that ghosts come back and govern our lives? If you do, then I feel sorry for you. Ghosts don't come back. The dead are just that. Dead. And to think yourself responsible is about the saddest thing I've ever heard.

"Yeah, run from the truth," Cole hissed.

Run from the truth? Why don't you try running towards the truth? he fought with himself.

Cole sat up straighter, letting those words sink in a little bit. He had always thought of the truth as his enemy, maybe it was time to think of it as his friend. Ruth had been telling him that all these years, but Ruth didn't know everything. Cole would never let her know everything. No, he didn't need the truth right now. He would never need the truth. He would do all he had to do in order to insure his daughter's happiness and he would do it on his own. The last thing he needed was belief, the one thing he didn't want was faith, and fate could take a dive for all he cared. He would run his own life and take control of his own destiny.

"Paranoid or not, I don't give a damn. I have to do what is right for my daughter and myself," Cole muttered. "I'm tired of getting myself riled up. I'm wound tight and feel like I'm gonna explode. Then, I'm so damned tired that I just want to let it all go. Say the hell with it and just let things go on as they are, oblivious to everything. Like living in a bubble! I'd love to wake up one morning and have nothing on my mind but taking care of Katie and running my ranch. I'm so sick of worrying about tomorrow," he sighed deeply.

Cole lay back staring up at the ceiling, feeling very vulnerable and overwrought by all he was facing. Thinking of everything he needed to do was too much. He knew it was better taking one thing at a time, but things had a way of piling up.

Ok, now that you know the root of the problem that has your nuts in a knot, do something about it! You're upset cause Danielle showed up today. Deal with it! She has no power over you and if she tries to take Katie, both she and Maggie will pay dearly. It's over. Everything is over and all you have to do is look to the future. And don't start spouting that sorrowful shit about how you have no future. Time to get over that. Don't let them take you down, his own voice argued to set things straight again.

"You're right! I know you're right. She did nuke me pretty good today. If I'd been expecting her, I would have been ready for her shit. But she really took me by surprise. And it wasn't a good one! And being tired, overexcited and nervous all rolled up into one didn't help. I was enough of a mess with all I had going on today and the party tomorrow that I didn't need any help from her! Shit, I'm just so damned tired," Cole sighed, his body trembling.

"Fuck, you're a goddamned mess," he swore at himself. "You gotta get a grip. You haven't been eating right and you sure as hell haven't been sleeping. What the hell's wrong with you? Why are you doing this? So you had a bad dream about Sarah! And who gives a damn about Danielle showing up? It's not the end of the world and you won't let it be," Cole said, sitting up a bit straighter.

He knew right then and there what he needed, but also knew what an impossibility that was. Cole needed to go off into the mountains alone, it was the only way he could heal. If he could just take a few days and get away by himself to really get in touch with his feelings and the world around him, then everything would be fine. He loved the mountains and had always found peace and solace in their embrace, loving and cherishing the world nature provided.

At times, Cole felt like he would become one with the universe as he sat on the edge of the plateau, overlooking the valley below. Over the years, that had turned out to be his place, the only place he could escape to where he was understood. Nature wrapped him in her arms, giving him the comfort that was denied him in this life. Ruth was always there for him, but there was a part of Cole that even she could not touch. Only his Nature's Mother could do that. She created the world, and she mothered her tiny beings when needed. Cole more than needed her now.

However, the only reason he couldn't leave was Katie. Cole used to go to his special place all the time after his arrival. While wandering and exploring the vast mountain ranges one day, he was drawn to his spot. The wind blew through his hair as he reined his horse in, dismounting and walking to her edge. The world spread out below him. Hearing the cry of an eagle, Cole knew that he had been summoned. She wanted him here; she had a message for him. That message was peace. If he could give of himself, then she could help him heal. And she did, to a degree. Slowly, he tried coming out of himself and facing life again. He came to his place more and more over the years.

Now, when he needed her most, even nature couldn't call him into her fold. Cole was scared, and couldn't leave his daughter. Another time he had left loomed in the dark corners of his mind. He had gone off for a little while, leaving everything he cherished behind. When Cole returned, Sarah was gone. She had been taken away from him and would never return. He couldn't do that again; he wouldn't leave his little girl. He was afraid of coming home, only to find her ripped from his life. He was afraid to leave and he was afraid to love again. Holding his face in his hands Cole wept, wondering if there would ever be a time in his life when he could stop being afraid ... when he would stop being afraid.

He sat, staring unseeingly at his hands, when a sound from the doorway caught his attention. He looked up, seeing his friend standing there. Somehow, Brent felt that Cole needed him there tonight. He had spoken with Ruth earlier, and learned of Danielle's arrival. That had to have Cole on edge, but Brent knew that somehow, he would find a way to hold himself together during the day. Night, however, was a different matter. Instead of leaving Cole on his own, Brent felt that if he came to speak with his friend, he could somehow keep some of the heartache away. He could at least help Cole work through his fears. Even Brent feared the day Maggie would resurface, and was just as shaken as Cole now appeared to be.

He walked in slowly, kicking a bale of hay from the pile. Rolling it across the floor with his foot, he finally settled in front of Cole, quiet for a moment. Cole looked up, remembering another time someone had saved him from himself while he sat in a barn, and now, Brent was there.

"You heard?" he asked his friend softly.

"Yeah, hope you don't mind, but Ruth called me earlier. I figured you needed someone to talk with," Brent nodded.

"Don't know what good talking will do, but I'm glad you're here," Cole admitted.

"Talk or not, it's being here for one another that matters. Remember? We made a promise to ourselves, and that includes everything," Brent replied.

"I remember.... How could I forget? But got nothing to say," Cole shrugged.

"So," Brent quipped, also shrugging. "Then don't say a thing. You talk too damned much anyway."

Unable to help himself, Cole had to laugh. If there was one thing Brent could do, it was to reach out and help him. He didn't even have to say a thing, which was good most of the time, for Brent had a way of sticking his foot in his mouth, whether he meant to or not. Cole knew that it was meant, Brent always sought to lighten things up, hoping in his own manner that he had helped. Tonight, it helped.

"Brent, what the hell am I going to do?" he asked, turning to face his friend.

"Cole, there is no easy answer for that, and it's not because you never explained Katie's mother to her, it's because she's still a baby and she's not capable of understanding. There is no right or wrong here, and there are no mistakes. It's simply called life. Life has a mind of its own and does what it wishes. Katie will see that herself as she grows older. Nothing's set in black and white, right or wrong, we just exist and we do what's needed, when it's needed. Even if we don't have the answers now, they ultimately find a way to come," Brent said, surprising even Cole.

"When did you become so astute?" Cole joked.

"Don't know, maybe it was over breakfast," Brent snorted. "I guess what I'm trying to say is—"

"What you're trying to say is that I should just go on as I am, raising my daughter. I shouldn't spend time best spent loving and enjoying her by worrying about tomorrow, for tomorrow always finds a way to help itself," Cole nodded.

"And I'm also saying that you don't have to do any of this alone," Brent said steadfastly, staring intently.

Cole met his gaze, and found a renewed strength. "Thanks. I mean it … thanks. Brent, knowing that I still might have to deal with both Maggie and Danielle one day is only made bearable cause of friends like you. I know that I'm not alone, and am glad for that. If I was alone, I'd be scared to death. I think that's my biggest fear. I don't want to be alone. It's not a nice feeling, but as long as I have you guys, I'll be ok."

"We'll all be ok, cause we have one another, no matter what comes along. Cole, don't ever be afraid to talk or to ask for help. That's what friends are for, and we're more than that. All of us are. We don't have anything but ourselves," Brent reminded him. "We have to stick together through anything that life throws our way, and muddle through the best we can. I'm not saying it's going to be easy, and I have no idea when or how you should tell Katie, all I can promise is that when you do, we'll all be here to help you through. And don't go selling your daughter short! She knows how much her Daddy loves her, a love like that can't be taken away."

"You think so?"

"Cole, it's one of the reasons I envy you," Brent nodded, laying his feelings out in the open for the first time. "I envy you your daughter, and hope that one day I can be as good a father as you are. It's sort of like taking notes, I see how you two are together, and the lessons you teach one other each and every day, and I try to remember those lessons for when I have a child of my own. I only hope that I can be to her what you are to Katie."

"And I hope that I'm half the friend to you that you are to me," Cole nodded, turning to face his friend. It was as if they were truly seeing one another for the first time. "You've given me something valuable tonight, Brent, whether you realize it or not. You let me know that I'm a good father. After all the times I've doubted myself, you let me know that I'm doing it right. Do you know how good that feels? Brent, on some level, I might be doing something right!"

"Yeah, it's a good feeling, isn't it? You seem to forget a lot along the way, that's why you have me to remind you!" Brent said, his face bright as he puffed out his chest.

Cole couldn't help but laugh at the way his friend preened. "Brent, believe me, I'll never forget a thing!"

"See that you don't! Now, what do you say we head on in for the night?" Brent asked.

"You sleeping over?" Cole quipped teasingly.

"Yeah, we'll have a regular old slumber party! Just like that night of the storm, remember that?" Brent grinned crookedly.

Cole grew quiet for a moment. "I'll never forget that night. You and Will came over purposely that night so that I wouldn't be alone, right?"

"Guilty," Brent shrugged, grinning.

"At a time when I needed someone the most, when the last thing I wanted was to be alone, you and Will came over, giving me someone to talk too. It could have been a very long, cold, dark night; instead, it was one I'll never forget," Cole said softly.

"Like I said, what are friends for? Now go on in and get some sleep, I'm gonna stroll on home now," Brent laughed at his own joke as he strutted to his truck. "I'm a prophet!" he chuckled, with Cole shaking his head and waving his friend off as he walked into his own home.

He couldn't help but turn and watch Brent driving away. Somehow, Ruth knew to bring him over tonight. She had more than one way to reach out to Cole, and her convictions never wavered. This was exactly what he needed. Brent had reminded him of something he had forgotten. He was a good father, and they were all in on this together. No matter what, he would put Maggie and Danielle out of his mind for now and enjoy Katie's party. That could not be taken from him. Without knowing how, Brent had managed to bring Cole back to himself.

The dreams were forgotten, along with any other worries. Now was not a time for worry. No one would ever know what he had done, and the dead did not come back to punish. Cole had to believe that. Even if he didn't, he wasn't going to let it bother him now. Now, he needed to be with his daughter. Katie slept soundly, but he still needed to be with her. She always kept him grounded.

She lay sleeping peacefully, the sound of her soft, raspy breathing filling the room, her innocence reaching out, ensnaring Cole. He sat by her side, lost in the wonder of her youth. Children were so trusting. Everything made sense to them in a simplistic way that was lost on adults. Cole desperately needed to be lost somewhere where everything was simple again.

"Maybe the world would be a better place if children ran it; us grown-ups have mucked it up enough. And we think that we're the smart ones," Cole snorted. "All we do is hurt one another. We forgot how to treat people. We forgot how to play, little Katie bug," he said quietly.

Cole sat quietly for a moment, catching a stray piece of Katie's hair between his fingers. "You know, baby, demons have a way of following you. I have my share of demons and I pray every day that you never find them out. What would that do to us if you did?" he shivered.

"I really don't deserve you; you know? I still don't know why you were given to me, after all I've done. If you only knew, but I pray that you never do. Those who do know are all far away. It's better that way. I can only hope that my demons don't touch you," Cole shivered, holding his face in his hands.

Chapter Fifteen

Matt Young sat at the dining room table, staring dejectedly at his wife, Shauna. Both were at a complete and total loss. It had been two days now with still no word; it was as if she had disappeared into thin air. Shauna watched her husband shut down almost completely ever since Becca left. They had looked everywhere for her at first, then finally resorted to calling the police and getting their neighbors involved. It was no use; it was as if their fourteen-year-old daughter had fallen off the face of the earth.

Becca had left willingly, that much they knew. She had taken the time to pack her clothes and took the almost $300 she had saved from doing odd jobs and babysitting. Plus, she had taken her diary, her portable CD player and, what puzzled Matt the most, a stuffed rabbit that Cole had given her when she was four years old. Matt knew that she treasured the animal, but not to this extent.

As hard as it was to admit, Matt and Shauna had to tell the authorities that their daughter had run away. They were ashamed, but neither was very surprised. Ever since the deaths of her aunt and grandmother almost 7 years ago, their house had ceased being a home. For seven long years, Becca was shoved aside, with her parents forgetting that even a small child felt pain. They knew loss and they grieved. They were smarter than adults gave them credit for.

Becca had never been given the opportunity to grieve the loss of her Aunt Sarah and grandmother, she had only been 7 at the time, but she picked up on everything that was said and done, and it had been eating at her ever since. Becca's house stopped being a home and had turned into something of a tomb. Her father barely talked to her anymore and he virtually ignored her mother. Her mother then kept herself locked in her room most of the time, thinking no one knew her dirty little secret. But Becca knew, she knew more than they ever thought. She knew that her aunt and grandmother were dead, she watched her grandfather grow old before his time and die, and she knew that her Uncle Cole was gone. The only thing she didn't know was why. So she ran.

"God, I need a drink," Shauna muttered under her breath.

At the age of 35, she looked at least ten years older, with her brown hair turning dull, shot through with streaks of gray she never bothered to hide, and years of sorrow and hardship etched in her face. Her skin was pale, almost to the point of being transparent, with large, dark eyes peering out from behind sunken cheekbones. Shauna didn't smile anymore, and she never laughed. What she did do, was drink.

"That's the last thing you need!" Matt muttered under his breath.

"What did you say?" Shauna countered, leaning forward accusingly. "Are you telling me what to do? You have the nerve to sit there telling me what I can and can't do? How dare you!"

"Give it a rest, Shauna," Matt said dejectedly. "You're being a bit overdramatic and I don't need that shit right now. And you don't need a drink!"

"How do you know what I need? You don't even know I exist anymore, let alone what I need!" she shouted, nervously pacing the room.

"I know more than you think I do. You think that I don't know about the bottle hidden in the bottom of your drawer? And no matter how many times you brush your teeth or chew on those mints, you can't hide the smell of the booze! Shauna, face it. I'm hopeless and you're a drunk," Matt said dejectedly.

"Then we make a very good pair," she said vehemently. "Just the perfect parents for a fourteen-year-old girl! Boy, we ought to be proud of the job we did with her! Tell me Matt, when did we die with...." Shauna caught herself, her eyes widening as she stared.

Matt sat back, sitting straighter as he returned her stare. "When did you become so hateful?" he quietly retorted.

"Matt, that was wrong of me ... that was so wrong," Shauna said, giving in to her emotions. She turned, her shoulders shaking as she tried hiding her tears. "Oh God, everything with our lives is so wrong. Matt, we have to get over this! If we won't do it for ourselves, we have to do it for Becca! This isn't the first time she's run away, and nothing's changed! Matt, what the hell's wrong with us?" she wept desperately.

Matt buried his face in his hands. "I don't know what's wrong with us and I don't know how to fix things anymore. Shauna, this goes deeper than what you think, this is all because of C—"

"Don't go there! Just don't go there! I've heard that every day since the fire and I don't want to hear it again! Every time you bring up that man's name and what he did, we relive that night!" Shauna yelled, spinning back around to face her husband.

"Not hearing what he did won't solve anything!" Matt fought back. "I know what I know!"

"Then keep it to yourself! I don't want to hear it! Matt, nothing will ever come of this! For years now you've been trying to prove that the fire wasn't an accident and you've gotten nowhere! It's time to stop! If you don't put this behind you, then you'll never get on with your life! We'll never get on with our lives! Look at us! You and I don't even sleep in the same bed anymore! We stay in the same house for the sake of our daughter, but even that has slipped through our fingers! Our daughter is gone! Matt, you have to fix this!" Shauna raged.

"I don't know how to fix this," he said quietly.

"Then find a way!" Shauna shouted, turning and abruptly leaving the room.

Matt sat dejectedly at his table, thinking back over the years. That wasn't hard to do. Lately, he had been unable to think of anything else. Cole left over six years ago and now Becca was gone.

"How many more have to leave before you snap out of this?" he shuddered, burying his face in his hands.

Matt knew that he had to find a way to set things straight, but it was already too late. Unable to face losing his home and family, Cole had vanished. Matt woke one day finding him gone. That was when the guilt and overwhelming depression took hold and had never left.

Feeling like a pariah, Matt kept his feelings to himself. Every once in a while Shauna was witness to his anger, but like everyone else, she turned a deaf ear to him. He knew that it was fear, after what had happened to his mother and sister, if anyone else followed his beliefs, then they feared meeting the same fate. Fear kept everyone from the truth as Matt knew it, crippling them emotionally. Matt was alone in his suspicions; he had no proof to back up his beliefs, so he kept them to himself.

They had tried getting back to a normal sense of life at one time, but no one knew what that was anymore. Cole was gone and Matt spent his days caring for his father, who had turned inward. Jeremy Young had never spoken to another soul. The loss of his wife, daughter and unborn grandchild had robbed the man of the will to live. His soul was broken and nothing or no one could fix it. Jeremy barely clung to his sanity, and spent his days staring idly out the window of his living room. No one could reach the man, he was broken and beyond consolation. Two years later, Jeremy died quietly in his sleep.

Too much loss in too short a time. Broken Arrow was nothing like Matt remembered from his youth. The town was now foreign to him, as was his home. He sometimes wondered how he ever managed to get out of bed in the morning, much less put one foot in front of the other. Nothing about his life was familiar or comforting. Happy memories of the past played out in his mind like a sad, forgotten movie. Cole was gone, his father had passed on, and now Matt had to find a way to make things right again.

There had to be a way, only he didn't know where to begin. Perhaps if he had been more understanding from the beginning, then things would be easier now. Cole had been faced with an impossible decision, something Matt realized now. However, at the time, he simply felt that Cole had given up on Sarah and walked out of the hospital after signing the papers the doctors shoved at him.

Myra's death was a little easier to deal with, if that was at all possible. She had been killed in the fire; they knew that she was gone. But Sarah had lingered on, yet they said that she was gone. When Matt saw her, she looked so peaceful. He simply couldn't believe her gone. She was warm to the touch; someone who was gone wasn't warm. Yet, they all told Matt that there was no hope. Eventually, Cole believed that very thing. With trembling hands, he took the pen the doctors held out for him and signed the papers that took Sarah's life. Unable to stand by any longer, Cole walked out of the hospital and Matt turned his back on him.

No comfort was offered, and Matt never spoke to his friend again. The funeral was quiet, with him keeping Becca between himself and Shauna, not allowing her to go to Cole's side. Cole stood quaking violently as silent tears streamed down his face. He never uttered a sound and sank to his knees when the prayers were finished. Matt, Shauna, and Becca left quietly. Friends and neighbors offered what condolence they could, but Cole was beyond feeling. Finally, his older cousin Dave placed a hand on his shoulder, urging him to stand. He brought Cole into his home, where he stayed until he left Broken Arrow a few days later. Cole never looked back.

The years passed and Becca grew, hating the silence of her home. No one ever knew how scared she really was. In her short life, all she had ever known was loss. She never told her parents or anyone how she really felt, choosing to keep her feelings bottled up inside just like she saw all the adults around her doing. None of them talked, so why should she? They went through life acting like robots, so Becca adopted the same mannerisms.

She never told her mother or father how scared she was at the funeral. She was barely seven at the time and all she knew was that there had been a huge fire and Uncle Cole's house was gone. Then they told her that her grandma and Aunt Sarah were also gone. She didn't understand, so Becca just stood back and watched.

She was petrified the day of the funerals. Standing at the gravesites,

Becca cringed, hiding behind her parents as the coffins were lowered into large, dark holes dug in the ground. She was scared that they were going to put her there too, and fought the urge to run. The sounds of dirt plopping onto the caskets still haunted her dreams, causing night terrors that robbed the small girl of sleep night after night. And everyone cried. That was the hardest thing for Becca to get used to. She never knew that grown-ups cried. They were supposed to be the strong ones. They were supposed to take care of everything and not be afraid, but all Becca felt was fear.

Jeremy had stopped talking and stood leaning against Matt as the service droned on. He wondered why they put themselves through this torture; as far as Jeremy was concerned, it would have been easier to just say goodbye in his own way and forget all this commotion. He only wanted to be home, surrounded by an entire community was the last thing the man desired. Everyone said that funerals brought a person closure, but for Jeremy, there would be no closure. He didn't want closure. He just wanted his wife and daughter back.

Becca had never seen her grandfather looking so old and sad before in her life. He was so silent that it scared her to death. She hated silence; no one talked and no one comforted her, so she hid behind her parents, except for the one time she tried going to Cole. Her father's strong hand stopped her, however, and Becca left the cemetery sandwiched between her parents and staring back over her shoulder. The last time she saw her Uncle Cole was when he fell to his knees, burying his face in his hands.

Matt and Shauna still lived in the house they had built on the southern section of their land, and closed up his parents' home. The light gray two-story farmhouse, trimmed with dark blue shutters, with a white, split rail fence bordering the yard and shrouded by tall, gnarled oaks that spread their leaves like a blanket overhead, sat empty. Mail was still delivered to the same box, flowers still grew in the beds along the length of the fence, and Matt still walked down the gravel lane every day at two. Only instead of turning right to visit his parents for a quick cup of coffee on his return, he bore to the left, heading to his own brick ranch-style home, set back from the road, barely visible, buried among a dense thicket of oak and pine. No one had set foot inside the old house since the day Jeremy died. Becca hated seeing it so empty and stayed away as much as possible. She also hated the silence of her own home and missed everyone she loved. She knew that she would never see her grandmother, grandfather, or aunt again, but she could go see Cole and no one was going to stop her.

Becca was barely eight years old when she ran away for the first time. She simply couldn't stand being home any longer. Her mother was quiet all the time and her father looked right through her. She was tired of being invisible and felt cheated. Becca wanted the truth and she wanted to be with someone who cared about her. One night she had had enough. Tired of living by rules set by adults, she decided to take matters into her own hands.

"If they won't take me to see Uncle Cole, then I'll go myself," she vowed, sliding her window open. "I don't care if I never come back."

Stealing out into the night, Becca started down the familiar dirt road she had walked all her life. She made her way by the light from the moon, kicking up dust as she went. So far it had been a hot, dry summer with no relief in sight. Even with the night half over, the heat pressed in around them. Becca didn't seem to notice, though, and even if she did, she didn't care.

Becca knew that Cole had been staying at his cousin Dave's house ever since the fire, so she took off in that direction. She hadn't seen him since the funeral when he had been so sad. People tried talking to him but all he did was cry. Becca tried running over to Cole, she had a special flower to give him, but her father wouldn't let her. That only served to confuse an already devastated child; her entire world had collapsed around her and she had no reason as to why that had happened.

Like any child, Becca thought that she had been bad, maybe that was why everyone was crying and all the bad things were happening. She never quite got over feeling that way, especially when her parents pushed her aside. No one seemed to want to bother with her anymore.

Becca missed Cole and she wanted to see him. He felt bad and she wanted to give him a special flower, knowing that it would help make him feel better. What seemed a lifetime ago, Cole had given Becca the flower, which she had saved exactly as he told her to. Now, she wanted to bring the same flower over to him. Pulling her book from the bottom of the bookcase, Becca made sure that no one was watching. Her flower was a secret only she and her Uncle Cole knew about. She never forgot what he had said the day he gave it to her. Becca had just turned six and he came over that morning, carrying a single red rose. He swung her up into his arms, twirling her through the air.

"How's the most beautiful birthday girl in the world?" Cole asked, smiling brightly.

"I'm fine, Uncle Cole," Becca had giggled. "Are you coming to my party later?" she asked excitedly.

"I sure am! Wild horses couldn't keep me away! But I just had to come early to give you a special present," Cole said, smiling at the way her eyes twinkled.

He then pulled the rose out from behind his back and handed it to Becca, watching her face glow with happiness. Her eyes fairly danced as she sniffed her flower.

"You just remember, this is a magic flower," Cole told the child.

"How is it magic?" Becca half whispered in all her excitement.

"Honey, it's magic cause it's only between you and me. I want you to take this flower and hide it in a very special place before anyone can see it. It's your secret. Whenever you hold this flower in your hand, you'll think of me. If you're upset or mad, just talk to the flower and it'll be like talking to me. It will make you feel better. So go on, go run and put it between the pages of your favorite book and it will last forever," he said, setting her down.

Becca turned to run, only to turn back. She wrapped her arms around Cole's knees, hugging him once more. "I love you, Uncle Cole!" she cried out brightly as she danced her way back into the house.

The night Becca ran away, she carried the flower in her hand as she made her way over to Dave's house to see Cole. He must have been really sad to stay away for so long. She was eight and she hadn't seen him in over a year, but at her young age, Becca had no concept of time, except that it sometimes seemed to drag on endlessly. No one would tell her why Cole stopped visiting; she didn't know what was happening. He just stopped coming over and her father never took her to see him, either.

Then Becca noticed that not only did her parents stop talking around her, they now whispered a lot. She hated whispers and secrets, that's all anyone did and no one told her anything. It just wasn't fair. Her father always stood by the fence of their corral, looking out over towards Uncle Cole's place. If he missed him so much, why didn't he go over? Becca just didn't understand.

"Cole's gone," was what Becca heard.

No one ever sat the child down and explained exactly what they meant by those words. Did her Uncle Cole go away on a trip? He used to do that all the time, only he used to go with her father; now, her father never went anywhere. Maybe Uncle Cole had to go on a special trip and that was what they meant; but since Becca had no idea what he would be doing on a special trip, she was more confused than ever. Maybe he was just gone for the day, but she had heard that phrase more than once to be satisfied with that answer.

All she heard was that Cole was gone, and she didn't understand a thing. He was staying at his cousin's house. Becca knew Dave Jensen, and knew where that was, so maybe that was what everyone meant. Maybe he went over to stay with Dave.

If she could only get to Dave's house, then maybe she could visit with him for a while. If no one else would explain things to her, then maybe her Uncle Cole would. He had always told Becca everything anyway. But when she arrived at Dave's ranch, Becca's heart was broken. She stood on the front porch of the large, sprawling farmhouse, knocking.

"Becca! What on earth are you doing here, honey?" Dave asked, kneeling in front of the small child.

"Hi Mr. Dave, I came to see my Uncle Cole. Can I please see him?" she pleaded, her eyes large and wet, her bottom lip trembling.

Dave took a deep breath, looking away. Taken by surprise, he had no inkling of what Becca was talking about. Everyone in town knew that Cole had sold his ranch and left ... that is, everyone except for a small girl of eight. Angered that her parents had never sat Becca down to talk with her, Dave had no idea of how to confront the child.

Sure, Matt had closed up after the loss of his mother and sister, but that was no excuse, he still had a family to take care of. Matt had refused to speak with Cole after the tragedy, not even to offer him any comfort or solace. There was just nothing left inside him to give. His own family floundered, thrust into a nightmare that never ended. Then Matt had been consumed with a thirst for revenge, something that Dave thought fruitless; it wouldn't change their lives and it would not bring back those lost. He was better off putting that kind of energy back into his wife and child.

Dave had always been close with Matt and Cole; he was a few years older than the two, but the three boys basically grew up together. Not only did they go to school, ride, work their ranches and do the rodeo circuit together, they were a large part of one another's lives. Cole could either be found at Matt's or Dave's home, depending on his mood and what their mothers had planned for dinner.

Cole's father had been killed in a farming accident when Cole was only 15, with the tractor hitting a rut in the field and rolling over, trapping Seth in a ditch. Two short years later, barely over his father's death, Cole lost his mother to cancer. It hit quick, or seemed to hit quick, for what saddened him even more was that she had been sick for a long time, only she never said a word about her illness. She simply could not subject her son to watching her die, not wanting to burden him with waiting day after day for the end to come. At the age of 17, Cole was on his own.

He never left the family ranch, however, choosing to remain and work the place as he had been taught. No one ever questioned Cole's ability to do so, for he was older than his 17 years. Dave's mother Thelma and Cole's mother Nan had been cousins, so it was only natural for Thelma to take him under her wing. Dave resembled Cole in looks, the only difference being his hair was a shade darker. Other than that, the boys could have passed as brothers. Many nights Cole could be found at either their house mooching a meal, or over at Matt's home, where it was slowly becoming obvious that Matt and the food weren't the only things he was stopping by for. Matt's younger sister, Sarah, soon began working her wiles on the shy man, eventually capturing his heart.

Even after their marriage, Dave went out to the ranch on a regular basis to lend a hand and visit. Cole still hit the rodeo circuit with him and Matt, but instead of competing, now watched his friends from the stands, cheering them on. Then Becca was born, and Cole lost his heart again, this time to a blonde-haired, blue-eyed waif. How he could be out of her life like he was also angered Dave. He knew how hard Sarah's death impacted his cousin, but like everyone else, Cole forgot about a small child and left, leaving Dave holding the bag.

"Just a minute, honey, why don't you come inside and sit down?" he asked gently, leading Becca into the room. He softened a bit, ashamed that he had been angry with Cole, no one knew better than he just how devastated Cole had been.

"Is Uncle Cole here?" she asked, her voice small and shaky.

"I'll be right back, ok? How about something cold to drink?" Dave pleaded, wishing that he knew what to say.

"No thank you, I'll just wait here," Becca had replied.

Dave left the room, running out to where his mother was finishing up with their dinner dishes. "Mom! You won't believe this, but I think that Becca has just run away!"

"Land sake! What are you talking about?" Thelma asked, wiping her wet hands on her apron.

"Just what I mean! She's in our living room and I don't think Matt and Shauna have any idea she's here! Hell, knowing them, I doubt if they know that she's gone at all!" he said through clenched teeth.

"David! That's not proper! We can't cast judgement and we have no idea of what those poor people are going through!" Thelma admonished her son.

"Mom, I know exactly what those poor people are going through, cause we went through the same thing! We knew how Cole suffered! Hell, I only wish that I could have stopped him from leaving like he did!" Dave exclaimed. He stood for a moment, running a shaky hand through his hair.

"Son, you did everything humanly possible! You took care of your cousin and his animals while.... Well, you were there for him. That's what matters!" she said, her eyes wet once again.

The tragedy of two years ago had turned the entire town upside down. Everyone cried with the families, there wasn't a soul who didn't feel a part of their torment and most people were left wondering how any one of them ever found the strength to carry on like they had. There was even a time when Dave doubted if Cole could go on at all. He wondered if his cousin even remembered the fire, the dazed look in his eyes spoke of a deep tragedy, but Cole never did.

His face had taken on a haunted look and he went through his days barely speaking a word to anyone, giving both Dave and Thelma reason to worry. It had been Dave who found Cole in the barn with a rope in his hands. With his heart in his throat, Dave ripped the rope from his grasp and tossed it across the barn. All Cole could do was stare dully at his cousin, not even seemingly aware of what he had been about to do. Without another word, he rose and walked out.

As far as Dave knew, Cole never went back to the ranch after that night. He had no belongings left to speak of, and the only clothing he owned was that donated by family and friends. And since he had Dave's promise to care for the animals until he was able to do so himself, Cole had no reason to return. Everything he owned was lost in the fire, with just a few pieces of odd furniture and heirlooms from his parents packed in the shed on the back of the property.

The only thing he had left of Sarah was the blue amulet worn around his neck. Cole never took it off, he had worn it every day since the night Sarah had presented it to him, and carried the tiny wooden box it came in whenever he left home. The box sat tucked away in the bottom of his suitcase, with Cole holding it in his hands every night before he went to bed. At home, the box sat in his top drawer. To Cole, both were a part of his wife and he would never part with either. But Dave had noticed that Cole no longer wore the amulet around his neck. Instead, he found him sitting in the spare room of his home, holding the box in his hands one night. Without another word, Dave left the room and went out into the kitchen with his mother.

None of them were strangers to death. Cole had lost his parents, and two short years later, Dave lost his father. Yet they had always found a way to give solace to one another. The grief went deep, but it never crippled them. When Sarah and Myra were killed, the entire town came to a standstill, paralyzed with a grief that spared no one.

The night of the fire, Dave had been unable to leave the farm and was home when the tragedy struck. He was also the one who accompanied the sheriff to the motel where Matt and Cole were staying, not knowing how to break the news. There was no way to tell a man that he had lost his entire family, and they had two men to give that very message to. Now, the unwelcome task of giving bad news to someone once again fell to Dave. Becca sat quietly, waiting.

"Mom, what the hell do I tell her? How could they not tell Becca that

Cole left?" Dave asked, running his hand through his hair.

"Honey, Shauna said that Becca knew! They told her that Cole was gone, but who knows what goes on in the mind of a young child! You tell them one thing, but they take it as something else. And the poor little thing, she's lost so much in such a short amount of time, it's no wonder she's confused! I just don't think she fully understands that Cole has left and isn't coming back," Thelma tried soothing her son.

"You'd think that they would make sure that she understood! Now I have to go out there and tell her that he's not here! Damn it, Mom!" Dave swore, as yet another unpleasant task was thrust upon him.

"Dave, we can't judge the decisions Matt and Shauna make and we don't have the right to question them! They were so broken after the fire, and not really that much time has passed! It's still fresh in all of our minds. We can live ten lifetimes and it would still hurt! Something like that always hurts! They are probably doing the best they can; it's not easy trying to go on with your life, especially when you have others who are depending on you. Just go out there and tell Becca as gently as you can. Tell her that she needs to talk with her father. I'll go call Matt," Thelma said. She then pushed her son to the door and went to the phone.

Dave went back into the living room and sat next to Becca. She turned a pair of large eyes up at him, wondering just what all the ruckus was about. "Honey, I ... uhhhh ... Becca, I have to tell you something, and it's going to be hard to understand," Dave began.

"Did something happen to my Uncle Cole, too?" she asked, with tears threatening.

"Becca, your Uncle Cole is fine," Dave lied. Truth be known, Dave simply had no idea if Cole was fine or not. No one had heard from him since the day he left. "But you see, he's not here."

Becca's bottom lip trembled as she tried digesting the news. "You're just like my daddy! He said that Uncle Cole was gone too! Did he go somewhere? When will he be back?"

"Honey, I don't know when he'll be back," Dave said.

"Where did he go? You have to tell me where he went! No one ever tells me anything! I'm not stupid!" Becca burst out.

"Honey, no one said you were stupid! Why don't you talk with your daddy—" Dave started, only to be cut off when Becca bolted. "Becca!" he cried out, chasing after her.

Thelma wept, watching as Becca disappeared into the night, with Dave running after her. Minutes later, he was back.

"Tell Matt that I'm going out after her! I don't know if she's hiding somewhere, or if she's on her way over to Cole's place! Damn it! They should have told her!"

"Where are you going?" Thelma called out after him.

"I'm gonna cut through the old service road! It's open field there and if she's just running scared, I'll be able to find her! I'll also get to the ranch quicker that way, if that's where she's going!" he said, then disappeared.

Matt couldn't believe his ears. One minute he had a call saying that Becca was over with Dave and Thelma, then mere minutes later the phone rang again, telling him that Becca had taken off. With a sinking feeling, he knew exactly where she was going, and left for Cole's ranch immediately. Pulling in, Matt found Dave sitting on the tailgate of his truck, staring over at the fence. Looking further, he saw Becca standing forlornly, crying quietly as she stared at the now empty ranch. The burned-out remains of the house had been cleared away, but that was all that had been done to the property since Cole had sold it. The house had never been rebuilt.

"She won't let me near her," Dave explained. "I tried, but she said she just wanted her Uncle Cole and would run away if I tried to come over. Matt, I'm sorry. I didn't want to tell her, but what was I going to do?"

"Not your fault," Matt said, reassuring Dave. "I should have talked to her long ago; she needed to be told the entire truth. Was stupid of me to think she understood that Cole was gone for good. How the hell I could have been so stupid is beyond me. The only excuse I have is that I've been so caught up in my own grief that I didn't even consider my daughter and what she was going through. Dave, I just don't know what the fuck to do anymore," he said tiredly, watching while Dave drove away.

Afraid that Becca would run again, Matt watched her for a few more minutes before slowly making his way to her side. She just stared; shocked into silence by the now stark emptiness of the ranch that was once teeming with life. Becca's world had changed and she hated it; not knowing or understanding why was the worst part.

"Honey, you had us scared to death! What on earth are you doing here?" Matt asked, reaching out for his daughter.

"I wanted to see Uncle Cole!" Becca answered, not knowing how those words tore Matt's heart out. "No one ever let me see him! Not even at the funeral!"

"You remember that?" he asked, shocked.

"Dad! I'm not a kid anymore! I'm not stupid! I remember everything! I remember how you wouldn't talk to him and how you wouldn't even let me go to him. He left because of you! He left and didn't even say goodbye! You and Mom didn't even tell me! Why didn't you tell me?"

"Honey, you were so young, we—"

"Oh Dad, please! Stop treating me like a baby! It's not fair, you know! You may be mad at Uncle Cole and you may hate him, but I don't! I still love him and I miss him! It's not fair that I can't ever see him again because of you! Nobody cares about me and how I feel! It's all your fault! I hate you!" she screamed, shoving past her father as she ran to the truck.

* * *

Matt now shuddered, thinking about that time. One of the biggest mistakes he had made was in not being truthful with Becca. She was right, he never considered her feelings back then, she was so young that they just seemed insignificant. He had operated under the assumption that even though you explained death and loss to a child, on some level, the real meaning never impacted them. They were blissfully innocent, and it was that innocence he wrongly believed protected them. He should have known that adults didn't corner the market on grief; on some level, the child also suffered the effects.

The one thing Becca didn't understand, though, was that Matt did not hate Cole like she had accused him of. Sure, he couldn't face him after the tragedy, but that didn't mean he hated him. Matt hated the decision that Cole had been faced with, one that he himself didn't understand. One part of him was angry that the decision regarding Sarah's life fell to Cole, and another side was grateful that he wasn't the one who had to sign those papers.

Wanting to shield her from the pain they were experiencing, he had underestimated his daughter. Matt simply thought that Becca had been too young to really know what was going on, so he ignorantly used silence as a way of dealing with her. They did sit with Becca the afternoon after the fire and explained what had happened, but that was about as far as he and Shauna had gone. When Cole left, they told her that he had gone and then just assumed that she would take them at their word.

How did one explain something to a child that they, themselves, did not understand? Cole's leaving had shocked the entire community; it happened so suddenly that they were all blindsided. He never even said goodbye to Dave and Thelma, who woke early one morning to find his room empty and his few possessions gone.

After a trip out to the ranch, they discovered that Cole had placed a 'for sale' sign in front of the property and had taken the few odd bits of furniture stored in the shed and his camping supplies from the barn. He simply disappeared. All the horses were left behind; Cole hadn't even taken his own horse, Midnight. Everyone knew that he had been beyond comfort, but his leaving in such a fashion further stunned the town and those closest to him.

Therefore, it was hard to tell a little girl that the uncle she loved so dearly had left, and not have any answers as to why. How did one tell a child that sometimes a person grieved so deeply that if they didn't shut down completely or if they didn't run from themselves, they would lose their minds? The entire world had gone insane, and Matt no longer recognized his own life. How could he explain anything to a child? They never realized the hurt she carried deep inside. So Becca ran off again; only this time, she was a lot older and better prepared. She was just a lonely child looking to reclaim a piece of her life.

* * *

The next morning Matt found himself back at Cole's ranch, staring out over the land. There was still no word on Becca, and he no longer knew where to turn. He shivered, everything in their lives had changed; people were wiped out as if they had never existed and the ranch lay in ruins. The fields and yard were overgrown, choked with weeds and dried, brown grass so tall, it bent double. Nothing turned green anymore, even though it was spring. The land was as dead as those on it.

Matt simply didn't have the heart or the desire for any kind of upkeep. The house was gone, with only the foundation remaining, and the barn was falling in on itself. He just stared, wondering how everything could be gone so permanently and so fast. Not only does life slip through one's fingers, sometimes it just fades into oblivion.

A lifetime had slipped by since Becca stood at this very spot, crying her heart out and breaking her father's. She still looked very much like a little girl, but for the first time Matt realized that they had to stop treating her as such. He now owned Cole's ranch, something nobody had any inkling of. All everyone in town knew was that the ranch had been sold, no one had moved in, and no one knew the identity of the secretive buyer. What made it even more puzzling was why someone would buy the place almost before the paint on the sign had the chance to dry, and then never bothered to do anything with the land.

Smugly, Matt nodded. He knew who had purchased the land; as a matter of fact, only he and those needed to complete the transaction knew, but they were sworn to silence. It was the least he could do, it wouldn't change things, but in some small way, he felt better just taking control of something. It made no difference that he had never done anything with the land, that wasn't why he purchased it. The transaction had been completed long ago and Matt never regretted it for one minute. At least he had this one small victory. Cole never wanted the ranch to fall into the wrong hands and had fought tooth and nail to hold out, refusing to sell. Matt had jumped the very second he heard of it being put on the market.

The shockwaves that rolled throughout the tiny town so long ago never seemed to ebb; a tidal wave of insanity had washed down over them all, leaving a trail of broken souls in its wake. One long, dark night shortly after the fire, Matt endlessly paced the living room floor. Every so often, he would go over to the large picture window and stare out into the dark. There wasn't a star in the sky, which was fitting. Stars no longer shone in their part of the world. The night was more than half over, but that didn't matter to Matt. Ever since the funeral three days ago, sleep stopped coming at regular intervals. He just drifted through his days and nights, only succumbing when his body was just too exhausted to stay awake. It wasn't a restful sleep, but it was sleep.

His face was haggard and unshaven; his eyes were empty and carried a haunted, hollow look. Matt wasn't the only one; it seemed that everyone had aged overnight, the shock and grief lining their faces. He hated meeting with anyone from town and hid out at home. Every time Matt saw someone else, all they did was cry. All he really wanted to do was scream, which was a luxury he denied himself simply because once he started, he would not stop until his mind snapped. If he didn't have to go check on his father during the day, Matt doubted if he would ever leave his house again.

Shauna was caught up in her own grief. She barely spoke with a soul, and only went on with the chores that still demanded her attention. Matt knew that he was doing the same thing, only it felt as if he were standing back, watching someone else controlling his body and tending the animals for him. He didn't see anything; the world had taken on a glassy, faraway look. Everything heard just drifted around him, coming to his jumbled mind garbled and incomprehensible. Faces faded in and out as friends and neighbors came over during the day, offering food and solace, both of which went unnoticed by Matt, who was numb. He was beyond feeling, and their words of comfort fell on deaf ears. There were no such words. There was only the madness they had been pitched into.

Cole had not been by since the funeral, but Matt never even gave that a thought. One part of his brain told him that he should go to his friend … that Cole needed him … but Cole was the one who signed the papers. He walked away from Sarah after taking her from them. Matt knew the sheer idiocy of those thoughts, but was unable to act on his feelings. The days drifted by, blending into nights that stretched on forever. Most of the time Matt stood staring out the window, or sat on his front porch until dawn started breaking through. Only then did he get up to feed his animals.

Shauna now slept alone nights, with neither giving comfort to the other. At a time when everyone should have been pulling together and helping each other through their grief, each went their own way. Becca stayed in the shadows, watching the strange way her parents and everyone around her were acting, her eyes large and scared. Every once in a while someone hugged her or walked by patting her on the head, but that was about the extent of it. She would go up to her room, wishing that someone would follow and tell her that everything was going to be all right again, but no one came and Becca had been scared ever since.

It all came to a head that night, when Matt once paced the floors. Everything was too quiet and the shrill ringing of the phone made him jump out of his skin. Fingers of fear played along his spine. Looking at the clock, Matt saw that it was almost four in the morning. No good ever came from a phone call at that hour, and he was too petrified to even pick up the receiver. Not wanting to wake Shauna or Becca, he jumped, catching it on the third ring.

"Yeah?" he asked, his voice hoarse and barely audible.

"Matt, you gotta get over here," Dave's voice came to him.

The world started swirling around him. They all were early risers, but even four in the morning was early for them. Dave would never consider calling anyone at this hour unless it was an emergency and since Cole had been staying there, Matt braced himself for another loss. It was at that moment sheer hatred for himself coursed through his veins. Something had happened, and it was his fault. He should have gone to Cole; he should have talked to his friend.

"Dave, what the hell—" Matt replied, his voice breaking.

"Matt, I've had a bad feeling all night long and I just got up. He's gone!" Dave sputtered.

"What the hell are you talking about?" Matt almost shouted.

"Cole! He's gone! Matt, the other day he left without saying a word, and I found him back at the ranch sitting in the barn," Dave shuddered, not willing to say anything else.

"And?" Matt asked, picking up on his hesitation.

"Well, he was just sitting there," Dave answered, refusing to divulge anything else. "He didn't say a word, he just sat there staring at the ground. Matt, it scared the hell out of me! I wish he'd blow up or something, but he didn't say a word! Not even around here! He just sort of drifts around the place, you know?"

"I know, we've been doing the same thing. Dave, I'm scared. I've never been so scared before in my life. I know that I wasn't there for Cole, and that was wrong. If it's any solace, I wasn't there for anyone, not even my own family. But I gotta pull myself together! I need to for everybody's sake! Dad's not even Dad anymore, if that makes any sense!" Matt replied.

"That more than makes sense; none of us are the same anymore, but we all have to be strong to get through this! We gotta find him, Matt!" Dave exclaimed.

"I'm coming over," was all Matt said before hanging up the phone.

By the time he arrived at Dave's front door, Matt found him already dressed and waiting. They drove quickly over to Cole's ranch, lost in the fear of what they would find. There was no good reason for Cole to return to his home at such an ungodly hour, but neither knew of anywhere else he would go. Dave tried swallowing past his fear, his throat constricting painfully. The one thing he didn't want to do was walk into the barn. Maybe this time, Cole would have acted on his grief.

But another sight greeted the men as they pulled up. Matt jammed on the brakes, skidding to a stop as they stared at the sign by the mailbox. 'For Sale' taunted them. Angered, Matt slammed the truck into gear and smashed through the offending sign. Those two words said it all.... Cole was gone. Dave knew that he would not find his cousin in the barn this time, all they found were the animals Cole had left behind. He had simply vanished, with a pickup truck and the few meager belongings still to his name. No one knew where he had gone and they had no hope of him ever coming back. Cole simply had nothing to return to.

"Thought he would rebuild someday," Dave muttered.

"Could you?" Matt asked, staring intently at the man.

"Fuck, don't know anything anymore," Dave answered, kicking at the ground as he walked back to the truck.

* * *

They rode back to Dave's in silence. Matt knew what he was going to do, but he wasn't saying a word to anyone. All he had done since the fire was make one bad decision after another. It was time to set things right. It might not change things the way they now stood, but it would solve an even bigger problem. No one listened so far, so his intentions were kept to himself. It wasn't anyone's business, not even Shauna's. No one needed to know and no one would ever know.

This was the only way Matt could preserve the land his family had

321

perished on and keep it out of the hands of the one person who had been the cause of their heartache. There was no time to waste; Matt had to get to Sally Kirl, the only real estate broker in town. He only had one shot at this and if the good Lord were willing, he would make it in time. Not only would it be the first thing that he had done right since their nightmare started, Matt somehow hoped that it would make a difference. It might not happen right away or even within the next few months or years, but it might someday. This wasn't something Matt was doing for himself; he was doing this for Cole, knowing what his family's land meant to him, even if Cole didn't realize that himself anymore.

Not caring that it wasn't even 6 a.m. yet, Matt dropped Dave off and without a word about his plans, drove straight over to Sally's home, where he pounded furiously on the door. There were no misgivings as far as the money was concerned; Matt had some put away that was given him by his father years ago. Jeremy had wanted to give both his children something for the future, and one year he presented both Matt and Sarah with a large share of profits from the ranch.

The only thing Matt had asked for in return was for his family to keep this between themselves; no one else ever knew of the gift. To this day, Matt had never mentioned a word about the money to Shauna. Prideful or not, wrong or not, the funds were his secret. It wasn't that Matt didn't trust his wife, he just wanted something that was his, and his alone. Shauna and Becca never wanted for anything and never would; the ranch was profitable and both were well provided for. Matt steadily put money away for their future so that they would have a nestegg upon retirement (if there was such a thing when one lived on a ranch,) and Becca's education was secured.

This money was his, to do with as he pleased. Besides, a part of him just didn't believe that Shauna would agree with how he was now spending it. Matt had made up his mind and there was no stopping him. All he had to do was pray that he was in time to make the purchase. Dave had said that as of yesterday morning, Cole was still at the house and the sign had not been put up yet. After dinner, though, he had gone off by himself for a few hours, without a word to anyone as to his whereabouts. He returned home as sullen and quiet as when he left, and closed himself up in his room.

Matt had no idea if anyone else had been contacted about the sale of the ranch yet or not, he only prayed that Sally hadn't had the time to do so. No rumors were flying around town, so maybe it was early enough and no one even realized that the property was available. That brought some consolation; talk spread fast in Broken Arrow, silent tongues insured Matt's chances of being the first to know.

For years now Matt watched his money grow, he had invested it wisely and never touched a cent. That was one saving grace. He shivered momentarily, wondering if the powers that be had already slated the money for such use the day his father presented it to him. That thought was just too chilling to think about, so Matt quickly shoved it from his mind.

Grief and the confusion caused by sudden loss had caused Matt to do a great disservice to those he cared about the most. Instead of being there for them, he had turned inward, shunning everyone that came near and not extending himself to those who remained aloof. This was a small way to atone for his sins. In his mind, he had let everyone he loved down. He wasn't there for his mother and sister, and they perished. If he hadn't dragged Cole away for the weekend, then they might be alive today.

"Hell, if I hadn't dragged him away, he might be gone too," Matt shivered. "Nice time to feel bad about that now, he's as good as gone already and the way he feels right now, he probably wishes he was with Sarah. God, why did you let this happen?" Matt asked, pounding on the steering wheel as he drove.

If he couldn't find Cole and make amends, then he could buy the ranch and hopefully turn it over to him one day. Maybe after Cole had had a chance to get his life back together, he might return to Broken Arrow. If that ever happened, Matt wanted him to have something to return to. A person often acted rashly and made impulsive decisions during times of stress. Matt didn't want Cole to spend the rest of his life regretting his actions; therefore, he jumped at the first chance to help. God willing, they would somehow find a way to deal with their grief and put it behind them.

"What in the world?" Sally's irritated voice greeted him. Flinging open the door, the tired woman glimpsed Matt through bleary eyes. "Matt Young! Do you have any idea what time it is?" she asked accusingly.

"I know very well what time it is, and that's why I'm here! Please tell me that I'm not too late!" he pleaded, ignorant to her anger.

"Too late? How the hell can anyone be too late at this hour? Don't you people ever sleep?" she asked, immediately regretting her words. Her anger softening, Sally reached out, pulling Matt inside. "Matt, I'm so sorry, I didn't mean anything by that, please come on in," she said, fighting back her own tears.

Clearing his throat, Matt looked away. He had cried so much lately that it was a wonder he wasn't dehydrated. And the one sight he loathed right now was the tears of another, he had seen too many of them this past week. Sally wiped her eyes and took a deep, shuddering breath. In the bliss of sleep, sometimes the grief that holds a town in its grip can be forgotten if one was lucky enough not to dream. Sally had been friends with Sarah and had been even closer to Myra. It seemed that every person in town who had lost their mother, father, or both, at an early age, was taken under Myra's wing, and Sally had been one of them. Only 11 when her own mother died of cancer, she became a welcome addition to the Young home.

Whenever in need of a mother's ear to listen to her fears and questions about growing up, Sally found that in Myra. Sometimes after school, she would walk home with Sarah and together they would sit in the kitchen with Myra, laughing while they prepared that evening's meal or baked a treat for the men. Most nights Sally took what she helped make home to her father so that they could eat together, but sometimes she stayed with Sarah and ate with the family. The leftovers were ultimately split between her and Cole, who always seemed to show up when his favorite dishes were made, and Sally would bring them home to her father. She missed Myra and had been paralyzed with grief and fear since Friday.

Frankly, Matt scared her. Through the gossip mill she heard what he believed about the fire, not wanting to believe it herself. Sally refused to think that anyone she knew and had done business with could be capable of such a heinous act, but deep inside, she sensed the truth. Sensing it and acting on those feelings were two different things, and she refused to act on them. If Matt came to talk to her about his suspicions, then she would have no choice but to send him packing; she was that scared.

"I know that it's early, but you have to help me. Besides, since when did you turn away from a sale? I've known you to go halfway across the state to pick up a buyer if you had to! And I know that you're very good at keeping your mouth shut if it means making a deal," Matt said. "Not that this is a threat! Please don't think of it as that! I didn't mean anything by it, and I won't bring up anything!" he quickly interjected, waving his hands once he had seen the way Sally's face paled at his words.

"Matt, I don't want to—"

"Sally, this has nothing to do with anything I believe in. Let me start over, you see, Dave called me a little while ago. Cole's gone!" Matt said, feeling the color draining out of his own face.

"My God!" Sally gasped, pulling him into the room. "What on earth do you mean Cole's gone?"

"You didn't know?" Matt had to ask.

"If I knew that Cole was gone or was leaving, don't you think I would have called you and said something?" she shot back.

"Then what do you know?" Matt needed to know before he made his offer. The one thing he needed was to get his facts straight.

"Matt, all I know is that late yesterday afternoon Cole came by saying that he was selling the place. I have to tell you, I didn't like the sound of it and at the risk of being teased, I did try to talk him out of it!" she stated.

"You? Talk your way out of a deal? That's a new one on me!" Matt snorted. "But seriously, did he really put the ranch on the market? Please tell me that he didn't!"

"Did you see the sign?" Sally countered.

"You mean, did I run over the sign?" he answered back.

"Oh no, tell me you didn't! Is this whole world going crazy?" she asked, sitting down and rubbing her eyes. There was no coffee ready at this hour, so both settled for glasses of orange juice.

"I did and I would again. So, I guess that answers my question. Cole just put the place up and he left. It's as simple as that, but it's the most complicated mess I've ever been in. Sally, what the hell am I going to tell everyone? They'll be heartbroken!" Matt said.

"As heartbroken as Cole was during the funeral?" she asked somewhat angrily.

Matt sat back dejectedly, "I deserved that," was his flat answer.

"No, Matt, you don't deserve anything that happened. None of you did," Sally changed her tone, taking his hand. "I can never tell you how sorry I am. You're hurting and I know that you will be for a long time. I hurt too, but they were your family; I have no right to judge how you acted. I don't know how I would have if put in your place!"

"That's why I'm here," Matt admitted sorrowfully. "I turned my back on everyone I love and look what happened! Mom and Sarah are gone—

"That's not your fault!" Sarah said quickly. "Please, don't go there!"

"Sorry," Matt replied. "I can't seem to reach my father, all he does is sit in his rocking chair and stare out the window all day long. I get this eerie feeling that he's waiting for Mom and Sarah to come walking up the lane! Sally, it's spooky! Mom left to spend the night with Sarah, and Dad's acting like he's waiting for her to come home! God, I can't take this! Now, Cole's gone! I wasn't there for him either!"

"Matt, Cole didn't leave because of you," Sally said.

"How do you know why he left? Did he say?" Matt asked, his voice almost pleading.

"Not in so many words, but he's so lost, Matt! He told me that he couldn't face rebuilding and going on as if nothing happened. He said that he had to get away from the place. I just assumed that he would be staying on with Dave and Thelma! It never occurred to me that he would leave like this!" she said, her voice taking on a shrill tone.

"Sally, how could you know? But it all seems so easy, doesn't it? I mean, he has nothing left! The only clothes he had were those he had on his back and what he'd packed for the weekend! The only other clothes he had were those that Thelma and Nell bought for him and what was donated! Sally, the man has nothing! He doesn't even have himself! And he left his animals behind!" Matt exclaimed.

"I can't believe it. Well, I guess that you and Dave will have to decide where they go," she shrugged.

"Dave's taking them. Told him so on the ride back to his place. Knowing him, he's already over there getting them as we speak. He can have them, he's family," Matt cringed.

"So are you," Sally reminded him.

"Not important now. What's important is the reason I'm here. I didn't come to whine about Cole's leaving or anything," Matt explained.

"Then why did you come?" Sally asked of him.

"I came to buy Cole's ranch," Matt said flatly, crossing his arms.

"You what!" Sally sputtered. "Buy his ranch! How in the world do you propose to do that?"

"That's where you come in, pretty lady. First of all, is it available?" he needed to know.

"I haven't had the chance to get word out yet," Sally nodded.

"Good! Thank God for dragging your heels! Now, I'm depending on your reputation for keeping your mouth shut. Sally, I intend to buy the ranch and I want this to be between you and me. No one else is to know! No one, understand? I don't even want word of this to get back to Shauna!" he pleaded.

"Matt, I don't understand! First of all, how do you plan on doing this and why would you want it kept secret?" she wondered.

"Easy," Matt began. "First of all, I want this kept between us simply because it's nobody's business and I don't want to answer to a bunch of questions. My life's complicated enough right now, thank you. And it's also my way of giving something back to Cole. I know how much he loves that place! I think he's making a big mistake, but I don't want him to pay for that for the rest of his life! If he decides to come back someday, I want him to have something to come back to."

"Sounds so much like you," Sally sighed. "Why else?"

"Sally, I want to keep the land in the family," he said, no further explanation needed. Sally knew exactly what he meant. "And I have some money invested that my father gave me years ago. I'll use that."

"Oh, you are the shrewd one! I bet you never told Shauna of that money, did you?" Sally asked slyly.

Matt leaned forward, staring intently. "Takes one shrewd one to know another! I never told anyone about that money. It's mine, and that's all I'm saying about it. I have enough to buy the ranch and keep it in the family. And I don't need Shauna blowing a gasket because of the money and what I'm doing today, so can I count on you?"

"Honey, you pay, I'll deliver the goods," Sally said seductively, leaning forward. "Money talks!"

"Good, then you give me what I have to sign now and I'll leave you a deposit. When Wallace opens the bank at 8, I'll be the first in line. Just tell me the asking price and I'll get the draft and come straight here," Matt said, his gaze never wavering.

"You know, I usually doubt a person's honesty when they say they'll be back with the money, I'd think it a ruse to get me to write up a contract, thereby stalling any future sales. People can get screwed that way," Sally said, her gaze just as intense.

"Oh, pretty lady, no need to worry; I fully intend to deliver. You have my word on that; I swear on my mother and sister's graves," he flatly stated.

"Then sign here," Sally said crisply, handing Matt the paper she had been rifling for. "But if you're not back by 11:00, I'll rip this up like it never happened and I'll be in the town square heralding the availability of the ranch!" she warned.

"You won't be making any trips to the town square today," Matt said as he signed, then walked out the door.

Three hours later, he was back with the check and left with the deed. Cole's ranch was his. Climbing into his truck, Matt couldn't help but sneer. "Beat you again, you bastard," he cursed, slamming the truck into gear. If things got ugly, he would just take his lumps. For once, he had won.

* * *

Now Matt prayed that he could finally do what should have done so long ago. He hoped to find the strength to help those he loved get their lives together again, and that included his daughter, whom he desperately wanted back. If he could only have one more chance, Matt vowed that things would be different this time. This time, he would listen to Becca ... he would really listen to her. Right now, she was the only one who mattered.

"How many more have to leave before you snap out of this?" he shuddered, burying his face in his hands.

Walking over to the remains of the foundation, Matt stood silently, staring down. After all these years of waiting and worrying, he had finally hired a private detective to search out his friend. Three months ago, the man returned with the requested information. Cole was now living in the town of Crater Mills, Montana. That was all Matt wanted to know; he was too afraid to ask anything else and chose not to dig into Cole's personal life. Knowing that he was alive and safe was enough for now. Anything else would have been an intrusion and Matt did not want to tread where he didn't belong. Even if they never made contact again, at least he knew where Cole was. Every night, he fervently prayed that Cole had found some sort of peace and happiness in this life. Lord knew that he had never known a moment of either, since the fire.

Kneeling, Matt spoke with his mother and sister, as he did so often now. "We all lost so much. What right did I have to think that I was the only one hurting? I didn't help anyone when they needed me, including my own wife and child."

Between bouts of depression, Matt felt his life slowly slipping further away with each passing day. He and Shauna were polite strangers and Matt had just come to the realization that he literally knew nothing about his daughter. The young woman who stared back at them now was demanding answers. She couldn't get them at home, so she left, searching for someone who would tell her what she so desperately wanted to know. Becca wanted her life back and unlike the adults, she wasn't afraid to reach out and fight for it. Where they cowered and hid, she faced life head-on. Matt had failed his daughter, and now Becca was gone.

"God, I can't lose anyone else," he sobbed into his hands.

There was nothing left to do here. Matt shook with fatigue. He drove home slowly, and tiredly climbed from the truck. Shauna came out to his side, greeting him. She hadn't succumbed to the bottle; it was hard, but she went and poured the golden liquid down the bathroom sink. Drinking would not help her now, it hadn't helped all these years and it wouldn't help now. Shauna knew that she couldn't hide anymore. She and Matt had to finally take control of their lives and they had to get their daughter back. Nothing else was acceptable. First, though, they had to find her.

"You know, I used to wonder why Cole left like he did. I can see him not mentioning his leaving to anyone else, but I never understood why he didn't at least say something to Dave and Thelma," Matt said quietly.

"Honey?" Shauna asked, massaging his shoulders.

At first, her hands upon him in such a manner felt foreign. It had been a long time since they had shared such a normal, nonchalant moment. He jumped, but settled quickly as her fingers kneaded into his skin.

"He lost his home, Shauna! How could he have stayed? I just figured he would've stayed with Dave and Thelma, and if he ever got strong enough to go back and face things, he would somehow find a way to rebuild. I should have realized how useless that thought was, how can anyone go back after such a tragedy? Our family died in that house, on that land, how can you rebuild and go on? There's just no way, for they're still there. They'll always be there," he replied eerily.

"He could have talked to someone," Shauna suggested, shivering inwardly at her husband's words and mood.

"Who? You name one person on the face of the earth Cole could have talked to that could have helped and taken away some of his pain? Shauna, that person doesn't exist. And that person certainly wasn't me," Matt shuddered.

"So? Matt, Cole's leaving wasn't your fault. How the hell could you have been there with words of comfort for any of us, when you needed them yourself? Honey, for years I was mad at you for letting this happen, but you didn't let it happen! Cole didn't let it happen! You both are blaming yourselves for something neither of you could ever understand and couldn't have stopped! You both are victims, and you both fell apart. You couldn't be there for Cole, any more than he could have been there for you! How can two broken men help one another? It's an impossibility! But time has passed! Matt, things can change! They can change now! We can make them change!" Shauna said, feeling stronger than she had in a long time.

"Change? How? Can you tell me how? Can we change so much that our daughter would want to come back?" Matt challenged.

"We can if we want to badly enough," Shauna adamantly replied.

"How the hell can we do that if we can't find her?" he asked, his eyes flashing.

For a moment, both fell silent. Shauna's hands slipped from his shoulders. He was right; she didn't have anymore answers the he did at the time. Both knew what they wanted, and both were at a loss of how to achieve that goal.

Shauna paced, trying to figure out where Becca could have gone, when she was besieged with a frightening thought. "Oh my God," she cried out, spinning around to face Matt. "She heard us!"

"What the hell are you talking about?" Matt said weakly.

"For God sakes, Matt, lift your head and look at me!" Shauna demanded. "Becca heard us talking last week! She had to have!"

Matt could feel the color draining from his face at his wife's words. "If you're right, then...."

"Then she heard us talking about the report from the investigator and she knows that we found out where Cole is! She probably heard us arguing about me telling you to go to him!" Shauna exclaimed.

"But she was supposed to be asleep!" Matt cried out.

"Oh come on, Matt! You know she heard us! We were very vocal about it, if I remember right! How could she not have heard? But as usual, did we give a damn? It's the only thing that makes sense! Where the hell else would she go? The only other time she ran away was to go to Cole's place, so it makes perfect sense now! She knows that you don't have the courage to go and face Cole, so she's going to go herself!" Shauna said.

Matt's hands fell from his face to the table, where they lay limply. "She told me the night I found her at Cole's that it wasn't fair that we kept her from him. She said that we didn't care about her feelings and it wasn't right that he left like that and we didn't tell her. God, she was barely seven when this nightmare started, but she still deserved to know. We always treated her like she wasn't smart enough to understand, but she has always understood more than we ever gave her credit for. How the hell did we expect her to just follow along and go on with her life as if nothing had happened?"

"Well, we better find her and when we do, we better start talking. I'm going to call the police," Shauna said, running to the phone.

* * *

Three days had passed since Becca left home and she was tired. The bus finally pulled into Landing, which was a mere two miles from Crater Mills. She would have to walk that distance in the morning, but that did not bother Becca. Walking two miles was nothing for her; back home, she and her friends easily walked that distance and more. Plus anything had to be better than that long, dusty bus ride. If she left just before daybreak, then she could do most of it under cover of the early morning shadows.

Getting to Cole's ranch would prove trickier; the sun would be up and Becca would have to keep to the side of the road, ducking into the brush when necessary. But if Crater Mills was anything like back home, she wouldn't have to worry much, one could walk the roads of Broken Arrow all day long and not see any traffic. At the most, only a car or two would pass by, bringing one of her neighbors home. It would be easy to duck and take cover; all she had to do was keep alert and listen for oncoming cars.

Becca was smart; she prided herself on that fact and on the fact that she had already outsmarted them all. They didn't know she had heard them the other night and they didn't know that when she was alone the next day she had written the address from the report down on a sheet of paper, and then memorized it. She also purchased a map, which she spent days studying,

330

along with mapping out a route. This time when she ran, she would do it right.

She would have her clothes, her money, and a bus ticket, which was purchased in a neighboring town one afternoon when cutting school. That was Friday; by Monday, Becca was gone. By the time anyone even realized that she was missing, she would be far from home. They wouldn't have a clue. Soon she was on the bus, leaving Broken Arrow and all her problems behind.

Becca had no idea of what awaited her or even if Cole would be happy to see her, but that was a chance she had to take. Anything was better than living at home the way things were now. Her father never snapped out of his depression and her mother drank. She thought that no one knew, but Becca did. She knew more than they thought; she knew where Cole was and she was going to him. Holding her flower in one hand and the rabbit in the other, Becca watched the towns slipping by.

It was late Wednesday night by the time she reached Landing, so Becca found a place just outside the station to sleep. She wasn't afraid to sleep outside alone; there was nothing here to hurt her. She slipped into a corner behind the building where it was dark and the ground was soft. It was a hot night, there was no need to worry about keeping warm. In the morning, she would get up early and walk into town, where she could hopefully find a place to wash up and get something to eat.

It was easy for her to go unnoticed, Becca had learned quickly that if she stuck to gas stations that had a convenience store; she could do all those things and leave without anyone questioning her. Most of the time the clerks running those stores were either tired, or just plain bored and paid absolutely no attention at all as to who was standing in front of them. They absently rang up purchases, stuffed them into a bag and yawned while handing over the change. Once she ate, she would then follow the route drawn out from the map and walk to Cole's ranch. Tomorrow afternoon she would finally see him again. Becca fell asleep that night wondering just how much Cole had changed, if he had changed at all.

Chapter Sixteen

"Wake up, Daddy!" Katie giggled, jumping on Cole's stomach.

"Oh God," he wheezed, rolling to his side.

After a few quick gulps of air, Cole felt a tiny finger slowly peeling his eyelid back. Peering through the slit, all he saw was a small face with a large grin. Rolling onto his back, the most he could manage was a tired groan. Looking over at the nightstand, he saw that it was barely four o'clock. He hadn't planned on getting up for another hour, but Katie had other plans. He knew she was excited, but this was the first time she had ever gotten up before him.

"Daddy, are you in there?" she giggled, poking at his forehead. "It's my birthday!" she whispered in his ear.

With a growl, Cole rolled over suddenly, grabbing her in his arms. "I know it's your birthday, you little weasel!" he exclaimed, biting at her neck.

Shrieks and cries filled the air as he tickled her until she finally gave in, "Daddy! Stop! Don't tickle...." she cried out, gasping for breath.

"You give up?" he demanded to know.

"I want my birthday! Are we going for our ride?" Katie asked, her eyes shining with hope.

"Of course we're going for our ride. I wouldn't forget that! Why don't you go get ready?" he said, swinging his feet down over the side of the bed.

"Can I wear my flower bracelet, Daddy? It's just like our flowers!" she asked.

"Sure you can, honey," he smiled softly at her. There was nothing better than seeing hope and excitement dancing in a child's eyes as far as Cole was concerned. "We'll get dressed and then I'll go get the horses ready. We'll eat breakfast when we get back, all right?"

"Ok, Daddy! Can I still go with Callie?" Katie asked not one to forget a thing.

"Where are you going with Callie?" Cole asked, forgetting about their plans.

"Callie is going to come get me! I have to be pretty for her, Daddy! Will you fix my hair?" she begged.

"Honey, I'll fix your hair, but can we first fix some coffee so that I can go feed the horses? And then we'll go on our ride. I'll fix your hair after breakfast," he said, slinging her over his shoulders.

Hearing all the commotion, Ruth met them in the kitchen with a smile on her face. "I knew that someone would be up bright and early today! It's always fun to start your birthday early, isn't it honey?" Ruth smiled, holding out her arms.

"I'm sorry we woke you! I wasn't planning on getting up yet myself, but we have a ride to take," Cole smiled apologetically.

"Honey, today is going to be a fun day! And fun days are supposed to begin early! So why don't you go get washed and dressed and take care of your chores? We have a lot to do!" Ruth said, pushing Cole from the room.

* * *

The sun began peeking into her room, but Callie almost didn't want to get up and face the day. In spite of talking to Cole right before she went to sleep, she was still upset. She had heard of Danielle's arrival and was shaken to the core. Callie doubted if she would ever get over her insecurities where Maggie was concerned, and even though the woman didn't come herself, having Danielle show up was just as bad, in her eyes. Callie feared a piece of Cole lost.

By now, Cole and Katie were probably on their ride. She had spoken with him around 11 the previous night and hoped that he had managed to get some sleep. The upset in his voice was plain to hear, and Callie knew that he had gone out to the barn to think. Cole always went to the barn when upset. It was his haven from the world. She also knew that Katie would be up early this morning, getting ready for her big day. She had promised her a trip to the beauty parlor, but Callie was still upset from her earlier conversation with Cole. Even though he had sought to reassure her, she could hear the distance in his voice.

Just when they found each other, there was still a part of Cole she could never claim. A part of him would never belong to her, it would always be with Maggie, whether he realized it or not. Cole had tried keeping the worry from his voice, but he could not fool Callie. He also tried joking about Danielle's visit, keeping the real pain from her, also. Not sharing felt as if he was slowly pulling away. She prayed that his old fears did not resurface and drive a wedge between them again, it was bad enough that Maggie was still a wedge.

Not only was Callie worried about Maggie coming and claiming Katie one day, she was worried that the hold the woman had over Cole would never loosen its grip. Where Cole feared losing Katie to Maggie, Callie feared losing them both. Even though she had spoken with Cole, she still worried. She would always worry. No matter how much he denied any feelings for Maggie, they still shared a common bond that he and Callie did not have. They shared Katie. Maggie was absent from her life, but Katie was still her daughter. Callie knew she could never compete with that.

It made no difference that Maggie had a husband of her own, that didn't stop her from sleeping with Cole in the first place, and Callie doubted if things had improved over the years. Who was to say that Maggie's marriage was not failing, or had failed? She could have sent Danielle to test the waters before she swooped in, snagging Cole and Katie in her clutches. There would be no further reason to keep their secret. What would happen to Callie if Maggie showed up one day, free of that husband? Would she be tossed aside while Cole turned to her? Callie's heart froze, Maggie had been unhappy for years and her children were growing older. Once they broke out on their own, they wouldn't need her as much. What would happen to Callie then? Would Maggie show up one day, ready to make a life with Cole and Katie?

It was not unheard of. She had shown up once before, rattling Cole's life. It wasn't so far-fetched that she would do the same thing again, only this time she would be offering herself. It was like a package deal. Cole would have Katie, and Maggie would have them both. Cole's life would be free from the worry of losing his daughter. How could Callie compete with that?

What makes you think you have to compete? You claim to love the man, how could you think so little of him? Callie shuddered. *Because he would do anything to keep his daughter,* she sighed heavily.

Even toss you aside like you never meant a thing? Do you really think that he would just turn back to Maggie after all these years, like nothing happened, and welcome her back into his life just because they share a child? Lots of people share the common bond of a child, but that doesn't make a relationship work! she fought with herself.

"No, but lots of times people use their children to make them work. Besides, Cole would do anything to keep Katie," Callie said.

Anything? Do you really think he would turn back to Maggie? I doubt it. And she hasn't left her husband. Let's face it, Maggie is a wealthy, world-renowned woman. She was born to money and she married money. Need I say more? If there's one thing you don't have to worry about, it is Maggie confessing to her family. Her father would disinherit her for ruining the family name and never mind how Ronald would react! Maggie won't do anything to bring dishonor to any of them. Maybe her children are grown, but that still doesn't mean that she would give up the lifestyle she has become accustomed to, just to live on a ranch in the middle of nowhere! Both of their families are rich, neither of them are hurting for a thing! She's not the type to turn her back on all the luxury, fun and excitement that she's used to! A person almost craves that kind of lifestyle once they've had it, she continued the argument.

"Yes, and a person craves their child," Callie sighed.

But she hasn't come for her child. She only asked about her child. There's a difference, she reminded herself.

Is there? Callie tiredly wondered.

The same argument had been raging through her mind since yesterday. Ever since Callie heard of Danielle's arrival, she fought the urge to go over to Cole's and snatch every hair from the woman's perfectly made-up head. If she hadn't been so hot and sweaty, and didn't smell like the barn floor, she would have. But she stopped herself. Once again, her day was spent going from ranch to ranch. How could she show up looking the way she did and confront a woman as exquisite as Danielle? The woman was world class and Callie saw herself a meager hayseed in her shadow. If she had gone over, Cole would have seen the difference too, then it really would have been over. Chiding herself vehemently, Callie finished her shower.

Looking in the mirror after she climbed out, Callie scowled. *Look at you and listen to you. You keep thinking like this, then you're not only going to look like a harpie, you're going to sound like a harpie. You claim to love Cole. Well, if you love him, then give him a break. Trust is the backbone of any relationship. Look at what he's overcome to let you into his life! Sure, it took a long time, but in a way, that only made things better. Maybe it made the bond stronger between you two, only you're too lame to see that. Whatever, the man loves you and he's not one to take things lightly. He has also thought of his relationship with Maggie as a nothing but a mistake, do you want him to start thinking of his relationship with you the same way? You better get a grip.*

Wiping the steam from the mirror, Callie brushed her teeth furiously. She had to get her emotions under control. She had to trust Cole. He had tried his best to reassure her last night, but there was still something missing. As much as she wanted to remain behind and not face anyone today, was as anxious as Callie was to go over to Cole's. She would be doing that soon enough. By the time she finished dressing and fixed a quick breakfast, it would be time to pick up Katie. At least she had this over Maggie. The woman may have given birth to Katie, but she was the one who loved her and shared in her life. With that thought in mind, Callie went in to dress.

* * *

They rode down through the back fields, watching the sun slowly rising in the sky. Katie laughed, pointing out all the colors that seemed to wash down over them from above. Her hair shone a dark, brownish red in the golden rays of light that covered her. Her eyes darted around looking everywhere, and her finger never stopped pointing.

"Daddy, that's east!" she proudly exclaimed, remembering how her father had explained how the sun rises in the east and sets in the west.

"You're right, honey!" Cole answered proudly, astounded that she had remembered. Then again, Katie's intelligence should come as no surprise, she hung on to his every word. "Do you know which way we're going now?"

For her age, Katie had a mind like a trap; once she was told something, she never let it go. A serious look crossed her face for a moment while she pointed to the rising sun and then over to her left. She then looked up, remembering her compass in her head. One night last summer Cole had sat down showing her all four points after they had taken a ride earlier that day. She had asked what east was and what it meant.

"Honey, the four points are to show us which direction we are going. It's called a compass," he had explained, wishing he had one in his pocket; but *the only compass Cole had was home packed with his camping equipment.*

"What's a point?" she asked innocently.

"There are four points, one is north, and one is south. North is on the top and south is on the bottom. To the right is east and to the left is west."

"I don't know what that is, Daddy," she said, confused.

They rode further on, with Cole thinking of an easier way to explain things. "Honey, it's like forwards and backwards. When we walk, we go forwards. And when you play your games and walk the other way, then that's going backwards. The four points are only directions, once we know and understand them, then we won't ever get lost. Like, the sun always rises in the east. Once you remember that, you can usually tell which way you're going."

"But what if it's cloudy?" she asked, causing her father to groan.

"What if it's cloudy," Cole mumbled to himself. "Honey, that's why it's always a good thing to carry a compass," he laughed as they rode on. "And before you ask what a compass is, I'll show you when we get home, ok?"

"Ok, Daddy!" she answered happily.

They rode on further, with Cole explaining everything she either pointed out or asked about. Later that afternoon, Ruth watched with an amused smile on her face as Cole dug out his compass and walked around the ranch with

337

Katie, explaining how it worked and how to understand it. It didn't take much, it was hard to believe that she was only three; she seemed to grasp just about everything he took the time to explain. Soon, she picked up on the concept of working the compass and slowly began to understand a little about directions and traveling.

Cole watched as Katie scrunched up her face, looking up at the sky. "We're going north!" she proudly exclaimed, looking up at her father for his approval.

"That's right, Katie bug," he said proudly, holding her closer. "Your flowers are to the north."

Cole felt his eyes misting over as they rode along. Katie's laughter danced out across the prairie as she watched the birds skittering about and the animals darting into the brush. This was their special day and Cole's mind slipped back through the years.

It was a long night, and he was restless and bored. Deciding to go to the Branding Hole for a drink, Cole sat alone at a table, trying to unwind. It wasn't long before a tall, lithe, dark-haired woman walked in. She caught his eye immediately, but remained aloof. Everything within Cole screamed to walk away, instead, he sat staring.

After fortifying himself with a drink, he walked over, his heart hammering. She turned, staring sadly upwards at him. Her deep brown eyes captivated him as they began to talk. For the life of him, Cole was unable to turn away. He escorted her over to his table, ordered a drink, and the words came naturally. The one thing that did not escape his attention was the sadness set in those deep, brown eyes. She was like a lost soul, looking exactly as he felt. It was that mutual loneliness that drew them together. There was no fighting it, sometimes the body had a mind of its own, driving a person to do things he would never consider otherwise. It reached out blindly, often confusing comfort for love, and taking both.

"Margaret, huh?" Cole said softly. You look like a Maggie to me!"

Those brown eyes looked sadly away again, making Cole think that she would run from her seat at any given moment. Both were silent.

"My father used to call me Maggie," she said brokenly.

"Your father?" Cole asked, ready to kick himself. "I'm sorry, if I said or did anything. ..."

"No! You didn't! Please forgive me if I gave you the wrong impression just now. My father is very much alive and he's doing well, thank you!" she laughed slightly for the first time.

Her smooth voice washed down over Cole, "Well, that's good to hear," he chuckled nervously. "Mind if I ask what brought you here?"

338

"What brought you here?" Margaret retorted.

"Touché! I guess neither of us are in the position to be asking questions," Cole grinned nervously.

"Maybe questions aren't needed," Margaret said, taking his hand. "And you can call me Maggie."

All it took was one final look in her eyes. They didn't ask any questions and sadly, they later came to regret their actions. They were together just that one night, but that was enough to change their lives forever. It didn't take long for both to realize the mistake they had made; each had been seeking something missing from their lives, but neither had anything to give. Both were looking in the wrong place. But life is a force onto itself and Cole loathed himself for letting things get so out of hand. He knew better, he had already lost so much when he lost Sarah a little over a year ago. What he was doing with someone else now was something there were no answers to.

Cole never meant for anything to happen with Maggie. That wasn't his goal the night he went out for a drink. He had been restless, but that's all it was. Then she walked into the room, and he couldn't help himself. The loneliness washed over him and he needed to be in a woman's arms again, even if it was only for one short night. There was no love between the two. Cole had never believed in love at first sight anyway, and they had not even spent enough time together to get to know or care about one another. Maggie blindly reached out to him that night, and he had been unable to turn away.

Both knew the enormity of their actions immediately. A deep-seated guilt began to form even before Cole pulled on his pants and stumbled from the room, apologizing profusely. Maggie was a married woman; she had never lied about that, but he had taken her anyway. There was nothing right about that night; he should have walked away the moment she came through the door, yet he let his weakness claim him. He had been searching for something lost, but had no right to take that from Maggie. She might have been just as lonely and vulnerable as he was that night, but that didn't make it right. Both were sadly lacking in their lives, yet they had nothing to give one another. They came together explosively, satisfying a deep primordial need that left them empty and riddled with guilt at the end.

Cole never begged Maggie to stay with him, knowing how wrong they were. There was no pot of gold at the end of the rainbow, and their story did not have the perfect ending. Their story never had a beginning. Maggie returned to her husband and Cole resumed his quiet life, pitching himself into work at the ranch. He never heard from her again, until one warm, dusty afternoon about three months later, when Maggie showed up on his doorstep, pregnant and alone.

Her husband knew nothing about the pregnancy; no one in her family, except for her sister, Danielle, knew. It was Danielle who crafted a plan to keep Maggie's secret from being exposed. Maggie was devastated. She could not let anyone know of her condition and she could not abort this baby. She had never believed in abortion to begin with, and had voiced her opinion strongly over the years. Already a mother of three, Maggie could not forget the fact that a new life now grew within her. To rip that life away before it even had a chance, would have destroyed her.

Now Maggie stood to lose everything, including her children. Neither woman would let that happen. After breaking the news to a stunned, confused Cole, Maggie moved in with Ruth until the birth of the baby. As far as her family was concerned, she was on an extended vacation with Danielle, who recently located to Europe for her job.

Everything played through his mind like it happened yesterday. What had started as a simple night out for a drink turned into an unexpected one-night stand. That, in turn, became the basis of Cole's worst fear and dreaded nightmare. He never forgave himself for his actions that night, and blamed his weakness for all he would ultimately bring down on them.

As angry as he was at Maggie at times, Cole knew that she had no other choice, and his anger was misplaced. He wasn't as angry with her as he was with himself. In spite of the fact that he now had Katie, that night never should have happened. Something beautiful had come from that night, but beauty was fragile. One couldn't hold on to beauty any more than they could hold on to happiness. It was all fleeting, and it all slipped away.

The sins of the father. Cole had heard that his entire life and never knew it to be truer. The sins of a father eventually visited upon the child, no matter how much that father fought against it. Sin and fate. Both went hand in hand. Both had a mind of their own, and neither showed any mercy. There was no mercy in his world, there was only the fleeting smile of his daughter.

Cole rode on, clutching Katie a little tighter as he looked down, kissing the top of her head. He couldn't help it; this tiny being had trapped his heart, and that was the one thing he could not escape. Still, his mind wandered back to the day that changed his life forever.

He had just come in after a long, dusty day of exercising and working the horses. It was towards the middle of November and the weather was unusually warm. They were being spoiled with another patch of Indian Summer, which was odd, but not unheard of for this time of year. So they enjoyed the mild weather while they could and hoped that they wouldn't pay for it later on when winter finally chose to hit. Cole had decided not to worry about the coming months, choosing instead to enjoy these few, brief warm days while he had the chance. Once it was gone, the days would turn cold and the nights would be long and even colder. Heading into the kitchen, he grabbed a cold beer to cut the dust.

Not expecting company, Cole was startled slightly by a knocking on the door. For some reason, his heart began racing and the hair stood up on the back of his neck. "You afraid of the boogey man? Wouldn't Brent and Will love to hear that one," he laughingly chided himself.

Opening the door, Cole's heart caught. Maggie stood there, with a suitcase at her feet. It had been months since he had heard from her, to say that her arrival surprised him was an understatement, and to find her carrying a suitcase further added to his confusion.

It seemed like a lifetime had passed since he had seen Maggie; their one night was all but forgotten, but now it was back. Being with her had been something both needed at the time, but Cole was ashamed of his actions and relieved when she returned to her family. She had helped fill a lonely night, as Cole knew he had filled hers, but that was all they shared. Besides, being alone had its own special rewards, as Cole learned slowly over the past few months. There were no pressing worries, no one to please, and no one to answer to. He could eat when he wanted, sleep when he wanted, and basically do as he wished. There was no one else to consider and that was the way Cole wanted it. He did not want to love again, but here she was, waiting to be granted entrance.

"Maggie! What the hell?" Cole gasped, unable to help himself.

"I expected a little better greeting than that," she tried joking.

"You just took me by surprise. I had no idea you were coming," he said dryly, wondering what to do next.

"Can I please come in?" Maggie pleaded.

"Yeah, I guess," Cole hedged.

"Cole, please, this is hard enough. ..."

"Maggie, look, not that I mind you coming, but frankly, I never expected to see you again. We made no promises to one another, and you went back to your family," he said, jumping in.

"No room here for promises," Maggie replied tiredly. "Believe me, Cole, if the circumstances were different, I wouldn't even think of barging in on you."

"Circumstances? What circumstances?" he asked suspiciously. "Are you here because your marriage didn't work out, and I'm the one to pick up the pieces?"

"It's nothing like that," she sighed. "I only wish that it were so easy. Things are ok with Ronald and I—"

"If things are so good with him, then what are you doing here? And with a suitcase?" Cole couldn't help but interrupt again.

"Cole, can I come in?" she pleaded.

"Yeah, it's all right," he said, realizing that even though he had given the same reply a few moments before, they still stood at the door. Then Cole began feeling uneasy, sensing another reason for the visit. "Maggie, what's going on?" he asked, his eyes narrowing.

She backed away, almost as if she were afraid. Cole had never struck a woman in his life and from the look on her face, he almost believed that she expected that very thing. If that was the way Ronald handled things, then she had another thing coming. That was not the way he dealt with things.

"Cole, I'm pregnant," Maggie said, her voice barely audible.

"You're ... you're. ..." Cole backed away, the blood draining from his face.

It took a few seconds. Time stood still as he tried swallowing past the lump deep in his throat. His stomach began churning and the bile rose, almost causing him to gag. He had never expected to see Maggie again, and now here she was, telling him that she was carrying his baby. The night they spent together was a blur in his memory, yet he thought that they had been careful ... at least as careful as anyone in that kind of situation could be, but nothing was foolproof, as Maggie's presence now proved. He barely heard her words over the pounding of his heart. Words were lost as Cole gaped mutely.

"You're. ..." he managed to croak out.

"Pregnant. With your baby," she whispered.

"Maggie. ..." Cole sobbed brokenly, turning his back. It took a few moments for him to compose himself and turn back.

"Don't! Do you think I wanted this? I can't have this baby! But it's too late! Cole, I never meant for this to happen! Damn it! It shouldn't be happening!" she shrieked suddenly.

Finding his voice, Cole struck back. "Fine time to think of that now! You're having a baby, but how the hell do I know it's mine?"

"Because Ronald had a vasectomy after Timothy was born," Maggie said flatly.

"Oh shit," Cole shook, running his hand through his hair. "But how. ..."

"Don't you dare ask me if I was with anybody else! I may have been with you but we both knew how wrong that was! I'm not a whore!" she yelled.

"I never said you were!" he shouted back. "But a baby! How the hell!"

"How the hell? You and I! That's how the hell!" Maggie shot back. "I can't have this baby!"

"Then what the hell are you doing here? If you can't have this baby, then why did you come here?" Cole asked desperately, grabbing her by the wrist. "To taunt me for my mistakes? Rub the thought of a baby in my face only to take off and destroy it? If you did, you have another thing coming. I won't let my child be destroyed! I don't give a damn if you can have it or not, there is a baby and that baby will be born!"

"Don't you worry, the baby will be born," Maggie hissed. "You're lucky, Cole. I'm not only a mother who loves her three children dearly and can't bear the thought of destroying an innocent baby, I don't believe in abortion. So I'll be having this baby. I couldn't live with myself otherwise."

"So I noticed," Cole said, his arm dropping.

"Cole, Ronald is moving the children and me back east. We're leaving next week. He has no idea that I'm pregnant and hasn't been home the past two months anyway. I sent the children to stay with my mother. I told Ronald that I was going on an extended vacation to Europe with my sister, Danielle. She just accepted a job overseas for the next five years and since Ronald knows how close we've always been and how much I'll miss her, he agreed that I should go. My mother has no idea of this pregnancy; Danielle is the only one who does, and she's covering for me. She knows that I can't leave Ronald! He'll take the children away and I'll never see them again," she sobbed.

Cole could see that nothing had changed where Maggie's marriage was concerned. She was still as lonely and upset as usual, and now the complication of her pregnancy only served to make matters worse. But he couldn't be concerned with that, the only thing Cole cared about was his child. His child. ... How those words rang through his mind.

"But my baby! Where does this leave me? You're taking my baby to Europe? Damn, I knew that this was so wrong from the beginning! I can't let you go! We messed up, but now there's a baby involved! We can't forget that, and I can't and won't let a child of mine go!" Cole said desperately.

"Cole, I'm not going to Europe! Don't you see? Danielle laid all the groundwork with the family. She has a private jet and all the bases are covered. My family thinks that I'm headed to Europe with her for the next six months or so, and I'm here, seeking your help," she said forlornly.

It was then Cole saw the desperate need in her panicked eyes. Maggie may have been pregnant, but stress had taken a toll. She was pale and had lost weight, something that she could not afford in her condition. Trying to understand the mess he had just been thrown into, Cole desperately tried to grasp the situation. His brain ceased functioning. Shaking his head, he tried making sense out of everything.

"My help? What do you mean?" he asked, almost too afraid to say the words.

"Cole, do you want this baby?" Maggie asked brokenly.

"Do I want this baby? Of course I want this baby!" he burst out.

"Cole, I can't have this child and I can't destroy this child. I'd never destroy a child," she said, looking down at her hands.

"Maggie?" Cole asked, taking her trembling hands in his.

"Cole, I'm going to have this baby, but I can't keep it. Would ... would. ..." she broke down, sobbing.

His anger gone, Cole swept Maggie into his arms, soothing her. He gave her the first hint of hope she'd had in months. His heart was heavy, this was something he had always wanted, but not in this manner. He knew that it had been wrong to be with Maggie, but that was in the past. Now, they had other things to consider. This was not the time or place to hash out whether their actions had been justified or not. Cole wanted this child, and vowed to help Maggie in any what he could.

"You can't keep this baby, but I can. I already love this child. Maggie, everything will be ok. I'm not the type of man to turn his back on his obligations. We may have been wrong, but is a baby wrong? I don't think so," Cole said, shaking his head slightly. "A child is never wrong. I'll take care of you and I'll raise our child. You never have to worry about a thing," he said softly.

"What about everyone talking?" Maggie worried.

"Maggie, no one here will talk. They're my family, all they'll want to do is help. They'll feel the same way I do and will do what they can and what is needed for this baby. Everything will be fine. What do we do?" he asked, stumped.

"Cole, my sister has her own private jet. One of the perks of her job," Maggie sniffed, smiling slightly for the first time. "She made arrangements with her pilot that no matter when, he's to fly me to Europe and no one will be the wiser. She took care of the paperwork and all, I just couldn't. Anyway, I'll be leaving after the baby comes—"

"So, you're giving birth and leaving?" Cole asked incredulously.

"I have to, Cole! I have no choice! I can't keep this baby! This baby shouldn't be, but it is! It is and we can't ignore that!" Maggie exclaimed.

"I guess you're right, but it all seems so. ..."

"Barbaric?" she jumped in, staring intently.

"For lack of a better word," Cole shrugged helplessly. "But what do we do? Where will you stay?"

All of those questions were soon answered, as Cole should have known they would be. As usual, he naturally turned to Ruth. She was at their side in minutes, embracing both. Even though she had never approved of their being together, this time a baby was involved. To Ruth, there was no greater blessing. She took charge, caring for all three. It never mattered how this baby came to be, the important thing was, it had come to be and would need all the love a child deserved. That was all that mattered. The good Lord had deemed that a child would come into the world and Ruth was there for when that time came.

Later that day Cole helped Maggie get settled with Ruth. She stayed in the spare room across the hall where Ruth could hear if she was needed. The months slipped by, with a long, cold winter bearing down on them. Even though Ruth could not understand why Maggie had to leave her child, she never questioned the woman. The two spent the winter in one another's company, sewing and talking to help pass the time. Cole came by on a daily basis, checking on Maggie and joining them for dinner. When the weather turned bad, he made sure they wanted for nothing.

A generator was up and running, ready to be put to good use in case the power failed and the furnace no longer worked. In this manner, they would still have heat and lights without resorting to candles, the woodstove in Ruth's kitchen, or a kerosene lantern. Ruth argued the necessity of the generator, saying how she had resorted to those means her entire life and Cole should have saved his money, he chided her by saying how it was about time she got out of the dark ages, which earned him a well-deserved swat across the backside. Smiling sheepishly, yet a little deviously, he nevertheless forged ahead and hooked the contraption up, filled it with gas and instructed Ruth of its use.

Wood was chopped and piled just outside the service porch in the back of the house, with a hearty supply carried in and stacked in the corner. Another, smaller pile sat to the side of the fireplace, waiting to be put to use. Cole wanted Ruth to do as little as possible, he always had. She argued, and he ignored. From the beginning she had been there for him, and since then, he had done what he could to make her life easier. Two stubborn souls drawn together.

Every morning, like the previous winter, Cole arrived early, walking Ruth up the hill to the small family plot behind her house so she could visit her little family, when the weather allowed. He stood back quietly, praying with her, then helped her back down the slippery, snowy incline.

He drove her into town for groceries when the weather looked ominous, not wanting her to be out on the roads by herself, and kept the steps and walkway shoveled and the driveway plowed, thanks to Will.

Ruth and Maggie sewed booties, knit little sweaters and hats, and made just about everything a baby needed. Irma, Helen and Sadie came by on a regular basis for the very same reason. Truth be told, all Ruth thought of was how her world would now have a baby to love. That winter was a little less lonely due to a tiny miracle that had yet to arrive.

The days drifted by and the cold winter was finally over. Soon it was spring and the days grew warmer as they neared the middle of May. Maggie woke one night, crying out in pain. Ruth ran to her side, then immediately called Cole. Brent, Will and Gris were summoned next and all converged on the hospital, leaving the nurses staring at the strange entourage gathered in front of her. While the three men paced the floor, Ruth kept busy stitching some quilting squares she had brought along. They had a long wait ahead of them.

In the delivery room, Cole held Maggie's hand as she pushed, sweat streaming down her face as she screamed. He had never seen such stark, selfless pain in his entire life. Everything Maggie did now, she did for their child. How Cole wished that things could be different; he had always thought that when this time came, he would be sharing it with his wife. Now, he would be bringing his baby home alone. He and Maggie had shared many long talks over the winter, with her deciding not to look at or hold the baby. Cole couldn't understand that at first, but he soon came to realize why Maggie felt that way. He prayed that she would change her mind as the baby came closer.

For a split second, he almost thought that she would forget she had another family waiting for her and would remain with him and their child. That thought was fleeting, however, when Maggie turned her eyes up towards him.

"I can't stay, please don't hate me," she whispered fervently.

Cole wanted to reply, but before the words were out, another scream burst from her lips. He held her from behind, helping Maggie focus. Her words tortured him. He could never hate her. How could he hate the woman giving birth to his child? With every push and every scream, he waited with bated breath for his child to arrive. Suddenly, she came into the world, crying and wiggling in the doctor's hands. Cole stared, seeing a tiny little being no bigger than a sprig screaming her lungs out. The cord was cut, and the baby was wrapped in a receiving blanket and placed in his eager arms.

A feeling Cole couldn't even begin to describe washed down over him as he stared at the squirming baby, still not believing that she belonged to him. A full crown of dark brown hair topped her head, her eyes were scrunched shut against the intrusion of their world, and she flailed her hands. Cole held her close, burying his face in her wonder. He felt her soft cheeks against his, her hair tickling his nose. Looking down at Maggie, he saw her turning away. Cole had his answer right then and there, but he didn't care. He had his daughter. He would not try to hold on to Maggie, it had to be this way. Suddenly, Cole understood. Looking down into his baby's face, he knew that he would never be able to turn away. No wonder Maggie couldn't look; for if she did, she would never be able to leave.

"Would you like to give your daughter her first bath?" the nurse asked Cole, laughing at the way his eyes lit up.

"Can I? I mean, how?" he quipped, looking like a lost puppy.

"Come on, Daddy, I'll show you," she laughed, leading him over to the basin.

Cole laid Katie down in the warm water, supporting her head as he was shown. She wiggled, almost sliding from his hands as he gently washed her. "She's slippery!" he laughed. "And she has everything! Look! All her fingers and toes!"

"They do come equipped!" another nurse came in, laughing at Cole marveling at the wonder of his child. "Come on, Daddy, let's wrap her in this blanket and get her footprints," she said, with Cole following.

"Time to get you all dirty again," he giggled as he placed her tiny foot in the ink. "My God! Her foot isn't even as big as my pinky!" he said with awe.

"She sure is a beautiful little one," the nurse said wistfully. "What's her name?"

"Katie Sarah," Cole answered softly, smiling at the masked faces around him. Picking up his daughter, he held her face close to his. She opened her eyes, staring into his. Cole melted, his heart was stolen and he would never be the same. His daughter looked at him for the first time, smiling. "Hey Katie Sarah, this is your daddy!" he beamed. "She's smiling at me!" Cole laughed, looking around the room.

They all shook their heads as he tried comprehending what was to become of his life. Babies only a few minutes old couldn't smile, but to Cole, they did. Katie knew he was her father and she smiled the minute she laid eyes on him. The two were now bonded for life.

Cole went out into the waiting room, still clad in scrubs. He stood wordlessly in the doorway for a moment, watching the pathetic pacing of Brent, Gris and Will. In her own patient manner, Ruth kept busy with her hands as she sewed. They all stopped, staring when they realized that someone had come into the room.

Cole giggled from behind the mask, then lowered it slowly. He stood staring with a huge grim plastered across his face. Brent was the one to crack, and ran over impatiently.

"Well?" he asked, running a trembling hand through his hair.

"It's a girl," Cole said softly, smiling at his friends before him.

* * *

"It's a beautiful girl," Cole thought to himself as they rode along, his heart swelling with pride and love as he studied his daughter. *What is life going to bring your way?* he wondered quietly.

So far, the world had not intruded on Katie's innocence, something that Cole prayed would never happen. He knew that he would have to let go one day, and he also knew how hard it would be. Yet, he would do it; life did go on. The years slipped away too quickly, four of them were already gone. Soon, four more would be gone and then four more. Cole would sit back and watch Katie growing more and more with each passing day. The only thing he did know was that no matter how much she argued about it or how big she grew, she would always be his little girl.

Katie was surrounded with love from the moment Cole brought her home. Will, Brent, Gris and Ruth were already a huge part of her life. None of them seemed able to keep their hands off of her, so they didn't. Cole thought that she would be spoiled, but then thought differently.

"You can't spoil a child by holding and loving them too much; there's no such thing as too much. Holding them close to your heart lets them know they're loved and that only brings happiness and makes them secure. Knowing someone loves them can never ruin a child. Not loving them enough to bother is what ruins them," he reasoned, thinking of Maggie.

"You'll have to tell her one day," Ruth said quietly.

"One day, but not now," Cole finished, closing the subject.

Looking down at his daughter now, he wondered how and when he would ever tell her. She was so innocent and knew what it was like to be loved. Would she even be capable of understanding why her mother had to leave? Or why her father kept the truth from her all along? Not wanting to go there, Cole shoved those thoughts aside. There was no room for them today.

I can only pray that when the day comes for you to find out, you will remember just how much I love you, and nothing has changed. You are a beautiful, smart, strong child and you are going to go far in life, Cole thought to himself as they rode along.

"Daddy! Our flowers! They came back!" Katie squealed, clapping her hands in joy.

Tears burned, and Cole fought them valiantly. His love for this small creature welled now, more than he ever felt it before. With all the ruckus in the world they lived in, he was astounded as to how something so simple as a field of wildflowers could bring such joy to a person, yet it did to Katie. One would think she was given the gift of the entire world at that moment, and she was. This was her world and she embraced it fully.

Cole climbed down off the horse, bringing Katie with him. He laughed while she ran, waving her arms in the air as she danced after a butterfly. He stood watching. His child was dancing in the golden sunlight, as happy as a child could be. The butterfly flew away so she ran off in search of something else. Cole ran over grabbing her hand. Together, they dove into the middle of the field of flowers, laughing and bathing themselves in the splashes of color that rained down over them. They then lay quietly, with Katie at his side and his arm around her.

Everything became hushed as the flowers danced over them, shielding them from the sun and hiding them from the world. If Cole had his way, he would hide Katie forever and the two of them would stay this way for the rest of their lives. This was his idea of heaven.

* * *

Becca walked into town, where she found a convenience store by a gas station. Entering, she was relieved that no one paid any attention to her whatsoever. She simply walked in, helped herself to the facilities, and came back out searching for something to eat. A plastic bottle of water, a package of sugar doughnuts and a container of milk were just the thing.

"Mom would have a hairy fit if she knew," Becca snickered sarcastically. "But when has she given a damn?" she shrugged, too angry at her parents to realize just how upset they were at the moment.

The police had been notified and were now searching for her. The bus station had confirmed that she had, indeed, purchased a ticket to Landing, but by the time the station was notified, the bus had arrived and Becca had disembarked. She hid in the shadows, missing the police that cruised by, but had already figured out that they would be looking here sooner or later, so she kept watch over her shoulder. Paying for her purchases, she ran out into the street, ducked behind the buildings, and quietly made her way to the other end of town.

* * *

Matt paced, wanting to call Cole, but upon calling information for the number, he was dismayed to hear that it was listed as private. He had to wait for the police, the operator just would not budge.

"No luck?" Shauna asked wearily.

"No, they refuse to give me the number. It's just as well, the police are going to notify the sheriff up there and he'll handle things. He can get word to Cole and if Becca shows up, we'll know. Besides, it's been six years since I've talked with him; the last thing he needs right now is to hear my voice on the other end of the phone."

"Don't you think that it would do him good?" Shauna asked of her husband.

"What good will it do to have him hear me? All it will do is dredge up everything he's tried to forget by leaving. Honey, we shouldn't have been surprised that Cole left after losing Sarah and the baby that way. Everything he did, he did for them! I should have known that he wouldn't have the strength to rebuild and move back in, reliving all those memories. A body can't get past something like that. Look at us! But maybe if we ... I mean if I ... well, I wasn't good for anyone. Maybe if I could have seen past myself, then I could have helped all of you. But I didn't. I'll never forgive myself for that. I'll let the police handle this, it's the best for Cole."

"What's the best for you?" Shauna wondered out loud.

"Right now, I don't matter," Matt answered dejectedly.

"Matt, everyone matters," she tried reminding him.

"I don't matter!" he replied, slamming his fist on the table. "How the hell can you sit there and say I do? Look at us! Becca is gone and you and I hardly bother with anyone anymore. You hide and drink and I sit and mope! We've both ignored our daughter, and haven't given her a thought all these years! She's a stranger to us, and that's the most shameful thing that I can think of. We have one child and we both failed her because we were too busy thinking of ourselves. I've failed miserably as a husband and a father, and because of that, you and Becca are the one's suffering! You can't even look at me anymore and my own daughter hates me! She left because I never even considered her feelings. I never considered anyone's but my own ... God, I was so wrong," Matt sighed, his shoulders heaving.

"Maybe if you worked as hard at fixing your family and making amends with Cole as you do wallowing and going after that stupid vendetta of yours, then things might turn around here and this place can start being a home again," Shauna said vehemently as she turned to leave.

Sunk in despair, Matt hung his head and wept. Tears fell onto the back of his hands and sobs filled the air. She was right, Shauna was always right. For years, he had only cared about himself. And now it might be too late. They all had lost so much and Becca was gone. He lost his daughter long ago and hadn't really made an effort to get her back. Instead, he just drifted through his days. His actions had been selfish from the beginning, and they still were. When one wallowed in self-pity, he granted himself the luxury of shutting everyone out.

Sighing deeply, Matt swiped his arm across his face and sat back. Shauna was right. If he loved his family, he had to do something about it; it was time he started acting like a man again, they were all he had left. Matt cried, not wanting to lose his family, yet he didn't make a move to change things. He was the only one with the power to do so. He had been the one to start this entire mess, but being the coward he was, he simply did not have the courage to set things right.

As he told Shauna earlier, he should have known that Cole wasn't strong enough to rebuild and move back onto the ranch. Even Matt felt as if the place was now haunted, with the ghosts of his mother and sister hovering at the site, unable to find peace. Their death had been too sudden and unexpected, leading Matt to believe they were still there. To this day, he got chills when visiting the ranch, which was done at least once a week. Every time Matt showed up, he expected to see Cole and Sarah running out to greet him; instead, only their apparitions came to him.

Cole had loved Sarah with all his heart; Shauna was right about that too. He had lived for his family, doing everything he could for Sarah and their new little one that was on the way. Cole hadn't wanted to leave Sarah that weekend, but Matt wanted to attend the rodeo finals, and had badgered him all week long. By Friday, Matt had finally convinced his friend to join him. Dave was unable to make the trip and Matt hated going alone as much as he hated missing the event. It was also his idea to have Myra spend the night with Sarah, and deep inside, Matt felt like the one who sent his mother to her death. Of small comfort was the fact that Sarah had not been alone. Matt liked to think that they were together in death as they were in this life. At least he could envision them both holding hands and drawing strength from one another in the end.

Everything perished that night. The red-hot flames consumed the house and wiped out their lives, leaving everyone standing in the ashes. No one had been able to put their lives back together yet. Some people said, 'It's been six years, don't you think it's time to get over it?' But Matt could not get over it. The only thing six years meant, was that he had six long years to think about what happened. He could live 600 years, and would never forget, and there was no getting over it. His mother, his sister, his unborn niece or nephew, and everyone else affected by this tragedy, were burned indelibly in his mind.

Since there was no getting over the trauma, then the only other option Matt had was to be strong and learn to live with it. Perhaps then, he could pull his family together again.... If only he could be lucky enough to have that chance. So much had gone through his mind ever since Becca ran away three days ago. Everything happened all over again, and everything needed to be fixed. Shauna needed her husband back and Becca needed a family that was strong. For a brief glimmer of a moment, Shauna reached out to Matt. There was hope after all. It did not last long, but it was more than they had given one another in a long time. Matt needed that; he needed that more than anything. And Cole needed the comfort, friendship, and solace that he had been denied all these years. They needed closure.

"It's time to fix things," Matt said, finally straightening.

He drew a shaky breath and sat back, trying to think of where to begin. The first thing that they had to do was find Becca. The police were watching for her, keeping an eye on the bus stations and roads leading into Crater Mills. Even so, it would still be easy for Becca to slip through; she was a smart child. If they didn't find her, Matt prayed that she would reach Cole's place safely, knowing that he would take care of her. Matt never questioned that for a second. Becca would be safe, and maybe, just maybe, it might pave the way towards reconciliation.

That left only one other thing that needed taking care of, and that was the basis of what was really destroying Matt inside. He knew that the fire had not been an accident. He knew that it was done coldly, deliberately, and with the intention of driving Cole from his land. Matt also knew the heartless bastard responsible. The only problem was, he couldn't prove a thing, and it had been eating him alive all these years. The need for revenge smoldered inside, driving him to the brink of an insane hatred towards the man responsible for all their grief.

With one deadly, malicious act, that man had robbed two families of those they loved, forever tearing their lives apart. Matt lived for the day to destroy this man with his own two hands. It was up to him; no one else would listen. No one else believed him. Matt wondered if he was the only person on the face of the earth who knew the truth. If so, then that was fine with him, because if he had to die to bring justice and peace back into their lives, then he would gladly do so.

Matt was alone in his vendetta. Even after six years, he had been unable to prove his theory. Shauna wouldn't hear of it, she turned a deaf ear to his ranting long ago, not wanting to constantly dredge up and relive that night.

But Matt couldn't stop reliving it. He wouldn't stop until the day he brought Culver down. Everyone told him to forget it and go on with his life. Shauna had begged him to stop; she pleaded endlessly for him to stop. Becca just remained silent and Matt couldn't stop. Now Becca was gone and Matt was left with his torment. Shauna was wrong, it wasn't time to put an end to things; it was time to finally face them once and for all.

Chapter Seventeen

"Irma, come on in!" Ruth excitedly greeted her friend. "I have some fresh muffins and coffee waiting for us and then we can get busy around here!"

"Won't Katie see what we're doing?" Irma's eyes darted around.

"No, she's out riding with her father right now and when she gets back and has her breakfast, Callie's going to take her out for the rest of the morning. They're going to get their hair and nails done," Ruth said, putting on a fancy air for both their benefits.

"Oh my, aren't they going to be the grand ladies of the day," Irma sniffed, laughing along with Ruth. "Seriously, aren't Callie and Cole becoming a hot item?"

Looking around, Ruth could not help herself. She leaned forward and whispered conspiratorially to her friend. "Between you, me and the fence post, things are heating up pretty good around here!"

"It's about time for the both of them!" Irma declared. "Lord, everyone in town could see how those two felt about each other! It's about high time they realized it and did something about it! Although I bet they already did!" she snickered wickedly with Ruth.

"Honey, I cannot tell a lie!" Ruth laughed right along. "I'm just so glad that those two have found one another. And little Katie needs a mommy so bad! She already loves Callie and if you ask me, I think they make the perfect family!"

"But does Cole feel the same way?" Irma asked.

"Oh dear, one can only hope," Ruth sighed. "But I won't push my boy! He's had so much hurt already, I'm just glad that he let a little bit of love back into his life."

"Is everything all right?" Irma asked, looking to make sure Cole had not returned yet.

"You mean with Maggie?" Ruth said, sitting with her coffee. "That's a hard one. He's been so upset since yesterday! Oh, he puts up a brave front for me, but I can see through it! For a little bit yesterday I thought that all was lost. He fell apart after Danielle left and I barely got through to him. He spent the rest of the day acting as if nothing was wrong, but I know he was hurting.

As hard as he's trying to hide it today, I can tell that he can't get her off of his mind."

"That's not good," Irma clucked. "He should be thinking of Callie now, not Maggie or Danielle. I know he's scared, but does he really think that they'll try something?"

"I wish I knew that, too," Ruth sighed deeply. "He's so afraid of losing that little one that he's running scared. I can see it in his eyes. I have to admit that I was upset too, but I really don't think Maggie will try to take Katie. Danielle said that she just wanted to know about her daughter."

"Isn't that only natural?" Irma asked.

"I suppose it is, but after four years?" Ruth worried.

"Ruth, would four years make you forget?" Irma challenged, seeing by the way Ruth's eyes snapped up that she had struck a nerve.

"You're right," Ruth shook her head. "How could I think that one would forget? Of course you can't forget. But there's a difference between wanting to know about your daughter and trying to take her, which Maggie hasn't done. She just sent Danielle to see how Katie was doing. But Cole took it as a threat. I only hope he's wrong."

"Ruth, maybe letting Maggie know about Katie will be just what Cole needs," Irma nodded.

"How's that?" Ruth wondered.

"You've always said how worried he was about Katie finding out the truth one day. He's scared that she'll be angry with him for keeping that from her all these years. But if he lets Maggie in on some level, then that worry will dissipate. That won't make things any easier to explain, Katie will still know that her mother had to leave and she'll need all the love and support Cole can give her," Irma nodded.

"You're probably right; at least you brought up a good point. But won't it make things more confusing? Cole already has to keep Katie a secret from Maggie's family, there's no such thing as a 'secret mommy'. What will it mean to Katie to know her mother, but know that she can't be a full part of her life? Her mommy will have another family that she will never be a part of and that is bound to hurt," Ruth pointed out.

"I never thought of that," Irma said quietly. "Of course that would hurt. So, I guess we're right back to where we started; there's no easy solution to this, is there?"

"No, but today is a party!" Ruth said brightly.

"And we have a lot to celebrate! Don't you worry about a thing, this will stay between us," Irma reassured her friend, meaning every word. The two loved to gossip, but it was kept between them explicitly. "I just want to see

Cole happy. He's had such a hard row that it's good to see things working out. Yesterday was such a success for him, I'm sure you're proud!"

"I'm more than proud of my boy," Ruth exclaimed. "He's worked so long and hard for what he's achieved, I am just so happy that things worked out as well as they did. At first, I had my doubts. Danielle couldn't have picked a worse day to come. It's almost as if she knew, yet came just to shake things up."

"And did she?" Irma asked over her coffee.

"She did more than that," Ruth said sadly. "She almost totally dashed his hopes. I really thought that Cole was going to give up for a while there. The joy and excitement of the day simply drained right out of him. But once I got him thinking in the right direction again, he did what was needed. That's one thing about my boy, he always does what's right."

"He sure does that with his little one. I've never seen a happier child. Are they on their special ride?" Irma asked with a small smile crossing her face.

"Yes, they went to see their flowers. She even had to wear the flower bracelet Cole gave her last week. They were both so excited!" Ruth exclaimed.

"They're quite a pair and speaking of quite a pair, here they come!" Irma laughed as Katie bounded into the room, chattering a mile a minute about the rabbits, the birds, her butterflies and most importantly, her flowers.

* * *

Ruth couldn't be happier than she was that morning. It was her granddaughter's birthday and she had a million things to do, all of which she looked forward to. The dollhouse was ready, as was the barn scene that Brent and Will had done to go along with it. Ruth also had a special present for Katie, which was started the night she was born. Two nights ago Ruth and Irma sat at her table going over the books one more time before Katie's was wrapped. Ruth's own book was placed carefully in a box, wrapped in flowered tissue paper.

"I started my memory book the day Cole came into town," she told her old friend as she ran her hand carefully over the soft leather binding. "I never had the chance to start a baby book of my own and from the beginning, I knew that Cole needed me. And I needed him more than he will ever know. Right from the start, I considered him my child; maybe it was because he was so lost to the world, or maybe because it was just destined that way. Whatever the reasons, I felt that way from the first."

"So you started your book," Irma said softly.

The two had gathered over coffee, putting the finishing touches on their own special presents for Katie. Irma had made two dresses, one done in a dark pink to bring out the tones of Katie's eyes and hair, and one done in tiny flowers in the very colors her bracelet boasted. Both women knew that Katie would love the dresses. Even though she spent most of her days in shorts or jeans while she ran and played, she still loved to wear dresses when she went out. At the age of three, she was already a little lady. Now, in a few days, she would be four, something that Ruth was finding hard to believe, in spite of herself.

"It all goes so fast," Ruth said wistfully. "That's why I started this book of mine. I wanted to have something to remember a child by. Even though Cole was a big child when he wormed his way into my heart, he's still my child. It doesn't matter how old they are, or when or how they come to you, you treasure them from the moment the good lord places them in your care."

"Have you ever shown him the book?" Irma wondered.

"No," Ruth shook her head. "I haven't yet, but I will tell him about it. And one day when my body is old and tired and the Lord calls me home, I'm leaving this book for him. And Katie's picks up with a small story of how her father came to me and how I loved both him and her the minute I laid eyes on them. Then it documents her birth up until today."

"You didn't mention. ... "

"Maggie? Lord no, woman! As sad as it may seem, I just didn't know what to say," Ruth replied. "Even when I wrote about Cole, I simply left her name out of it. I very tastefully spoke of how a lonely man met a woman one day and from that union my baby was born. But by the time Katie reads it, she will be older and will already know about her mother."

"God help her," Irma whispered fervently.

"She'll be fine," Ruth patted her friend's hand. "Her father will see to that. Anyway, tomorrow I'm giving Katie her own book which her father can help her keep until she's old enough to write her own thoughts and dreams down in."

"A memory book," Irma said dreamily, "how precious for a special child. ... "

"How precious indeed," Ruth now smiled as she placed the present on the table in the living room.

Breakfast was over and Callie had arrived, taking Katie for the rest of the morning. Ruth had never seen the young girl so excited. She was now like the 'big kids' as she put it, when she excitedly told her father about their plans.

"Soon I'll be all growed up!" she exclaimed, skipping to the door with her hand in Callie's.

Cole swallowed against the lump in his throat, a brave smile pasted on his face as he watched her leave. She was getting 'all growed up', and it was happening too quickly for him.

"We can't keep them frozen in time forever," Ruth said softly. "Life does go on," she finished, hugging him softly.

"Yeah, but when you realize just how fast it goes by, it hurts," he said quietly.

"But she'll always be in your life and she'll always need you. She has an entire lifetime of love, surprises and dreams to share with her father, whom she'll never forget," Ruth reassured him.

"Think so?" he asked, questioningly.

"I know so," Ruth shooed him out the door. "Now, we have a party to get ready for!"

"HEY! Here they come!" Cole cried out, bounding off the porch as Brent and Will pulled in, honking wildly.

Ruth ran to the door, shaking her head at the sight. It was supposed to be a party for Katie, but the three men were acting like they were the kids and it was their party. She frowned when Brent backed a trailer up to the empty corral, where Cole had opened the gate. Will pulled to the larger corral, where his load was led into a separate area. Almost immediately she knew what they were up to, something she should have expected.

"Now why did I think that this was just going to be a quiet birthday party?" Ruth groaned, running over to the men. Nobody ever partied quietly in Montana. They played as hard as they worked. "What are you three overgrown hoodlums doing?" she demanded to know, jumping back when the trailer gate came crashing down.

"It's wild horses! Oh, and some broncs from Bill, but I'll explain our deal later," Cole exclaimed brightly as the animals bounded down the ramp into the corral. "Aren't they great?"

"Just what are you three planning on doing with them?" Ruth asked, her eyes narrowing.

"We're riding them!" Brent quipped, running out from behind the trailer.

"Today?" Ruth exclaimed. Brent pulled forward, and Will took his turn backing up to the gate.

"Why not? Everyone's gonna be here, it's gonna be great! We'll see who the real cowboy is!" Brent answered, strutting around. "Don't you worry none now, Ma'am. After I show the fillies here what a real cowboy can do, I'll come back for my lady," he said, planting a kiss on Ruth's cheek.

"Oh you three!" she cried out, chasing after the bunch. "You better come back here and take these animals away!"

"Can't! Gotta go! Lisa's waiting for me!" Will laughed, jumping into the truck.

"Gotta run! Have a party to get ready for!" Brent said, dumping the keg from the back of his truck and jumping in behind the wheel. "Bye pretty lady!" his laughter rang out as he pulled away.

"Now, they made me do it!" Cole put up his hands, backing away as he defended himself. "Honest! They made me do it!" he snickered, making his break before Ruth could catch him.

All she could do was stand there trying not to laugh at their antics. It was their party, too. It had been a long time since any of them had let their hair down, partying into the night. Ruth confronted Cole in the barn, barring the way out.

"You just make sure you don't fall on your ass! We're gonna party today and we're gonna party Montana style! And my money's going to be on you!" she declared, leaving a gaping-mouthed Cole standing in her wake as she strutted away.

"Hmmmph! Men! They think they're the only ones who know how to have fun! I'll show them all how to party!" she snorted, strutting into the house.

Cole just stood there in shock; it was definitely going to be one interesting day.

* * *

Gris lay back against the large oak, his line floating lazily upon the surface of the water. A few bugs danced across the top, only to disappear into the mouth of a fish looking for his breakfast. The only blemish to mar the smooth surface was the ripples left in its wake. It had been the kind of morning Gris needed. Although they were a quiet town, people still kept him hopping.

Lately, the biggest complaint came from town, where one of the neighbor's kids had a penchant for playing the drums when his parents weren't around. There was also the reported stolen calf, which was later found wandering down Main Street, and 14 reports from Mrs. Mayhew, who, at 88 years of age, swore that someone was breaking in.

'I hear noises! There's someone breaking in. I know it!' she complained on an almost thrice daily basis.

Poor lady, Gris couldn't help snickering. *She's convinced someone's after her, but I know better. Oh well, better to pacify her and make her feel better. That's what we're getting paid for, all part of the job,* he thought as he settled back.

Other than that, he had been assailed with town meetings about his budget, which was still a sore point, and a stack of paperwork that just wouldn't quit. He hadn't even had the chance to make it out to Cole's since last weekend, when he saw Katie the night she had spent at Ruth's. Since today was her birthday, Gris had decided to take the day off and turn the town over to Ted, who was both excited and nervous to the point where Gris thought Ted would wet his pants. The young man was bright and eager, needing nothing more than a bit of experience. Gris had reasoned that today was as good a day as any.

Since nothing much had been going on, Gris was shocked to see the car pulling in, with a red-faced Ted racing down to him. "Sheriff! Sheriff, we got us a problem!" he cried out breathlessly.

"Now hold on there, no sense in getting yourself all riled up like that. Take a deep breath and tell me just what's going on," Gris urged, calming Ted down. All the time he fought his own panic, this was one part of the job he would never get used to.

"Sheriff, just got a call from that place in Wyoming where Cole came from," he began to explain between huge gulps of air.

Gris felt his skin prickling, "What's that you say? Broken Arrow?"

"Yeah, that's the place! Sheriff up that way says that we gotta watch out for some young girl of 14 who's run away!" Ted gasped.

"A runaway! You get a name and description?" Gris asked.

"Yeah, they say her name's Becca Young, and she's a tiny little thing. About this high," he gestured with his hands, "and all of 75 pounds soaking wet. Has sort of shoulder-length brown hair and blue eyes. They sent her picture over the wire, it's back at the office."

Gris couldn't believe what he was hearing, the name Young set off warning bells in his mind as he remembered all Cole had told him of his past. Becca had to be Matt's daughter, who had been about six or seven when Cole left. Gris had never given this type of scenario a thought, and the last thing he wanted to do was mention anything to Cole, especially today of all days. Anything from the past was enough to send him into a tailspin, something Gris did not want to see happen. He had seen Cole at his worst and had no desire to go there again.

"Now why the hell would a young girl like that be all the way from home up in this area?" Gris scratched his head.

"Beats me! Isn't that the fella who was a friend of Cole's?" Ted asked.

"Yeah, Cole knew of him, but what his daughter is doing here is what puzzles me. Poor kid, guess she's pretty upset to do something as drastic as running away. I'd hate to think of how bad things were for her at home."

"Who knows with kids! Sometimes it doesn't take much for them to get upset and leave," Ted shrugged. "What we gonna do? Run over and tell Cole?"

Gris practically jumped out of his skin, and grabbed Ted by the arm, "For now we take things easy. We really should go on out to Cole's place and take a look around, but I don't want to raise his suspicions yet. So you go back to the office and see if anything else came in. I'll go to Cole's and scout around. Will just pretend that I'm checking on how things are going for the party later on. Oh, and don't mention a word of this to anybody. I don't want people to get wind of this and go running to Cole, I don't want to see him upset on Katie's birthday. If this girl didn't show up, then there's no sense in alarming him right away. Won't be anything he can do anyway. There's no sense in ruining his day, especially if she doesn't show up," Gris said as Ted turned to leave.

"But Sheriff, he has to know!" Ted argued.

"And he will! Just not right now, and not till I check a few things out first! I'll meet you back at the office," Gris said.

"You're the boss," Ted shrugged, obeying but not understanding the reasoning behind it.

Gris bent over with a groan, picking up the equipment. A morning of fishing a bust, and another new worry. Tossing the empty creel into the trunk, he followed Ted back into town. It had taken both him and Ruth over a year to finally draw Cole out of himself. Gris had never seen anyone as devastated and broken before in his life. He was the only person besides Will and Brent who knew Cole had considered suicide that night in the barn, something Gris vowed never to tell a soul, not even Ruth. Especially Ruth. She worried enough as it was.

So did Gris, and he didn't need more. He cared for Cole deeply, and had to pursue this matter the right way. A little girl's welfare depended on that, as did his friend's. Deep down, Gris chided himself, for Cole was more than a friend, he loved him like a son. Both he and Katie were a special part of his life and he felt badly that he had not taken the time this past week to make a trip out to their place. If someone from Cole's past showed up unexpectedly, it would rock him to the core. Not knowing how he would react, Gris decided to take things one step at a time.

Sitting at his desk, the first thing he did was contact the State Police, who he knew were already working on the case. It took a bit of doing, but he managed to convince them that he would be the one to contact Cole. In the meantime, he would speak with Ted and make sure they had patrols out watching.

"Some patrols, assholes cut me to the bone. Have but two men and myself, and if I pull Troy from the party, Cole would want to know what's going on. Shit," he mumbled, turning back to the officer droning on endlessly. Mumbling a hasty, less than courteous reply, Gris slammed the receiver back into the cradle.

Everything was in place. The State Police were combing the area, Ted was handling everything in town, Troy would keep an eye out on things from his end, and further watch the ranch, and he would go out to see Cole, giving him the chance to gauge the situation, and hopefully spot Becca. If she hadn't shown up at the ranch, then he would tell Cole after the party. In the meantime, everyone was out looking. That brought some—very little—but some, comfort.

Gris would scan the area leading into the ranch, for that was where he knew in his heart Becca would try to reach. It now looked like Cole wasn't the only victim of the fallout six years ago. It had taken this long, but it appeared that things still had to be pretty bad at home for Becca to have left. She was caught up in the mess as deeply as Cole and the others. She probably did not understand any of it and that didn't surprise Gris any, for Cole didn't understand either, and was still reeling from the trauma. It only made sense that Matt's daughter felt the same way and was trying to make sense of things. It also spoke volumes about the quality of life in the Young home.

Apparently, Matt had to be just as upset as Cole was, or even more so. This latest twist was enough to make Gris think that Matt was suffering from a guilt so deep, it had been eating him alive for years. Like Cole, he was probably unable to put the past behind him and now it was affecting his family. Also, like Cole, Matt needed a way to find peace and get on with his life. Gris had always felt that to be the case, and his suspicions were proving true. There was no anger on his part, for both men were suffering a tragedy so deep, so unspeakably heinous, it tore at his heart.

Good God, how far does this mess stretch? Just when I think I have a lid on things, there's another fly in the ointment. And how come I have the damnedest feeling that we've only begun to scratch the surface of what happened? Damn, this is just too damned much to think about. Especially on a day like today! I can't let anything ruin the party for Cole and Katie, yet I can't forget the fact that a young girl might be wandering around here somewhere. Gonna have to keep my eyes open, he thought on the drive over to Cole's.

* * *

"Hey Gris! What brings you out here so early? If it's to sneak some of the food they've been getting ready, don't try it! I've already lost two fingers doing just that! Those women are dangerous!" Cole teased.

"As tempting as that sounds, I just came over to see if you needed any help setting things up," Gris offered, looking around.

"Nope, everything's just about ready! Brent came over a while ago to help set up the tables. You just missed him!" Cole grinned widely.

"Looks good! How's our birthday girl?" Gris asked, his eyes quickly scanning the ranch.

"She's probably having the time of her life!" Cole threw his head back, laughing. "She's all 'growed up' now, as she puts it, and she and Callie are off getting their hair and nails done for today!" Cole laughed.

"Oh my, it starts already," Gris shook his head.

"What starts already?" Cole asked hesitantly.

"Nothing, you'll find out soon enough," Gris chuckled, looking out over towards the corral. "Oh my, my, my! Now I know what you were admiring when I drove in! Wild horses! I should have known!"

"Well, been thinking of increasing my stock and picked these beauties up at the stockyard last week!" Cole proudly explained. "I knew I was taking a chance, but Bill got hold of me and we worked out a deal. Wasn't really planning on this, but couldn't pass it up. He took me aside while Brent and Will were checking cattle prices. Gonna screw me up a bit, but I'll be ok. Besides, got one hell of a deal, Bill was willing to let them go pretty cheap, for reasons we all know."

"Oh, his vendetta again," Gris moaned, knowing full well how both Bill and Cole felt about the wild horses. "Did Ruth or anyone know about this?"

"Nope! And that's the beauty of it! Brent's eyes almost fell out of his head when I told him! He and Will couldn't get there fast enough to pick these guys up for me! Don't know who was more excited! And figured that since Katie's party was coming up, what better time to bring them home!" Cole exclaimed.

"Ah ha, and them broncs, bringing them home for something like a wild horse race?" Gris asked, glaring knowingly at Cole.

"Damn, it shows that much," Cole shook his head. "Can't lie to you! They're on loan from Bill. Headed to the rodeo, but we thought we'd have some fun, first! Besides, I played on his sympathy a bit! Even promised him one of my first colts from the mustangs! That was the ticket! But seriously, you know I have a soft spot for these guys, and with the way they're being driven off their land, and with the chance of them falling into the wrong hands when brought to auction, I couldn't let them get by me."

"Wrong hands? Son, they're protected by the government when they're rounded up and brought in," Gris replied.

"You think so?" Cole asked, shaking his head. "I know better. So does Bill, that's why he took me aside. No one can prove it cause like we all know, the government is great at keeping their little secrets. When horses like this are brought in they're supposed to be protected from being sent to slaughter, but are they really? I've heard too many tales of how for some reason or another they're being rounded up and brought to stockyards all over the place. Someone either wants the land, or the government claims that it's their way of thinning the herd, which I never believed in to begin with. The herd has taken care of itself for hundreds of years, who the hell does the government think it is to come in and take over?" Cole said passionately.

"For their own good?" Gris asked, knowing the futility of that question.

"It would be for their own good if the government left them alone!" Cole declared. "But since they don't and since I'm looking to expand my stock, then I couldn't pass this chance up. Like I said, it's gonna take a bite out of my bank account for a while, but it's worth it just knowing that these guys are safe! Gonna keep some for breeding and then will train and sell a few to other breeders in the country, and hopefully keep a strong line going."

"Sounds like you're on the threshold of making one hell of a name for yourself!" Gris said proudly.

"Always been my dream! Gris, I'm only beginning. If I can breed the mustangs successfully, thereby creating a strong bloodline and eventually moving the herd to other breeders to increase the chances of an even stronger bloodline, then we'll have one hell of a horse! Look at that bay over there! And that black stallion is magnificent! Can get more bays by breeding that black stallion with the chestnut. And that creme beauty over there! Isn't she a beauty?" Cole gushed.

"Son, you do me proud," Gris shook his head in amazement. "Oh, the choices!"

"One lucky stallion," Cole smirked. "But really, I want to gain their trust, that's the most important thing. Once I'm finished helping Brent and his Dad this weekend, I'll settle in and start training, get these guys used to me. Slowly, the trust will be built up. They're intelligent, won't take long."

"So I've heard," Gris nodded.

"Their herd is one hell of an intrastructure!" Cole beamed proudly. "They're proud, have a mutual respect for one another. I want to extend that respect to us, let them know we respect and admire them."

"You'll do that, and I have no doubt you will. You'll have one hell of a herd," Gris smiled warmly.

"You know, Gris, if I could take in every wild horse and protect them, I would. People should be made aware of their plight," Cole said sadly. "But since I don't have the power to do that, I can do this one small thing."

"Son, if everyone does one little thing, then that trickles down into the bucket and before you know it, that bucket's full," Gris said, clapping Cole on the shoulder. "And in the meantime, you've got yourself some beautiful animals here," he beamed.

"I sure do! And there's a method to my madness!" Cole exclaimed brightly.

"Now that's a scary thought!" Gris guffawed.

"In bringing them home today, I got extra hands helping me get these guys settled in! Plus, they'll get one hell of a ride on the broncs!" he joked.

"And who can pass that up!" Gris had to laugh.

"You got that right!" Cole replied.

"Well, like they say in the movies, I'm gonna get while the getting's good! I'll see you in a bit," Gris bellowed, walking to his car.

"Don't be late!" Cole cried out, waving as Gris drove away.

Cole watched, still thinking of his words regarding Katie. Lost in thought, he leaned against the corral fence, watching the new horses running through the pasture. It had started already. As excited as he was today was as saddened as he was about the passing of another year. Katie was another year older, only this time it was different.

This time, she knew that she was her own little person, and that she was growing older. She had already lumped herself into that category, forgetting that she was still a tiny girl. Cole shuddered, not liking the thought one bit; he actually feared the day he would see her coming out of her room all grown up, dressed like a young woman ready for a date. Just the thought of that broke his heart; right now he was the most important man in her life. One day, Cole knew that he would have to concede that role and take a step back, letting another in.

"My baby's growing up," he said sadly as he went in to shower.

Ignoring Ruth and Irma, Cole went into the bathroom with an armful of clean clothes. It wouldn't do to go strutting around in a towel today. His life was changing before his eyes, and he hated change. He had had enough change and just wanted things to stay the way they were. Change meant coming and going. It also meant different people coming into one's life, which took some getting used to, especially when that person came into your daughter's life, moving her one step closer to crossing the threshold forever. Once she did that, she would be gone; the little girl would be a woman in her own right, with her own life. Now, Cole was still the center of Katie's world

366

and he vowed to make the best out of each and every single moment. Since the good Lord only gave him this chance once, he was determined to savor every treasured second.

The women noticed his mood, but kept to themselves; sometimes a man just didn't take to things the way they did. They knew the world went on and it did not necessarily mean the demise of the human race as they knew it. Children were born, children grew and children struck out on their own. What seems like the beginning of the end to men was really another chapter in the book to women.

They looked forward to every single stage, reliving a part of themselves over again as they watched their little ones dealing with the day-to-day trials and tribulations that they, themselves, once faced. That didn't mean the child grew out of your life, they still needed you no matter what age or stage they were in at the moment. They needed your guidance, your approval, your knowledge and expertise, and most importantly, they needed your blessings and love, something they couldn't possibly live without. Your ties grew stronger and you reached a new understanding, gaining mutual respect for one another.

The daughter then looked at the mother as a friend. Someone who had gone through the very same thing she was now experiencing and could understand her feelings. She could turn to her mother for advice and come to her with her tears, knowing that they would be understood. She looked at her father with pride, reaching a new level of understanding with him, also. She realized that she was more like him than she had ever thought, and was learning to be proud of that fact and embrace the knowledge. They were now friends, companions, and stood up for each other, with both giving a shoulder to lean on. The child had grown up.

Shaking all sad thoughts about growing up from his mind, Cole quickly dressed. Today was Katie's day and he was not going to let a dark mood slip in, robbing him of sharing that with her. Life went on, children grew, and so did your love for one another. Their lives went on; as well as the lives of their children, as had the life of his parents and grandparents before him. They were all part of a cycle that was never ending.

Life was as old as time. Generations came and generations went, but what did not go was the love shared by each one. That was what carried on throughout the years, passed down from parent through child year after year. Now it was Cole's turn. He was the one enjoying the special love of a child in his life. One day, he would look back on this day with a mixture of happiness and sadness, but he would then look down, seeing Katie enjoying the same kind of love with a child of her own. Then, he, too, would be kin to that love. His grandchild would reach his or her hand out to him in very much the same way Katie did now.

"See, it doesn't end," Cole shook the feeling off as Katie burst through the door, vaulting herself into his arms.

Callie followed, laughing as she watched the two. Katie's hair was curled, with the sides pulled back in new barrettes, which had pink strands of ribbon lying delicately upon her curls. Her face was radiant with joy and she talked a mile a minute as Cole tried keeping up with her.

"Whoa! Hey, hold on there! You're telling me ten things at once," he chuckled, bouncing Katie on his hip.

"Daddy! My hair got curled just like Callie's!" Katie proudly announced.

"And you look every bit as beautiful," Cole winked at Callie, sharing a smile.

"Look, Nanny!" Katie cried out as Irma and Ruth came into the room. "I got curls and she washed my hair with strawberry shampoo and made it real shiny! And look at my fingers!" she ran on, wiggling her digits in front of Cole's face.

He had to grab hold of them in order to see.

"Oh Daddy, be careful of my butterflies," she gasped, smiling as Cole loosened his grip.

"Your butterflies?" he asked, staring closer. "Hey! You got butterflies on your fingernails!" he laughed as he listened to her tale.

It had been Katie's first real trip to a beauty parlor, one of many, which was something Cole reluctantly resigned himself to. From now on, every special occasion would start with a trip to the beauty parlor. It was just a way of life. He was relieved to know that she really did not have nail polish on, just a thin layer of clear glaze to shine them up a little. And through Naomi's patience and expertise, Katie sported a tiny butterfly on each nail, which Cole discovered was nothing more than minute decals, which were patiently placed upon the almost dry surface. All in all, it wasn't too bad. Katie did not return 18 years of age, which was something Cole had feared at first. She was still Katie, and today she was four.

"Come on, honey, let's go get you dressed for your party!" Ruth said, taking Katie from Cole's arms.

He had to laugh at the chatter that still flowed from her, which would last all day and into the night. As a matter of fact, Cole had the feeling that she would be talking about today for weeks to come. Turning, he took Callie by the hand, pulling her to the side.

"You don't know what this means to me," Cole said softly, tracing her face with his finger.

"Yeah, I think I do and I had so much fun doing it! Cole, she's so happy and she's getting so big!" Callie gushed.

"I know, but I've gotten used to that!" he said proudly.

"Yeah, I bet," Callie scoffed, seeing the hope dancing in his eyes.

"All right, I just keep on telling myself that," Cole admitted, laughing with her. "Honey, you're not still upset about yesterday, are you?" he finally asked, seeing the way Callie lowered her eyes. "Callie?"

She felt the way his hand gently cupped her chin, tilting it back up towards him. A warm smile greeted her, melting Callie's heart. "Cole, I...." was all she could manage to stammer.

"Honey, I'm just as upset as you are and believe me, I was, and still am, scared to death. Just the thought of either woman coming around asking about Katie is enough to put the fear of God into me. But I have to put that fear aside and go on for my daughter. And it doesn't have anything to do with you and me. I love you, Callie. That won't ever change. Do you know what got me through yesterday and then last night?" he asked softly.

"No, what?" Callie asked, her eyes burning through his.

"What got me through yesterday was seeing your face. I never put your face out of my mind for a moment. I saw you with a tiny piece of hay sticking out from your hair and I saw you bathed in candlelight the night we went out...."

"Oh Cole," she sobbed, falling into his arms, everything else forgotten.

"I've seen you in every sort of light a person can be seen in and I don't know which I love the most. I guess what I'm saying is that I adore everything about you. Callie, you're real, your love is real. When you reach out to love me, I know that it's true. When you sit by my side at night tending sick animals, I feel your love and concern enveloping me. I never want to be without that. Honey, there isn't a woman on this earth that can compare to you. You're one hell of a woman, did you know that, Callie Marsh? Nobody can take care of all of us and our livelihood like you can. We put everything in your hands where our animals are concerned and nobody can love my daughter and me like you do. You make my blood boil," Cole said, groaning as he drew her close.

Everything was forgotten. All Callie had worried about earlier flew out the window when she saw the stark truth hidden in the depths of Cole's eyes. They grew quiet, with his lips coming down softly on hers. At first, they shared a quiet kiss, their lips barely brushing against one another, more like a whisper than a kiss. It was there, but they were almost afraid to believe so, nothing could feel that good and not disappear, yet it did. And when they parted, they were still there, as was the memory of their lips on one another's. Cole lowered his head, taking her mouth more insistently this time, his body involuntarily curving into hers. He breathed deeply, not wanting to break apart, yet they had to. They'd had very little time to themselves lately, something both their bodies screamed out, reminding them.

"How the hell are we gonna get through today?" Cole asked, sighing in resignation.

"We can always hide in the hayloft for an hour," Callie giggled.

"They'd miss us. And Brent would come looking! That, I don't need!" Cole cringed.

"How about tonight? Is Ruth staying over?" she asked hopefully.

"Yeah, she is! I'll have her watch Katie and will sneak over on Ontario! We'll take a ride down to the lake!" Cole exclaimed.

"Ooooh, skinny dipping! I can't wait to get you in the water," Callie growled lightly, sucking on Cole's bottom lip before pulling away. Staring longingly, she slowly pulled her hand from his.

Cole's body was already burning with pent-up passion as he let her go, her touch searing through him, her hand leaving her brand on his skin. It wasn't there for anyone else to see, but in Cole's eyes, it existed. He belonged to her, body, heart and soul. They had been apart for too long and planned on doing something about that later on that evening. Cole could not think of a better way to end a perfect day.

"You better not break your ass during that wild horse race," Callie said, her voice sultry and low. Her eyes danced around the room quickly before she advanced, grabbing his crotch firmly. "You better remember that, cowboy," she said, leaving Cole shaking where he stood.

All he could do was watch helplessly as she sashayed out the door. His body was numb, yet thousands of shards of electricity surged through him. He was wound tight; his skin feeling like it belonged to somebody else, his nerves prickling just beneath the surface. Every sense was highly tuned and quaking, right down to the familiar tingling in the pit of his stomach as his groin tightened, just from the mere thought of this woman.

Her touch did not help; unexpected, yet more than welcome. It literally rendered Cole paralyzed where he stood, unable to do anything but gape and stare as Callie walked away, her eyes boring through him. She was pure vixen, she could love like a woman, and she could torment like a minx. Cole had the feeling that tonight, the minx would be on the prowl and he would be her helpless prey.

"Are you ready, honey?" Ruth asked softly, not getting any response. Smirking at Irma, she reached out, tapping Cole on the shoulder.

"Geez! What the...!" he cried out, jumping out of his skin. Taking his breath in deep gulps, Cole looked at the two and began blushing furiously.

"Did Callie leave?" Ruth asked, already knowing the answer from the state Cole was in.

"Yeah! She went home to get ready!" he answered. "For the party!" Cole choked out as an afterthought, hoping that the women had not witnessed the scene he had instigated.

He had better be careful from here on in, there were too many prying eyes and nosy imaginations that needed feeding milling around. It was bad enough everybody else knew his feelings before he even made a move; now every move would be known to all.

"I'm living in a frigging fishbowl," Cole grumbled, going outside to wait for his friends. "Women! Why do they have to know everything?"

They laughed as he left, knowing just how Callie was working her wiles. Ruth swore she could feel the lightning snaps in the other room, knowing that they were together. She could feel the tension that surged between the two, neither could hide it no matter how hard they tried, and Ruth couldn't be happier. A love like that was rare and she was glad to see someone she loved finding it.

She had found it once with Gerald and even though she had lost him at an early age, Ruth still carried that love in her heart. And Gerald was waiting for her. He sat in their home in the heavens that he was preparing for her. He was in his rocker watching their children running and playing in a place where they would never lose their innocence. Ruth's rocker was waiting by his side. When she was called home, Gerald and their children would be waiting patiently. But that was a long ways off yet. Ruth still had too much she needed to do and two people who still needed her here taking care of them.

"See, the good Lord always does know what he's doing," she winked at Irma.

"I never doubted it for a moment," her friend smiled back.

* * *

That was the end of their quiet. Cole was out sitting on the edge of one of the tables when Brent pulled in, with Will and his family following close behind. Katie flew from the porch, squealing with delight as Lucas and Jordan ran to her side. Within minutes, the children were running through the yard, happily chasing after one another. Brent did manage to wrangle a hug from Katie, who had to show off both her flower bracelet and the butterflies on her fingers. That didn't last, however, for as much as she loved her Uncle Brent's undivided attention, she was just too excited to stay in one place for long.

Cole laughed as he greeted his friends and they watched the children running in the golden sunshine. Their faces were bright and radiant and their laughter sang through the air. The tables were heavily laden with every kind of food imaginable from roast ham and turkey, to two large platters of fried chicken, a pot of chicken 'n dumplings and a pot of Irma's special Texas chili.

"What about Montana chili?" Cole had teased earlier.

"Honey, Montana's good at turning out gorgeous cowboys, but nobody can beat Texas when it comes to good old-fashioned tongue burning chili!" Irma laughed, walking away with a swing in her hips.

Another table boasted an array of cornbread, homemade biscuits and gravy, and freshly baked bread ready to be dredged with golden honey from the jar Hec had brought over earlier. An array of salads from a green salad, compliments of Sadie, to a potato salad from Gil, were also on hand. Rounding out the side dishes were large bowls of stuffing and gravy for the turkey, a pan of candied yams and a generous amount of mashed potatoes, dripping with sweet butter. An assortment of vegetables awaited their pleasure, with everyone digging into their gardens and cooking up a hodgepodge of secret family recipes. They were so secret that the women spent the afternoon trading and passing them along for everyone to enjoy.

But the table that caused the most trouble with the children, as well as the men themselves, was the dessert table. Mountains of cookies, pies and cakes sat covered until the main meal was finished. The birthday cake stood in the center, with someone always sneaking over and stealing a peek. At one point, Cole got his ears boxed for sneaking a taste of the creamy, sweet icing. Turning a pleading smile in Ruth's direction, he gave her a quick peck on the cheek and ran off before he got into any more trouble.

"They just never grow up! I don't know who's worse, the men or the kids!" Ruth snorted.

"Hey! Where's my birthday girl!" Gris' booming laughter greeted them.

"Papa!" was Katie's happy greeting as she ran over.

Her legs couldn't get her there fast enough; just watching the way Katie flitted from one person to the next, Cole knew she would sleep well that night. Katie then proceeded to go through her morning again as she tossed her curls and displayed her decorated fingers for Papa to see. He beamed, hanging on to every word, his own eyes as bright as hers. Then, just as quickly as she jumped into his arms, she was out again.

"So, where's the party?" Gris roared.

"Over here by the keg!" Brent answered loudly, raising his glass in the air.

"Now, that's my kind of party," Gris grinned excitedly, rubbing his hands together. "Come to Papa," he spoke to the mug. "Ahhhh, that goes down real smooth! Now, boys, we have a lot to toast to! First of all, let's drink to Cole's successful sales of yesterday!" Gris raised his mug, along with the others.

Mugs were emptied in what seemed like one long swallow and were immediately filled again, the frothy foam spilling over their hands.

"And here's to Cal and Brent's success on Saturday!" Cole raised his glass. "Even though they're gonna be working my ass off!"

Glasses were raised once more, drinks went down and the foam flowed as they were filled to the brim again. Shouts and hollers greeted everyone, with the arrival of each new body a reason for the men to drink. Callie arrived amid a flurry of cat whistles from the men, who drew dirty looks from the women. She just shook her head at the gang and went off to join Ruth and the others. The men were really cutting loose today and it was not a pretty sight.

"To the women!" Brent cried out, whooping and hollering.

"Now, that, I'll drink to!" Cole joined in.

"I bet you will!" Gris teased, ignoring the red flush that crept over Cole's cheeks.

"And here's to Walt! Hey Walt! You come on over and grab yourself one of these here beers!" Cole shouted, waving his glass after he spotted Walt and Zach driving in. "We gotta fortify ourselves for the race!"

"Oh Lord, that's all we need is a bunch of drunken cowboys running around on the backs of wild broncs," Ruth winced. "Any takers on who breaks their ass first?"

"Oh, my money's on Cole, judging from the way he's pounding down the beer," Callie giggled.

"Yes, but Brent seems to lose control of his limbs when he drinks. Believe me, his father and I have seen him stumbling around plenty of times! And besides, he's just naturally clumsy!" Helen said, laughing at her son.

"If they keep this up, none of them will be able to stand on their own, let alone ride!" Irma clucked her tongue. "Damned fools!"

The rest of the women laughingly agreed, but no one made a move to stop the men. They couldn't if they tried. It was good to see them enjoying a day off as well as cutting loose and acting uninhibited for the first time since anyone could remember. The ranches and farms in the area demanded hard, 24-hour-a-day work, which sometimes drained a body and soul no matter how much they treasured their way of life.

They needed to step back for a moment, or an afternoon of partying, and not even think about their work. It wasn't often that they could put things on hold for a day, but for an occasion like this, they did. Morning chores were done and most of the men had things set out and ready for their evening tasks. Everything else could wait until tomorrow, where time would be spent catching up on what did not get done today, whether their heads pounded or not.

Cole couldn't remember a time, other than when Katie was born, when he was happier. His daughter was four today, his friends were here and everyone was healthy and sound. Plus, things could not be going any better than they were now. Everyone was having a good year with very few setbacks, if any at all. For once, it felt good knowing that they would be putting money in the bank instead of spending the winter wondering how they would make it through the following year.

Cole would spend Sunday putting his bills in order and getting them ready to be sent out. He would then make his deposit up for the bank. At least now he was secure in the knowledge that the funds were there when needed, getting him through the next few months until the next sale. That promised to be even bigger and better than this one and would bring enough money to carry him through the winter.

Walt was readying his heard for shipment the following week, with Brent and Cal shipping their cattle out that coming Saturday. Both men were nervous, they had skimmed through the winter, refusing any financial aid from anyone, and Cole had tried. He had managed to put a little away the previous summer, which he had tried lending Cal and Brent. But pride stood in the way, and the offer was graciously refused. Cole shouldn't have been too surprised at the refusal, for he, too, had been guilty of the same thing.

They all walked a thin line, and so far, no one had fallen off. They had come close, though, and some years had been harrowing, to say the least. But through hard work, strength and perseverance, they always found a way to make it through. This had already been a good year for Cole and had the promise of being the same for the others. Will's herd was doing well and he hoped that the market price of beef would hold steady until he brought them in a week from Saturday. Again, Brent and Cole promised to be there to help in any way they could.

"Hey, know what?" Brent said, swaying on his feet a little.

"I can just imagine," Cole rolled his eyes.

"Instead of sending our cattle on trucks this Saturday, why don't we have an old-fashioned cattle drive?" he asked, his eyes bright as he looked around.

"You've had too much beer," Cole retorted, plucking the mug from Brent's hands. "Either that, or you got kicked in the head by one of your heifers this morning. Did he get kicked in the head?" he asked of Cal.

"Beats me, he's always been a mite bit touched," Cal shrugged both men off and sat back to enjoy his drink.

In the midst of their banter, Gris kept a smile on his face, a drink in his hands, and a watchful eye on the ranch. The last thing he wanted was someone from Cole's past showing up and possibly ruining today for him. Cole was happy; for the first time in a long time, Gris could see how his defenses were down. True, she was only a scared, lost child; but her effect on Cole could be devastating. Gris couldn't look around as much as he would have liked without raising suspicion, so he had to be content with scanning the surrounding hillside, at the same time praying that Becca was safe. What he had failed to catch, however, was a flash of blue as a tiny slip of a girl darted out from behind a bush, moving her way closer to the back of the barn.

Chapter Eighteen

"Now remember, boys, keep your ass in the saddle and your feet off the ground!" Gris whooped as they ran to their mounts.

Everyone gathered around the fence yelling wildly as the men chased down their horses ... all saddled, all running from their grasp, and all thoroughly wild. Katie sat on top of the fence between Callie and Ruth, cheering for her Daddy. The horses stampeded about trying to buck the imposing obstacles from their backs. They fought when they were saddled for the first time and now they fought to keep from being captured. Ropes were not allowed; they had to dodge the flailing hooves, each other, and the charging horses, until they were able to grab on to their mount. Snorting wildly, the horses bucked angrily while the men approached, some of them wobbly on their legs due to the beer they had ingested.

"At least if they fall they won't feel any pain," Callie snickered with Ruth.

"Is my daddy going to win?" Katie asked, her eyes brimming with excitement and energy.

"He sure is, honey," Ruth nodded. "That's if he survives," she then whispered to Callie.

"GET OUTTA HERE! HE'S MINE!" Cole yelled, shoving Brent aside.

"WHAT THE HELL YOU MEAN HE'S YOURS? I HAD HIM!" Brent shouted back, plucking Cole's hands from the rein he had managed to grab.

"I'LL SHOW YOU!" Cole screamed, shouldering Brent and carrying him as if he were no bigger than Katie.

"He wouldn't!" Callie gasped, seeing them heading towards the water trough.

"He would and he did!" Ruth hooted.

Amid cheers and yells, Cole plucked a screaming Brent from the horse he had his own sights set on, and carried him across the corral. Fists pounded his back, but Cole ignored them. Cal couldn't believe his eyes, all the other men were playing fair, but neither Cole nor Brent could manage to behave. Screams filled the air as Cole bent forward, unceremoniously dumping Brent shouting and writhing into the water.

"I can't believe you f— you did that!" Brent sputtered, shaking his head.

Ignoring the shouts around him, Cole dashed back to the animals, fighting for the horse he had claimed as his. Brent vaulted from the trough and was right on his heels, tackling his friend. To everyone's delight, Brent became encased in mud and Cole wheezed as dust assailed his nostrils. He clawed forward, but felt himself being dragged back. Brent jumped up, stepped on Cole's backside and leapt, barely clearing his head. The horse was within his grasp, but Cole had reached up, grabbing Brent's booted foot in mid-flight. He tugged; Brent grunted, but pulled free as he fell to his knees.

Cole held on for all he was worth, but all he was rewarded with was an empty boot in his hands as Brent dashed forward, finally grabbing on to the horse. Just as he was about to mount the animal, the horse reared, flailing his legs and turning to the right as he came down. Brent was knocked into the fence and Cole was waiting for that very thing to happen. He shoved Brent to the ground and made one last desperate attempt for the animal, when another pair of hands intruded, shoving him aside.

"LET A REAL MAN HANDLE THIS!" Will shouted, flinging a stumbling Cole to the ground.

He fell on top of Brent, with both men tangling. Will mounted the horse in one jump and was off, his arm high in the air to steady his swaying body. Walt had managed to mount his horse and Zach was off on one of his own. Kaitlin had snagged a mount and was struggling to hold on. Seconds later, she was bucked off, rolling quickly out of the way. Callie shrieked as she fell, almost rolling towards Brent and Cole, who were too busy wrestling each other than fighting the horses.

Gris strode over with a pitcher of beer, which he dumped on their heads, and pulled the sputtering men apart. "NOW! Get your asses on a horse! You wanna fight, you can fight later!"

"What'd you do that for?" Brent whined, sputtering against a mouth full of mud and been. "He started it!"

"You stole my horse!" Cole fought back, his heart racing. It felt good to let loose, they were like kids again, fighting as if they didn't have a care in the world. And right then and there, they didn't."

"HEY!" Brent screamed, pointing. "He's got our horse!"

Looking towards Will, Cole was rewarded with the sight of their friend flying through the air and the horse triumphantly storming off. Both men sprinted forward at once, this time Brent was a little quicker, but Cole ended up stumbling over Kaitlin. With a frustrated cry, he flew over the top of her, landing face first in the dirt.

"Oh, Cole!" Callie burst out, laughing too hard to even breathe.

"You better get yourself up!" Ruth cried out, trying very hard to act like a lady.

Katie made a move to jump to her father's aid, but Gris intervened, holding her back. "Hold on there, pretty lady, you don't want any part of that!" he laughed. "Why don't you sit on Papa's shoulders?"

He hoisted Katie high and stood back out of the line of fire. No one inside the corral was safe. In the midst of the melee, Walt was thrown from his horse and, ignoring the threats from his wife, immediately ran to catch another and ride again. Irma winced, peering through fanned fingers when Zach was pitched forward off of his, landing and rolling in front of his father. In a huff, Walt went down like a sack of potatoes, grinding his own son into the dirt. Cole had managed to grab a mount when Jake came flying off of his, driving him face first into the ground.

"Oh no! Cole, you did it again!" Callie howled hysterically, laughing at the stricken expression that had crossed his face.

So far, in spite of his best efforts, Cole had been unable to get his hands on a horse and attempt to ride. He had been shoved, pushed, plucked from and stomped in his endeavors to mount one of the animals. Kaitlin was back on her feet and was on a quest for her own mount. Brent had finally managed to clear his head from the muck which was quickly drying to a caked-on, crusty surface, and Jake, Jared, and Troy each managed to grab the reins of their own horse. Will had just plopped his seat down into one of the saddles, when he was sent flying through the air again. Jared was in the saddle, Cole had his foot in the stirrups, but the animal started spinning in circles much to Callie and Ruth's dismay, and Jake finally vaulted upon a horse of his own.

However, he slipped and wound up face down on his stomach, holding on to both the tail and the saddlehorn while the animal spun him in a crazy circle, his legs cutting through the air. One foot came up, the heel of the boot clipping Brent on the side of the head and toppling him off over the rear end of the first horse he had just managed to snag. Cole was still stuck, but was making headway.

This time, he was on but had misjudged when the horse lunged to the left, making him overshoot the saddle. Hanging on sideways, he fell to the left and held on for dear life. All of a sudden the horse darted forward, snorting as he lowered his head and charged towards the gate. Cole's cries filled the air when the ornery beast stopped short and he flew over its head, arms and legs flailing as he pitched over the fence, landing on one of the smaller tables that Helen had left her plate of salad on. Covered in potatoes and mayonnaise, Cole rolled over, spitting the offending mess of grass and food from his mouth while Katie ran to him, landing on his stomach.

"Daddy! You're dirty!" she squealed, jumping and running off before he could catch her.

"You were supposed to keep your ass in the saddle! Now how am I going to hold my head up around here?" Ruth sniffed, walking away in a faux snit.

"Break anything, cowboy?" Callie licked her lips sensuously while leaning down and blowing softly into his ear. He shuddered, staring helplessly as she strolled away, swinging her hips teasingly.

He had hoped for a bit of sympathy from Callie, who was laughing too hard and left before he could even reach out for her hand. Propped up on his elbows, Cole cringed at the mess smeared over him and watched the outcome of the race. Will was down for the count, rubbing his backside as he limped towards the fence. Jared was giving it a good run, but was tossed off mere feet before the finish line. Jake was giving Troy and Brent a run for their money, but at the last minute his horse had a change of mind and direction, turning and heading the other way. Walt and Zach were sitting along the side of the fence, nursing their aches and bruises. Being too cocky for his own good, Brent turned to laugh at Jake, and wound up flying from the side of his own horse when it turned quickly to the left, throwing him clear.

With a triumphant whoop, Troy shot across the finish line and jumped off the back of his very irate, foul tempered mount. Bellowing a hearty, victory cry, he waved his arms in the air as he ran to claim his prize. A tall, frosted pitcher of ice cold beer sat at the ready. Holding the drink high, he turned victoriously, shouting his defeat before downing a quarter of the brew in one, long breath.

"Whoo! All it took was a deputy to show you cowboys just who's boss around here!" Troy whooped for the entire county to hear.

"Son, you do the department proud!" Gris shouted, strutting over proudly. "See! Just another facet of our public service!"

"He's just lucky!" Brent groused, limping away.

"No! He's just that good!" Gris laughed, walking away with the winner.

* * *

Becca wasn't aware of the tears streaming down her cheeks as she hid behind the corner of the barn watching. While all the women shouted, laughing at and cheering on their favorite rider, a young girl cried for all she lost that was now found. The air was charged with energy, their laughter floating by on the breeze, yet her heart was confused by the maze of emotions rippling through her.

One moment she felt all her longing welling up as she saw her uncle for the first time since she could remember, and the next she was seized by the fear that after all these years he might be angry with her for showing up unannounced. He did not look like he would be angry, Cole was laughing as he raced for his horse. Becca remembered that laugh, almost smiling at the ton of memories the sound brought on. She had missed him dearly and could not tear her eyes from his face.

Then she was angry … angry over what she had been cheated out of all these years. It just wasn't fair. The way her family ignored her wasn't fair and the way her uncle left without a word wasn't fair. She had missed so much, and nobody cared. She should be in on all this fun; she should be a part of things. She had always been a part of things before but now she was left out and forgotten. Uncle Cole never called for her and he never came to see her. Then she felt an almost instant remorse as she remembered his losses. No wonder Cole had never come back, being home was just too sad anymore. He now had a new home and new friends he seemed to love very much, and no one was sad.

It was with a mixture of sadness and pride that Becca came to the slow realization that the tiny girl the party seemed to be for was Cole's daughter. She looked just like him, with brownish gold hair and dark eyes. Her nose was pert and cute, and her mouth had the tiniest hint of an uplift that seemed to tug at the sides, making her smile slightly crooked and very endearing. Becca cried dearly then, her heart aching that she was now the unwelcome stranger her uncle did not want to see. She almost turned and ran, but held back. Uncle Cole was like her; he had lost everything once, too.

Becca wished that she had been older when the tragedy struck; perhaps then, they would have listened to her and maybe she could have helped. She had so wanted to comfort Cole back then. Now, she didn't know if he even wanted her here; maybe it had been a big mistake in coming. Becca prayed that she could work things out with Cole and that he wouldn't send her back to her parents.

She tried summoning up the courage to face him, but it wasn't the right time yet. She needed to compose herself and get over the shock of seeing him again. And she needed time to digest the fact that he now had a daughter to love. Becca was happy for him, yet she was scared. She couldn't help but laugh at the men's antics as they fought with one another in their quest for a horse. She almost shrieked out loud when Cole dumped Brent into the water and then turned, only to fall flat on his face … not once, but twice. Then when he went flying over the horse and landed on the table of food, she could hardly contain her laughter and had to resort to clamping her hand over her mouth and falling back against the wall of the barn so she could not see any more.

Then Becca realized that she was hungry, her stomach ached and it was getting hot. Her canteen was empty and she desperately needed something to drink. Looking at the food, her mouth watered. Everyone was either inside getting washed up or they were over talking by the horses and toasting the winner. The kids were oblivious to anything but each other and the mountain of presents they were slowly sneaking closer to, and the rest of the crowd was off eating and talking amongst themselves.

"Maybe they won't see me, I'll just blend in with the crowd. As long as Uncle Cole doesn't see me, then everyone will just think I came with someone else," Becca reasoned as she slowly made her way over.

* * *

Brent had just come out of the house and was fixing a plate of food. Cole had graciously lent him a set of clean, dry clothes and the use of his bathtub to rid himself of the caked on muck.

"I know the feeling and it's not a pretty one," he laughed, dragging Brent inside.

"Hey, it's your fault that I'm a mess!" Brent had whined.

"I'm giving you some of my clothes, aren't I?" Cole asked, dumping everything Brent needed into his arms. "Just make sure you wash your stench off before you return them," he teased, snorting as he walked away.

"Just get your stench out of them," Brent mimicked, making a sour face as he locked himself in the bathroom.

Once he was finished, Brent went back out to join the crowd. Ravenous, he had just emptied one plate and was going back for a refill when a movement behind the barn caught his attention. Thinking he was seeing things, he did a double take, only to find no one in sight. Yet, the hair prickled on the back of his neck, giving him the eerie feeling of being watched. Setting his plate down, he quickly wound his way around the other side of the barn, spying a young girl with her back towards him.

"Now, do you mind telling me what a little snippet like you is doing hiding here?" Brent asked softly, causing Becca to jump and run in fright.

Darting after her, it didn't take much to catch up and grab her by the arm. "Now hold on there! Nobody's gonna hurt you!" Brent said, holding Becca firmly.

"Let me go! I want my Uncle Cole!" Becca fought, kicking Brent in the shins.

"Yeeeowww! What'd you do that for? I didn't go kicking you!" he yelped, staring at the beginning of a mystery.

One thing Brent never expected was someone from Cole's past showing up. He doubted if his friend did, either. Especially in the form of a slip of a girl who called him Uncle Cole. Brent paled slightly, this could only mean one thing; this had to be Matt's daughter. Hearing about people from a tragedy not so far in the past was one thing, seeing one in the flesh was a totally different matter. It brought everything to light, including the brutal suffering all had endured, and were still. Everything was suddenly too real, a legend brought to life, one Brent had just fallen into. And judging from the pain and fear in the young girl's eyes, Cole wasn't the only one still reeling from a loss that chilled him to the bone just thinking about it.

"Now do you mind telling me just who you are?" he asked, still holding her arm tightly.

"I don't have to answer to you! I'm looking for my Uncle Cole!" she stood defiantly.

"Well, if you'd quit kicking me, I'll take you to him! Geez, that's no way to assert your independence, you know! That hurts!" Brent whined, staring at the defiant youngster. "Come on, this is gonna be good," he quipped, dragging her along.

No one paid them any mind at first as Brent strode out from behind the barn, dragging Becca behind him. Gris's eyes flashed. Dropping his plate, he ran over attempting to intervene, but it was already too late. Spotting Cole over by Ruth and Callie, Brent made his way towards the small group.

"Cole, this one's been a looking for you. She's got quite a kick too," he grumped, standing back out of range as he handed Becca over.

Cole's mouth fell; his throat became dry, and his body started trembling. The small child he had left behind had turned into a young woman without his giving it a thought. With a strangled cry, he broke from Ruth's worried grasp and ran to Becca's side. Tears streamed down both their faces as he picked her up, holding her close. All of Becca's arguments about her age dissolved when she fell into Cole's arms. She wept; for the uncle she had loved and missed so much had her in his arms again.

He wasn't mad and he hadn't forgotten her in the least, not any more than she had forgotten him. He only cried as he held her close, like he used to. Becca wound her arms around Cole's neck, not wanting to let go. Slowly, he went down onto his knees, heedless of the fact that everyone was slowly gathering around. He set Becca on her feet, still keeping both hands on her shoulders. Cole couldn't believe his eyes; he had never forgotten this child he had always treasured, and the guilt welled up deep inside. It was now clear to him that she had been suffering, also. If not, then she would not be here right now. And how did she get here?

"Honey! My God, what are you doing here? And how?" Cole gasped.

"Oh, Uncle Cole," Becca sobbed, breaking down in his arms again. "You're not mad at me, are you?"

He pulled her face back up, staring deeply into her eyes. "Honey, of course I'm not mad at you! My God! Let me look at you! Becca, is it really you? Is this really my little Becca?"

"I'm not so little anymore," she managed to sniff brokenly.

"No, you've grown into a lovely young woman," Cole said softly, gently running his hand down the side of her hair. "But you still didn't answer my question.... Wait! The questions can wait, honey, are you all right? How did you get here?"

"Cole, let's get her into the house," Ruth suggested, seeing how Becca was beginning to tremble.

"Uncle Cole, I don't feel so good," she burst out, tears streaming heavily down her face.

"Honey, it's going to be all right, I have you now. Everything's going to be all right," Cole soothed, scooping Becca up in very much the same way he would Katie. Carrying her into the house, he felt Katie following, tugging at his legs.

"Daddy! Daddy!" she cried out, trying to understand what was happening.

All of a sudden everybody had stopped having fun and had grown quiet. Then this strange girl was crying in her father's arms. Katie didn't know how to feel at the moment, but curiosity was quickly outweighing her fear.

"Katie bug, it's all right! Why don't you go with Callie and she can help you, Lucas and Jordan play a game. Then we'll get ready for your presents. Daddy will tell you all about this in a minute, ok?" he asked, grateful that the game and the thought of the party continuing weighed on her mind at the moment. Flashing a quick smile in Callie's direction, Cole knew that his daughter was in good hands.

He ran into the house with Ruth at his side. Gris followed close behind, as did Brent and Will. Nothing ever happened without those two nosing around. Cole worried about how frail Becca felt in his arms and nightmarish thoughts filled his mind at how she could have possibly gotten here. As far as he knew, no one even had the vaguest idea of where he was and now Becca showed up seemingly out of nowhere, alone, frightened, and crying. How could this be?

"Honey, let's get you settled on the couch," he said gently, seeing Ruth running for a glass of cold water. She returned a few seconds later with the drink and a wet cloth, which Cole gratefully plucked from her hands.

"Becca, try and drink a small sip of this. You feel all right?" he asked, brushing the cool cloth across her forehead.

It only took a few minutes for her color to return and her smile to beam back up at him. Cole felt his heart lifting as he realized that Becca was going to be ok, it had to have been the shock and excitement surrounding their reunion that had gotten the better of her. His questions could wait for a moment, yet they couldn't. He not only needed answers, he needed to contact Matt ... he needed to stop trembling and help a little girl who had been denied for too long. His apprehension about calling Matt had to be put on hold for now, that was the least of Cole's worries. It would be hard, but it would be done; Cole had to do it for Becca, if not for himself. In the meantime, he had to gather his thoughts, calm his rapid heartbeat, try breathing normally, and face Becca smiling.

"Now, what in the world are you doing here?" Cole asked

"Uncle Cole, please don't send me away! I don't want to go back! I hate it there, I hate them!" she pleaded.

Her very words chilled him to the core, Cole winced at the thought of Katie saying those very same words about him one day; nothing scared him more. "Becca, I'm not going to send you away, that I promise. You're here and you're safe. Haven't I always taken care of you?"

"Yes," she answered, hanging her head.

Cole's hand gently clasped hers, "Haven't I always told you the truth and been honest with you?"

"Yes, Uncle Cole, but you left! I missed you so much, but you were gone! And you never said goodbye! How come you never said goodbye or called me?" Becca asked.

Taking a shuddering breath, Cole paled. Both Ruth and Gris made a move towards him, but he waved them back. "Honey, we have a lot to talk about, but that can wait till later. But I never left because of you and I never stopped loving you. I sometimes dream of seeing you one day and you'd be all grown up and we would be together again. And here you are! You're all grown up just like I imagined and we're together again," he smiled weakly.

"I'm not mad at you, Uncle Cole, it's not your fault. Everything that happened is Dad's fault. He screwed up everything. I hate him." Becca angrily declared.

Cole grabbed her gently, but firmly by the arms, "Becca, it's ok to be mad at your father, but don't ever say you hate him! Being mad is one thing and it can make you think you hate him, but you really don't! Don't ever say that! Let him know how you feel! Let him know how mad you are and how all of this has made you feel! But please, don't ever hate him!"

"Do you hate him?" she asked so quietly, Cole barely heard the words.

"No, honey, I don't hate your father," Cole said quietly, shaking his head. "I could never hate him. Honey, your dad had nothing to do with my leaving. He didn't make me leave, do you understand? That was my decision, and mine alone. I left for reasons that we can talk about later, ok? Believe me, it had nothing to do with your dad," Cole gently explained.

"I guess I don't hate him either, but I don't want to go back!" Becca cried out.

"Guess there's no sense in asking if he knows you're here," Cole asked of her.

"He probably figured it out by now," she shrugged. "He had a detective find out where you were, and one night, I stole the file and wrote down your address," Becca replied.

"And you came here," Cole finished for her. "Honey, you can tell me all about that later, but right now you look like you need something to eat and some rest. And...." Cole hedged, running his hand through his hair. He took a deep breath before continuing. "And I have to call your father."

"NO!" Becca screamed, jumping from the chair.

"Honey, I have to! That little girl you saw out there is mine...."

"I know, I heard her calling you Daddy," Becca said in a hushed tone.

"Anyway, if she were gone and someone knew, I'd die if they didn't tell me! Becca, I promise not to send you away; you can stay here as long as you like. You can sleep in Katie's room with her, or I have a spare bedroom if you want. I'll even tell your dad that I think it's best to leave you here for a while. Do you trust me?" Cole asked, looking intently into her eyes.

"You can call him," was her reply. "But I don't want to go back there. It's not fun being home anymore," she finished.

"Tell you what, this is my friend Ruth, and this is Gris," Cole nodded between the two. "And the ones you see standing behind us being nosy are Will and Brent; but I hear you already met him and have one heck of a kick," he snickered.

"I'm sorry I kicked you," Becca smiled an apology that melted Brent's heart.

"Ahhh, that's all right," he scoffed.

"He's a pushover," Cole giggled. "Guys, if you haven't put two and two together by now, this is Becca," Cole finished the introductions.

"Hi Becca! If I shake your hand, you won't bite, will you?" Brent teased, putting Becca at ease.

"Hi, I'm Will," Will quipped, holding his hand out next.

"Man of few words," Cole still snickered. "His boys are outside playing with Katie. You're right in time for a party, so I hope you don't mind."

"Uncle Cole, I don't want you to stop her party cause of me," Becca replied.

"Honey, we won't stop the party! You're more than welcome to join in. You're still family, you know! I know that it's been a long time and we both have a lot to talk about, but I promise that everything will be ok. So why don't you go on out and get something to eat? You're too skinny!" he teased, tweaking her nose like he used to.

"Oh, Uncle Cole!" Becca gushed, falling into his arms again.

"I still love you, baby," Cole said softly, his own breath catching.

Winking at them, Brent took Becca by the hand. She joined the party, sandwiched between him and Will as they walked to the door. In their usual fashion, both men grunted as each tried taking the lead by being the first one to squeeze through. That led to both becoming stuck and flashing each other a look of defiance. Cole just shook his head. Those two never learned. Gris reached out, settling matters in his own way. A beefy hand grabbed Brent by the collar, pulling him back, and another shoved Will forward. Like a popped cork, the two sprang free. Becca then made her escape by running out between them.

With the initial shock over, Cole felt his body going slack as all the tension and shock drained from him at once. He began trembling almost violently, falling into Ruth's arms. Huge choking sobs burst forth unheeded, rendering him helpless. It had taken all of his self-control to keep his mind sane as he caught sight of the little waif he had left behind so long ago, standing right in front of him. Guilt and remorse consumed Cole; he should have been man enough to go to Becca instead of causing so much grief that she had to run away and seek him out. Then he had to call Matt, which would be just about the hardest thing he had to do.

Cowardice and shame gushed through him. How could he have thought that he had been the only one hurt? Sure, he had been brokenhearted, but so had everyone else. At the time, Cole didn't consider anyone's feelings except his own, and he ran. He never went back and he never even contacted those closest to him. They all had enough to deal with; Cole should have realized that his leaving in such a fashion would have only added to their hurt.

His head ached. That time was still muddled and he did not want to remember. He had stopped remembering what happened the day they buried Sarah. The few times Cole had gone back to his old home, he just stood staring, trying to make sense of things; nothing was the way it should be and that hurt. Contacting Matt now would only bring those memories back, and Cole did not want to do that. Sarah was gone; she had been gone for a long time now and that was all he wanted to think about. He did not want to think about anything else, yet it was thrust upon him. Regardless, that wasn't important now. What was important was a little girl who had enough courage to take her life back.

The adults had been floundering all these years, as Becca's arrival was testament to. Things had to have been pretty bad at home for her to have left like that. Becca had always been close to her parents, she was the center of their world. But like Cole, the center of Matt's world had fallen out. For years now he had avoided any contact with his friend ... friend ... that was the first time in a long time that Cole had thought of Matt in such a manner. So much was left behind; so much had been lost, that everything impacted him at once. He knew that he would wake one day and his past would be staring him in the face, yet he prayed that he could always keep that day at bay. Now, it was here, and Cole had no choice. Remembered or not, it was here.

At that moment, Cole hated himself. He should have been braver, he should have stayed and faced his losses, instead of letting a little girl down. He just thanked God that she had arrived safe and unhurt. Becca wasn't any worse for wear and with some food and a good night's rest, she would be fine. But he still had to call Matt.

Cole then prayed that Matt would listen to him and let Becca alone for the time being. She needed time to regroup and get her feelings sorted out. She had run because of the way things had been at home, a part of which, Cole blamed himself for. He thought that everyone else had just simply gone on with their lives, not caring that he had left. He never even contemplated the fact that Matt would be suffering from all of this also; further proving how selfish he had been in his actions.

"You were right," he said brokenly, looking over at a very worried Gris.

"About what, son?" Gris asked, coming to his side.

After all the times he had been with Cole when he broke down about his past, after all the times he and Ruth had struggled to get Cole back on his feet, Gris was needed again.

"You once said that I wasn't the only one hurting, that maybe they were hurting too. I was so wrapped up in my own pain, I never gave it a thought. Maybe if I did, Becca wouldn't have run away," he said, feeling the shame coursing through him.

"Cole, it's not your fault," Gris argued back.

"Maybe it is, maybe it's not; but the fact remains that a little girl ran away from home because of all that's happened, and I just thank God that she made it here in one piece! I should have gone to her instead of making her come looking for me!" he retorted.

"Honey, how were you to know?" Ruth soothed.

"I'm supposed to be the adult here! I should have known. Maybe I never should have left in the first place! I could have at least kept in contact with Becca! Or my cousin Dave! My God, there were people back there who cared about me, and I simply shut them out and took off! I never contacted a single person back home, how could I have thought that no one would worry or at least wonder what had become of me?"

"Cole, I'm not going to lie and say that no one back home was worried after you left," Gris replied in a hushed tone. "But I don't think they hold it against you, and I'd bet my life on it that they understand, considering all you lost," he blanched, turning away quickly.

"For years it's been about all I've lost, but now it's time to go beyond that. My actions were selfish! How could I have been so selfish? And don't say that it was grief, and that grief causes a person to do things they wouldn't do otherwise!" Cole snapped, staring intently at Gris.

"Say it or not, it's the truth. Other than love and hate, the strongest emotion is grief. Like the others, it can bring us to our knees, guide our thoughts and actions, and make us do things we never would have thought of in order to escape it. We all base our lives on emotions! Sometimes, they are so overwhelming that they get the better of us, so we run. It's more than natural, it's a part of self-preservation. Cole, Matt had his home. Your wife died in yours," Gris said, looking away quickly.

"Ok, so I have a good excuse," Cole replied brokenly. "Nonetheless, Becca was only a baby at the time! Can you imagine how confused and scared she had to have been? Or still is?" Cole asked, standing back. After taking a deep breath and rubbing his eyes, he looked at his friends. "Why don't you two go out and keep an eye on things? Katie's probably bursting at the seams. Just tell her that Daddy has to make a phone call and will be out soon," he smiled, squeezing Ruth's hand.

Ruth gently caressed his face and together, she and Gris made their way back out to the party. Cole turned to the phone, his heart skipping a beat as he picked up the receiver. The last thing he wanted to do was to hear Matt's voice on the other end. Doing that would only dredge things up again. He had hurt so much back then; he didn't want to hurt anymore. He didn't want to remember. Cole's heart slammed against his chest as he tried remembering the number.

With shaking hands, he began dialing. Hitting the wrong numbers, he clasped the receiver to his chest as he jammed the button down, cutting off the connection. He had to do this; if it were Katie he would want Matt to call him, regardless. No matter what came between him and Matt, Becca was his daughter. Cole knew that Matt loved her as much as he loved Katie, this had to be tearing him apart. He had to swallow his hurt, look past his pride, and make the call. Right now, nothing else mattered but Becca.

The question now was, how did he approach Matt? With all they had shared growing up, it should be so easy. Yet, Cole was at a loss of what to say. How did you begin talking to a friend that you had left behind years ago, and never contacted him again? What did you talk about? You simply couldn't call and ask, 'Hey, how ya doing? Nice day, huh?' That was just too clipped and informal. Yet, he and Matt had grown up together and never stood on formality. Did Cole start with an apology? Did he say how sorry he was and what a coward he had been? Or did they act like nothing happened, make amends, and talk as they always have with one another? Cole just wasn't sure anymore; Matt wasn't the stranger here, he, himself, was.

Becca was here; Becca was crying out for help. She had been crying for years, with no one listening to her. Maybe Matt was the same way; he had lost his family. His mother and sister were gone. His father was all Matt had left, and he had been just as broken and lost. Everyone was shattered, yet no one had ever reached out to the other. Matt turned from Cole, Shauna cried silently, Jeremy shut down, and Cole ran. And Becca ... Becca just stood by, witnessing it all.

It was time Cole stopped fearing his past and faced the consequences of his leaving. He had no choice, they were here and they were staring him in the face. There was no ignoring anything now. They had to think of Becca; she was the one who needed their help and attention now. The adults had had six years to screw things up; it was about time they started thinking like she did.

Suddenly Cole wanted to help; he wanted to reach out to Matt and help with Becca in any way he could. He didn't want to see her so angry with her parents. He didn't want to hear how badly her life had turned out; she was still young, they could fix things if they tried. It wasn't too late.

Could Matt listen? Would he be receptive to the call and Cole's pleas, and allow Becca time to heal? Or would he come storming down to reclaim his daughter? Cole didn't know whether Matt trusted him with Becca or not. Regardless, it was a chance he had to take. "Maybe he's mellowed with age," he muttered, finally dialing the number.

Beads of sweat formed across his forehead as he waited, impatiently brushing the moisture from his skin. With every ring, Cole's skin prickled from nerves that were already stretched to the limit. Feeling the nausea rising, he fought the impulse to just hang up and let things stay as they were

"Come on, just answer the frigging thing and let's get this over with," Cole muttered, wishing he could be anywhere else at that moment.

After what was only the third ring, a familiar voice greeted him. Cole froze, unable to utter a word. It had been so long, and so much had happened. How did he break in and just say, 'Hey man, I know we haven't spoken in years, but guess what? I have your daughter and she wants to stay!' Time stood still as Cole tried gathering his wits.

"Hello?" Matt's tired voice came over the line.

Cole swallowed deeply, his voice betraying him. He moved his lips, with only a slight croaking sound erupting. Feeling the need to be patient, Matt held his own breath as he waited. Sensing who was on the other end, he knew instinctively not to hang up.

Mustering all his nerve, Cole tried again. "Matt?" he asked, at a loss for anything else to say. His world was spinning beneath him again, plunging him back to a place he had no desire to be.

Matt closed his eyes tightly, this time his turn to remain quiet while gathering his feelings, and Cole's to wait patiently. It took a few moments for both men to regain their composure; yet each was patient and understanding, something that both frightened Cole and offered a sense of relief at the same time. He didn't want to fight, he was tired of being scared, and he was tired of hurting. If he had to talk with Matt, he wanted to talk amicably and put their anger behind them. They had to consider Becca. This time, their feelings didn't matter. The seconds stretched into minutes before Matt finally cleared his voice enough to talk.

"Cole?" he managed to choke out, his voice raspy, throat hot and aching.

"Yeah, it's me," was all he could think of saying.

"Cole, how ... how.... Oh God," Matt broke down, dropping the phone.

Cole winced, throwing his head back as he fought his own emotions. This was Matt ... this was the Matt he had known all his life. No, this was a broken stranger. His friend was just as broken as he, Matt's voice portrayed that fact. He was just another broken spirit in the wake of an unthinkable tragedy. Loss and grief had robbed both men of their lives. Cole could hear the sound of sobbing coming from the other end and then someone else picked up the phone. He held his breath, hearing Shauna's voice coming over the line.

"Cole, is it really you?" she asked breathlessly. "Are you all right? Did you hear from Becca? Please tell me you heard from Becca!" she pleaded.

"I'm fine, don't worry about me. And stop worrying about Becca, she's with me and she's safe. She showed up a few minutes ago, scaring the hell out of me, but she's fine," he quietly reassured her.

"Cole, we're coming—"

"NO!" he cried out, cutting Shauna off and causing a brief moment of silence.

"Excuse me?" she asked quietly.

"Shauna, I know that I have no right to tell you what to do or to offer advice where your daughter is concerned. I'm only asking this for Becca. You don't know anything about me or my life anymore, so I'll have to ask you to please trust me on this. Shauna, we've all been through hell and that's an understatement; but it seems that we've all forgotten one important thing," Cole began his pitch.

"Becca," was all she could say.

"Yeah, she's hurting deeply from all of this and she's reached her breaking point. Shauna, she needs time; she wants to stay here, and I agree. I don't know what's been happening up there, but she's really upset now and I'm afraid that she might run again if she thinks she has to go home. I know that I'm the last person on this earth that you want to talk with or consider letting your daughter stay with, but that's what she wants. I'm only asking for her; she has so much to work out," he pleaded.

"She missed you, Cole. We all miss you," Shauna whispered softly.

"Yeah, well … she really wants to be here. But I understand if you don't trust me. But my life has changed, I'm not what you think...." he winced at his poor choice of words.

"Cole, hold on, Matt wants to talk with you," Shauna said, handing the phone over before he even had the chance to decline.

"Cole?"

"Yeah."

"How are you? I gather Becca's there," he replied shakily.

"She's here, and she's fine. Matt, what the hell's been going on up there?" Cole asked, his tone harsher than he wished.

Matt winced at the tinge of anger still present, "I don't blame you for being angry—"

"Matt, I'm sorry if it came out that way; believe me, I'm not angry. It's just that this whole thing sort of caught me by surprise. Besides, my feelings don't matter now and to put it frankly, neither do yours or Shauna's. All three of us are to blame for the way Becca's feeling, and have our brand of guilt to carry. I shouldn't have left like I did and in spite of how you feel about me, I should have kept in contact with her. Now look what happened."

"Cole, you don't know how I feel," Matt replied.

"No, I don't know how you feel, but I know how Becca feels and I know that she doesn't want to come home right now."

"She wants to stay with you?" Matt replied, not surprised by that revelation.

"Does that surprise you?" Cole asked, almost reading his mind.

"No, that's the reason she left," Matt admitted.

"Matt, she's your daughter and I have no right to tell you what to do, but please consider her needs. I have a pretty good spread here and I'm not alone—"

"You're married?" Matt asked too quietly.

"No, I'm not married and it's too long a story to explain. But I do have...." Cole hesitated, trying to find the right words. "Matt, I have a four-year-old daughter that I'm raising alone and I have a woman who comes in every day helping take care of her and the house. What I'm trying to say is that Becca will be well taken care of; she can sleep in Katie's room with her and Ruth and I are always here," he said, finishing.

Matt rubbed his eyes, a feeling of elation mingled with loss as he learned of Cole's daughter. If Sarah had lived, she and Cole would have a child of their own, making him an uncle. Now Cole had a child with someone else, news that further accentuated his hurt. Yet it brought a sense of peace knowing that he had found somebody to carry on for. In spite of everything he had suffered, Cole had been strong enough to carve out a life for himself. Maybe he would be strong enough to help Becca.

"Matt?"

"Cole, I'm not going to argue with you," Matt answered tiredly. "Becca hasn't been happy for years and you're right about one thing, we should have considered her, but we didn't. But you're wrong about something else, you're no stranger to me and she's still a part of your life. That hasn't changed."

Cole sighed deeply, "I gotta tell you, Matt, I really didn't ... didn't...."

"You really didn't expect me to be human again, did you? But who can blame you? Especially after everything I've done," Matt explained, much to Cole's intense relief.

"Well, yeah, since you put it that way," Cole snorted.

"Cole, things aren't the same here; I'm not the same. I can't expect you to know that, since you've been gone all this time ... but things are just ... different."

"They are for all of us Matt," Cole replied quietly, the anger draining from him. The relief brought by hearing Matt's voice went deep, healing a part of him that had been broken for years. "Matt, I ... shit, I didn't know this was going to be so hard."

"Cole, I'm sorry ... for everything. I'm so deeply, terribly sorry that I can't even begin to convey the words," Matt said, feelings he had been fighting for years tumbling from his mouth.

"Matt—"

"No! Let me finish! If I ever see you face to face again, I might not be able to say this! I might clam up and not be able to get the words out! Please let me get them out! I know that over the phone isn't the best way and I certainly don't expect you to forgive me! I don't want forgiveness! I just want you to hear me!" he pleaded fervently.

"Go on," Cole rasped, his voice hoarse.

"Cole, I've hated myself since ever since I turned away from you that day at … at the hospital. I knew then that nothing was your fault! It wasn't only unfair, it was inhuman. I know you stopped living when Sarah died and I haven't lived since then, either. You needed me; you were faced with a decision no one should ever have to be faced with. I didn't understand that then; in my weakness, I thought that you had simply given up on Sarah and walked away," Matt began explaining.

His skin prickling, Cole tried shutting out those words. His dirty little secret still threatened him to this day. No one in Crater Mills knew the entire truth and he wanted to keep it that way. If they knew what he had really done, nothing would be the same. Everything he built up the past six years would vanish like his previous life had. Everyone would look at him differently, forever doubting his word and never trusting his intentions again. He had failed Sarah, and that could cause Cole to lose what he had now. Even Katie would turn away in disgust one day when she was old enough to know what had happened. One little secret could destroy so much.

"Matt, please," Cole pleaded, practically choking on the words. It was happening, just like in his nightmares. A thousand faceless figures stared, knowing what he had done.

"Cole, we needed each other. Yet you were alone at a time in your life you needed everyone you loved around you the most. How I could have thought that you never cared about…. God, I won't go there now. I'm sorry! I promise not to go there! Cole, I don't want forgiveness, I don't deserve it. I just want everyone I've hurt to know that I didn't mean it! God, Cole, I didn't mean for any of this to happen! I didn't know what I was doing! I still don't know what I'm doing! Cole, please help me! I know that I don't have the right to ask, especially after…."Matt's voice broke completely again, becoming muffled. The minute he heard the phone striking the table, Cole knew he had his face buried in his hands.

He held on and sure enough, Shauna's comforting voice came over the line, "Cole, can you take care of Becca for us?" she asked quietly.

"Shauna, I'll take care of her. I love that little girl. That's never changed," he answered brokenly. "And please tell Matt that I'm ok! Shit, that sounds so stupid! God, Shauna, I was so scared to talk with him!"

"I know you were. Cole, he's really not the same! I don't even recognize him anymore. Just please find it in your heart to remember that," Shauna replied sadly.

"I will, Shauna, I will. And please, tell him ... tell Matt that ... just tell him that I don't hate him, I never did. My life really is ok now, this is the road fate led me to and there was a reason. I now have a little girl I adore and ... well, I'll explain it all later, but I'm doing ok. Matt didn't hurt me as much as I think he destroyed himself. Please tell him not to be too hard on himself anymore, we all still need him."

"Cole, I can't believe you're saying that after all he did to you," she whispered.

"Shauna, he didn't do anything to me that he hasn't done to himself. It was a bad time for all of us and one that's best forgotten. I'm ok, really, so don't worry. Tell Matt for me, will you?"

"I will, Cole," she replied.

"And tell him that Becca really is safe. As a matter of fact, she came in the middle of a birthday party," Cole explained, with Shauna holding the phone out for Matt to hear also.

"A party?" Matt's voice came back over the line.

"Yeah," Cole replied, his voice cracking. "My girl, Katie, she's four today. Becca sort of crashed the party and is helping herself to the food," he laughed lightly, hearing the same, strange response from Matt. It was obvious that it had been a long time since he had laughed too, if he ever laughed at all anymore.

"That's my little girl," Matt sniffed.

"Yeah, she's something. Matt, she said ... well, she said that she doesn't hate you," Cole told his friend, hearing a quiet sob.

"She did?" he asked as soon as he found his voice.

"Yeah, she did. But she needs time, Matt. She just needs time to be here and get herself together. It's best not to push things right now, but she's a smart girl and she loves you guys. As hurt as she is, I can still see that. She just needs time; I hope you understand," Cole asked.

"Yeah, I do," Matt replied.

"That doesn't mean she won't be coming home soon, time heals all wounds," Cole said, having more meanings than just one. "Matt, she's just scared and confused right now, but she'll be all right. We'll all be all right, can you believe that?"

"I don't deserve it, but I believe it," was his reply.

"Matt, none of us deserve the hurt that's become a part of our lives. We didn't bring it on ourselves, it just happened. We were faced with things that no one should ever be faced with and we had no idea of how to deal with those losses. I know that now, and I know how very precious life is. Please, just remember that, ok?" Cole said quietly.

"Cole?"

"Yeah?"

"Take care of my little girl for me?" Matt then asked.

"You got it," Cole answered, feeling the years melting away.

"She needs you right now," Matt said softly.

"She needs all of us, she just doesn't know it," Cole replied.

"I hope that's true," Matt said.

"It is, Matt, it is. And don't worry, I'll call again soon. Things will settle down here. She'll be fine once she gets the chance to think things out. Matt, she's a good girl and she loves both you and Shauna. Once she realizes that even adults make mistakes and that we're trying to make things right again, she'll come around."

"Is that what we're doing, Cole? Are we making things right again?" Matt's plea came over the line.

Cole was quiet for a moment, trying to still the numerous thoughts racing through his mind. "Matt, that's what we have to do," he replied, knowing then and there that he wanted nothing more.

They were a long way from healing and being as close as they were before, but both men had managed an odd sort of peace. In a matter of minutes, six years of sorrow had been dealt with, even if on such a small scale. All involved knew that they had a long way to go, for this was merely the beginning. So much more loomed on the horizon, but they had taken the first step.

They were a long way from what they used to be, but maybe in time they could find a common ground once again. They talked for the first time in years, bringing a bit of peace, understanding, and hope into each other's hearts. They spoke for a few more minutes, thanking God that he had found a way to intervene. Where the adults were at a loss of how to get past their own feelings, a small girl stepped in, showing them the way.

She showed them that nothing mattered but love, family and friendship. Feelings didn't die and it wasn't right or fair to toss them aside like they didn't matter. They did matter; when that was forgotten, everyone suffered. Now, they put their hurt aside and looked into the eyes and heart of a young girl, seeing the truth that had been denied all along. The more they talked, the more they began putting the pieces of their lives back together. There was still so much to say and do, but now they had time on their side. Whatever the future held, they would work together.

Cole hung up the phone, suddenly realizing that what he had thought would be the hardest thing he ever had to do in his life had really turned out to be the easiest and most rewarding. How he wished he had seen Gris's side years ago. Instead of thinking of Matt with anger and bitterness, he wished he thought of him as broken and in need. They could have helped each other, but it was better now than never. At least they had a start.

Cole was surprised that Matt had given in so quickly. He had expected a fight, but instead, received the chance to reach out to a broken, forgotten friend. True, he never wanted any of this and had always prayed for things to be different, maybe this was that chance. Who was he to turn away and not make the first step on the road to their recovery?

That thought alone was shocking enough. It was then he realized that in spite of all the pain he had suffered all these years, he had been the strong one. He wondered why he couldn't have seen that before.

The more Cole thought, the more he realized needed to be done. His personal life still had a lot to be desired. He had made a mistake with Maggie, but that was over. Anything that came along later would be dealt with. He had no idea how he would go about doing that and if he should think of explaining things to Katie. He also knew that if Matt and he ever came to terms again, that it would be a long hard road, but they would walk it together. How it would effect his friends here, Cole could only begin to guess.

It would never change things in his eyes. Brent, Will, Ruth, and Gris were such a dear part of his life now, his feelings would never change. This was now his home; no matter what, Cole would never leave. Yet, he wondered how they would accept Matt if he came back into his life. For years his friends have helped him over his grief and were there to help put the pieces of his shattered life back together again. They would always come first in his heart and in his mind, but he had hoped that there was still room for Matt and his family. Then Cole thought of Ruth and that worry was put aside; she was right, the heart always opened up to add one more. In Ruth's mind, love was limitless and spread, touching everyone you let in.

There was still a lot of work to do with the ranch, especially with the new stock he had just purchased, surprising even himself. He had always planned on expanding, but was shocked that he had jumped in, doing so right away. But like Ruth said, there was no better time than the present and Cole now knew that she had meant more than just the horses. He also looked forward to helping his friends, hoping that their upcoming sales were as successful as his had been. How things with Sinclair would work out was beyond them all. The man had been absent for days now, so maybe he took the hint and had given up.

Then Cole had Callie to consider. Just the sound of her name sent his heart soaring. He loved her beyond belief and knew she felt the same way. But he was not in any kind of a hurry, and wanted to take things slowly, not knowing what he wanted yet, or how to approach it. Or if he would ever approach it. He was tired, that would take a long time. Callie always said she would be there for him, for now, this was all he could offer. His heart was still healing. Cole hoped she would understand.

With a little luck, Maggie would fade away once again. Sadly, Cole remembered her words the night she gave birth to Katie. '*I can't stay, please don't hate me.*' He had never hated Maggie. At times he pitied her and at times he feared her, but he had never hated her. Maybe time would help him deal with all that was facing him where Maggie was concerned. Maybe in time, his fear would lessen and the sound of her name would not send his heart racing. One could only hope.

As for the rest of his life, well, somehow that, too, would fall into place. None of them knew what the future held, but did anyone? It was in that second that Cole knew he had to live his life one day at a time, as he faced everything that came his way. It was the only way. So after putting the first genuine smile on his face in a long time, he strode proudly out the door, finding Katie, Becca and all those he loved waiting for him. Everything else could wait. Today, he had a party to attend.

*